PRAISE

"Nobody writes like Tijan. With [. . .] [. . .]eled prose, she's always an autoclick author for me."

  —Rachel Van Dyken, #1 *New York Times* bestselling author

"Tijan knows how to create addictive, fun, and exciting stories that you simply cannot put down!"

  —Elle Kennedy, *New York Times* bestselling author

"I can always count on Tijan to write an action-packed, intense, emotional story that will have me invested until the very last page."

  —Helena Hunting, *New York Times* bestselling author

"Tijan delivers on the fun, edge, and angst. Her books never fail to please!"

  —Kylie Scott, *New York Times* bestselling author

"Tijan delivers a power punch with *Anti-Stepbrother*—angst, tension, and an emotional conclusion that'll have you glued to every page. The characters jump straight from the story and claim your heart. You won't be ready to let go."

  —JB Salsbury, *New York Times* and *USA Today* bestselling author

"One of my Tijan faves, with a hero to die for and a heroine you'll want as your best friend."

  —Katy Evans, *New York Times* bestselling author, on *Anti-Stepbrother*

"5+ *riveting* stars!!! The chemistry between Dusty and Stone was *off-the-charts electrifying*. I was completely absorbed from the first page to the last. Tijan didn't just get a touchdown with this story—she won the Super Bowl!"

  —Beth Flynn, *USA Today* bestselling author, on *Enemies*

A Cruel ARRANGEMENT

ALSO BY TIJAN

Kings of New York

A Dirty Business

Mafia Stand-Alones

Canary
Cole
Bennett Mafia
Jonah Bennett

Fallen Crest / Roussou Universe

Fallen Crest Series
Crew Series
The Boy I Grew Up With (stand-alone)
Rich Prick (stand-alone)
Nate
Aveke
Frisco

Other Series

Broken and Screwed Series (YA/NA)
Jaded Series (YA/NA suspense)
Davy Harwood Series (paranormal)
Carter Reed Series (mafia)
The Insiders (trilogy)

Sports Romance Stand-Alones

Enemies
Teardrop Shot
Hate to Love You
The Not-Outcast

Young Adult Stand-Alones

Ryan's Bed
A Whole New Crowd
Brady Remington Landed Me in Jail

College Stand-Alones

Anti-Stepbrother
Kian

Contemporary Romances

Bad Boy Brody
Home Tears
Fighter

Rockstar Romance Stand-Alone

Sustain

Paranormal Stand-Alones

Evil
Micaela's Big Bad

More books to come!

A Cruel ARRANGEMENT

TIJAN

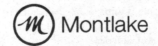

Montlake

Published by Montlake, Seattle

www.apub.com

Amazon, the Amazon logo, and Montlake are trademarks of Amazon.com, Inc., or its affiliates.

ISBN-13: 9781542038591 (paperback)
ISBN-13: 9781542038584 (digital)

Cover design by Caroline Teagle Johnson
Cover photography by Regina Wamba of ReginaWamba.com

Printed in the United States of America

For Kelly and Justin.

CHAPTER ONE

MOLLY

I had a problem.

I was pointing a gun at a guy with green makeup on his face, and I kept thinking how he looked like that goblin guy from one of those superhero movies. A bubble of laughter was coming up in my sternum. I tried stopping it, I did, but once it was past my throat, it was hopeless.

I bent over, my gun still in the air, and the laughter was *kapoosh!* Totally coming out of me.

I winced, hearing a note of hysteria on the edge of it.

"Molly!" That was my employee who was on the ground, his arms folded behind his head as he lay on his stomach, and I could hear how horrified he was.

I raised my head back up, steadied my arm, and cleared my throat. "Let's review the changes that just happened here. You"—I shook my gun, indicating the green guy—"came in here, to my bowling alley, to rob us. Correct?"

He had a rifle aimed at me, and it was at this point I realized how crazy I *really* was.

Like, seriously crazy.

A rifle against my handgun. *And* I was laughing.

I was verging on lunacy. A lunatic. Me.

But he was wearing green makeup, so there could be an argument about who was the more irrational one in this situation.

"You do this sort of thing often?"

"Molly, my god." That was from a different employee. "What are you doing?"

We had a good situation here. Not the robbery, obviously, but what I'd built in this business. Easter Lanes. This was my place. My business. I was proud of what I'd done for the bowling alley when I took it over from my dad. He'd already run it into the ground, so I seized an opportunity when he was particularly vulnerable, and he was a lowlife street gambler, so those moments were fairly common. We were talking twice a month, but this time was when he was up a literal shit creek and he had no one to come and save him. So, me, being his daughter, well, I took a page from his book—I conned him. Meaning, he called me for bail money and he seemed *extra* frenzied to get out of there, which probably meant there was someone on the inside who wanted to give him some sort of beating.

I told him I wouldn't post his bail until he gave me the bowling alley. I was aware that some debts came with the business, but at that point in my life, I had nothing to lose. So I got the bowling alley, renovated what I could, and have continued renovating it over the years as profits got better. I paid off the bowling debts, but that was it. Anything to do with Easter Lanes was all mine. Added a whole pub part and gaming section so families could come here too.

I made sure it appealed to all ages to maximize our customers.

And it worked.

This robber guy had no clue what he was threatening here. This was my life. My only life.

This place was in my blood, and because of all of that, yeah, I went a little unhinged when I looked up and saw a rifle pointing at me.

"What are you playing at, woman?! I told you to give me the money. Why are you waiting? *Give me the money!*"

Oh, boy.

Boys, girls, don't try this at home.

The register drawer was closed. The key was right next to it. I looked at my staff because they knew where the extra keys were, but . . . I could grab it, so quick. I could—I did something. That I was going to regret.

"Molly!" from my one employee.

And my second employee. "What did you do?!"

My staff was shouting and gasping, but one scream drowned out the rest. The green-faced robber was shrieking at me, shaking his gun. "*What did you do?! You crazy psycho bitch!*"

I swallowed the key to get into the register.

That's what I did.

I was still holding my gun up, but it was shaking because my hand was shaking because my arm was shaking because *I* was shaking. My whole body was trembling, and I was tasting tears.

Enough!

Screw this. I'd not endured my whole tragic, sad story of a life to get it all taken away from me by this guy. "You come in here! Thinking you're going to *rob my place*! This is mine. And I'm not going to take this. You know who my dad is?"

I had temporarily stunned the green-faced robber, because he began backing up, slowly inching away from me. He'd forgotten he had the rifle in his hands, but he paused at my question. "Your dad?"

I could see the realization start coming to him.

His eyes were flickering, skirting, panicking, and he was beginning to remember that some businesses in our neighborhood were hooked in. I'm talking Mafia-style hooked in. I wasn't above using some of *that* intimidation if it meant I wasn't going to be arrested for homicide today.

"Who's your dad?" His voice rose, more shrill, and I could see green face paint start to drip.

"Shorty Easter. You know who he is?"

His eyes jerked to the name of my bowling alley. I had it in neon letters above the bar. Easter Lanes. Anyone who was anyone knew that Marcus Easter, a.k.a. Shorty, was basically owned by the Walden family.

He gambled at their establishments, but he also gambled *for* them. I knew his debt to them was so deep that he'd have to live nine lifetimes before paying anything back, but he had other uses, and I knew they used him for those. What they were, I never asked and never wanted to know, but I knew he did jobs for them.

The robber backed all the way up until he hit the door. His rifle slumped down, and he almost dropped it to the ground. "Oh, shit."

It wasn't my dad's name that was causing this change of mind. It was who owned him. I never wanted to use their name, ever, but this was a life-and-death type of situation. A girl had to do what a girl had to do to not get ripped off.

"The Waldens own my father. You coming in here, threatening his daughter, his business. That's going to have some consequences for you."

His eyes were really bulging out now. "Oh, fuck. Fuck!" He was plastered against the door, shaking his head. The desperation was edging in him because I was also feeling it, just in a different way. Easter Lanes was the only place I had that *was* me. Out of all my other homes, nothing stayed. Foster. Shelters. Nothing held.

No one stuck, but this place did. I would not let someone take that away from me, and hear me roar because I was a mama lioness protecting my cub. I was desperate and a lunatic right now, but I didn't care.

He was going to leave. It was the only play he had left. Get out. Run. Get away as far and as fast as he could go. I was waiting for him to accept that choice, but suddenly he jerked away from the door. His rifle snapped back up.

"If what you say is true, then I'm fucked! Fucked, lady. So I figure you owe me. You want me gone? I need money. If not, I'm dead anyways, and we both know it. You give me all your cash, and I'm gone. Yeah, yeah. I'll go, but I need cash. What do you have?"

He reached forward, trying to grab me, and I recoiled, feeling the switch happening.

Oh, no.

———

I blanked.

Coming back, the sound of screaming was all around me, and there was red. Everything was dark red. My hand. My arm. I—

"Oh, good god! Molly!"

I felt a body rushing toward me and jerked around. They stopped, almost falling backward to halt their momentum. Their hands went up, and they were shaking. "Molly."

It was Pialto, my bartender.

"Molly." He dropped his voice, low and calm. Soothing. His hands lowered a little, and he took a step closer to me. "Move back, Molly. Back up. One step."

I started to step to the side, but my foot caught on something, and my gaze jerked downward.

A foot was there.

A leg.

Blood.

There was blood everywhere.

Terror sliced through me.

A body was there. Spread out.

My other employee, Sophie, was on the right side of the body. She had a phone in her hand as she bent down and picked up the rifle. Her whole body was shaking too.

Oh, no.

What had happened? What had I done?

"Is he . . . is he breathing?"

"Molly." Pialto was beside me now. I could feel him and hear him, and I knew he wasn't going to hurt me. He touched my arm. The touch was off. Felt weird. I looked at him, for some reason wanting to tell him that, but I didn't.

A part of my brain was still working while the other part of my brain was turned off.

I was numb while also half feeling at the same time. That didn't make sense either. It was all very weird.

I'd shot the green-faced robber.

He'd reached for me. I'd panicked, and my finger had pulled the trigger.

I hadn't known what he was going to do, and I'd reacted.

I'd done my thing again. My switch.

It wasn't the best name, but the best way to describe that sometimes, when I felt backed into a corner, I did *things*. I reacted or overreacted or irrationally reacted, and most times it made things worse. It was something I was working on, but I'd swallowed the register key. I'd shot a guy. Both big "switch" moments, and oh boy.

I was officially freaking out.

I. Shot. Someone!

"She's freaking."

Pialto was a genius. He was tuned in to my mind.

"Oh, man."

I always liked Sophie.

I'd miss her. I'd miss Pialto too. He'd have to manage the place for me. Or I could ask Jess. Yes. I'd ask another friend of mine. She had, well, she had some flexibility with her new work, or she'd know someone who could run it for me. Her man might help. But not my dad. He'd try to take over the bowling alley while I was in prison. I couldn't let that happen. No. I needed to call—

I reached for my phone. *"Whoa! Hold right there. Stop! Don't move, Molly!"*

That was Pialto yelling at me, but I heard Sophie gasp before she dove for cover.

I looked up, still dazed, and saw both were staring at what was in my hand.

I still had the gun in my hand.

I started to drop it. *"Don't do that!"* Pialto shouted.

His hands were out, and he was half-crouched as he approached me. I didn't know when he'd stepped back from me, but it might've been out of a sort of life-preservation instinct. I mean, at this point, chances were high I would accidentally shoot myself.

"Molly." His voice dropped again, low. "I need to take the gun from you."

I was nodding before he even finished. Yes. Yes, he did, before I did any more damage.

I held it out and he took it, quickly unloading it before he backed away again. Sophie had removed the guy's rifle so it was almost on the other side of the bar. That was good thinking on both their parts.

I slumped down on the barstool behind me, staring at the unconscious man on the floor. God, I hoped that's the reason he wasn't moving.

I heard the sirens a second later.

The cops had arrived.

CHAPTER TWO

ASHTON

The screaming started again.

Three hours into this interrogation, and he hadn't given up a name.

"He doesn't know." Trace pushed up from where he'd been leaning against the wall and dropped his arms. He raked a hand over his head, frustration coming off him, but I understood it. I did. It'd been three months since the bodies had been pulled from the water. While Justin Worthing had been a good employee, we were here because of Justin's woman. Kelly. She'd been best friends, roommates, coworkers, and everything to Trace's woman, Jess.

They'd been sisters.

"How's Jess handling everything?"

I was guarded in my approach.

Jess and I, we weren't on friendly terms. We weren't on any terms, and for a valid reason. I'd put her through a torture session, more psychological than physical, but it put a rift between Trace and me.

He and I had been best friends all our lives, attending the same private high school, same undergrad college. When he moved west for graduate business school, I went with him and started my first business. After that, he joined in, and we'd built our own empire separate from our families, but as much as we wanted to distance ourselves from the family business, it never quite panned out. Both of us were standing in this warehouse, watching a man being tortured because of those same family businesses we tried to get away from—the Walden and West Mafia families. That was me and him. In one night, he and I went from breaking free and taking the legal route of living, to each of us stepping into our respective roles as heads of our families.

In one move from our enemy, the Worthing Mafia family, my uncles and my grandfather had been killed. I made the decision. I stepped up and took over. Despite being put in the same situation—his uncle killed on the same night—Trace still considered not taking over and getting out.

He'd been thinking of leaving, for her. His woman.

Then one phone call changed everything.

Justin's and Kelly's bodies were found, two people we thought had been hidden by the 411 Network. That network was known for smuggling people and hiding them if they feared for their lives. They usually helped abuse victims, but over the last few years, they'd started hiding potential victims from the cartel and the Mafia.

Justin and Kelly hadn't been taken by them, and we were in the process of trying to find out who'd killed them.

"What do you think?" he snapped at me.

I steeled my insides, knowing he was in pain because his woman was in pain, though that was putting it mildly.

Jess Montell had been a parole officer when we met, and then she went legit, becoming an in-demand painter. But that one call set her on a different path, and she was now helping to run the West family Mafia business alongside her man, my best friend.

He sighed, his eyes flashing, before he came to stand next to me. We were in a second-floor office, a one-way mirror acting as our window so we could oversee the torture taking place beneath us. Trace rubbed a hand over his forehead, cursing under his breath. "She's not eating. She's not sleeping. I don't mind taking over the business, but Jess is acting like a vigilante on our behalf. She's going to hate herself when she stops, when she starts thinking clearly again."

I grunted, understanding. It'd been her intel that had given us this guy to question. Her intel was wrong. She was starting to lose it. She was pushing for information just to get information, whether it was real or not. That was bad business for everyone, *dangerous* business for everyone.

"Goddammit!" Trace stepped back, picking up a knife and flinging it at the far wall. It embedded from the blow, and I watched below as they heard that happen. They paused, glancing up. I reached over and flashed a light, signaling them to keep going.

This hadn't been the first time an incident like that happened.

Prior to my own interrogation of Jess, I'd been a lot less quiet on this matter, but that time was gone. I was in a precarious position, and I needed to curtail what I would say to my best friend, who was slowly becoming my best friend again. My brother.

Still, I knew I had to say something. "You need to let me take over."

"I have been!"

I turned, slowly, locked down.

Trace was anything but. His eyes were wild. He was on the verge of losing it.

I gave him a look, saying quietly, "I need to take over, Trace."

"God—" He stopped, swinging back to me, and his eyes narrowed. "What the fuck have you been doing if you haven't been leading this?"

"I've been following Jess's intel, but this isn't the first time her intel was wrong. This is the *third* guy this week. You have to rein her in."

He let loose a myriad of curses. "You rein her in. She—"

"She's in love with *you*."

"They killed her best friend because of *me*." Agony flared in his expression.

I couldn't let myself feel anything, not right now, not when I needed to steer him to the sidelines. He and his woman. They were too emotionally involved. It was blinding them. "Trace."

"Stop it, Ashton. I know what you're going to say."

I almost grinned. "Probably. You're the analyst, after all." I took a step toward him, softening my tone again. "But you know I'm right. It's been three months. Jess isn't helping anymore."

He turned away, his shoulders tightening. "Be careful where you step next, Ashton."

I had been, for three months.

I took another step closer. "She's hurting and she's making it worse. You know this. Pull her back. She's on the edge."

"How am I supposed to do that?" He winced as he said it, his head moving back.

I'd lost family, but it hadn't been my family that had helped to kill my own people. That's what his father did. And Trace had to carry that, knowing his father was part of the reason everyone was hurting now. But while we could trace back the killings of my family and his uncle to the Worthing family, we couldn't with Justin and Kelly.

The Worthing family blamed us, saying that we'd killed one of their own, even though Justin had been an innocent. He wasn't in their family business, and he'd been in our employ for a while before he realized how both sides escalated. He took himself out of the equation, himself and Kelly, but now no one knew what was happening. Jess's involvement had gotten back to the Worthing family, so while they thought we might be behind it, they also weren't totally sure anymore. I knew this because I'd been on the end of a phone call from Nicolai Worthing, the new head of their family, and he said as much to me.

It'd been a fishing call, trying to find out what he knew, but also a tentative truce had been offered until we found the murderer. I'd not accepted, but I hadn't fully rejected the offer either. Because of that, there'd been a ceasefire of deaths in the last two and a half months.

We were both looking for who killed them.

"I don't know, Trace. She's your woman. She's suffering. You have to be the one to pull her back." I waited until he looked my way. This time, I couldn't be soft anymore. "And you know that."

Enough time had passed, at least between him and me.

He was struggling. That much was obvious, but he closed his eyes before swinging back to the guy strapped to a chair below us. "They turned her mentor against her. They tried to kill her mother. That was my father who did that, because he was working with *that* family, but whoever killed Kelly—that destroyed Jess. Kelly was the good part of her. That's how Jess sees it. She's slipping, and I have no idea how to pull her back."

I stepped to him and placed a hand on his shoulder. Just one. For comfort. "You have to, because if you can't, she'll never come back. I *will* find Kelly's killer. I will do this, for Jess. For you."

"Ashton."

I heard it. He was giving in, in that one word, one name.

Knock, knock!

My hand fell from Trace's shoulder as my main security guy, Elijah, stepped inside. His eyes went straight to me. "There's been an incident—" He looked at Trace and faltered.

I frowned but went to him. "What is it?"

"At Easter Lanes."

"Molly's place?" Trace stepped next to me.

Molly Easter was good friends with Jess, and they'd gotten closer until Kelly's death. I didn't know the current state of their friendship, but seeing Elijah falter in Trace's presence, I was taking that he worried about sharing.

"Is she okay?"

He nodded, his eyes darting back to Trace again.

Right. She was alive, but something more had happened.

I turned to Trace. "I'll handle this."

"Molly—"

"Marcus Easter is owned by my family. I'll handle this."

"You told me you'd handle that." Trace's jaw clenched as he pointed out the one-way mirror/window.

"Molly falls under my territory."

"She's friends with Jess."

"They're not *that* close, and you know it." They were friends, but I wasn't totally lying. They weren't best of friends, not like Jess and Kelly, not like Trace and me. "Her father's debt to my family extends beyond the grave at this point. I will handle it."

"Ash—"

"I've been lenient regarding Kelly's killer, but not with this one." My tone was firm, and my gut sharpened because he had better not push this. Not with Molly.

Reading me, Trace nodded and stepped away. "Fine, but when Jess finds out, I'm telling her to call you directly. *You* can answer to her about Molly."

A new fire had started in my stomach.

It was low and simmering, but it was always there when Molly Easter came into play. I smiled, knowing how deadly that would look because that was how I felt inside. Deadly. Lethal. And a part of me wanted to come out to play.

Unlike Trace, I liked being cruel. I liked killing. I liked the ruthlessness of this world, but I'd been holding back for him, for my brotherhood with him, for his woman, for my very delicate relationship with Jess, but Molly—she was a whole other factor.

Seeing that, he cursed softly and shook his head. "Don't break this one."

Another scream sounded out from the man, and I went back to the mirror as I heard Trace leave.

The guy arched backward, his back almost breaking in half as my man held a knife to his stomach. I saw the blood dripping down, and finally, *finally*, a part of me was being let free.

I inhaled the freedom, but I knew a dead end when I heard it.

Elijah was still in the room, waiting for my order. I gave it: "Release the man."

"Kill him or . . . ?"

Our men couldn't be identified, but it wouldn't matter. This man wouldn't say anything. He didn't dare, so I shook my head. "Drop him off at the doctor's parking spot. She can take care of him for us."

"Will do."

"Elijah."

"Yeah?"

"Make sure to call ahead so the security cameras are turned off."

"Got it."

But it wouldn't matter because there'd be no investigation into the man who was almost killed by torture. There wouldn't be because everyone already knew who'd done it.

Me.

CHAPTER THREE

MOLLY

"Okay." Dr. Sandquist was rubbing the top of her nose where it flattened between her eyebrows, and she had her other arm wrapped around herself. Her elbow was resting on her own arm. She looked tired, but that could've been because it was four in the morning.

I first met Nea Sandquist in a pottery class. I met a lot of friends in pottery classes. It was kinda my outlet. I liked to take an edible, put on my headphones, and get all spiritual with the clay. I felt a connection to the movie *Ghost* that I didn't think was healthy.

"You are in shock, Miss Easter."

"Molly," I piped in, kinda hoping for an edible right now.

She sighed. "Molly. You're in shock, but it doesn't look like you've been physically harmed. The key you swallowed should make its way out of you within a day or two." She shared a look with Nurse Sloane, the head honcho of all the nurses at the hospital. "I'd like to introduce you to our social worker. He can help you go through the emotional aftereffects of what happened to you. I'd really, *really* suggest talking to either Matt, our social worker, or he can refer you to someone else, unless you already know someone you could talk to?"

The two detectives were outside the door, and she glanced over her shoulder at them before her head ducked. She stepped a little closer to me, quieting her voice. "I need to let the police in to question you, but in the meantime, is there anyone you want us to call?"

Sloane closed in on the other side. "Jess, maybe?"

Head honcho. Sloane knew everyone and everything.

I shook my head. "Not unless . . . no." I changed my mind. "I have time to call her myself. Where are my employees?"

"They were released and sent home after they gave their statements."

I loved Sloane. I had a mentor crush on her. Sometimes, when I was little and I was brought into this hospital, I liked to pretend that Sloane was my mother growing up. She could put anyone in their place, take charge of any room, and make police jump at her instructions. She was a big part of the reason the two detectives, Worthing and Monteyo, were still outside the room and hadn't barged in.

They'd tried in the beginning, but she'd taken one look at them and snapped her fingers. "Outside. Now." Her tone was super sharp, and they did what she said.

No one messed with Sloane.

"Molly, do you want us to call a lawyer for you?"

Most people might be confused about why she was offering this. I'd been the victim. It was my place that was held up—no. Never mind. I just remembered that I had indeed shot someone. This suggestion made total sense, but for a minute I thought maybe Sloane was referencing the other elephant in the room.

Everyone on the street was aware of the Mafia war going on.

When that robber had first come in, I'd thought that Easter Lanes would be collateral in the war because of my loose connection to the Walden Mafia family. I was relieved to find out he was just a typical run-of-the-mill idiot criminal.

"Is that guy I shot—is he dead?"

Sloane and Nea stiffened before sharing a look.

"No. Oh gosh. No, Molly. From what we were told, your hand jerked, and the bullet grazed the side of his face." Nea motioned down her cheek. "He'll have a nasty burn for a long time, but it was mostly superficial. He's handcuffed and in police custody at the hospital."

My shoulders sagged. I felt like I just gained back five years of my life. "Are you serious?"

"Yes. Did you think—"

I shook my head before she could even say it. "I didn't know. I was . . . never mind. Thank you." I shared a silly smile with both of them. "I didn't kill someone. Phew. I mean, they probably won't charge me with much for self-defense, right? It was self-defense. It's not like I'll get assault with a weapon or something, right?"

They were doing that look-sharing thing again before Sloane spoke, and her voice was curt. "No. They will not be charging you with anything. I will make sure of that."

Okay. Who knew a nurse had such pull with the police? But go Nurse Sloane. Mentor slash crush.

I gave her another smile while starting to think maybe I *had* ingested an edible and didn't remember it. "You're super cool, Nurse Sloane." I was starting to feel rainbows and unicorns. That was a momentous feeling. I'd be up for meeting a yeti at this point. "I always wished you were my mom. Did I ever tell you that?"

The ceiling was moving. The clouds were coming in.

I was sure I was seeing Mount Everest too.

"The drugs kicked in."

A hand went to my arm and another behind my back. I was being lowered down to the bed. "You can take a nap, Molly. I'll handle the detectives and get them out of here. When you wake up, everything will be fine. You don't need to worry about a thing."

I was trying to tell Sloane that was amazing, and thank her for it, but one of the unicorns started to talk to me. I was going to shut up.

I didn't want to miss this conversation.

CHAPTER FOUR

ASHTON

I should be exhausted from hospitals by now.

My uncles. My grandfather. All had been gunned down three months ago, on that night. And I had been here, watching from a similar hallway as each of them flatlined. Over and fucking over again.

And the blood. Everywhere.

I had to give the hospital staff their due, because they'd tried to save each one of them, but Jesus. They came out one by one, all covered in blood, and that feeling right there, watching each of them and seeing how they didn't want to look my way—I would never ever forget that feeling. It fucking haunted me, every morning, night, and day.

I couldn't get that out of me, no matter how I tried, no matter how I focused, how I obsessed, how I thirsted, but now. Now, I had a new mission, one just for me.

Molly Easter.

She was sleeping, curled on her side and the blanket tucked over her shoulder.

I had mixed feelings concerning Miss Easter, and they stemmed from a day that no one, including Trace, knew about. But right now, I was letting the current thought come through. And that was that

Molly Easter, among other things, had been a pain in my ass for nearly all my life.

"What are you doing here?" A hiss came from my right, and I stepped back from the opened doorway where I'd been standing, smirking at Dr. Nea Sandquist, who was clutching a tablet to her chest. Her eyes bugged out.

"Dr. Sandquist."

"You can't be here, Ashton." She moved closer, her head ducking down as some of the nurses went by, all attention on us. "Get out. I mean it."

My body had been churning, a mix of emotions surging through me, but at her command, I went cold. "Watch your tone, Doc."

She drew back, her eyes sparking. Pain flashed before the doctor shuttered her expression. She clutched her tablet even tighter, her fingers turning white. "I was stupid when I first met you, believing you were interested in me. I know who you are. Since our couple of dates, I've been *educated*." She spat out the word. "I know exactly who really runs this hospital, but I won't leave. I don't care if you threaten me. I won't go." She nodded inside Molly's room. "She's good people. Leave her alone. She's innocent from your business."

My lip curled up. "Molly is a lot of things, but innocent is not one of them."

She quieted, frowning.

I moved into her space, and she had to take two steps backward. It was enough where I could turn my back to Molly's door, and I leaned down, making sure the doctor saw my intent. "In this situation, I would suggest you walk away."

She was bristling, getting ready for another argument, when Sloane's voice cut in. "Nea." She said it low and calm, but everyone here knew the reason behind her interruption.

Sloane knew all. She knew the details.

"I'm handling something—"

"Nea." Calm. Low again, but more insistent. "You need to step back from him."

Nea's eyes flashed wild, and she turned, hissing at the head nurse, "Are you kidding me? Do you know—"

I met Sloane's gaze, my head finding hers over Nea's head. She was walled off to me. Good on her. I knew the nurse enough, had known all sides of her from growing up. She could be loving and mothering at times, but she still understood what needed to be done, even now knowing what my family stood for and hating me for it.

"Molly's father called. He's on her file as a person of contact, and he said Mr. Walden would be coming in his stead. We need to honor the patient's wishes and her father's. Mr. Walden needs to be briefed on Molly's situation, and then release her into his care."

"I am her doctor. I say when she's to be released."

Sloane's eyes briefly blinked. She wasn't showing any emotion, speaking in a monotone. "I'm aware, but you know what the hospital board will expect in this situation."

Nea drew her breath, hearing the underlying threat. Yes. My family had a long reach, even to this hospital's board. "Sloane." She dropped her voice, walking over to her, but I could still hear. "You can't be serious. You know who he is—"

"*Yes.*" Sloane broke now, that word being hissed back and her eyes flashed fiercely. "*I* do. Do *you*? You're forgetting—" She bit off, casting me a furtive look. "Don't forget, Nea."

Nea fell back a couple steps, blinking rapidly. She took a second, breathed in deeply before the same tone came over next. "You're right." She turned, her eyes glazed, but she refused to meet my gaze.

"The only physical harm to Molly was a key she ingested, and her gun went off so close to her face. She might have some burning in her eyes and ringing in her ears, but I've prescribed ear and eye drops to help offset those effects. The key should pass within a day to two. I'd suggest she keep a liquid diet until it does, just to be safe, but the biggest concern for me is the emotional stress she might be under from her ordeal. You're aware of what happened?"

I nodded, dipping my head down a bit.

Key. Burning. Ringing. She shot someone.

Jesus Christ.

"She felt threatened, under attack, and she worried she had killed a man. I'd like her to meet a social worker from this hospital to see if she feels safe to talk to him."

Him. "No."

"Ashto—" She stopped herself, closing her eyes again, drawing in a breath. She tried again. "Mr. Walden, I've already given Molly his card. It will be her choice if she meets with him or not, but she should talk to someone. No one was severely harmed, but it was still a traumatic experience to a *normal* person."

I got her dig—a normal person, unlike me—but I didn't care. I watched Molly continue to sleep.

"Ashton." She dropped all pretenses, stepping close again. "Please leave this woman alone. She's good. She doesn't deserve whatever you're planning on doing to her."

Unlike what I had done to Nea.

There'd been another patient, one that Nea had wondered why the police hadn't been called because of his state. Trace had dispatched me to "educate" the new doctor on how our families ran business through the hospital. I'd done my job, but I took her on a couple dates to really cement the fact that she could not touch us.

Our paths had not crossed since that day. I saw that I'd left an impression.

I'd done my job.

"Start her discharge papers. We'll take her home as she is."

She sucked in a sharp breath.

"You made your argument, Nea. I do not care. Discharge her."

She cursed as she stalked away from me.

"I took care of you and Trace when you were both boys. I've helped you many times." Sloane stepped up in Nea's place. "I'm aware of the changes to both of your families and what's going on." She was saying that as she was eyeing the four guards standing behind me in the hallway. There'd been a time when I didn't use guards. "I can't imagine the stress and responsibility put on both your and Trace's shoulders, but I need to echo Nea's sentiments. Molly is good people. She's kind. Loving. Pure. It's not her fault who her father is. Don't punish her for Marcus's failure as a father," she added, her voice low.

I didn't respond. That, in itself, was a kindness to Sloane because I did remember the kindness she'd given me when I was growing up.

"Ashton."

She was going to push it. I turned to her, letting her see some of the darkness that I knew scared so many others. She stopped when she saw it. "Do not say anything more, Nurse Sloane. For *your* sake."

Her chest jerked up in a ragged breath. "You've never threatened me."

I stepped toward her, but unlike Nea, she held her ground.

"I let you have your say."

She was very still, her throat moving as she swallowed. "I've been wary of you. You and Trace. I've been nervous around your family members, unnerved by Trace's father, but I've never been scared. Until today." Her eyes flashed hard, and she took a dramatic step back. "We'll ready Miss Easter to be discharged. You'll have to bring a car around for her to be transferred inside."

Yeah. Yeah. Hospital policy.

I turned around as Sloane went to do as she said, and I moved to stand over Molly's bed.

Both of them were right. Molly Easter looked like an angel sleeping. Tiny. Five five in height. A little over a hundred pounds. Strawberry-blonde hair that was matted and greasy right now, framing under and around her head on the pillow. When those eyes opened, I knew they were a deep sky-blue color. There'd been a time when I swore that I could even see the clouds in her eyes.

Freckles over her face.

She was beautiful sleeping, but she was stunning when she turned those eyes and that smile on you.

They were all right. Molly *was* kind and pure, to them.

To me, she was a cross that I'd been forced to bear all my life.

I was done bearing it.

CHAPTER FIVE

MOLLY

I did not recognize the sheets I was lying on, and I'm picky. I liked my warm sheets. These were cool and smooth but not silk. They were cotton, but like the most expensive form of pure cotton there was. Another odd thing about me. I knew my bedsheets. I'd worked in a bedding store one time, and I could outsell everyone except Marjorie Jones. Damn that Marjorie Jones. She also had a side business selling Tupperware that was killer. I didn't like Tupperware, so I was cool with that, but the bedding crown was still a sore spot.

I sat up and looked down.

Total déjà vu moment, because I had on silk pajamas, and the room was the nicest room I'd ever been in. Where was I?

I went to the bathroom and gulped at how nice it was.

Or I tried, because I was fully focusing on where I was and not how I was feeling, because if I started thinking about how I was feeling, I'd not be getting out of that bed for another whole week.

My whole body was stiff and in pain, and I felt like a walking black bruise. Throbbing, but nope. I was focusing on the positive. Functional thoughts. Those were the only ones that mattered in circumstances like this. The way I grew up, sometimes when you woke, you had no idea where you were, and you didn't have the time to wallow in your misery.

That old survival skill was kicking in right now, but kinda in the opposite way because I wanted to wallow. This place was off the rails.

The sink looked like a water rock fountain you'd see in nature. It was glorious. And the shower, oh my goodness, the shower. A clear glass partition separated the bathroom from it, and there were five shower heads. Some lined the entire wall from floor to ceiling. I was looking at the one set right where my butt would be. That would be . . . yeah.

Then, taking a breath, I did look in the mirror.

I winced at myself. My face looked swollen, red, patchy eyes, and I grimaced as more pain rushed through me, half knocking me over.

I grabbed onto the sink, steadying myself.

Deep breath in. One. That was all I was giving myself. Just one breath, and I pushed back, on to the next.

I knew I should be freaking out that someone must've changed my clothes, but I wasn't. A part of me was just in awe. Go to sleep in the hospital and wake up at the Ritz-Carlton. That's how I was feeling, and my eye caught a button on the wall that was blinking.

I pressed it. I had to.

A female voice came over a speaker system. "Good morning, Miss Easter. Would you like breakfast and a beverage brought to your room?" She sounded soothing, like Alexa.

I leaned over. "Yes. I'd like a coffee—"

"Press again for a list of the full menu."

I frowned, straightening back up. She kept going, giving me all the options, but there was only one button to press.

"I'd like a coffee."

She kept talking. I could do a burrito, pancakes, a croissant, or an omelet. There were other options, but I didn't want any of them. I pressed the button again, but she kept speaking.

I should really—my staff! The robber. The rest of last night (was it last night?) was coming back to me, and now a little panic was setting in.

I finished up in the bathroom, then looked around for my clothes. They were folded and set in a pile on a couch in the corner of the room. I lifted one and took a good whiff. I loved the smell of fresh laundry, but who had done all of this?

After changing clothes, I left my pajamas on the bed, half considering trying to take them with me because they were the softest material I'd ever had on my body. I left the room and saw I was in a back hallway, and as I moved down, lights lit up ahead of me on both sides.

Soft music played ahead, so I followed, coming across a giant dining room with floor-to-ceiling glass walls. At least I knew where I was now: in a high-rise in Manhattan, and we were seriously high up. The Hudson River below was right next to us.

There was a giant waterfall island. All the cupboards looked sleek, like something that I would've imagined being on a spaceship. There was a room on the other side of the kitchen and a second sitting area, so I went over, coming to an opened doorway, and through what looked like a library was another door.

I followed, finally seeing whose place I was in. I was floored.

Absolutely.

Truly.

Gutted.

Sitting behind a large mahogany desk was Ashton Walden.

The fuzzies started.

That's what I felt when I was around him. My body always did a whole swoop, feeling like I stepped into my own vortex, because he had the ability to make me want to lose myself, to flip my switch, and make me want to throw him down on the nearest bed. Plus, he always looked at me like he half wanted to fuck me or half wanted to strangle me. It'd been like that since as long as I'd known him, and it had only intensified over the last six months once he'd come back into my life.

He was the new head of the Walden Mafia family. *The* head. Not a head. The head honcho over it all. I was rambling in my head because I was freaking out that I was in Ashton's home. Power, control, danger. Those three words clung to him, walked with him wherever he went, and I'd seen him walk.

I'd seen him do a lot over the years. I was aware of him growing up, every time I saw him with Trace or their other rich friends. How everyone knew not to mess with them, and if they did, it was never Trace who handled their enemies.

It was Ashton. Always.

He got a reputation because of it. No one messed with Ashton. I think the only person who wasn't aware of how truly deadly he could be was his actual best friend, Trace West. Though, none of that mattered now since both were the heads of their families, and I was breaking out in a cold sweat because how the hell had I gotten myself here?

Sensing me, he lifted heated eyes my way, but they switched to the cold and dead eyes I always associated with him.

Dead. Cruel. Ruthless.

I suppressed a shiver and tried not to take in his cold beauty, but dammit. I couldn't stop.

"What am I doing here?" My voice was hoarse, coming out raspy.

Ashton didn't respond, instead taking his time as he studied me. Another cold flicker of emotion passed in his gaze before he stamped that out and stood, coming around his desk toward me. A predator stalking his prey.

I always had that feeling when he was around me, but this time it was the worst it'd ever been. I was in his home. Not the giant house his family ran their business out of, but his personal home.

Ashton and me. He didn't think I remembered him, but I did.

I remembered the day we'd met when we were kids, though I didn't remember a whole lot about that day. It was fuzzy, another reason I got the fuzzies around him. There was a whole theme going on. I had some gaps in my memory about that, but him, I remembered. Even back then, he was cute and striking and I'd liked him, immediately.

Liked him—that wasn't the right word for what I felt that day, but I'd been a kid.

He was angry and cold now, and I guess not much had changed.

He'd come into Easter Lanes one night, looking for Jess, and I'd never forget that night. How he looked like he wanted to murder her, and how I had been reaching for my bat under the counter before Jess went with him. She reassured me everything was okay, but I knew it wasn't.

It never was with Ashton Walden.

He'd come in flanked with his security guards, and then the other time at the nightclub when he'd yelled at me before having me whisked away. I wasn't altogether sure what went down that night, but I'd felt zapped from him. He had pierced me inside, and that feeling never went away.

I felt it again, all over again.

"What am I doing here?" I asked again, cursing internally as my voice dipped. A slight tremor slipped out.

Hearing it, Ashton stopped. His eyes flared slightly. "You and I have some things to discuss."

I was shaking my head as he went past me, heading through the library and to the kitchen. A shiver trailed down my spine at the same time. "No, *I* don't. I want to go home."

I followed him, hugging myself in the opened doorway.

He acted as if he hadn't heard me, pressing a button. A deluxe coffee machine appeared, and he pressed another button. It began rumbling, and soon the smell of brewing coffee filled the space.

God.

My stomach did its own rumble because I really loved coffee. It was a weakness for me. I never got that order in from my room.

"We have things to discuss." He lifted his head, those dead eyes lingering on my clothes. "Business and your father."

My toes curled in. "My father?"

There was another flash of emotion in his gaze, and was I imagining it? I thought I saw a softening come over his face, but then it was gone. He took out a cup and motioned to the island. "Sit, Molly."

He angled his body so he was half leaning against his counter, half turned toward me.

God. His face was always so unreadable.

Nearly black eyes. Dark hair. A face that could've been an angel, though I knew he was anything but. Dangerous. Powerful. Sleek. A toned body, but it was so much more. He was both beautiful and so dark, so deadly, that I couldn't contain a shiver. At every phase of his life, he'd always been good looking. He was pretty when he was young. When he was a teenager, he'd been *hot*. But now, my mouth was almost watering, and I hated that, but I couldn't deny it. Now he was a masterpiece to look at, and my stomach dipped because I knew how ruthless he could be at the same time.

He was a dichotomy. That's what he was.

I seated myself at the island, taking one of the barstools that lined the far side. "Did you hurt her that night?"

I wasn't looking, but I felt him grow still. Very still.

"Hurt who?" he asked quietly.

I looked up. "That night. You came in and took Jess. You looked like you were going to hurt her."

He didn't answer, but his jaw clenched, and his eyes narrowed.

The coffee beeped that it was done. He set the mug down in front of me, surveying me in silence for another second. "I thought your friend was a mole."

I took the coffee, pulling it closer to me before looking down at it. "Then you were being stupid."

I still felt his gaze on the top of my head as he murmured, "It's nice to see you have a spine. I wasn't sure."

I shoved back from the counter. "Fuck you."

Gone were the functional thoughts from earlier, the nice thoughts of whose place I was in, and all the anger, the bitterness, the resentment swirled up now. Because of him. Because of what he thought about Jess. Or my dad. Probably more my dad, but Jess was the tipping point.

"You thinking Jess was anything but loyal just shows the asinine way of thinking your family operates. Your family," I spat. "They could've put my father out of his misery long ago, but you didn't. Your grandfather didn't. You just kept adding to his debt until he'll do anything for you now. That's how I got here. My dad's my contact person. I meant to change that, but I keep forgetting. I'm betting they called him, and he called you. Am I right?"

Ashton's eyes narrowed even more. "I'd be very careful about how you insult family members of mine that were not long ago put into the ground." Ashton was still leaning against the counter, but his head inclined forward. "And you're wrong about your father. I called him."

I flushed; my whole body felt it. "Why?"

"Because, Molly Everly Easter, you just became a part of the war that my family is involved in."

I frowned. "How? It was a random robber. I'm assuming you got the CliffsNotes from someone. That guy had nothing to do with your war."

"Detective Worthing does. I was told that he tried to question you about the robbery."

"Because it was a robbery and he's a cop."

"He's in the organized crime unit. He's not a beat cop. He knows our family connections. That's why he was there. So him showing up brings you into my business."

I had no idea what he was talking about. "What?"

Ashton tilted his head to the side. "I was told Detective Worthing tried to question you at Easter Lanes?"

My body suddenly grew tired. "The ambulance got there first and took me to the hospital."

"They weren't at the hospital when I arrived."

Right. To the hospital, because that made sense how I got here now.

"I guess? I remember talking to Nea and Sloane before I fell asleep. I woke up here, and—" I swallowed my register's key! I gasped, grabbing for my stomach and looking down. Oh, god. That was in there. "I have a foreign object inside of me."

"It'll pass out of you within a day to two days."

I jerked my head back up. "What does that mean? I'll—"

His lips thinned again. "You're going to shit it out. That's what that means."

Oooh. That was comforting, but also uncomfortable at the same time. I eyed him warily again. "You got the 411 on me?"

"Your father appointed me in his stead. It's why they released you to me."

I shot him a look as those fuzzies in my stomach started to warm up. He and I both knew I got released to his care because of his last name. "What am I doing here? I'd like to go home. I'd like my phone. I'd like to call my staff and make sure everyone and everything is okay."

He reached behind him and opened a drawer. He lifted my phone out of it and leaned over, putting it on the island and shoving it to me. It glided over to me smoothly. "Your staff is fine, and I have a man at Easter Lanes, running it until you and I have concluded what we need to conclude."

I started to unlock my phone but I stopped. "You have a man? Easter Lanes is not a part of your family's business. You have no right to send a man over there, or to pick me up, or to have anything to do with me."

"Except that's where you're wrong. Besides talking about Detective Worthing, that's the other business you and I have to discuss."

"What is?"

"Easter Lanes. The bowling alley your father 'sold' you."

"What about it?"

"It wasn't his to sell."

CHAPTER SIX

ASHTON

The blood drained from her face and her body jerked before she grabbed the counter to steady herself. "Wha—"

Buzz! Buzz!

I frowned, hearing my door buzzer. My men hadn't called, and the concierge would never buzz anyone in if they weren't important to me. Casting her another frown, I went over and pressed the intercom button. "Yes?"

"I'm sorry for the interruption, but a Ms. Montell and Mr. West are here to see—"

I cursed, then hit the speaker button. "Let them up." As soon as I was done, I went to Molly and ignored how she jumped at my closeness. "You will keep this between us. Got it?"

She frowned, bristling, and I could see the thoughts forming before she opened her mouth. She was going to fight me on this.

"If you want even a shot at getting Easter Lanes to be yours and yours alone, you will follow my lead when Jess and Trace get here." Her eyes lit up at my offer, and she nodded before cursing and smoothing a hand down her hair.

"I look a mess."

She looked stunning. "You're fine."

Trace knew the code for my door, so I was unsurprised when I heard it open. I braced myself.

They were quiet, but I felt their intensity—or I should say hers, as Jess Montell, the love of Trace's life, came in.

Her eyes were blazing. I'd expected nothing less and half smirked. "Officer Montell."

"Jess!" Molly's delight was evident, but Jess gave her a cursory look. Up and down, before she rounded to me.

I stepped up to meet her, and as she was about to put hands on me, I flashed her a grin. "All her body parts are attached."

She stopped, holding back. "You took her out of the hospital when she was unconscious? Are you kidding me? Then you smart off to me?"

Molly was frowning.

Trace was studying me over her head.

Jess Montell was in mourning because of her friend's death, but I'd be lying if I didn't admit that there were other reasons for her frostiness, especially toward me. But I meant what I'd said to Trace. I was dedicated to finding Kelly and Justin's murderer.

As if reading my mind, which he probably did because it was something we did often over the years, Trace gave me another grin before shrugging, but he gave a little nod in Molly's direction.

Jess had rounded to her, and she was approaching with caution. "How are you feeling, Mols?"

Molly's eyes jerked to mine over Jess's head, and they narrowed before she responded. "I'm okay." She went around Jess, coming to my side, and linked her arm with mine, stepping closer. *Fuck.* I felt that touch down to my dick. "Thank god Ashton was there to help me out."

Jess went still.

I stiffened.

I heard Trace smother a laugh before turning away. He walked into the library, his head and shoulders shaking.

"What?" Jess's voice was flat.

"Oh yeah." Molly laid it on. Her arm tightened around mine. "He's been great. Bringing me here. Taking care of Easter Lanes. We were just about to have breakfast when you guys showed up. Are you hungry? I'm starving."

Jess took a step backward. "Breakfast?"

I stifled a groan but reversed Molly's hold on me. I wrapped my arm around her, taking hold of her hip, and brought her even closer to me. Her front was to my side. Another scenario and I'd be tempted to rest my cheek on Molly's head.

I kept my hand firmly on her hip, anchoring her to me. "I could make breakfast or have something delivered. Would you guys want to join us?"

Trace was stepping back into the kitchen. "No." He went next to Jess, putting his arm around her shoulders and drawing her into his side similar to how Molly and I were standing. "Jess was worried, but Molly seems like she's being taken care of."

Jess started to argue. "I think—"

"We're supposed to meet your mother."

Her mouth closed. "Oh. Yeah."

Trace jerked his chin up to me. "Before we go, can I have a word?" He motioned toward my office. "In private?" His eyes skirted from Jess to Molly before coming back to me and flashed briefly with extra emotion.

I held Molly close again, ignoring how her body shuddered against mine. "Sure." But before leaving, I turned so my back was to Jess and Trace. I looked down at Molly, who tipped her head up to me.

Right now, in this moment, it was her and me. I was barricading the others off.

I gazed down at her, my eyes a little narrowed.

What was she doing? Was she going to keep playing along? How'd I handle it if she didn't? All those questions flashed from me to her, silently. A deep warning from me.

I felt a second shiver come from her body to mine, and I didn't know the reason, but we held that look for a full three seconds before I pulled away. She never gave anything away. She banked down whatever caused that sizzle, and I got a wall right back.

Fine. On to my best friend.

Trace was already walking into my office. I followed behind, shutting the door, and as he started to speak, I held up a finger. After hitting the seal button, I looked back to him. "We're soundproofed now."

"What the fuck are you doing with Molly Easter?"

He wasn't wasting time. I almost had to smile at that.

"I believe we had this conversation not long ago."

"Jess got a call and was livid. I would like for my best friend and the love of my life to be somewhat civil toward each other, and I'm aware that's going to take time, but *Jesus*, Ashton. Taking Molly from the hospital when she was still unconscious?"

My gut shifted. "Did the doctor call or did Sloane?"

He held my gaze for a beat. "Dr. Nea Sandquist has become somewhat friendly with Jess, but no, the doctor is as terrified of me as she is of you."

So the nurse. Good to know.

"I see," I replied.

He snorted. "You don't see shit. Sloane is close to Jess, was close to Kelly. She used to volunteer at the hospital. Her death hit Sloane hard too."

I glowered at him.

He shook his head. "What are you doing with Molly?"

I half growled. "To be frank, Trace, that's none of your business."

"Don't give me the crap that your family owns Marcus Easter. You know he's been a horrible father to Molly. I shouldn't have to remind you that Jess *just* lost her best friend. She doesn't let a lot of people in. One of those that she has"—he pointed out the door—"is in that room with her, and fully lying to her. Which Jess knows. She's got a BS radar, remember? She was a parole officer. Why is Molly lying to her? What are you holding over her head?"

I was gritting my teeth tighter and tighter the more he talked. "I love you. I hope to one day be on good footing with your woman again, but listen to me carefully right now. I need you to *get out* of my home." I'd already told him Molly Easter was my business, not his. He knew this, had already agreed to it, so he was the one stepping wrong in this instance.

His head drew back. He gave me an assessing look before his eyes hooded over. "Let me remind you what is at stake here. If you destroy *her*, Jess will never forgive *you*."

The unspoken sentiment was where that would leave him and me.

I drew in a breath, my nostrils flaring. "Noted. Now get out."

CHAPTER SEVEN

MOLLY

My body was aching and stiff when I let myself into my apartment later that night. My head was pounding. I dropped the bag of clothes I had with me on the table, heading straight for some wine.

God.

My dad. My bowling alley.

My staff.

Even Jess.

My life was a total conundrum, but one thing at a time, and right now, I needed my painkillers and oh crap. I had to nix the wine. Water would have to do, and after, I headed for the bathroom.

My clothes were stripped off, and I stepped under the shower.

God. Warmth. Ashton's place had been warm. I wasn't physically cold, but emotionally cold? Oh yes. So much yes. And just thinking about him, I felt a wave of panic sweep my body. But no. I couldn't indulge in that. I needed to think clearly, needed to get through the next few weeks.

I remembered my time at Ashton's place.

As soon as Jess and Trace had left, I'd whirled on him. "What did you do to Jess?" Because she was hurting, and Ashton had done something to make her hurt even more. I could feel it, sense it.

He had frowned at me, studying me before he tilted his head to the side. "What did *you* say to her? I'm assuming you played along in order to save Easter Lanes?"

Right. Easter Lanes. One battle at a time here. I lifted my head up, squared my shoulders. "I want to know what you meant that my father didn't have the right to sell Easter Lanes to me."

I thought I'd been prepared. It was Shorty Easter, after all.

I had endured him all my life and I was still standing, but I'd been wrong.

Nothing could've prepared me for what Ashton Walden told me. "Your father sold Easter Lanes to *my* family. My grandfather. It's something he used to bargain for his life at one point. I don't know what he said or how he convinced you, but he didn't sell the bowling alley to you. It's in one of my family's company's names, and it hasn't changed since you were sixteen."

I felt struck in the face. "Sixteen?"

"You'd already been in foster care for a number of years by then."

God. A deep ache took root inside of me, but it was the same one that was always there whenever my dad got involved with my life. I called it the Shorty Ache. It was there in place of where my soul should've been. He took that from me. "I gave him money for the bowling alley."

"He gave you paperwork?"

The words hurt to speak, but I said them. "We met in a back room at an office. There was a person there. I signed. He signed. It all looked legit. I never questioned it."

"How much did you pay?"

I didn't want to tell him. He had no idea it'd been everything for me. I had nothing.

"I paid him thirty grand." I swallowed over a knot in my throat. I didn't tell Ashton, but I'd almost felt bad for my dad that day, like I had been the one actually conning him.

I should've known. No one out-conned Shorty Easter.

"What do you need from me?"

"I need to use you to do something."

"With the police?"

He hadn't answered. He only stared at me.

He wouldn't tell me anything more, but I didn't have a good feeling about any of this.

Buzzzzzzzzzzz!

Crap. Hearing the doorbell now, I got out of the shower and headed to the door.

I already knew who that was, and after letting them up, I had a robe on when Pialto and Sophie both swept through the doorway.

They stopped and turned as one to me, and both threw their arms around me.

"Oh my god!" Pialto exclaimed before sounding off on a Spanish rant. I wasn't even trying to catch up with him. I just let him go as I recognized a few words: "madre," "dios," and "por favor."

Sophie was shaking as she brushed her frizzy hair away from her face. "Are you okay, sweetie?"

Pialto stepped back, but Sophie moved in, framed my face with her hands, and searched my eyes as if she could read me from there.

Seeing them again, feeling them, that's when the tears started.

I felt them rolling down and tried to rally myself. I did, but with everything going on—my dad, the robber, Ashton—all of it was flooding me now, and I teetered.

My knees shook.

"Madre, she's going down." Pialto grabbed my arms as Sophie lurched for a chair.

I was lowered down, but I kept moving, sliding off the chair until I curled up in a ball. God. I'd been trying to be strong, but I was done for the night. I had nothing more in me.

"Oh, baby." Pialto moved, pulling my head to rest over his folded knees.

"Who's—" I started to lift my head because—Easter Lanes. Once Ashton told me that he had someone watching over it, I hadn't worried about it, and now I was horrified because that should've been the first thing I thought of after I left his place. "Easter Lanes."

"It's okay. It's okay." Pialto pushed my head back down, his hand smoothing over my hair. "There's big scary men watching it."

"Wha—"

"He's joking. Your cousin said he got a call and he's covering for you. Ben and Taj are helping him run it tonight."

I relaxed a little. That was my usual Saturday crew. My cousin wasn't really my cousin. He was from one of my foster homes. Glen. I never worried about my kitchen staff. They always showed up. I was blessed in many ways.

I nodded a little and pushed up so I was sitting. "Thanks, you guys."

Sophie grabbed a blanket from the couch behind her, handing it over to me.

I spread it over my legs, but stretched it to cover Pialto, who turned so he was mirroring me, sitting with his legs crossed. Sophie, too, and the blanket covered her legs as well. The three of us, still on the floor, half huddling together.

"So." Pialto was staring at me, his big dark eyes not blinking and wide.

Sophie moved closer. "What happened?"

I frowned, wiping a tear away. "What happened with you guys?"

They shared a look before Pialto shrugged. "We got checked over at the hospital, got the clear to head home, so we did."

"Did the cops talk to you?"

They shared another look.

"Some cops were there before we went to the hospital, and we gave them our statement, but that was it. Two detectives came in just as your ambulance was leaving, and when they found out you were in there, they took off. They didn't stay or come back," Sophie said.

"Did you guys go home after the hospital?"

"We went back to Easter Lanes. The cops were cleared out, so we started cleaning up, and then we went home. When we came to work today, two big guys were at the counter talking to Glen. Your cousin's the one who told us we could go home, but we didn't want to. We were worried about you."

"How'd you know I was back?"

Sophie grinned, ducking her head a little. "I asked your neighbor Mrs. Tulip to let us know. As soon as you got back, she was blowing up our phones. Said you got out of a big black SUV and looked tired. She also said if you want, she can make some Vietnamese noodles and bring them over."

Oh. That warmed me. My neighbor was nosy, but I liked her. I didn't worry about my place knowing she was always on the lookout.

"Spill, girl. What happened on your end?"

Now I had to make a decision. Should I tell them about Ashton? That'd mean bringing them in on Mafia business, but then again, they were my employees, and most times we acted like we were family. So . . .

"Ashton Walden kidnapped me."

Both sucked in their breaths, their eyes bulging out, and they leaned back almost as one person.

"No way." Pialto.

"Oh good Lord." Sophie.

"Wait. How? Like, for real? How are you here then?" Pialto was looking around.

"Yes, for real. He took me from the hospital, and then no because, well, I can't get into it, but there's things he wants from me and . . . I can't tell you guys. Not yet, anyway. But we came to an understanding, and now I'm here."

Sophie's eyes went cold. "He wants things from you? Like what things?" She gave me a once-over.

"No! Not that." Or I didn't think so, but when he'd touched me, the literal tingle that went through my whole body—gah. Stop it. He was dangerous and an asshole. He was Mafia, for fuck's sake. And cruel. And mean. And my body was weak. Weak, that was. Weak and pathetic. "Not that, but other stuff. My dad. Stuff like that."

"Wait. Wait. We know your dad is involved with that family, and you're friends with Jess Montell, and we all know who she's involved with, but—" Pialto stopped talking, instead starting to gape at me.

I know.

It was a lot.

Maybe I shouldn't have included them, but if I were working somewhere and it had Mafia ties in a whole new way than I'd originally thought—I'd want to know. I swallowed over a lump. "So." I moved closer, huddling farther down. "I'd understand if you guys don't want—"

"Oh my god!"

"Are you serious?!"

"Who do you think we are?!"

"For the love of Mrs. Tulip!"

They both exploded, talking at the same time, but I just started blinking back more tears. I couldn't hold back my smile. My family. That's who they were.

Pialto pressed his hand on my leg, leaning in and making sure I was looking right into his eyes when he said, "We're not going *anywhere.*"

I got all choked up. "Thank you, guys."

Pialto was blinking back some tears, patting my leg again. "No problem, Honey Bunny Molly. You know we're here for you."

I turned my hand under his, linking our fingers, and I squeezed his hand.

Sophie was blowing snot bubbles, but she placed her hand on top of ours. "I love you guys."

Okay. We were all for one and one for all. The solidarity pact was established, but then we fell into silence.

Sophie asked, "So. What do we do now?"

I shook my head. "I have absolutely no idea."

Pialto sighed. "This would be a really great time for you to discover that you have a superhero power."

Agreed.

CHAPTER EIGHT

MOLLY

I was back in Easter Lanes Sunday afternoon going over what I'd missed from the day before, but one good thing: the key passed.

Yep. I was now the weirdly reluctant owner of . . . you know.

We had a copy of the key already, so we were using that one, and Pialto was coming in shortly, so I'd have him take it for a copy of the copy.

Maybe I should have completely changed the locks on the register. But at this point, I didn't trust even a locksmith coming in to do that job.

The door opened, and assuming it was Pialto, I shouted out without lifting my head, "I'm thinking we should redo our whole system."

"Since I'm considering a more active ownership role of Easter Lanes, I think that would be a great idea."

Dread shot down my spine, and I looked up, seeing Ashton walking toward me, taking his very expensive-looking coat off and leaving it on a table as he moved closer to me. Man. Did he have to look as delicious as he did? I hated him, like despised him on a cellular level, but I couldn't deny how seriously good looking he was.

I'd heard rumors he used to model and wasn't surprised.

His security men were spreading through the place. I watched one giant guy walk toward the back of the bowling lanes, and another dipped into the bathrooms. Another went to the employee staff room. The kitchen. A fourth was checking the booths, walking past where I was standing.

Ashton's eyebrows went up, and he tilted his head to the side. "Usually you don't let it be known that you're plotting someone's murder while you're looking at them."

I flushed, my hands grabbing onto the side of my register as a new wave of humiliation went through me. "Get used to it if you're—" What had he said? "An active role? What do you mean by that?"

He moved behind the counter, heading to the coffee machine. He lifted the top lid and saw it was empty. "Do you not make coffee? Does this work?"

"What are you doing?" I stepped toward him.

He reached to take the coffeepot out, and I took it from him, putting it back. "Don't touch that." I put my hands on my hips, glaring at him.

He ignored me, reaching around me for the pot once again.

"Hey!"

I followed him to the sink, standing to the side as he filled it up and then took it back to the coffee machine. He watched me. "Where do you keep your filters and coffee grounds?"

I opened my mouth, totally ready to tell him where to put his coffee filters when I realized I did need to make some coffee. We had thirty minutes before we needed to open the doors for the day.

I growled but turned and grabbed the coffee and filter. After putting them in place, I hit the brew button and whipped back to Ashton. He hadn't moved—if anything, he was closer.

I jerked back, hitting the counter, but I didn't feel it.

I was fully engrossed in how close Ashton was to me. "What are you doing?" My stomach was doing a weird acrobatic performance.

He continued to study me, looking almost captivated, before he muttered something under his breath and moved away.

I frowned. "Why are you here?"

The door opened, the bell jangled, and two more large guys stepped inside. One began walking around the room as the other approached Ashton. Of course these guys were Ashton's. Large. In charge. The one guy who was talking to Ashton now lifted his head, and I caught a flicker of a grin at the corner of his mouth before he gave a nod and left again.

As if all in sync, the other four guys emerged from the building, and each headed outside.

The other one was still walking around, looking up, down. Pausing. He was studying all the doorways and windows.

"What are they doing?"

Ashton glanced down at me as I stepped next to him. "He's security detail. Those four will watch outside. These two will be in here."

I shot him a look. "They go everywhere you go?"

"He's not mine." He indicated one of the men.

"Whose then?"

He flashed me a grin, though his eyes were hard. "Yours. For the day, at least."

He took off, heading to my office, and it took me a minute before I hurried after him.

"Mine?" I went inside as he was at my desk. "Hey!"

He motioned behind me. "Can you get the door?"

I did, then cursed my own self. I was following him around, doing what he said, and for what? This was my place, damn the technicalities. Still, though, I locked the door before stepping behind the desk and behind where he was standing.

I scooted in and used my hip to push him out.

"What are you doing?"

I huffed, putting some extra oomph into my hip. "Moving you."

"Why?"

"Because this is my office."

He was looking down at me, his top lip slightly curled up. "Are you having a late reaction to the robbery? Should I take you to the hospital again, get checked out?"

I paused. "What?"

"You're acting odd."

My chest swelled up. "I don't care what you say about my place. This is my place. Mine. I've put the work into it. I've renovated it. Upgraded it. I have great staff—"

"I doubt you've upgraded everything."

I flushed, ignoring that insult, *if* it was an insult.

He shifted so he was facing me squarely. "You paid your father thirty thousand for this bowling alley. Since then, you have turned it around so it is thriving, but you were still conned out of thirty thousand. I'm going to look through your accounts and see where else you made not-smart decisions." He started to go around me again, reaching for the computer.

"Agh. Stop." Dickhead.

I reached for his hands and tried to maneuver myself so I was in his way.

He cursed under his breath before he wrapped his arms around me. I squealed.

Then he was picking me up, and oomph! I was pressed back against his chest. A tingle shot through me. He took three steps back and pivoted, and I was placed back on my feet again. His hands went to my hips, and he urged me in front of him. "The coffee is almost done. Why don't you grab both of us a cup so you can cool down?"

Heat flamed inside of me. "You did not just treat me like I'm the secretary. Who do you think you are—" And I stopped talking because he was fully trying to hold back a laugh, waiting for my reaction.

And, oh god, his whole face transformed.

I had to stop and blink for a beat before my mind caught up with what was happening.

"You're trying to piss me off."

"Well, no, but the last comment, yes." He sat in my chair, and I'd missed when he turned my computer on, but the screen was asking for my password. He motioned to it. "I want to see your books. Let me in."

I drew back. "No way. I don't know what you're going to do in there."

"Molly." His voice was low, almost soothing.

I hated it. Or I hated how I should've hated it.

He was the enemy.

"What?"

"My first company was in cybersecurity. Did you know that?"

Oooh. Whoa. No. But also not surprising. "I didn't know that."

"Me asking for your password was a sign of courtesy. I'm able to get in with or without you. Let me see your books. Right now it's under my family's name, so if the police come in, I need to see what they're going to see. That could happen. OC knows this place is connected to my family. When that criminal came in here, that gave them an opening to actually coming in here themselves. Are you following me?"

"How do I know you won't plant evidence or something? Or steal from me again?"

"I'm not the one who stole from you." His eyes flicked upward. "Just open your computer."

I did, even though my head was yelling at me not to, but what was I going to do here? He was the mob, for freak's sakes. You didn't say no to the mob.

I typed in "IHATEASHTONWALDEN23" and stepped back.

"Really?" He gave me a dry look.

"I might've changed it this morning."

He rolled his eyes, moving in and starting to click through my computer, and he was going fast. I looked at these things like they were trying to speak to me in an alien language, but not him. He was an alien.

I was remembering what he'd just said. "You think the police will come and look through my books?"

He never stopped studying the computer screen. "They could, yes." He paused, glancing at me. "You had no incoming calls last night, and your only visitors were your two employees. Detective Worthing hasn't tried to talk to you?"

How did he—never mind. "You have my phone tapped?"

"I have a man on you, and he's able to track who is calling or texting you, yes. We put your cousin in charge yesterday, but even he didn't try to contact you. Why not? He was told you'd been held up at gunpoint. He wasn't concerned?"

"Glen and I aren't really cousins. We were in the same foster house for a while."

"I'm aware of this, but if you call him your cousin, that implies there's some form of kinship there. Why didn't he call to see how you were?"

I shrugged. "He'll come in today or tomorrow to check on me. He knew if I needed him, I would've called. It's not the first time we've dealt with police or being held up at gunpoint. It was just the first time it happened here."

Hearing voices from the other side of the door, I recognized Pialto's raised tone. "I'm going to go and make sure P doesn't murder your man."

Ashton had gone back to the computer. "Sure. Because *that's* the likely scenario. And for the time being, Elijah's not my man. He's yours."

Yeah, yeah. I had no idea what that meant.

Pialto was just inside the doorway, his one hand raised when he saw me. "Who is this? What's going on?"

I motioned to Elijah. "He's family to me."

Elijah was watching me back but didn't react and only stepped aside.

Pialto smoothed down his shirt and his hair before craning his neck as he walked around Elijah. I motioned to the farthest end of the bar, and we huddled there.

"What is going on?" he hissed.

50

I hated to say this, but, "Ashton Walden is here."

His head reared back as he gave me the same look he'd just given Elijah. "Have you lost your mind?"

"Keep your voice down, and no." I put my finger to my mouth before saying quietly, "I don't exactly get a say in the matter. He's here whether I want him to be or not."

"Where?" He was looking around.

"My office."

"Your office?!" Another hiss from him.

"Ssshh." Though, the Elijah guy didn't seem concerned. He was focused on the door leading to the back exit. "Listen, I know you're supposed to work, but I don't want you here—"

"You shut up. You hear me?" So many hisses. "Sorry. Hush it. I'm not happy about this new development, but we're family. We have each other's backs. If you're here, I'm here, but again, why is the Mafia guy here? He's got a sudden new crush on you or something?" He held up a hand, stepping back, and his voice rose a little. "And for the record, I am not down with that development if it happens. You hear me, Miss Molly Everly Easter?"

"Okay." I held up a finger right back. "One, it is so not like that. And two, I don't want him here either."

"Good. Then let's plot to get him out of here. How do we do that?"

All good points. "I have no idea."

"What does he want?"

Another solid question. "I'm not sure about that either."

His eyes bulged out, and he let out a frustrated sound. "What do you know that can help in any way?"

"He's been asking questions about Detective Worthing. I think he's here because he thinks Worthing will come back."

"Well, *that's* something."

I nodded.

"Let's call the detective. Have him come here sooner rather than waiting." He started to pull his own phone out.

I stopped him.

"What?" He paused on his phone.

"I don't know. I don't like cops." I was not sharing how Ashton had already said he needed me to do something for him. I was assuming it had something to do with Detective Worthing because the truth was that I was just playing along until I figured out a way to get Easter Lanes fully in my own name. I had no clue how to do that because I knew going the legal route would not work in this situation.

"You're friends with one."

"She wasn't a cop, and she's no longer a PO."

"Still. She was here a lot."

"I know, I know, but something feels weird. Maybe we should let it all play out how it's supposed to?"

"Hmmm no. No, no, no. I've learned many things in my thirty-three years on this earth, and letting things play out when you know catastrophe is coming your way is not a smart move. You don't let it happen organically. You take control and you contain that shit." He held his phone up and stepped back. "Now, you want deniability?" He motioned behind me. "Take a step back and stay busy."

I groaned. "P."

"Now, Honey Bunny." His tone went soft. "Let me do this. It's better to get both wolves out of our henhouse, if you know what I mean."

I did not have a good feeling about this. I did not, did not, did not, and I couldn't get that phrase out of my head as I walked back behind the counter on wooden legs. My whole body locked down, but then the bell jangled above the door again, and I saw the first customers come in for the day.

No matter what, I still had a business to run.

CHAPTER NINE

ASHTON

Her entire system was decrepit. She was still operating on a handwritten ledger. The bare minimum was computerized. I was getting a headache just staring at her computer screen. It looked as old as the first computer ever created.

My phone was buzzing.

I pushed back the desk chair, which had a good view into Easter Lanes as I reached for it. "Yes?"

Silence, then a growl. "You're at Easter Lanes?"

This was Detective Worthing.

I stood up, phone pressed to my face as I stared at the window where I could see Molly behind the counter. She was helping a few customers, but there. I saw it. Her head was folded down. Her shoulders hunched forward. She was looking around. The customers left, and she remained in the same spot, her hand reaching for a rag and wiping the same circle over and over as her eyes were skirting around the place.

What did she do?

"Should we expect a surprise visit from you soon?"

A dry laugh again, caustic at the end. "Can't say it would be a surprise, considering I got a call to my personal cell saying that if I wanted to question Miss Easter, today and within the hour would be a good time."

My body went cold. "She called you herself?"

"Not her. Thinking it was one of her employees. They both seemed real protective of Miss Easter when we questioned them the other night."

I wasn't liking the way he said her name. "She's not a part of this war."

"Beg to differ. By the way, what are you doing at her place of business?"

I grunted. "I'm fucking her. How's that for an answer?"

He was silent for a second. "Are you kidding me?"

Now my body went on alert. "Why would I joke about who I take to my bed?"

"Jess Montell was a good PO. Leave another one like her alone."

"Unless my gut is lying to me, I'm pretty certain Molly Easter has absolutely no affinity for being in law enforcement."

"You know what I'm saying. She's an innocent."

"Then why the call, Detective Worthing? Why the sudden interest in her? You're assigned to organized crime. Why would you be assigned to a simple robbery if you thought she was so innocent?"

He bit off a curse. "You know why. Everyone knows why. Now listen, I got the call, and I have to report it, so that means that my partner and I will be coming into Easter Lanes to interview Molly Easter. This call is a courtesy because you used to pay me."

I went back to being cold. "Yes, I did, until your family killed mine. Remember that. I'll be seeing you when you get here."

"Ashton, I didn't make this call for war purposes. I'm aware that there's a ceasefire—"

"But you still want to interrogate Molly Easter because of her connection to my family."

"'Interrogate' is a strong word. Question, yes. It makes sense. Her father has ties to yours. You know where I was transferred to."

"We both know it would've been an interrogation. I was told you were at the hospital to see her, but you weren't there when I arrived. Why did you leave?"

"When Nurse Sloane tells you to leave and come back later, you leave and come back later."

Nurse Sloane again.

"Have you gotten any leads for my brother's murder? I know there's an understanding between you and my cousin."

And that was it for me.

I ended the call, still watching Molly as she was pretending to wash the same spot once again.

Her whole body was tense. Her eyes were darting around. She was nervous.

Why was I here? Like I didn't have other items to handle today. Other businesses. Other family members wanting answers for events I still didn't know. But I was here.

What was I doing?

That day, that morning so long ago. We were kids, and she'd had no idea what had happened that day, but I had. I knew who she was. I knew why she was there. I didn't know the specifics, but I didn't need to know. Grew up watching con men coming in and out of my grandfather's house. Could clock them the second their cars pulled onto our block. Knew the rank they held among my family's workers, how very little anyone thought of them or how much respect they carried. Her father had none. He was the bottom of the bottom, and I'd always known it, but then he brought her, and I knew what she'd lost that day.

She looked up, scared, all alone in a house of Mafia men. She shouldn't have been there.

Then she saw me, and I recognized the look. She thought I was a cute boy, but more. Like I was a knight in shining armor. For a brief moment, so brief, but burned forever in my head, she looked at me like I was there to save her.

That's what pissed me off the most.

Her father's job was to protect her, and he was selling her out in the office I just left.

She had no clue about any of it, still didn't.

That's what I was doing here, and I needed to acknowledge it. I needed to get rid of it because I'd been feeling it since that day. Carrying that shit. It was time. Finally. Fucking tell her everything so she and I could move forward without holding someone else's burden, whether we knew we were carrying it or not, and this one had nothing to do with her father.

It had to do with her mother. And mine.

But that was something to untangle another day.

I was here. I'd already told her enough to start this process.

Molly hadn't even needed to know about the real ownership of her business. Her system was old, but the business was doing well. She'd continue to make it do well. It was profitable, and I could've made our claim known at a later date, demand payment for profits that hadn't been paid to us, or I could've transferred everything legally into her name, and she never would've known.

I could still do that.

Then again, that wouldn't be very Mafia of me.

CHAPTER TEN

MOLLY

"You close early on Sunday nights?"

I almost screeched as I jumped backward.

I grabbed onto the counter, glaring at him behind me. "Why are you still here? What do you actually want from me?"

I was scowling as he stilled, his own eyes narrowing, and I had an image of a cobra raising its head, eyeing who it was about to attack.

A chill went down my spine, and I shook my head, trying to clear the unsettling image from my mind. Then I remembered what he'd originally asked. "We do. Ten." I looked at the clock. I'd made Pialto leave an hour ago, along with the rest of the staff. I could handle the last three customers, but they'd just left as well. I was ignoring the pit in my stomach because I didn't think Ashton remembered what usually happened on Sunday nights here.

"Why?"

The bell above the door jangled again, and I looked over, half expecting one of our customers coming back. A lot of people forgot their jackets, but it wasn't a customer. Two men were coming in, their badges flashing under their jackets as they moved. Dead eyes.

Cops. I would've known without the badges or their guns on their sides.

Also, I knew one. Detective Worthing had finally shown up.

Police always made me feel the same way, like my life was about to get fucked sideways. Again. It was a pattern that repeated.

"Molly Easter?" The first cop approached, showing me his badge. This was the one I didn't already know. He had sandy-brown hair, looking like he could fit in at a country club or in the middle of a shoot-out. Pretty blue eyes. White. His nose had been broken at some point in his life. There was a dip on the bridge. The other cop who came with him was the opposite in a lot of ways. Dark features. Hair. Eyes. There was a dangerous air that surrounded him, a bit more than his partner.

He was also staring at Ashton. Hard.

"I'm Detective Monteyo. It's nice to officially meet you." The first one was introducing himself before he put his badge away. "Mind if we ask you a few question—"

"What are you doing here?" Worthing cut in, his voice rough. The question was directed to Ashton.

A whole new slew of shivers went through my body, and I had a distinct impression that nothing was what it seemed right now.

I heard Ashton's cool response but could also hear some dark amusement from him. "What do you mean? We had a conversation hours ago that you were coming in. You said soon, yet it's almost closing time. What took you so long?"

I sucked in my breath.

I felt a whole edge slam into place as Worthing's eyes took on a rageful effect. "Excuse me?"

Monteyo had frozen in place, but he coughed, giving Worthing a look before speaking. "We got word that Miss Easter had returned to her place of employment, and since we were grabbing food in the area, we decided we could stop in." He focused on me; his smile was forced. "Get some preliminary work out of the way before the week starts tomorrow, you know?"

I had no idea what he was talking about. "I own this business. It's not just my place of employment." I sent Ashton a withering look because it *was* going to be my business again. At this point, I would do anything and everything to get this away from his family and away from my father, and away from even the West Mafia family too.

I was so tired of this world.

Ashton was unreadable. His face was made of granite, but his eyes met mine before they slid over my head and landed back on the detectives. "You have questions for Miss Easter?"

Neither of them moved, but Monteyo coughed again, clearing his throat, and took a step forward. He pulled out a pad of paper and questioned me about the robbery. I answered with honesty except vaguing up the bit where I'd used the Walden family name to scare the robber away.

Monteyo frowned. "So you think he changed his mind because of your father?"

I snorted. "Have you met Marcus Easter? He's Satan's spawn. If you haven't met him, I'd stay away. He's a curse that you'll never get rid of, no matter how much you try to shake him. He's like lint that's immune to a lint roller." I shuddered at the magnitude of truth there.

I'd never be done with my father's shittiness in life.

"Uh. Yeah." Detective Monteyo scribbled one last thing before putting his pad away. "Want to explain why a businessman with prominent and known Mafia ties is standing behind you right now?"

I opened my mouth, but yeah. I had nothing.

A hand touched my side. Ashton was moving.

Both the detectives saw the motion, their eyes falling to his hand, but at that moment, the bell above the door jangled again, and my dad's voice rang out, "Daughter! Daughter! You here or—" He skidded to a halt, his oversize cargo jacket flopping in front of him.

Marcus Easter always looked half-homeless, mostly because he ended up sleeping a lot of nights on the streets, but tonight he looked worse than normal. Ratty and greasy hair a mess, half-smashed to the left side of his head. He had jeans and a sweatshirt underneath his jacket, but the ends were in holes. The jeans wore him, not the other way around. The ends trailed on the floor, and it looked like he was wearing moccasins on his feet.

"Oh, whoa, whoa, whoa." He gaped at everyone before his eyes bulged and he turned, already lunging back where he'd just come from.

I felt movement at my side, and then Elijah moved in from behind him, his hands clamping down on the sides of my dad's arms. His hands were huge and half on my dad's shoulders.

"Hey! What are you doing?! Let me go. Let me go, I say." My dad was wiry, and he was trying to get untangled from Elijah's hold, but Elijah was six four and solidly built where I didn't think he had any fat on him, that kind of built. My dad didn't stand a chance.

Then my dad got a good look at Elijah, and his voice trailed off. "Wait a minute . . ." He tensed again. His head popped up, like a bird's, and he whipped around, looking, looking—seeing me, clocking me, and then switching behind me, and my father looked like his eyeballs wanted to really pop out of his skull. I saw the whites on the back end of his eyeballs before he started shaking his head, recoiling backward, but Elijah was there, and he merely grunted before picking up my father and bringing him closer to the group.

"Hello, Marcus." That came from Worthing.

My dad's gaze was riveted on Ashton before he turned to who had spoken, and his eyes closed, his head fell back, and he made a whole dramatic groan. "Are you jerking me around?"

"Shorty. How's it going?"

Monteyo moved in on the other side. "Pretty certain we've got three warrants out for your arrest." He reached behind his back and pulled out a pair of handcuffs.

"Oh, come on, guys! Not like this." He waved a hand to me. "In front of my daughter. And on Sunday? I was hoping to come in for a warm meal. With my daughter."

A warm meal? With me?

I.

Was.

Seeing.

Red.

RED!

Sunday night?

With me?

A warm *fucking* meal?

After *what he did to me*?!

I growled and started for him, or I would've if Ashton hadn't held me in place. "Relax," he said under his breath. He had an arm around my waist, clamping me to him. His chest was firmly behind me.

I couldn't.

I just couldn't. What my father did? He wasn't a dad to me. When had he ever been a father to me?

I wanted to murder him. I wanted to take his head, twist it, and yank it off his body.

I wanted to bathe in his blood.

I was unhinged. Fully aware of it, but this was him. This was what my dad did to me. He had the ability for me to flip the switch, and my switch was all the way flipped.

"Marcus Easter, you're under arrest." Monteyo motioned for him to turn around, and as he did, Monteyo put the handcuffs on him.

Worthing was watching Ashton, who was as cool as a fucking cucumber.

I wanted to commit murder, in front of these cops, but no. The Mafia head guy was all nonreactive and Mr. Cool Joe. Then again, that's probably why he did what he did.

As Monteyo was reading my father his rights, my dad turned his head my way. "Sweetie. Honey. I heard what happened to you, and I was worried—"

I burst forward, but Ashton had ahold of me still. I yelled, "Two days ago, Dad! Dad. Dad, my ass. You—" A hand clamped over my mouth.

I wasn't having it; I wasn't dumb, though. He was smothering my words for a reason, the law enforcement for one, but I was beyond seeing reason. I hated Marcus Easter. Hated him. Loathed him. I was planning his funeral on the joyous occasion of when he was killed. By me.

By me and my shovel.

Yes. Me. My shovel. My dad.

Monteyo finished reading my dad his rights and glanced over, his eyebrows pulling low. "You got her under control?"

My dad's eyes enlarged. "Under control?"

I was still shouting at him, Ashton's hand covering my mouth, but now I started reaching for him. Ashton was like a cement wall. I couldn't move an inch, so I tried kicking for him, though that was just a comedic experience by now because Monteyo started taking my dad to the door.

Worthing stayed back, moving backward until his partner and my father were through the door. He stopped.

Ashton's hand fell from my mouth, and I almost fell forward but caught myself.

I quieted because a whole new awareness had fallen over the room, with just those two staring at each other.

"Really?" Worthing asked, though it sounded more like a statement.

Ashton's words came out like ice. "Really."

Worthing moved closer to the door. "We don't have to be enemies."

"Your last name says otherwise."

His phone made a buzzing sound. He grabbed it but gave one last lingering look at Ashton before leaving.

I swung around to Ashton. "What was that about?"

No reaction. Nothing. He just turned to me. "He thinks we're fucking, and now your father does too. That's unfortunate, for him."

Fucking?! What?

Why—

"Heading out, boss?" Elijah asked.

Ashton gave him a nod, and Elijah left as well.

My blood was still pumping, but I was able to think a bit clearer. I followed Ashton as he went to my office. "You told him what? Why? You told me that you wanted to use me to do something for you. I thought that was about the cops. Is that what that was? But sex? You and me? What was all of that about?"

My heart was speeding.

Ashton went over and began shutting down my computer, which I was now clueing in had a whole new look on the screen before it went black. I pointed at it. "What'd you do to my computer?"

Ashton ignored me, coming back and folding his coat over his arm. He gestured for me to go ahead of him, and he locked my office behind us.

"You're taking over everything."

He barely blinked, his hands finding my hips and gently urging me ahead of him. "Where's your coat? Your things?"

I was still frowning at him, looking beyond him to my office, so he stepped away and went behind the counter. I'd already closed out the register, but he dipped down and straightened, my coat and purse in his hand. "Your keys?"

I motioned to the purse. "In there."

He held it out to me, coming back to me. "I need you to lock up behind us."

"What?" I reached in my purse and pulled out the keys. I went to the back door, tested the doorknob. Everything was already locked up. I had either Pialto or Elijah to thank for that. The last door was the main door, not the one I usually exited out of, but today seemed like the whole theme was out of the normal routine. We stepped out, and I hit the locks as we did.

A black Escalade pulled up in front of us. Ashton opened the back door. "Come on."

"You're giving me a ride home? Because that'd be nice. I mean, I take the train."

He waited until I got in, got in behind me, and shut the door. "No. We're going for dinner."

"I don't want to have dinner with you." Maybe talking to him about my dad would be a good idea. I'd like to know if I killed him, whether there'd be repercussions against me. "I mean, sure. I'd love dinner."

"It's time we talked about the day you were at my grandfather's house."

I blinked at him. Then blinked again. "Huh?"

His mouth tightened as he looked out the window. "Exactly."

We pulled away, and I looked back, feeling something sinking in me.

Tonight would've been the night Kelly and Justin came to bowl with their friends.

CHAPTER ELEVEN

MOLLY

He took me to Pedro's, a very exclusive small restaurant that most people only heard about. As we pulled up, going down an alley and then stopping at what looked like their back door, I could attest to how special I already felt. A back entryway. Two members of their waitstaff came out, dressed in black pants and shirts and nice-quality cream aprons, to greet us. The chef stepped out as we got to the door, and he embraced Ashton, speaking in Spanish.

We were getting this special treatment because of Ashton, because of who he was. Ashton was Mafia. I caught the looks from the staff through the windows. These people knew it.

They were all watching.

I couldn't catch what was being said, but it was beautiful to hear, a touching moment to witness, and then the chef came to me and took my hand in both of his. He was speaking again, blinking back tears.

I thought Ashton would translate, but he didn't. His eyes were on me, and they'd gone back to their normal hardness. A chill started to go down my spine, but it stopped halfway because Pedro was still talking to me. He was shorter than Ashton but taller than me. Maybe five seven, and he kept himself trim. His hands were strong. When he was done, he reached up and tucked a strand of my hair back behind my ear, saying a last phrase before turning back to Ashton. He clasped him on the sides of his arms, gave him a bright, beaming closed-mouth smile, and gestured for us to follow him inside.

Ashton stepped back, letting me go ahead of him, and he placed a hand at the small of my back.

A whole different kind of shiver went all the way down my spine this time, and I was cursing myself internally because hello. I did not need to keep finding this man attractive or letting his touches affect me in a certain way. But as his hand pressed a little more firmly down there, I couldn't stop myself from envisioning if he kept moving south and how I might've liked that touch too.

The inside of Pedro's was dark, lit with candles everywhere. I was hoping they were LED candles, but they looked like the real deal. I could hear other customers as we passed, but only by a very low murmur of conversation and the clinking of silverware on plates. I never saw anyone, and then we were taken to a back area that almost magically opened up to a courtyard. There was a gazebo above, but higher than that, stars. Vines ran the length of the walls around us and intertwined the wooden posts overhead. A small fountain was set in one of the walls, the water running as we stepped out. The floor was made of rocks, looking like Europe with cobblestone.

A small table in the middle of the courtyard.

The table was already set with candles. A wine bottle at the ready. Bread. Oil for dipping.

My heart paused for a brief moment because I envisioned how this would feel on a date. Romantic. The girl would be like Cinderella. Ashton was acting like a prince, helping me sit in my seat first before he went to the other. Swoonworthy. The wine was poured. Water was being poured at the same time, and one of the waitstaff said something to Ashton.

But this wasn't a date.

He nodded, his eyes never meeting mine until the second she left and closed the glass doors behind her. We were alone.

Those eyes flicked up and found me.

I was zapped in place. "What?"

"Pedro is a family friend. You will keep your reactions to me and what I'm about to tell you to yourself."

He wasn't asking. He was commanding. I flushed because *damn*. "I would've anyways. You didn't need to reiterate that. It's obvious that Pedro is like a celestial being on this plane. Can feel that the second you approach this restaurant."

He frowned but didn't comment on that.

I glanced over my shoulder. "Are they coming back for our order?"

He shook his head, leaning back in his seat and for the first time heaving a breath. "Pedro would never let that happen. He's making a feast for us. If you lose your appetite during our talk, I can have it boxed and brought to your home for you."

He was already planning for me to lose my appetite.

His eyes had started to lower, but they lifted back up. I was pinned in place again. "What do you know about your mother?"

I tensed but jerked up a stiff shoulder. That came from left field. "She was a drug addict all her life. Why?"

"What do you know about how she died?"

Now I was the one becoming like cement. "She died getting drugs. It was a drug deal gone bad. Tried to rip off the dealer. He killed her instead."

He was studying me. I couldn't shake how he seemed to be seeing inside of me.

"Were you aware our mothers were friends?" His voice was almost gravelly but unyielding.

"What?"

He tilted his head to the side. "Your mother. My mother. They were friends. Did you know that?"

I was going through my memories.

Laughing with my mom.

Hugging her.

She read to me, tucking me in at night, but then she was dead, and my dad filled in the blanks afterward.

She was a drug addict.

He told me that I couldn't believe what I remembered.

My memories were wrong.

My mom was cold. Harsh. She just used me. My dad gave me the truth about her.

I turned eleven when my mom died. I lived with my dad for a few years after, but he kept telling me how she was and I . . . I stopped thinking about her. Then I went into foster care, and I stopped thinking about both of them.

Or I tried . . .

My mom, though.

I felt so small right now. "I didn't know she was friends with your mom."

"The morning she died, your father brought you to my grandfather's house. Do you remember that day?"

I frowned, swallowing a lump. My throat was burning. My chest felt like it was going to implode on itself. "I remember that morning. I remember seeing you, but . . . it was that day? I don't remember that part."

His gaze was burrowing into me. I could feel it. "You were sitting on the bench in our hallway, the one that's attached to the stairs. Your father walked into my grandfather's library as I was leaving, and I saw you. You saw me."

The memory began to flicker, more clearly.

A room. A wall.

Men. A lot of men were there, all standing around like they were waiting for something. They were on edge.

I'd been scared. I hadn't wanted to be there.

I frowned. "The wall behind my bench had a pattern on it. Wooden stairs."

His voice went flat. "Yes."

"That was the morning my mom died?" I was starting to remember. "My dad told me later. She left us, me and Dad, and she went to get drugs—"

"No." That came out flat. Hard.

I lifted my eyes to his, stilling.

A cruel glint showed from his eyes. The rest of him was back to being encased in stone. "She died the night before. It was the night before your birthday." He was almost unrelenting now. "They both died that night. Your father showed up the next morning. He offered a deal to my grandfather."

I felt sick.

My limbs were growing numb.

"The deal struck was that your father would be allowed to keep gambling at our casinos and through our bookies, and he'd always be given time to pay back his debts. He knew his time was running out with us. He made a deal regarding your mother to keep my family off his back."

No, no. I didn't—I didn't like this, whatever he was about to say. I felt it in my gut. "I don't understand. What are you saying?"

"I'm saying that my mother wanted to get drugs and insisted that *your* mother come with her. Your mom didn't want to go during the day because it was your birthday. That's when they would normally go to my mother's usual dealer, but because of your birthday, they went to a new dealer the night before. The deal went bad. They were both killed."

I was frozen.

No—

"The other truth? Your mother never did drugs. My mother did. Your mother was just stupid in trying to be a kind friend, but your father offered to flip the narrative. To say that your mother went to get her own drugs, because she was a drug addict. My mother died in the crossfire trying to save yours. That was what your father offered for his own skin. He offered up your mother's reputation to my grandfather."

My eyes were stinging.

My mom?

Those memories of her? They were real?

I shook my head. "Why would he—" I knew why he would do that.

"Your mother was homeless when your father met her."

I nodded, dazed. I wanted to say that she had people who cared about her, who would know her, but it wasn't the truth. What he said was true. She had me, only me.

"No grandparents. Your father was an only child. 'It's easy to spin another lie. The kid's already been lied to all her life. Easy as pie.' That's what your father said to my grandfather. He laughed about it."

I was on that bench, sitting. Hugging myself. My dad went inside, and all those giant men moved around to make room for him. They didn't like him.

I was almost there again, *tasting* my fear.

They hated my father, but that wasn't new. I barely registered it, but I had that morning because it felt wrong, not wanting my dad to go inside when normally I knew it was only better when he was away.

Then Ashton came out. They bypassed each other, and the look Ashton gave my father.

He hated him. He wanted to kill him. The sneer. The disdain, and a surge went up in me.

He was cute. So cute.

I didn't remember what he was wearing that day, just how he looked and how I knew, no matter how old he was, that he had darkness in him.

He could do what I couldn't, and even back then, I hadn't wanted to admit what I wanted to do.

That darkness inside of me.

I wanted to be away from my father.

Ashton, this boy going past him, could do that for me.

I knew it then, and that's why I never forgot him. I couldn't.

He was the prettiest and cutest boy I'd ever seen. Beautiful black hair that he'd been raking a hand through. Eyes that were so dark I was sure they were black. Eyelashes that framed them that were long and curled perfectly. And even back then, as an eleven-year-old, I knew he would grow up and be mesmerizing.

Which he had been.

Which he was, and that sculpted jawline clenched as he took me in.

"You were my birthday wish," I whispered.

"What?"

So dumb. "It was my birthday. I saw a cute boy." I looked at him. "My dad bought me a birthday cupcake afterward, and when I blew out the candle, I wished for you."

His eyes turned stricken, and then he blinked, and they were back to being cruel. Easy as pie.

"Why are you telling me this?" I asked.

His nostrils flared. "Because I hate my mother, and I hate that everyone thinks she's a good person when I know the truth."

Why would he—what son wanted their mother's true reputation to come out? I was shaking my head. "That makes no sense."

"I have my reasons."

"Why now, though? Why—" I couldn't wrap my head around all of this. My father. My mother. His mother. The lies.

The brainwashing.

My father had brainwashed me for how long?

"I'm telling you this because I need your help with something."

"With what?" I didn't want to hear any more. I didn't want to get pulled even more into this than I was, whatever this was.

I started to push back my chair. My hands were beginning to tremble.

"I need your father to do something for me."

"What?"

"I need a rat on the street, and that deal was struck between your father and my grandfather. I've always loathed your father. I've never made that a secret, so now when I need something from him, I don't believe he will deliver. If he did, I couldn't believe it was the true information. This is too important. He could easily con me, what he does best. There are other avenues I could go down, but . . . I'm trying a different way, a less-torture type of way. You."

"Stop." I wanted nothing to do with this. With him. Not with what he'd just told me.

I shoved my chair back the rest of the way and crossed for the door. I reached for it, my hand touching it, and then I was pulled backward. "No!"

"I am telling you the truth. Truth for truth. I hated my mother. I hated what was said about her. I was forced to swallow those lies, while *your* mother was taken from you. I'm giving her back to you. All cards are on the table right now, and I need your help." He turned me, in my space. His hands were surprisingly gentle as they touched my arms. He moved me so I was leaning against the wall next to the door. His head was angled down, peering at me.

I looked beyond him, to the gazebo, to the vines. To the stars.

"She'd read me books about the stars. The night sky."

I barely registered those words, sounding broken. They came from me.

Ashton's eyes flared briefly, in pain, but he schooled them again. "There's only one person who your father cares about other than himself. Only one other person who *might* be able to get him to do something."

I focused on the stars above. Pretending I was among them. Floating free. Flying.

He moved in even more, but I didn't mind. I liked the warmth. It made me feel closer to the stars for some reason.

"You're his daughter. If there's anyone he might do something for, it's you."

My father. He took my mom away from me. He took Easter Lanes away from me.

My father was the reason I was alive, but he was also the reason this world was so hard.

"What do you need me to ask him to do?"

I wanted to keep looking at the stars.

For the first time, there was no cruelty shining back at me. He was looking at me like I was a real person. Funny how that wasn't his default setting.

"I need you to ask him to find out who killed Justin Worthing and Kelly. Too many doors are closed to me, so I need a rat on the street. Your father is the best kind of rat there is, and if *you* ask, he'll do it. For you. You're the only one."

Kelly. Justin. Another lump was back in my throat.

"I was friends with her too," I murmured.

"I know. It's the reason your dad won't question why you're the one asking him to find out."

"Then what? If he finds out?" This was his less torturous way?

"I'll give you Easter Lanes. You won't owe my family anything after that."

"What if Shorty doesn't find out?"

His nostrils flared, and he gave me a hard look. "Make sure he does."

I nodded, closing up inside, walling myself to everyone and everything because it was all too painful, but I needed one more thing. "How do I know you'll actually give me Easter Lanes?"

"I will. I don't break my word."

I stared at him, holding his gaze, because of all his reputations, I hadn't heard one where he went back on his word.

Also, I had no other option.

I gave a small nod. "I'll get him to find out, but I don't just want Easter Lanes."

His eyebrows pinched together, just slightly. "What else?"

My darkness. It was in me. Sometimes it made me uncomfortable. Tonight, I was just fine with it. I let some of it out. "I want my father gone, as far away from me as possible, and I don't care how you do it."

He never blinked. "Done."

Good. We had a deal. It was a cruel arrangement in a way.

They brought the food out once we sat back down, and he'd been right. I never ate it.

I wanted to keep looking at the stars.

CHAPTER TWELVE

ASHTON

It was a local neighborhood street festival, but it was late, nearing midnight. So many had retired for the night, but not my family. My cousin Marco asked for me to stop by.

We parked at the front of the carnival and walked in.

My men got out first, with Elijah opening my door.

I was out next and felt the attention. I wasn't surprised. I was used to it, having been watched all my life, but this time was different. There was more weight, more responsibility.

Some little kids were still playing, kicking a soccer ball around. A couple chased each other, wrestling with balloons. They were squealing, laughing.

That was nice to see. A moment of lightness amid this heavy night.

"Ashton." Marco was coming toward me, smoothing a hand down his shirt. He was dressed up, like me. His hand was out, and we shook hands but moved in and did the typical cheek kissing. Because of our grandmother, it was a family tradition. He stepped back, taking me in, and nodded. "You look good."

I nodded, meeting his gaze briefly before looking past him to the rest.

Our aunts were back there, all sitting at the same table.

Our grandmother perished long ago, but the loss of Benito and our uncles was felt by everyone. It would be for a long time. Seeing some of the other men from the neighborhood, I knew their judgments. It should've been Marco who took the lead. Not me. I was the outcast among them compared to him. Marco, whose mother was still here, whose father had been executed that night. My own father left years ago, and my mother dying how she had . . .

Anger flared up inside of me as I remembered how I'd broken the news to Molly earlier this evening.

The shame from my mother was heavy, so heavy it sank inside of me, but I cracked myself open, speaking of her again.

It went against our family to feel such disrespect for your elders, but fuck anyone who didn't know, because they didn't understand. And they would if they knew the truth.

The world would understand.

"Come on. Unless you want to get stuck talking about politics or fútbol, let's grab some food. There's still some empanadas left. Or choripán and asada." He led the way, nodding to people as we went to the table, picking up his fernet, his small drink, on the way.

My men spread out, half walking beside me, but as Marco began to take me to the food, I stopped at the men's table. I had to. It was out of respect. I was showing it to them, and they were showing it to me as one by one, each stood. They clasped their hands to mine, saying their condolences. Each one. I thanked them, giving them my respect back.

Marco stepped back, waiting until I was done.

I went the entire way around the table until I reached the last man, who offered a sip of his Malbec. I declined, and stepped back.

Marco moved in. "I have a plate ready for you."

He was pulling me away, and I knew the reason. We had business associates who were waiting inside one of the local cafés. They came specifically to spend time with the Walden family, and it was why I had come because they wanted to know the plans for the future. I was here to tell them that our future was safe. I would make sure it was enforced, but giving Marco a small nod, I went to the women's table first.

My aunts needed to see me as well.

Right now, business could wait. Family would come first.

CHAPTER THIRTEEN

ASHTON

Two days later and I was walking *back* into Easter Lanes.

The guy worker, Pialto, shrieked when he saw me, and his hands flew up. The papers he'd been holding went everywhere.

The female worker rushed out of the back kitchen area, the door swishing behind her, and she also shrieked. Hers was more of a quacking sound as she jumped backward right through the doors. More shouts ensued. Clanging and shattering noises soon followed.

Curses.

Curses in Spanish.

I frowned, pretty sure I heard a German curse word as well, but then I felt *her* coming. Which was unsettling, but it happened, and she came out of her office, her hands already finding her hips. "What in the he—" She saw me. Her hands dropped; so did her tone. "Oh."

I raised an eyebrow up. "Hello to you too."

She turned, but I caught the quick flash of fear in her eyes right before she did. She was heading back to her office, and her door was closing as I got there. I caught it, pushing my way in, and I was the one who closed it. Locked it.

"Leave. You told me what to do. Now let me do it."

I moved into her space.

Her eyes went wide, but I moved us both back against the wall. I placed an arm on one side of her, next to her head, and leaned in. "Your father is still in jail."

She pursed her lips together, her throat moving up and down. "I'm aware." She was focusing on my chest, and her hand started to reach out, to touch me.

Yes. I wanted that. I wasn't questioning it. And if I was here, I was going to be touching her. I decided then and there. I leaned in even closer, but she pulled her hand back.

I frowned at that. "Why have you not bailed him out?"

She shrugged, biting her lip. "I mean, jail seems like the best option for him, don't you think? He can sit there and rot, forever."

"We have a deal."

Her jaw clenched, and she tipped her head up now.

There. Right there. I liked having her eyes on me. "You're being stubborn."

Her chin lifted.

Madre de Dios. I tried again, moving my head down a little closer. "Your father can't find out who killed Justin and Kelly if he is still in jail. Post his bail."

Her eyes flashed at me, defiant. "He deserves to sit in there and his insides rot out of him and mold with his cell and—" Her hand went to my chest. She held it there. I didn't know if she was aware that she was touching me.

I pressed harder against her hand. "Bail him out or you're never getting Easter Lanes in your name. I don't get what you're doing, or not doing. I'm trying to find out who killed your friends. I'm trying to do this for my best friend, for Jess, and then I have a whole war to handle. Bail your father out of jail. Why are you waiting?" My phone was buzzing, and I knew that was Trace or my cousin needing something. I didn't want to take it. I'd been annoyed that I needed to come back, find out what was going on in her head, but I couldn't lie to myself. I could've called. I could've issued a threat or a reminder, but seeing her in person had been what I needed.

I wanted to see her. I wanted . . . I liked these interactions with her.

My phone kept buzzing. The world was pushing in. I had to go. I had to do my duties.

Feeling almost cold, I reached for the door and started to open it.

"I can't."

I turned back. "What do you mean?"

She had moved to her desk. She wasn't looking at me, but her shoulders were down, and she was picking at the pen that she'd used for prodding her papers. "I can't. I just—if I see him right now, I will kill him. You—he took away the good memories I had of her, and that's just the latest he's done to me, that I know of. You can't—I don't know your grandfather or your father. I know you had uncles, but I can't stomach the idea of talking to him. Not yet. It's too soon."

Well. Fuck.

I shut the door behind me. "What do you need from me?"

Her eyes flickered, seeing me, and the ends of her mouth curved down. "What do you mean?"

"I need you to ask your father to do something. That means I need you to bail him out, first step. You are blocked from doing that. What can I do to help remove that block so you can stomach the idea of seeing your father?"

She lifted a shoulder. "Beat him up? I don't know . . ." She looked away.

I frowned, moving closer. "That'd make you feel better? If I beat him up?"

Her head folded down, and she was tapping her pen down onto her desk.

I looked her over, seeing the rigidness. The tension, so I took a moment, one moment, and put myself in her shoes. I considered what I'd told her, what she'd said. Her mother. The truth. Her father. His hand in how he helped to take away her mother.

My gut flickered. "I could have that done. Easily."

She looked up, her eyes clouded over. The tension still visible on her face, tightening around her mouth.

She didn't agree, but she didn't disagree either.

I took another moment, just one, before I said, "I would not judge you if you wanted physical violence against your father. He hurt you. He has continued to hurt you. There's nothing wrong with wanting some vengeance."

Her eyes closed, and she flinched.

"I would think there would be something more wrong if you didn't, if nothing ever happened to someone who took away the kindness of your mother. Her love. Because he tainted that, along with my family."

Her eyes opened, and there was agony there, briefly, before she snuffed it out.

My voice went flat. I did not like seeing that look there. "One might even insist on it, could be a sort of payment from my family to you. If that's what you were asking?"

She continued to study me. I let her see there was no judgment from my end. There would never be judgment from me.

She bit her lip and lifted a shoulder. "Or had *someone* beat him up. Maybe not you, personally, because yeah . . . but someone else."

I gave a small nod, but still felt I needed to tread with care here. "After you posted his bail or before?"

"What do you mean?"

"How soon would you want that done, if you did?"

Her eyes got big, and she stopped picking at her pen. "You mean—"

I stifled a sigh. "This is what I do. I'm in the Mafia."

Her eyes narrowed, and she jerked her head in a nod. "Right. Right. That's kinda the foundation of what you do." She looked away again, biting down on her lip once more. "I could handle seeing him when I posted his bail, if he was beaten up. Yes. That would help me. Before I posted his bail."

A ball of tension unwound inside of me. "Done." I began reaching for the door *again*.

"But, like—"

I stopped and turned back. Her eyes were still clouded over.

"Like—how beat up are we talking about? Still walking? Face all swollen up? Jaw broken? At least both his eyes swollen shut so he can't see?"

She wasn't hiding now. I *liked* this side of her. I cocked my head to the side. "We need him to be physically able to do what we need him to do."

She waved that off, a sound of disgust coming out from her mouth. "Put him unconscious in the hospital and he'd still be able to be a rat on the street. Trust me. His abilities of rat-hood know no bounds."

"Rat-hood?"

"You know what I mean. Slime of the earth. A weasel." She was getting heated, throwing down her pen.

It bounced back up, hitting her on the chin.

"Agh!" One of her hands flailed for it, but the pen was gone. It eluded her grasp, rolling to the edge of the desk and falling to the carpet. It ended near her foot, and if I was starting to get to know Molly Easter, she was going to somehow kick it forward. It would careen off her desk and end up impaling itself in her leg.

I went forward and bent to pick it up. "I'll have someone take care of him. When can you bail him out?"

She sighed, shoving her hands in her pockets. "Tomorrow."

"Thank you." I put her pen back into the cup with the others. I went to leave again, and I got halfway to the door, when—

"Do you—do you think I need to worry about the police coming again? You mentioned they might try to see my books or something."

I tilted my chin down. "I don't think so. The showdown that was going to happen already happened. Worthing gave me a heads-up that you called for them to come and question you on Sunday."

"You knew that?" She went still.

"I did, but I don't know why he did that. I know why he said he did, but I don't believe it. At the end of the day, I'm still in a war against his family, so I need to use all my resources right now to find out who killed Justin and Kelly. That's job number one."

"Why are you being honest right now?"

"Because I made the decision at Pedro's to be honest, thinking that would motivate you to help me better. Was I wrong?"

She shook her head, just slightly. "You were right. I wouldn't have trusted you, and I wouldn't have done anything you wanted."

My mom. Her mom. It was a tangled shit show that I'd known about all my life, but she hadn't. She was still processing.

I reached for the door. "I'll have your father handled tonight, so bail him out tomorrow, sooner than later. And for what it's worth, don't think about what your father's done to you when you see him. Think about Kelly. Justin. I'm aware that last Sunday would've been the night they used to come here." She sucked in a breath. That was the emotion I needed her to utilize. "Use *that*. What you're feeling right there, remember that feeling when you talk to him, and you'll get him to do anything you want. Con *him* this time."

My phone was ringing once more. I *really* needed to go, but I couldn't deny there was a feeling inside of me. An itch to stay. An itch—she was the itch. She'd become my itch.

I left, answering my phone as I did. "Yes?"

I didn't need to scratch that itch, at least not yet.

Trace was on the other end. "I need you at Katya."

CHAPTER FOURTEEN

MOLLY

I wasn't drunk, but I wasn't totally sober when I went to bail out my dad the next morning. I knew what Ashton said, use Kelly and Justin, only think about Justin and Kelly, but it was hard. So because I'd had a few shots, I had Pialto drive me.

Then my dad came out, and Ashton had done his job. Half his face was covered in bruises and swollen so I could barely recognize my father. I loved it. Thank you, Ashton. And bonus points because Shorty Easter was limping as he approached me. "Heya, little Molly bean." He lifted his arms to hug me, but I turned my back and started for the parking lot.

I motioned for him to follow. "We're out here."

"We?"

I ignored him, walking to the car.

My dad followed, and he slowed, taking in the car. "Whose car is this?"

It was a battered old Buick. We'd found it in Pialto's grandma's garage. It was his grandfather's, but rest his soul, he wasn't using it since he was buried in New Jersey and had been for the last six years. His grandmother kept up the tags and insurance, and when Pialto pulled up to Easter Lanes with it, I didn't ask. It was better not to know sometimes, though I didn't think his grandmother knew it wasn't sitting in her garage.

"It's your ride." I got in the front passenger seat. "Get in, Shorty."

I was ignoring how my dad's attention jumped to me. He got into the back seat, moving at a sedate pace. "Peter, right?"

Pialto shot me a look. My dad had been introduced to him eleven times over the last two years. He never used the same *P* name. By now, Pialto replied, deadpan, "Hi, Mr. Shorty."

My dad grunted, and then we were off.

I was just now realizing I could've taken the train, paid his bail, and had our conversation on the street. We could've parted our ways from there. This, the whole car thing, was overkill. I'd been acting on the basis that he was in prison and we needed to drive all the way there to get him.

Yeah.

Totally not planning ahead.

The seat squeaked as my dad leaned forward, his hand settling on the barrier between us. "You can drop me off—"

"We're going to Easter Lanes. You can leave from there."

"But—"

I raised my voice over my dad's. "Easter Lanes, Peter."

Pialto suppressed a laugh as he hit the turn signal and merged into the other lane. Three taxis whizzed past us. One was laying on his horn, his fist in the air. None of us reacted.

It was silent in our vehicle the whole way. Silent and tense, or maybe that was just me because I was having daydreams about me and my favorite shovel.

When we got to Easter Lanes, my dad got out first.

Pialto touched my hand. "I need to take the car back, but, you know." He motioned to my dad, who was now trying to get into Easter Lanes even though it was before opening, so the door would be locked.

We both watched him.

He tried the door. It was locked. He tried again. It was still locked. A third time, but this time, he cursed and raked a hand over his head, calling over his shoulder, "Something's wrong with your door!"

I was going to kill him. Full out. Full blast. Just take that shovel, grip it with two hands, hold it like the bat I never learned to use in softball because I didn't play softball, but I was going to do it, and then, whack! One good swing and his head would be the ball. I'd send it sailing, clear off his body and into the infield. Home run for first-degree murder.

I knew people. I'd be okay on the inside.

"Girl." Pialto's hand squeezed mine. "Go in there. Fix yourself a drink. Ask Justin's and Kelly's spirits to come through for you. You do what you need to do, whatever Ashton asked you to do, even though I know you don't want to do it. You totally got that."

Right. I squeezed Pialto's hand back. "Thanks, Peter."

He snorted, winking at me. "Of course, sweetie. Me and Sophie, we got your back. Always."

That's right. He was my family, not that douchebag now banging on my door and yelling inside.

I got this. I could do this. Totally.

I got out, and Pialto sped off.

My dad turned to me, pointing inside. "You should do a scanner so I can just use my thumb and voilà, your door opens for me. Way easier to get in then."

Murder. Yes. I'd start formulating my plan for how to get away with it as soon as I unlocked the door.

I opened the door, and my dad brushed past me, heading to the bar and dropping his bag on one of the stools. "You have no idea how good it feels to be inside friendly walls." He was heading for the bathroom, shaking his finger in the air as he went. "No idea, honey. Then again, you'll never need to be worried about going to jail. It's not like you'd do anything to get thrown in there. Hold on. I want to wash up."

My phone buzzed.

Ashton: My sources tell me Shorty Easter was bailed out by his daughter. Also, you'd been drinking.

Oh, good idea. I went behind the counter and poured myself another drink.

I could hear the water running in the bathroom.

Me: You know people in the slammer. I'd be protected if I went temporarily insane in the next five minutes, right?

Ashton calling.

I answered, leaning my hip against the counter so I could see when my dad came back out. "I'm going to do what you want. Don't worry."

He was quiet for a second. "How much did you drink?"

"A few shots. I forgot to take a breath mint, but don't worry, I had someone drive us."

"I assumed you'd take the train."

I needed another sip after the reminder. "I'm aware of that too. Now."

He smothered a laugh on his end. "Text me when you're done."

The door opened. My dad came out, pulling up his pants and fixing his buckle. His head was down. "You got any food in this place? I'm starving after my ordeal. I can't believe they kept me in there for a whole four days. You must've been going out of your mind with worry that they weren't processing me or something."

"Yeah. Sure," I spoke dryly. I ended the call with Ashton. "Food?"

Shorty's head lifted, and he frowned at me putting my phone away. "Who was that?"

I raised an eyebrow as I took another sip. "You want food?"

He focused on my drink. "It's early for you to be drinking." A whole new awareness was entering my dad's gaze now. Wariness. "You okay, Molly Holly?"

God, I did not want to be here.

I did not want to do this with him.

Be fake. Be a con woman.

I didn't want to become him.

My heart rate was rising.

My blood was boiling.

"Why was Ashton Walden here the other day?" His tone was quiet now.

Fuck him! Just, fuck. Him.

I was going to flip the switch.

Justin. Kelly. Justin. Kelly.

Remember.

"Forget Ashton. You know who should've been here that night? *They* would've been here that night." I could feel *them*.

Kelly, her laugh. And Justin was always so nice.

My dad fell quiet, but I kept speaking, knowing he had no clue who I was talking about, knowing in his mind everything was about him and his questions and his needs and his desires and him, him, him, but not right now. Right now was about me and what was burning up inside of me, and that was hate and longing, and murder. And pain. "Did you know that?"

"You're on a first-name basis?"

"That's not who I'm talking about."

He scratched at his chin. "Huh?"

"Justin Worthing and Kelly."

"You knew them?" Of course he knew about them, but he shouldn't. He had never met them, but he knew about them, about their death. Ashton was right. My father could find anything out. He was *such* a rat.

"Kelly and Jess Montell came here every Sunday night. It was their thing. They came with friends who weren't any of their normal friends. Jess told me it was her night away from her work. She needed it like church. My place"—my voice broke—"here. It was a sanctuary for them, and then Justin came in Jess's place later, so I got to know him too." A tear slipped out. I didn't dare look at my dad. "He was a good guy. He wasn't in the life, like his family was. She was too. God. They both were so good. They didn't deserve what happened to them. Whoever did it."

"Why are you talking about this? Why was Ashton Walden here that night?"

I lost it—turning, I heaved my drink at him.

His eyes bulged out, and he ducked. The glass went over his head, crashing and shattering against a chair. I let it go, glaring at my father in a way I never had before. He saw it and sucked in his breath. "Honey—"

"Don't fucking 'honey' me! *You conned me out of thirty thousand dollars!* I want to murder you." I was gritting my teeth at the end. Fuck this man.

I bent, grabbing whatever was closest to me, and I came back up, a broom in my hand.

"Molly." His hands were up. He was backing away. "Honey. Sweetie. Let's talk about this—"

"You want to know what Ashton Walden was doing here the other night? He told me the truth. Easter Lanes belongs to his family, to him. You made me pay for it! I hate you. I loathe you. I am currently planning on how to murder you. You asshole, narcissistic dirtbag who was never a father. You were worse than a father. You—" God! I stopped, horrified at myself. I'd been about to let him know how much I knew about Mom.

"Molly! Come on! I'll—help you get it back. How about that?"

"Get out!" *Don't get out, not yet. Stay.*

I needed him to do what I needed him to do.

"Molly." His voice was breaking. "I hate to see you like this. I— what can I do? Tell me what I can do. I'll go to Walden. I'll get him to give it back. I'll—"

"Who killed Justin and Kelly?" The words ripped out of me, and I was saying things before knowing I was even going there. None of this was planned.

"What?" He started to drop his arms, straightening back up.

"Who killed them? You find out, and I can use that to get Easter Lanes back."

"Honey, I—"

"Who killed them?"

"I don't know!" He threw his hands up in the air. "I don't know."

"But you can find out."

"What?" He turned, shaking his head. "Don't ask me to do that. That's serious business. That's—that'll put you in danger."

I threw the broom at him.

"Come on!" He ducked but glared at me. "Why do you have to do that? I'm your father."

"I grew up in foster care."

"I—" He winced. "Well, maybe you had it better there than with me. Maybe I was doing you a favor? Ever think of it that way? I was doing you a favor—" He ducked again because I threw a shot glass at him. When his head popped back up, I had another one already in the air. He threw his whole body to the side to avoid it. "Come on, Molly! Stop it! *You're going to have to pay for those!*"

"I don't care." I jumped to the top of the bar. I was about to launch my whole body at him when he saw and he cursed, rolling backward.

"Molly! Stop it!"

I was going to use my elbow. I would jump, my body would land next to him, and I'd slam my elbow into his face. That's what I was going to do, and I bent my knees, readying.

"Okay! I'll do it."

I froze. "Do what?"

He shot his hands in the air from the ground. "I'll find out who killed them, but when I do, you can only tell Walden. You hear me on that? You can't say a word to anyone else. You'll get yourself killed."

"Okay."

"I mean it!"

"Yes! I know." I growled, reaching for another shot glass.

He saw it, jumping to his feet. He pointed at it. "Hey, now. No more of that." His hands were up, his palms toward me, and he began edging to the door. "You want me to find out who killed your friends? I'll do that, for you, but no one can know. I mean it, Molly. No one."

I nodded. "Yeah."

"I mean it!"

I growled and let loose with the shot glass.

My dad ducked, opening the door and jumping out of the way. It smashed into the doorframe.

"I'll start looking today," he yelled through the door. "I can see you're still upset with me, so I'll let you cool off, and I'll find out what you want. I'm doing this for you, honey. I love you! I'm a good father, in my way. I know you know that—" *Shatter!*

Another shot glass shattered against the door.

He was quiet before he said, "I love you, honey. I'll be in touch."

I was still raging inside. Wanting to cry, wanting to commit murder. I was a whole mix, and I was suddenly and completely exhausted, too, but I didn't move from the bar top. I couldn't.

I sat there, moving to sit cross-legged, and I pulled out my phone.

Me: It's done. He said he'd find out.

Me: I should've played softball growing up.

Ashton: Keep your head down from here on out.

He didn't reply about the softball, but that was okay. I knew I was right. I would've been amazing.

I promptly started crying.

CHAPTER FIFTEEN

ASHTON

"One of our judges got picked up by the Feds."

Marco was on speaker as I was at Katya, a nightclub Trace and I owned. The same nightclub where Jess's second job had been as well. I was in our private area, the windows overlooking the club below. We had a box to the side with a patio that extended out with a bench by the back wall. I was standing at one of the walls overlooking the section that Jess Montell used to cover. It was being handled by another bartender, but not one as good as Jess. I never cared much for the employees at Katya, one of the legit businesses that Trace and I both owned. It seemed pointless. They were fine. The business was fine. There was no worry about it. My attention went toward our other endeavors or the family business because I'd always been more active than Trace had been in the earlier days. And by earlier days, I meant in the time before the Worthing family put out a hit against both of our families.

Those days. Back when we still thought we had a choice.

I missed those days, and I hated to admit it, but I missed seeing Jess's disapproving face behind one of our bars. The guy working there now was fine. Steady. But he didn't have the attitude of threatening bodily harm like Jess Montell had.

Those were the good ol' days too.

"Ashton?"

"I'm here."

"What do you want done about the judge?"

I sighed, taking a sip of my bourbon. "He's been compromised. Do what we always do."

"Okay."

"Marco."

"Yeah?"

"Who sent us this information?"

"One of our cops."

I frowned. The West family and the Walden family worked as two units in the city. They handled distribution and transportation. We handled the legal system and anything else that fell in between. Because of it, our hands were in a lot of pockets, but since the Worthing family had their own detective, I'd been starting to wonder who else Nicolai Worthing was using.

"You're questioning the information?"

"Maybe."

"That'd be a big hit for us, if they're using one of our judges and one of our cops against us. I think the information is legit. We should act on it before the judge turns on us."

"Unless that was the point? To make us turn on one of our judges."

"You think Worthing gave the judge up?"

"Let's get better eyes on Nicolai Worthing, better than what we've already tried."

"We already have a team watching him."

"Maybe a specialist on him, then. Someone who will get close and only focus on Nicolai. I want to know everything he does and everyone he talks to. I want to know how far their reach has gotten in our city. I want to know his fucking psych profile."

"I'll make the call, but what do you want done about the judge?"

"Grab him, bring him to the Box. Use Manny for the pickup."

Marco was quiet on his end. "He might be in South America."

"He's not. He's in New York, waiting for this call from us. I had him come back."

"There's another matter I gotta bring up. Personal."

I frowned, tossing the rest of my bourbon back, because usually when Marco used that terminology, he was going to bring up Trace or Jess. The rest of our family loved Trace, understood the benefits of our friendship, in a way that Jess refused to. She'd been a harder obstacle to overcome. That was one of the only silver linings of having half my family wiped out in one night. Most of those naysayers were gone.

Pain sliced through me, but I ignored that. "What is it?"

"Abuela. Tías. My own mother. They want you to come around for family dinner. They said your visit wasn't long enough the other night. They need more reassurances."

"When?"

"Tomorrow night?"

"Will that give them enough time for the food?"

He barked out a short laugh. "You kidding me? They had a whole pizza festival with fainá yesterday."

I started to grin, because that would've been fun to attend, but then I remembered—they were in mourning. We were all in mourning. No. It wouldn't have been fun. "Set it up. Let me know when and where."

"On it. How are you doing, primo?"

My gut shifted because I didn't like being asked that question. Trace stopped early on. He was focused on his own family losses, and then he was swept up with Jess, and eventually Marco stopped trying too.

"I'm fine."

There was movement at Jess's old bar, and I leaned in, not believing what I was seeing. Molly Easter was bellying up, her two workers/friends next to her, watching her. She hopped onto a stool and almost slid off.

"I gotta go, Marco. Let me know about family dinner."

"Got it. Be safe."

"You too." I hit the button ending the call and headed for the elevator. Elijah's head popped up when I came out of the room, and his eye twitched, taking me in.

He pressed the elevator button and followed me in after the doors opened. "Is there a problem?"

"Molly Easter came into the club. Do a search—let's make sure no one followed her."

"Am I looking for anyone in particular?"

"Just do a search for anyone questionable."

The elevator arrived, and four guards were waiting for us. Two followed me as I went to the main floor of the club. The other two went with Elijah. Anthony was leaving his office as we passed by him, and he winced, seeing me. "I gotta tell you something."

"I already know."

"You do?"

I stopped, frowning at him. He had no idea about Molly Easter. He wouldn't be talking about her. "What are you talking about?"

"What are you talking about?"

I growled, low and swift. It was a reminder who was the boss.

His head straightened. "Right. Sorry. I was talking about Montell. Security just called. She's heading inside."

Jesus. Molly probably called her.

I started forward again, saying to Katya's manager, "Call Trace."

Anthony nodded, heading back into his office, and I kept on. This was going to be a shit show, whatever was about to happen.

I was almost looking forward to it.

CHAPTER SIXTEEN

ASHTON

She was drunk.

I could see that as I was crossing the floor to the bar they were sitting at, which was Jess's old bar. Molly's hand went up in the air and slammed down on the counter. She was doing a Thor impression. "Barkeep!"

That's when her friends saw me, and both converged on her.

It was like watching chickens squawking, but instead of running away, they stuck like glue to her.

"Miss Easter."

She lifted her head up, her eyes glazed, and she stared at me for a moment. She was weaving on her seat, and I began to move in, wanting to steady her, but she grabbed onto the counter herself. Then she gave me a once-over, all the way down to my dick and back up.

Fuck's sake.

I was already hard, at just that look.

This woman. A serious pain in my ass, in more ways than one. Good pain. Bad pain. Annoying pain. Sexual pain. All of it, and growing, the more interactions I was having with her.

I narrowed my eyes. "Molly."

"You." Her head tipped back, and she smiled.

I stifled a groan.

Her smile turned sexy, though I was sure she wasn't intending for it to be that way. "Heya."

Heya. That's what she said to me.

"You didn't stop drinking today, did you?"

She shook her head, her eyes drifting back to my dick. "Your thing."

"My thing?" I didn't want to ask her train of thought.

Her friends were alternating between watching us and sharing looks with each other. I was ignoring them.

I moved in closer. "How many drinks have you had?"

She held up her hand, all five fingers, and then closed it and opened it once more.

"Ten?"

She shook her hand. "Más o menos."

Right. Jesus. She was obliterated.

I zeroed in on her workers, on the guy. Pialto. "You brought her here in this state?"

He shot upright, blood draining from his face. "I—"

The girl rushed in: "She's upset about her dad." Sophie. These people were important to Molly. I was making a note to have my PI look into them. Any information was always good information in my world.

Molly had no idea I was conversing with her employees. She went back to studying my dick. If she kept looking at me like that, I was going to do something about it. I began to reach for her arm, saying to Sophie, "I'm sure she often has ten drinks every day."

"No. Today was weird. She—oh. I get your point."

Pialto leaned forward. "Get off her back. It was a stressful day."

I moved in, a part of me just needing to touch her. My chest brushed against her back, and she leaned against me. She looked up at me. "Pialto was there. We took his car."

The dad. She'd been upset. She'd texted me about him, and I knew there'd be repercussions about having her send him on his way, to do what I wanted, but I hadn't realized it would result in this. If I'd known, well; I would've handled her personally, maybe. But, this would've still happened.

Her drunk. And me being here.

I touched her arm, starting to draw her from the stool, when another voice cut in from behind.

"Hello, people."

I knew she was coming in, but having Jess Montell interrupting wasn't welcomed.

I shot her a look. "Go away, Montell."

Her eyes went flat, and her mouth went firm. "Watch your wording toward me, Walden. You and I are still on shaky ground."

I pulled Molly the rest of the way, just needing to touch more of her. Needing to make sure she wouldn't fall off that stool. Her employees didn't protest. Their eyes were enlarged, and their heads were bouncing between Montell and me.

"Jess!" Molly clued in on who was here. She tried throwing her arms up, but her purse got in the way. "What are you doing here? I came to see you."

Jess's eyebrows went low, taking in how I was touching Molly and taking in Molly's state. She said, slowly, "You sent me a text saying you were coming to see me because your day sucked. Since you don't know where Trace's place is, I pinged your location and saw you heading here. Not liking what I'm seeing here. I love my friends." She glared at me. "I *protect* my friends."

The bartender came over then, gesturing to Jess. "Drink?"

She gave him a distracted glare, then shook her head. "What? No." Her gaze lingered behind him. "You're low on your bottles. You should keep it better stocked." Her gaze went back to Molly before lifting to me. "Not her."

"Yes." A whole possessive need was pounding inside of me. Molly was mine. She was either my target, my mark, my woman, or my cross to bear. Any and all ways I split it, she was mine.

"No." Her eyes narrowed into slits.

"Yes." I pulled Molly's barstool back and stood behind her. Sophie got off her stool and went around so she was standing behind Pialto. Both were a captive audience, watching every move and making sounds at every exchange. They were both sipping their drinks at the same time.

I moved my hand to Molly's hip, and went lower, cementing her against my chest. She was fully sitting back, leaning against me.

Jess shook her head, her lips thinning. "No, Ashton. Come on."

"Jess, Jess. I'm okay." Molly was trying to reassure her. "For real. You gotta know that. I'm an Easter. We're indestructible. I have Shorty Easter genes in me. We're like roaches. We survive anything. If an explosion went off, and everyone landed in a pile from the blast, I'd be the one crawling out from underneath and probably still holding a candle for my birthday cupcake."

Jess was nodding, a shadow crossing her gaze as she kept staring at where I was touching Molly. And how Molly was leaning back against me.

She looked at me, swallowing. "I already lost one friend because of a guy."

That was a hit to my sternum. I growled. "Too low, Montell."

"Was it? Really?"

"Jess."

Both of us looked up. Trace had arrived.

She stared at him, shaking her head. "You knew, didn't you? About them?" She gestured to Molly and me.

His eyebrows dipped down. "You knew too. At his place."

"No. Molly was lying to me. I knew she was lying, but I didn't know why. This—" She gestured to where I was touching Molly, low on her hip. "This wasn't happening then. My bullshit radar was blasting. But now? If you hurt her, Ashton . . ." She let the warning hang between us.

Molly was back to trying to order a drink.

The bartender wasn't paying her attention. He was transfixed by Trace and me, and Molly's friends were ping-ponging between the exchange.

Trace's gaze darkened. "I think it's time we had this out. Upstairs?"

Jess was already stalking for the door, and I suppressed a curse.

Trace lingered. "Jess is a lot of things, but she'll let you have your say. She'll listen. She might not like what you say, but she'll still listen."

I locked my gaze on him. "You know full well none of this is about Molly."

"Even so." Trace cast her a look. "Some of it is about Molly. Most of it's about what you did to my woman."

He left after that, and I had to make a choice. Go or stay.

I growled but said to Elijah, "Watch her."

He clipped his head in a nod.

CHAPTER SEVENTEEN

ASHTON

"Goddammit, Walden."

Jess was seething when I got upstairs. That was her greeting as I came through the door.

Trace was at the bar, pouring himself a drink, and he slid one across the counter for me. I picked it up, taking a sip before focusing on the love of his life.

"Trace explained to you that Molly Easter is my business. He told you the situation. I was told you agreed to step back because of it. What is your issue?"

"My issue?" Her hands went to her hips, and her eyes narrowed, and she looked like she was daydreaming about pulling her weapon on me. "My issue is that you look like you're fucking her. Are you?"

"You were at my place. You saw that we get along." I was lying then, and I was lying now, or . . . somewhat. "Why are you pissed about this now?"

"Because despite what you wanted me to think at your place, I knew you hadn't fucked her. She just got out of the hospital."

"She's my business."

"A cruel business." Her hands went in the air, and she twisted around, her back rigid. "I'm aware of that. God, I'm aware of this Mafia-business bullshit."

Trace came to stand next to me, taking a pull of his own drink. We were both watching his woman. I raised an eyebrow at him. "You want to step in here? Help out?"

He shook his head. "Not one bit. You both know the situation, and you're both pissed. You're pissed she's wading in because she cares about someone. She's pissed because she cares about someone she thinks you're going to fuck over. And she's pissed about what you did to her, which I'm still pissed about. You're not as apologetic as you should be." He turned, his back to his woman, and he faced me squarely, his eyes glittering. "Yet." Then he smiled before he took a second drag from his drink. "But unlike Jess, I'm cluing in to the real situation, and you'll be sorry for what you did to Jess. You'll be real sorry about it."

I frowned at him. "I already am."

"No. Not quite, not until you imagine someone doing to someone you love what you did to mine. *Then* you'll get it." His eyes flashed. He was finding this amusing, but there was a hardness to him too. "I'm looking forward to that day."

I quieted, but dammit. I turned fully toward her. "I am sorry, Jess. I am truly sorry for what I put you through. I thought I was doing the right thing for my best friend and for our family—"

"That's not good enough." Jess stepped forward, her hands back on her hips, her chin up in the air. She was staring at me, almost challenging me. "That's not fucking good enough. I'm aware of why you did it, but apologize and leave the last part off."

Goddamn!

I was being forced to swallow my fucking pride. It tasted like battery acid. "I'm sorry for torturing you." I took a step toward her, my eyes narrowing. My voice went soft.

Trace growled next to me.

I ignored him. "I'm sorry for doing it for hours."

I was challenging her right back, but I'd already apologized. I'd already had my ass beaten and put in the hospital because of it, by my best friend, and how many times did I need to apologize?

"You are such a fucking dick." Jess was shaking her head, but some blood drained from her face, leaving her looking ashen.

Guilt moved into my chest.

I lowered my head. "I *am* sorry." I looked up because I was. I truly was, but it was hard to take back damage that you inflicted.

Jess shook her head again, and a hollow laugh came from her. "The thing is—you're not sorry you hurt *me*. You're sorry you hurt someone Trace loves, and that I wasn't the traitor. That's what you're sorry about. There's a difference, and this, you and me—we'll never get along until you're actually sorry that you hurt *me*."

She started to leave, but I blocked her. Or I started to, until Trace growled. "Think about that, brother."

I threw him a look, but I didn't move. Not when he just called me brother again.

She started to leave again.

"Jess," I called after her.

She reached for the doorknob, but she didn't pull the door open. Her hand on it, she looked back at me. Some of the fight had left her. "Do not hurt my friend. You do, I will shoot you." She let out a soft breath of air. "And you know Trace will let me."

I threw him a sideways look. He only smirked at me before finishing his drink.

She left, and we heard the elevator arriving not long after.

I watched Trace as he went to the windowed wall and looked down. We both knew who he was watching.

"You're not going to say anything?" I asked, moving to stand alongside him.

"About what?"

I looked down, seeing what he was seeing.

Molly was laughing with her friends. The bartender seemed infatuated with her.

I wasn't liking the bartender and made a mental note to see if he *really* needed to have his job or not.

Trace shook his head. "I've said enough on the matter of you and Jess. It'll get worked out. I'm seeing that now. It's just a matter of time."

I frowned as he went back to the bar, pouring himself another drink.

Jess had been one of our last bartenders up here, and since then, neither he nor I had let anyone else take her place behind the bar. Him, because he didn't want anyone else up here. Me, it wasn't for sentimental reasons like him. I just liked the extra privacy. I began enjoying making my own drinks when I came here.

"You're seeing what now?"

Trace just grinned, holding up a bottle of vodka. "You'll see. Want another one?"

I looked at my drink. I had half in there but tossed it back.

Life was crazy right now, but if my brother was offering to make me a drink, I was going to take him up on it. Jess wasn't the only one I was still trying to make things right with.

I handed him my empty glass. "I *am* sorry for what I did."

He took it, somber, before he nodded. "I know."

Then, he made us both drinks.

CHAPTER EIGHTEEN

MOLLY

My cousin texted just as I was letting myself into my apartment.

Glen: All good. Had a good night. You need me tomorrow?

I paused in the open door, putting my purse on the floor.

Me: No. I'll be good tomorrow. Thank you so much.

Glen: Rest. Hope you feel better.

I stepped all the way in, letting the door swing shut behind me, and I was reaching up to lock it when my brain clicked on. I'd stepped into the space my purse had been. Meaning, it wasn't there anymore. Sheer panic exploded in me at the same time—a body was in my space. I was upended, hanging over someone's shoulder in the next second, and that's when the scream left me.

The guy grunted as he shut the door the rest of the way and hit the locks on. "It's me."

I froze. Me?! As in, I tried to twist around to see him. "Ashton?"

He'd already been inside my apartment. How? What?

He walked a few more feet back into the living room before he tossed me on the couch. He followed me down, almost landing on top of me, but as I was sprawled out, he was holding himself just above me. One hand to the couch's arm behind my head and the other on the back of the couch. It was an impressive plank, and he didn't seem winded.

Then I clued in on how angry his eyes were. His jaw was clenched. His eyes seared into mine. "I told you to stay put. Why was I then told that you'd left?"

I opened my mouth, indignation quickly replacing the terror that he just gave me, and then my body got heated. I poked a finger against his chest. "You're the one who left. And you didn't tell me anything. You were all hands-on and in my space. I was feeling a sort of way, and then bam, you're gone. What's with you and Jess?"

The alcohol was still there, still affecting me, but we'd stopped for pizza on the way home. That was helping.

His eyes narrowed to slits. "Montell and I are none of your business. And I didn't want you to leave. I was coming back."

"Then you should've said that." I gave him a little sheepish look. "We went to the bathroom and then just kept going." I pushed him back so I could sit up, and I tried to fold my arms over my chest. Tried. He was very close to me, close enough where I could feel his body heat. "I want to know about you and Jess."

"She's worried about you."

"It's more than that."

"That is none of your business. It's between her and myself."

I frowned. "Not even Trace?"

Ashton pressed his mouth into a very firm and disapproving line and gave me a meaningful look. Okay then. I wasn't totally sure what that meant, but it was between him and Jess.

"Why did you come to Katya tonight? Did something new happen with your father?"

I frowned. Something *always* happened with my father. "No. Nothing new except he's scum that doesn't deserve to be walking the streets. He should be in prison, or forced to hand milk a goat, on a mountain, in a yurt, all by himself. Can you make that happen?" He was still so close, and my body was all sorts of reacting to him. I had fuzzies going on in my tummy, and they were in a tizzy. "Can we talk about the body-claiming stuff? Why are you always so close to me? Not that I'm complai—"

He was staring at me, but then he went on alert.

His head snapped toward the door, and he held still like that for a second; then with a curse, he grabbed me and rolled. His body fell to the ground, but with the momentum, I was up and on my feet before I knew what was happening. He let me go, was up and took my hand in his.

"Wha—"

He twisted around, his hand covering my mouth, and he yanked me against his chest. "Be quiet. Someone's at your door."

My door?

It was probably my father. I hoped it wasn't him. Shorty wasn't supposed to know where I lived.

I pushed away from Ashton, taking a step toward the door. "It's probably—"

The door swung open, and a guy was there. He froze, looking right at us. He was on his knees, his hands up, working on my door handle, but then a *beep, beep, beeeeeeeeeep*—

The door exploded, toward us.

Ashton flung himself in front of me, shielding me. Then he was up and on his feet, running back toward where the door should've been. Instead, a huge hole was there. A guy was lying down in the hallway, but he looked up. His tools were blasted around him, and one was in the wall behind him. He paled, his eyes big as he saw Ashton, and was up, on his feet, running to meet him.

The two clashed. He threw a punch. Ashton dodged and threw one of his own, and then that guy was bringing up a gun—

Pop! Pop! Pop!

The guy fell back, his body jerking with each bullet—that was coming from Ashton! I hadn't even seen him pull a gun, and where had he even had that on him? The guy collapsed on the floor, and Ashton kicked the man's own gun away, toward me. "Leave that alone."

Kneeling, he checked his pulse before moving to pat him down. His wallet was taken and pocketed. His phone. Some keys. Ashton did a thorough job before he seemed content.

Walking back to me, he put his own gun away, slipping it into wherever he'd pulled it from. He knelt, grabbed the man's gun, and emptied the chamber before pocketing it. His phone was ringing, and he answered it, moving into my bedroom. I was in shock—I knew this. My mind was working, but I wasn't feeling.

That was weird.

I was watching Ashton going through my room. He rummaged in my closet, grabbing a bag. Some clothes were tossed in my bag. Shoes. He was talking to someone on the phone as he went into my bathroom and came back, another bag zipped up. I didn't even know whose bag that was—no. It was mine. It was my Happy Earth bag. I was so proud of it because I'd bought enough clothes that the company put money toward cleaning the ocean.

"—no . . . body . . . yes."

Ashton's voice was registering with me, slowly. In pieces.

He was motioning to me, pointing at my book on my nightstand.

"What?"

"Do you need this?"

"Need what?"

He held something up. I didn't know what it was. None of this was making sense.

A body—a body was in my hallway! I gasped, turning to go and look. Had I imagined all of that?

"No." A firm hand had my arm, and I was being held back.

"No. I need to—"

"No, Molly." He stopped in front of me, his hands holding my shoulders in place, and he gently walked me back a step until I was against the wall in my own doorway. "That man was trying to pick the lock, but he's not the one who blew your door. I think that was someone else."

"Who?"

His mouth was in a firm line. "I don't know. I missed it. I didn't see it either so it must've been small."

His phone was ringing again.

Oh—that was mine.

"How do you know that guy didn't do the door?"

Ashton stepped back but took my hand. He entwined our fingers, pulling me from the room. My Happy Earth bag over his shoulder. "Because he was just as shocked as us. Do you need anything from in there?"

He motioned for the kitchen.

Need? Like I was going somewhere. I shook my head, starting to tell him that was silly, but he took that as the answer to his question, and he led me back to the living room and entryway.

Another guy was there, bending over the man.

I gasped, braking, but the guy lifted his head, speaking to Ashton. Oh, good. It was Elijah.

"—dead . . . her?"

Ashton stepped in front of me, responding to his man before he lifted his hand, moving so he was half hugging me to his chest again. His hand went to cover my eyes, and he spoke, surprisingly gentle. "We're going to step around the body. Don't look. You won't get that image out of your head."

I readied myself as we were walking past. I couldn't help myself. I looked, though Elijah was there. He was moving as we did, an extra barrier between us and the body.

Body. As in deceased.

Jesus.

Ashton had killed a man in my apartment. And I'd seen the whole thing. I was a Mafia witness.

But—this was at my place.

My home.

That guy was trying to pick my lock. If Ashton hadn't . . . I started shaking. My knees were knocking against each other, and my legs were getting all wobbly.

I was going down. I'd fainted enough times to recognize the signs.

Suddenly, Ashton stopped running in front of me. He muttered a curse before bending and sweeping me up in his arms.

I gasped, my hands flying out, grabbing for his back. He kept moving, hitting the emergency door exit, and we were running down the stairs fast.

The door below opened, and Ashton paused until a male voice called up, "Boss?"

We kept going. Or I mean, Ashton kept going. I was carry-on luggage.

Another two men met us as we ran down the last set of stairs. They didn't say anything. Ashton didn't either. We got to the main floor, and Ashton carried me out into the side alley.

Two vehicles were waiting for us. The back door opened. Ashton deposited me inside before shutting the door and hurrying to the driver's side. He got behind the wheel. Just as he was putting it into drive, the front passenger door opened. Elijah threw himself in, and he yanked the door closed as Ashton was peeling out of there.

There was a slight pause when we got to the street, but just barely. There was a small opening in traffic, and he used it, gunning the accelerator again.

Elijah looked back at me. "How's she doing?"

I could hear him this time! Go me.

"In shock."

Elijah gave me a small smile before turning to face the front. "She saw a lot tonight."

"Don't start."

He glanced at Ashton. "I'm not. Just saying . . ." He shrugged. "You know."

Ashton's jaw clenched. "I'm aware."

I had no clue what they were talking about, and then I didn't care. Everything went dark.

CHAPTER NINETEEN

ASHTON

Molly fainted in the car, which turned into sleeping. I let her be.

The plan had been to take her to my place and stash her there. No one, or very few, actually knew where I lived. I could name them on one hand, but when she passed out, I decided to go a different route. I was bringing her to a compound very, very few knew about. She'd be safe.

We met with two of my men.

While she was in the back, all bundled up, I went over the plan with Elijah.

Elijah's phone buzzed. "Body's been handled, and I checked with our men. There were no 911 calls from her neighbors. Police were not notified."

Even better. "I want her place cleaned out within the hour."

He was typing on his phone. "On it."

"Relocate her stuff to storage."

"What about the bowling alley?"

"Notify her cousin. Tell him we'll double his pay if he keeps his mouth shut."

"Got it." He continued typing, but his gaze met mine over his phone. "You sure about this?"

No. "This has to be done."

"And Trace and Jess?"

Jess was already not happy with me, but she was holding back. Grudgingly. Still. I didn't want to push my luck. If she found out about Molly's apartment, she'd come barging in again. The "talk" between us had not gone well.

"Let's keep this quiet for now."

"You think this is because of Molly's dad? You think he found something out already?"

"I think he kicked a hornet's nest, yeah."

It was the only thing that made sense.

"Well, looks like if he doesn't get the information himself, you could always use her as bait . . ." He stopped when I gave him a sharp look. "Oh."

Oh. As if I wasn't already considering it.

We were at war. There were no innocents in war.

My gut tightened on that because I was finding myself starting to second-guess my decisions. I was getting irritated by the speed and the frequency with which I was questioning myself when it came to Molly Easter.

I turned to where I could see just the back of her head, as she was tucked into a ball in the back seat.

Sleeping. Resting. She looked like an angel again.

She would be perfect for bait . . .

I'd have to control it, contain it.

I would.

"Wait until we arrive, then let the information leak that I have her," I clipped out. "Let it spread that I have her in one of our warehouses by the water. Set up a security system. Let's see who comes looking for her."

Elijah's face closed off as he nodded. "Will do, boss."

I went and got into the back seat next to Molly. The guys had wrapped her up in a blanket, and a pillow was under her face, but as we began moving forward, she moved around in her sleep. Finding my shoulder, she nestled in.

I let her stay.

That itch for her only kept intensifying.

CHAPTER TWENTY

MOLLY

Oh. No, no, no. I woke up, but unlike last time, everything came flooding back.

My dad.

Me drinking. Lots of drinking.

Katya.

Ashton.

Jess.

Jess left.

Ashton left and *bam*! Exploding doors. Lockpicking strangers and *pop, pop, pop*. Ashton killing a man in my apartment.

I was in a bed but flung back the covers. I wanted answers, and I wouldn't stop until I got them. I headed downstairs, following the sounds of chopping and cutting, until the room completely opened up. A guy was in the kitchen and waved a knife at me. "Hey." This man was beyond pretty. Blond hair. Green eyes. High arching cheekbones. He was wearing a merino polo shirt, and I would not be surprised if he had on some Italian loafers.

"You work for Ashton?"

His smile faded, and he nodded. "I do. My name is Avery."

A male Avery? I liked it. "I'm Molly."

"I know." He motioned around the kitchen with his knife. "Want something to eat or drink?"

I shook my head, biting my lip because damn. He was cutting up vegetables. I loved vegetables, and my stomach growled, reminding me of that.

"You sure?" His grin was knowing.

"Where's Ashton?"

He lost his grin again. "Can't tell you that." Ignoring my insta-scowl, he held up a bowl from beside him and showed me what was inside. Rainbow-colored frosted cupcakes.

My stomach was growling again. "Then call him."

He lowered the cupcakes, studying me a little. "Okay."

Avery was reaching for a button when we could hear footsteps coming from down a hallway. Ashton appeared, putting his phone away. He perused me before walking into the kitchen, passing behind Avery. "You look well."

Avery paused in his cutting, watching for my reaction.

I shifted on my feet. "I want answers, Ashton. What happened last night?"

He motioned for the coffee machine. "I can make you an espresso. Do you want one?"

My mouth was instantly watering, and dammit, but I nodded. I gave in. Why was I feeling this was a tit-for-tat kind of situation? That's not at all how I lived. You were all in or all out. You either gave or you didn't. This keeping track of what I won versus what he gave was exhausting and making my headache worse.

Also, I had a headache. I didn't even know until now.

I was blaming the rainbow-frosted cupcakes for distracting me.

"You killed a guy at my place. And where am I? Just . . ." God. My head was now killing me. "I'm developing a sixth sense with you. I feel like you're planning something. What are you planning, and most importantly, how does it involve me?"

He stared at me a bit before slowly and calmly, which was irritating the fuck out of me, programming an espresso in his fancy machine that looked like I needed a PhD in alien language to figure out how to work it myself.

"Why don't you sit? Avery is my cook when I'm here. He can make you an omelet."

Gah. I could not get distracted by that omelet, though I wanted to be. "I want to know what is going on." My throat swelled up. "Is this because of my father? Because what I asked him to find out?"

Ashton and Avery shared a look just as the espresso machine started sputtering to life.

He nodded to the machine. "Can you do two? Bring them to the office? Also, maté for myself."

"Maté?"

"It's like a tea, from my grandmother's country. It's a common drink."

Avery nodded. "I can bring the food in as well?"

Ashton was eyeing me as he said, "Yes. I don't care what she says. She needs to eat."

I wasn't about to protest because hello, I was not one to turn down food. Ever.

Ashton was heading back along the hallway he'd just left. "Come on, Molly. Unless you don't actually want to get those answers after all?"

Nope. No way. I followed him into his office, and I was the one to close the door as he went to stand behind his desk.

"Who was the lockpick guy?"

He frowned at me.

I held up a hand. "Don't lie to me. Your men were there. I'm not stupid. Between you and Trace, you're the one who gets shit done. You wade in and get your hands dirty. Trace was a Wall Street guy before he took over his family's business, but you, you were always more *in* than he was. I know you know who that guy was. Your men probably identified him and have already done a complete investigation into

116

everything about him. This was all started because I sent my father out there to find who killed Justin and Kelly, isn't it?"

I was the one to blame.

My throat was burning.

Ashton stopped frowning, but he gave me a more contemplative look before nodding. "I think your father kicked a hornet's nest, but—" Now he was the one to hold up a hand as I'd been about to interrupt. He kept talking, softening his tone. "I was the one who did this, not you, not him. You want to blame someone, put it on me. I'm the one who decided to use you to get your father to do this job. We've talked about all of this."

My head started pounding, and I needed to sit down. "There's a different feel when you have someone trying to break into your apartment, and what was that on my door? A bomb? It must've been a small one. That means someone else was there because you said the lockpicker guy wasn't the one who did that. That means two guys were sent, by two different people. What did I get myself into? What did I get my dad into?"

Ashton's eyes went flat. "If anyone will survive this, you know it will be your dad."

That was true. We were cockroaches.

"Who was the guy, Ashton?"

He came back around the desk and handed me a file before sitting on the seat next to me. "His name is Wallace Birchum. He goes by Walleye."

I took the file, opening it. He looked different from when he was kneeling before my exploding door. His picture was rougher, his hair a mess. He was unshaven. His eyes glazed over. Dark hair. Dark eyes. "So who is Wallace Birchum?"

Ashton didn't reply at first, until he took the file away. "He's a hit man."

A hit man?!

Oh, god.

I sank back in my chair.

"He's also a CI for the police."

A CI. Confidential informant, and a hit man. "He diversified his street résumé."

The corner of Ashton's mouth twitched. "We got into his phone, and he received a call four hours earlier from Detective Worthing."

Every muscle in my body snapped to attention. "What?"

"I sent my men to pick up the detective so we can have a talk about this man."

Alarm sirens were blaring through my whole body, but also a whole different type of alarm was sounding. "He's a cop."

"Yes."

"You're picking up a cop to talk?"

"Yes."

I was remembering when they were at Easter Lanes—"Wait. Easter Lanes? Is someone still covering me there?"

"We're paying your cousin to run Easter Lanes while you're with me."

"He can handle covering for a shift, but not any longer than that. He'll mess everything up."

But wait again, Detective Worthing. "Worthing called you that day, and you said that he did. I saw the look he gave you and how his partner reacted." I was a little slow, but this was clicking at least. "You wanted his partner to know."

"I did."

"Why? You guys had an exchange at the end, and you said it was about him thinking we're sleeping together. That wasn't the truth, was it?"

"I didn't want him to guess what I was going to have your dad do."

"But his partner? What was that about?"

He studied me a moment before getting up and returning behind his desk. His hands went into his pockets, and his shoulders hunched forward and down. It gave him a whole different vibe, more relaxed, more trusting, but I knew not to believe it. No matter my own messed-up attraction, no matter how many times I enjoyed the feel of his body against mine, Ashton Walden was still Mafia.

"My family works with the West family, and both of us run this city. I handle a lot, but one of those roles is the authorities. Do you know what I'm referring to?"

My mouth dried. I nodded. "You got cops on your payroll."

"Cops. Detectives. Feds. Judges. Lawyers. Paralegals. Anyone in a place of authority, and if I don't have them in my pocket, I have someone right next to them in my pocket. Before his family declared war against mine, Detective Worthing was one of those men."

"You said that to out him to his partner."

"I said that to drop a seed in his partner's mind. Worthing is good at his job. He used to walk the line real well, but yes, now he'll have to worry about what his partner is thinking and observing. And if Worthing is the man who ordered Walleye to break into your place, I want to know why, and I don't have time to waste."

"What about the bomb?"

"It was sent to be analyzed. We were told it was faulty. It was supposed to go off when you opened the door. There was a delay in the switch, so whoever bought it, put it together, or installed it messed up. I'm hoping to get to whoever messed up before *their* boss gets to them."

Right. Yeah. Okay. A bomb that was supposed to kill me.

A bomb . . .

Pressure was attacking me from all sides.

Hands touched me on my shoulder. "Breathe, Molly."

I couldn't. That was the problem.

I was totally hyperventilating.

I heard someone cursing next to me, and I was being picked up.

I tried fighting, twisting. Reaching for anything, but I was being carried out of the room. We went through a doorway, I reached out, my nails dug into the wood paneling, but he didn't stop. We didn't stop. My nail tore. I saw it, registered it, but didn't feel it.

My body was burning up.

I couldn't—water was turned on.

Water?

I lifted my head, but we were stepping inside a shower, and the water hit us hard.

I jerked out of his arms. It was Ashton holding me.

I tried getting away from him, away from that water, but he held me against the wall, leaning over, and I gasped again; this time I could get air into my lungs. I drew in deep breaths, trying to fill my lungs as much as I could.

I never wanted to feel that again, never ever.

I felt burning at my eyes but ignored it. The water was cascading down my face. The tears were camouflaged. A firm finger tipped up my chin, lifting my head. That water poured down, washing everything away, and I moved back enough so I could open my eyes just outside of the stream.

He was watching me, his own eyes dark and somber. His thumb moved over my chin. "I'm sorry all of this is happening to you."

His hand cupped the side of my face, his thumb brushing up and over my cheek before he held the back of my head. His palm was firm, his fingers spreading out, and I felt fully anchored in his hand.

God.

My breath caught again, but my body was warming up.

He moved in, closer, blocking the water.

The air electrified.

We were in our own pocket, like under a waterfall. I could go there, let the world fall away. Let reason and sense fade, wash away with the water, and I wanted that.

I wanted that desperately.

I began reaching for him as his other hand went to my hip, pulling me against him.

His eyes were so intense, molten. They were firmly fixated on my lips.

I wanted him to kiss me. I wanted to feel the pressure of his lips on me, the texture. How he'd taste. How he'd taste me, and I was standing up on my tiptoes as my thoughts ceased.

I was just feeling. Needing.

"Boss—oh shit! Sorry." Avery's voice came from the doorway, but I felt Ashton pulling away before he moved back.

The pocket was gone. We were back to this world, where there was murder, bombs, disappointing dads, and the Mafia. Right. That was the world I was now in, fully and completely.

Ashton drew in a ragged breath, and he'd been watching me as reason settled over me, like a wet blanket. His hand slipped from the back of my head, but he drew it around my throat, his thumb grazing my jawline, the side, until he ended it at my chin before letting it drop all the way and taking one more step back.

"You should eat." He turned and left.

I stayed and let the water pour down on me for a minute longer before I turned it off.

CHAPTER
TWENTY-ONE
ASHTON

Avery was still in the office when I returned, finishing buttoning up a new shirt. He glanced to the bathroom, where Molly remained in the shower. I lifted my chin to Avery. "You have news?"

His eyes were carefully masked. "They got him. They'll be arriving in thirty minutes and want to know where to put him?"

I heard the water turn off behind me. "Warehouse one—put him in the back office and keep the cell jammer on."

"You think he'd call for help?"

I shook my head. "I no longer think I know anything."

Molly was coming from behind me. I'd become so tuned in to her every motion, movement, emotion, that I could almost guess what she was thinking. That was until now. She had a glossed-over expression on her face, and she was shivering.

Avery indicated the two trays behind him. "I brought the espresso shots and your omelets. Your maté as well." He frowned at seeing Molly step behind me. "Would you like a change of clothes? Blanket?"

"Uh, yeah. Sure." She said it so distracted. "Thank you."

Avery dipped his head, leaving. I knew he'd make sure the clothes he brought would be freshly warmed as well.

Molly stepped around me, walking to the tray, but she didn't open it. She stared at it. "Where are we? You never answered me." She continued watching the tray lid. "We're not in the city, are we?"

"North. My family has a compound here. We're safe, if that's what you're worried about."

She snorted out a laugh before covering her mouth. "God, no. I mean, I should. I was freaking out until the impromptu and fully clothed shower, and almost make-out session." She sighed, lifting her gaze to me. "But I'm not anymore."

"About what almost happened—"

She dropped her gaze and waved her hand. "No. I don't care. I, just, I want Easter Lanes back in my name, and I want nothing to do with any of this. No more bombs. No more people trying to break into my place—" She stopped. "How did you get into my place? You said it was supposed to go off when I opened the door, but wouldn't you have . . ." She trailed off, confused.

"I didn't enter through your door."

"How?"

"You live on the third floor. Your bedroom window was unlocked. I thought that was odd, but now I'm thinking that's where he entered and exited. The bomb was placed on the inside of your door, so you wouldn't have seen it."

She closed her eyes, and I could see how she was bracing herself.

I didn't like thinking about what thoughts were going through her head. "Have your espresso. Eat your omelet."

She didn't move. "Who is Avery to you?"

"What do you mean?"

"I heard him before I came in. You guys were talking about Worthing. He doesn't sound like just a cook for you."

"He is my chef, but he also oversees everything in this compound. Elijah is my right-hand man in the city. Avery is my right-hand man here, among other things. I have others, as you know, because of the new family changes, but those are my two main ones."

She grunted, now lifting up the lid for her omelet. "So don't mess with him, huh?"

A soft knock sounded at the door, and Avery opened it, bringing in a pile of clothing in one hand and a blanket in the other. His face was schooled, but I knew he'd overheard her. "Warm clothes for you, Molly, and a blanket as well. What chair are you thinking of using?"

She took the clothes and moaned. "Oh, goodness. These feel wonderful." She moved for the bathroom.

Avery looked my way.

I motioned to the chair she'd been standing by, and he nodded before spreading the blanket out so she could sit down and pull the ends to cover her. When he was done, he passed me and said under his breath, "They'll be here in twenty minutes now."

I gave the briefest of nods as he left, and Molly returned, a fresh glow coloring her cheeks.

Whatever shock she'd been in earlier was gone. She sat, a small smile on her face at the blanket, and dug into her omelet. She tried the espresso, and another whole moan left her mouth. "This is pure bliss. Oh, dear god. What coffee do you use for this? I need it for Easter Lanes. Forget alcohol. People will come in for this. Forget bowling! It's the espresso shots. I can see it happening."

I had to smile, just a little. She didn't dwell. Whatever bad shit happened, she freaked, and now she was enjoying her espresso shot. "Wait till you try the omelet. Avery's cooking is the best I've known."

She shot me a little grin as I went to sit next to her. "You mean after Pedro, right?"

I laughed, just a little. "Yes. Of course, after Pedro."

Her eyes were twinkling, but she was waiting for me to eat too.

I frowned but used my fork for a bite of my own omelet. When she saw I did this, her eyes lit up, and she took her own bite of the food. "Oh!" She fell back against her chair, her hands framing around her mouth, and her eyes were closed. "This is delicious. You were right. Sorry, Pedro, but Avery's omelet is on another level. Though, maybe Pedro can do a mean omelet too."

She was remembering Pedro because of the impression he'd left on her. She'd never eaten the food, and I'd forgotten to give her the leftovers.

I was finding out a lot about Molly Easter, details I'd never considered before.

"You're not eating." She pointed at my plate while a third of hers was gone. She gave me a closed and full-mouth smile, waving her fork in the air. "It's the little things, Ashton. The world might be imploding around you, but when you have an outstanding omelet to eat, you gotta eat the outstanding omelet. You may never get another like it."

She was right, but that's not what was surprising me. It was her. At every turn and twist, I was meeting a new side of Molly.

Outstanding omelets?

"Is that what you learned growing up in the foster system?"

She paused in midchew but blinked once and went back to eating again. After swallowing, she reached for the rest of her espresso shot but just held it. "Yeah. I mean, I guess. Some were okay, some were decent, but yeah. There were some where you just survived. Day by day, you know." She was bobbing her head from left to right. "The one nice thing about when you're fighting to survive is that the feelings don't creep up on you. You don't have time to feel 'em. It's after, when you're stable and secure, that's when the feelings hit you sideways. But yeah, in both worlds, you learned to live. Small things. Small blessings. Sometimes those are the only things you got to make you smile, and you have to smile. You always have to smile. You don't, and you don't want to be in the day, you know?"

I did, but I also didn't.

"Eat your omelet, Ashton." She said it with a smile. "Then you can go and be the bad guy after."

I did as she said. And she was right, though I already knew. Avery's omelets were amazing.

When we were done, my phone beeped. They'd arrived.

Molly had been eyeing me. "You gotta go to work?"

I nodded.

"Okay."

I glanced at her and raised an eyebrow in question.

She was finishing the last of her food and put the napkin on the tray before standing up. "You gotta go, you gotta go. Take me back to my tower."

"You don't want to know what he's going to say?"

She was chewing her bottom lip before she shook her head, slowly. "No. I think in this case, I'm going to go take a nap and let you do what you do. But I *will* nag you after so you tell me everything he says. Consider this your warning."

"You're going to nap?"

She nodded. "Yep." She was the one leading me to my office door. "Show me the way, Jeeves. If that omelet and espresso shot were any indication, I have a feeling my bed is a whole other form of heaven. I didn't appreciate it before, but I will this time."

Yes, indeed. Molly Easter was surprising me at every different corner.

I was finding that I liked it. A lot.

Molly went to take a nap, and I headed to be the bad guy.

CHAPTER

TWENTY-TWO

ASHTON

"Are you *fucking* kidding me?!" Detective Worthing growled as soon as I walked into the room.

I took note of him before responding. There were some bruises on his face. His jacket was torn in a couple places. Scuff marks on his jeans. His eyes were wild, and he was scowling. He was also zip-tied to a chair in four different places.

He had zero chance of escape.

"I see my men were thorough."

He growled again, shaking the chair as he jerked around. "I'm going to kill you, Walden. The second I'm free—"

I walked to a table set up in the corner. We had all my toys here, but as I scanned them, a zing of disappointment went through me. I wasn't looking forward to torturing him. Molly was right, what she'd said earlier. I *was* the one who liked to get my hands dirty. Torturing was my thing, but . . . it wasn't today.

Why wasn't it today?

I stepped to the side and swung my head his way.

It was then that Worthing realized his predicament, and who I was. He stilled, the wildness in his gaze diminishing. "I'm a cop."

I scoffed. "Like that matters to me."

"I'm a Worthing. You know what my cousin will do if you kill me?"

I narrowed my eyes to slits. "You mean it'd be worse than him killing my uncles and my grandfather?"

He was really realizing his predicament now because we'd not had our payback. Yet.

He coughed, clearing his throat. "We're in a ceasefire, remember?"

I was starting to get my hunger for torture.

It'd just been too long, that's all. I'd forgotten the taste, and I went back to studying which weapon I wanted. I ran my finger down the length of the table, stopping at a lethal but compact knife. It had a selenite handle, which always made me smile about the irony of that type of crystal on a blade used for killing.

I picked it up and began turning it around in my hands. "What are the chances that the day I send a rat scurrying to kick up a hornet's nest is the same day a man tried breaking into Molly Easter's apartment hours later?" I'd been watching him through a mirror in the corner, one that he hadn't spotted, and he'd been moving around, trying to get free, until I picked up the knife. He began watching me more uneasily, but once I said Molly's name, he froze completely.

I turned now, holding the knife loosely in one hand. "Or the odds of the coincidence that that same man received a phone call earlier from your phone."

His eyebrows dipped. "What? I never called—" He grimaced, his entire face twisting before a whole new level of wariness hung from him as he watched me. "I heard a rumor that Shorty was sniffing around, asking questions he shouldn't be asking, and I got worried about Molly. I asked a guy I knew to watch her, that's it. I swear."

"Your man is dead."

He went rigid all over again. "What?"

"I killed him."

"What?"

I flicked the knife up, caught it in midair, and sent it through the air. It nicked the side of Worthing's ear. He ducked, hissing, before looking to see where the knife landed. Three inches behind him. "I see those rumors are true. You do your own interrogations. You're a sick fuck, Walden."

I reached behind me and brought out a size bigger. Same selenite handle. Same just as lethal blade, but this one was more jagged. I held it up. "This one causes more of a mess."

He swore under his breath, starting to pale a little bit. "Why did you kill my CI?"

"Because he was trying to break into Molly's apartment."

He frowned, shaking his head. "Jesus. You really are fucking her. I hoped you were lying."

"Why would I lie about that?"

He snorted. "It's you. You're all about the mind games. I never know what the fuck you're going to do."

That made me smile.

But I still wanted to hurt him. That was coming back and growing. I liked it. The old me was still here. "You used to be one of my men. Now you're the enemy, sending men after the woman I'm fucking."

"I'm not your enemy."

"Your last name says differently."

"My last name—Nicolai, what he does—I don't have a choice."

"Bullshit."

"I don't! It's different for me. He wants to use me to push his way in. Justin . . ." He swallowed, pain flaring in his eyes as his whole face tightened. "My brother was always out. I was the cop, but he was the conscience for all of us. Nicolai is just as torn up as the rest of us. He wants to know who killed my brother. I'm saying that because the cease-fire is real on our end. I didn't send Walleye to do anything except put eyes on Molly. I was worried, *am* worried, about her. If her dad is out there asking questions, that shit's going to get to her immediately. She's his only weakness. She has to be protected."

He was sounding like he actually cared. That made me want to impale my newest blade into his stomach. "I liked my uncles. I liked my grandfather."

He cursed again, flinching before looking away.

"I say 'like' because in my family, what we do, if you 'love,' then you're considered weak. My family wasn't weak. I might admit that I 'cared' about them, but love . . . I'll never say that word. Once you 'love' someone, you will lose them. You were destined to lose your brother how you did *because* you loved him."

"That's so fucked up, and you're lying. You loved your family. You love Trace. You guys are like brothers. How you love him, that was Justin for me. Someone took him away, and when I think how he died—" His voice cracked. He choked off. "I want to be here that day, with his killer. I want them in this chair, and I want that tiny-ass knife you threw at me, because I'm going to cut them to pieces. Inch by fucking inch."

He almost had me believing him. Almost.

"Who told you about the rumors?"

He went still again. "Why?" More wariness.

"Who told you?" I was firmer.

He didn't reply, his mouth thinning.

I was losing my patience with him, and I didn't want that. The game would stop being fun. Because of that, I went over and pressed a button. "Bring me his phone."

"What?"

I waited.

"What are you doing? You can't get into my phone."

The door opened, and Elijah handed me first his phone, and then my programming equipment.

"What are you doing?! What is that?" Worthing was starting to struggle, trying to get free. The chair scraped against the floor.

I ignored him, giving Elijah a nod that he could go back out. I spoke as I plugged my equipment into the phone. "Do you know my first business that I ever started?"

I enjoyed asking people that question.

"What does that have to do with anything? Stop fucking with my phone! That's my phone—"

Beep, beep, beeeeeep!

I smiled, showing him his own screen as my program found the passcode. "It was cybersecurity. I know a thing about passcodes and passwords and firewalls."

"Don't! Ashton, please. Come on—"

I tuned him out as I went through his phone log first.

There was the call to Walleye, and after that, six calls to his partner. That was expected. A Laila popped up three times. But right before his call to Walleye, I knew that number. He didn't have it saved, but it didn't matter. I held up the screen. "I know who that is."

Nicolai Worthing.

He cursed, slumping back against his chair. "I know where you're going, but it wasn't Nicolai. He would never hurt Justin. Ever. I mean it, Ashton."

I didn't care what he had to say. I'd find out one way or another, and I switched over to his messages. Some sexting with Laila, but nothing else incriminating. "Don't you have a wife and kids?"

"How the fuck you know about them?"

I gave him a look, raising one eyebrow.

He cursed under his breath. "We're divorced. She's in California. And save your breath, I know you don't go after kids. That was the deciding factor why I went on your payroll. I never would've if I knew you used kids like the cartel."

Yes. That was our one redeeming quality being in the Mafia business.

I pressed a button, and Elijah came back in. I handed everything over to him. "Clone his phone. What else did he have on him?"

"You want me to bring it in here?"

I considered it. "No, but reach out to Shorty Easter. Tell him I want to see him."

"You? Not—" He motioned in the direction of the house. "You know."

"I want to see what he says to me."

"What do you want to do with Detective Dick back there?"

Him? I narrowed my eyes. "Didn't think I'd be gambling today, but I've decided to play a hand. You know my little surprises, my newest little invention?"

"The tape?"

I gave a nod. "Put a tiny piece on the detective's gun, where it won't be found."

Elijah shot me a look, nodding.

The door shut, and Worthing's head moved back, waiting. He swallowed, but a wall slammed over his face. "I know your games, Walden. I'm not going to give you the satisfaction of begging. You want to kill me, set off this war again, go ahead."

I took my knife and knelt, cutting through his zip tie in one swipe.

He quieted.

His gaze shot to me, watching intently with the second zip tie.

I moved behind him and did the last two.

He shoved off the chair and was reaching for his gun when he cursed, remembering we'd already taken it. "I want my gun back."

I took the knife out of the wall. "I want you to go back to your cousin and ask who told him about Shorty."

"Are you serious? Your guys jumped me, brought me wherever the fuck we are—and trust me, I *will* find out—and now you're giving me orders?"

"I'm not killing you."

"And you're joking?! If I didn't know your men would swarm in here in two seconds, I'd pummel your face into the pavement right now." He cursed again, eyeing the door. "I'm still half a mind of barring that door and going out with a bang."

I smiled. "Now you're being foolish, thinking you could pummel my face into this pavement." I gave him a wink. "Want to try? I'm game. I'll even tell my men to *only* come in if you're winning."

He swore, rolling his eyes. "So twisted in the head. I never understood you."

"Cheer up. You'll probably live." I smiled.

He was back to scowling at me. "Why do you want me to ask Nicolai about Shorty Easter?"

"Because before your man got to her apartment, a bomb had been placed on her door."

His scowl vanished. "What?"

Some might say it was a stupid move, having a cop kidnapped, but not me. Not with this life, and like Worthing thought he knew me, I also knew him. For a reason that I wanted to investigate at a later date, he was worried about Molly.

I was willing to let him go because like I'd planted a seed with his partner before, I was doing another one. To him, about his own cousin.

"If I hadn't shot your man, the bomb would've taken him out anyways. Either way, your man was the one to trip the bomb, not Molly. Seems like she's got the good luck that both of us don't."

"I didn't know about the bomb."

"I know. I want you to help me find out who put it there, and since I can't question your cousin . . ." I let it hang as I opened the door. Elijah and Avery were both there, along with two of my other men. They came in, forming a cage around the detective.

Avery started to zip-tie his hands behind him.

"My men will escort you back to the city."

They led him out, but I motioned for Elijah. "Bag over his head, like I know you did on the way here, but take him the long way back. I want him thoroughly confused when he checks his GPS later."

"We put his phone on airplane mode when we grabbed him. We should still be good."

"I know, but I still want him confused. No one knows about this place. I'd like to keep it that way as long as I can."

"Boss." He lingered.

"What?"

"What about the leak you wanted me to do? We spread the word that she's at one of the warehouses in the city, but you mentioned using her as bait."

"Has there been any movement yet?"

"Not yet, but if you're thinking of using her as bait, do you want her there?"

I didn't answer him. I knew what I should do, what would benefit the business, but there was the issue of what I wanted to do.

I walked away because I didn't know the answer myself.

CHAPTER
TWENTY-THREE

MOLLY

If Ashton Walden actually thought I was going to go and take a nap, he was—well, I was being positive here. The exception was my father. I would always allow myself to be negative with him, but back to what I was currently doing.

He was doing Mafia stuff. I was snooping.

Ashton or one of his guys must've scooped up my purse after the explosion because I found it next to my bed. I'd been elated, grabbing for my phone, only to find no reception.

So carrying my purse, my phone in hand, I was tiptoeing around the place.

At one point, I was in the east wing. Yes. They literally had a north tower, south tower, west, east, and it looked like there was a whole middle section where the kitchen was set at. The place looked more like a spaceship than a house. Ashton did say it was a compound, so kudos to whoever paid for all of this. It was a bit overkill in my opinion, but then again, I'm not the head of a Mafia empire. And anyways, I was in the east wing when I heard voices, and looking out, I saw Avery leaving the main building and heading into the distance. There was a road that led in the same direction, so I was guessing Ashton was back there, being Ashton.

First thing, or second, since the first was to call Pialto or Sophie and check in. I couldn't do that, so the second item got bumped up, and that was being the normal nosy person anyone would be in a place like this: get the lay of the land. I was doing that, and also oohing and aahing at some seriously and ridiculously amazing pieces of furniture, art, sculptures, even the mugs in one of the guest kitchenette areas. They were ceramic and adorable. They probably cost a fortune, but now I was in the last of the wings.

Um . . . gah. I didn't know what to do. If I kept nosing around, I'd get myself in trouble. It was my switch. It was a problem. I needed a distraction. I could call Pialto or Sophie from the phone on the desk.

I tried Pialto first.

"This is who you're trying to get ahold of. Leave a message and I'll text you back—beep!"

Crap. I wasn't sure if I should leave a message or not. That'd be one benefit, knowing what situation I was currently in. I'd be more committed to an escape plan, if that's what was called for.

I sighed and tried Sophie instead.

"Hello?"

"Soph!"

"Wha—*Mollyomgwhereareyou?Whathappenedtoyourapartment? andyourcousinwon'ttellusanything!*"

Oh, whoa. I had to unpack that a bit.

Oh my god! She knew about the apartment! "You were at my apartment?"

"*Yes! Where are you?!*"

"*I'm okay!*" Why was I yelling? "I'm okay. I'm safe, I think."

"What do you mean, you think? Where are you?"

"How do you know about my apartment? Did the police go to Easter Lanes, looking for me?" I mean, of course they would. That would be common sense.

"Glen is working, again, and not to be negative about your cousin, but he's not that great at watching over the place. He told Pialto and I we could take the week off, but he wouldn't tell us why, so we went to your place, and what do you mean the police?"

"The police? Because of my door."

"Your door? Well, it is gone, but *all your stuff is gone*! Where are you?"

I frowned and pulled back to look at the phone. I was talking to the right person, wasn't I? "What are you talking about?"

"What are you talking about? Your apartment—"

"—there was a bomb on the door—"

"—everything was gone! It was clean—*there was a bomb on your door?!*"

I was so confused. "Wait. All my stuff is gone?" My throat gagged. I must've heard that wrong.

"Yes! That's why I've been calling and calling. Pialto was fed up, and he went to find your cop friend. Jess. He's terrified of her, but he said he needed answers. Where are you?"

"I don't know."

"What do you mean you don't know? Who's there with you? And where's your stuff?"

My head was ringing, again. I was having a bad acid trip of déjà vu. "I'm with—" Shit, shit, shit. I didn't know if I could tell her or not. Wait. She knew everything else. "I'm with Ashton Walden."

"Oh, Madre de Dios. What are you doing with him? And *again*? Though, he is so gorgeous."

I gripped the phone tighter. "I know, and he shielded me from the bomb."

"He did?"

"He did."

We were sighing together.

"I can't believe there was a bomb."

"Same," I quipped.

"You don't know where you are?"

"I can't say. I don't think he want—" The line went dead. I looked at the phone again, checked the cord, made sure it was plugged into the wall, and it was. But the line was just gone.

A hand reached around me, taking the phone from me, and I turned, already gulping because the whole room got chilled. Ashton was glaring at me, his eyes seething and his jaw clenched to where I thought he might've been close to grinding his teeth.

I winced, thinking about that.

"Are you goddamn kidding me?"

Yep. He was furious.

"What?"

"What?" His eyes widened a fraction, and he stepped to me, his head coming down. "Are you joking with 'what'?"

"Uh . . ."

He threw the phone against the floor, breaking it into pieces.

I was gulping again. "You need to tell me what I did wrong if I'm going to answer your question."

"You called your friend?" Another step my way. His eyes were glittering from his rage. "You told her you were with me? Do you want to die? Did you actually comprehend anything that happened at your apartment?"

I raised a finger, but still using the timid approach, I kept my voice light. "About the apartment. Soph said all my stuff was gone—"

"*Fuck the apartment! There was a bomb that could've killed you. Why are you not comprehending that?*"

"I—I wasn't sure."

"About what?" Still snarling from him.

"About the whole protection we have going on here?" I made two circling motions with my hands.

"What the fuck did you think we were doing here?"

"Uh. I wasn't sure. Think of all the craziness that's happened to me lately. I'm a little flustered. That's all. I called my friends. I wasn't going to tell them where I am. I don't even know where I am."

His eyes were back to slits, but he didn't comment.

"Why are you so upset? I don't get this." Okay. I was going on the offense. That felt good. A better plan here. "None of this would've happened if you'd just told me what we were doing here." I poked at his chest, and yeah, that felt good. It felt great. I did it again. "It's called communication." Another poke.

I was trying for some intimidation here, so I approached as I poked, but he wasn't moving.

I tried it again. "I woke up from passing out and you were all like, 'Here's my chef. Want an omelet?' There was nothing about that we're here for your protection or—"

"You freaked the fuck out about almost being killed, and then bam, you're talking about appreciating the simple things in life."

"I mean, yeah. There's no point in letting the negative weigh you down. It's evolution. Move on."

Ashton's neck and shoulders were getting tighter and tighter, and he started eyeing my neck like he might be considering wrapping his hands around it. Maybe I shouldn't have been poking him.

I edged back a step, and immediately knew that hadn't been the right move. A whole different air came through the room, circling us, and I tensed. The hairs on the back of my neck stood up. I was getting the whole vibe that I was in the room with a predator, a very beautiful and sleek-looking predator, but one that was a killer nonetheless.

What had I been doing? Poking him. Talking back to him. Forgetting he was dangerous, because I wasn't right now. Ashton was very much glaring at me as if he could snap my neck right now and then just step over my dead body on his way to the bathroom.

A cold shiver went to my toes.

"Ashton."

He lowered his head, his eyes still on me, and his voice came out low and soft. "Do you have any idea what you just did? That I brought you somewhere no one knew about for your safety? That you didn't think the person who tried to kill you might also be watching your 'besties' on the off chance you might contact one of them? That you might tell them where you were? If their phones were tapped, if you were on long enough for a location trace?"

Right. Crap. I did all of that. I was aware that I had a problem. I hadn't thought about that stuff. "I'm new to this Mafia stuff. I'm sorry, but next time give me some lessons."

His nostrils flared. "Lessons?"

His tone was sending a whole new set of chills down my spine.

I wrung my hands together. "I said what I said. I'm sor—"

"Do *not.*" He leaned in, his head moving so he was a breath away, and he placed a hand behind me against the wall. "It's not my life that's going to be snuffed out if they find you. It's yours." He looked down, seeing my cell in one hand and my purse in the other. "You said you were going to take a nap. Were you planning to sneak out instead?"

That sounded really foolish when he said it.

"I was snoo—"

His hand moved in a flash to the side of my throat.

I gasped, straightening up, but he didn't tighten it.

His hand spread out, smoothing over my skin until he had a firm grip on me. It was just there, resting against my skin. One of his fingers could feel my pulse racing, which was pounding like a stampede right now, but his thumb began stroking up and down, just slightly. A soft graze. I wondered if he knew he was doing that.

"Ashton," I murmured.

He looked down at my throat and moved in closer so his chest was almost touching mine. "Do you know how many times I've considered being done with you over the years? Knowing what you stood for, what your mother stood for. Do you know how much that haunted me growing up?"

I frowned. "What?"

He moved all the way now, his hips touching mine, and I whimpered, flattening against the wall. His back was arched over me as his head was bent, his forehead almost resting against mine. His thumb kept caressing, growing bolder and firmer with each stroke.

My pulse was almost skyrocketing out of my chest. I had no idea what was happening here, but a part of me liked this, and that part of me was even more confused by it.

"I *hated* my mother. Loathed her, and I despised that my grandfather accepted your father's offer. It's not normal for a son to want everyone to know their mother is a monster, but I did. I fucking yearned for that to happen, and it didn't. She was a goddamn saint for the rest of her life, and you—so innocent. I watched you, too, hating you. Hating you because you had the mother I wished I had and it was all so unbelievably fucked up and here I am, holding your neck in the palm of my hand, so exasperated with you because you put yourself in danger when I—" He cut himself off, a darkness emanating from his gaze.

I was riveted, holding my breath, needing to know what else he'd been about to say. I *had* to know. "When you what? What were you going to say?"

Why did he hate his mother so much?

"Why aren't you angry about your mother? I told you the truth, and you've not said a thing about it. You should be enraged, and *nothing*. You don't feel anything about what I told you?" His thumb went back to moving over my throat.

Warmth was flooding me. A need for him was starting to grow deep inside of me.

"I grew up not wanting to know my mom, and what you said kinda . . . I've just not had time to digest. One crisis at a time right now."

He frowned at me, his eyebrows dipping down. "What do you need to process? She was your mother."

"I grew up mostly hating my dad except on the occasions that I realized I might actually love him despite him being the worst ever. The whole mom factor seemed so far away. I was surviving. That's all I focused on back then. Surviving. Nothing else mattered."

My heart began beating faster.

The need. The ache. It only grew.

His hand. It was right there. He was stroking me, gazing down at me, but he wasn't fully seeing me. He was seeing—I reached out, placing my hands on his chest, and he froze at the touch, looking down at them. "Ashton."

His eyes refocused, seeing me again.

Pain flooded there. It was raw and real and visceral, and I gasped. A surge of need to take it away flooded me.

Anything. I had to help.

"Ashton. Your mother—"

"Hated me," he clipped out.

"What?" I froze. "What did you say?" I reached up, catching him with both of my hands, but he blinked, and it was gone. That small window, so fleeting. It closed up, though he remained where he was. He stood, holding me, touching me, as I was framing his face—he could've been on the other side of the room.

I slid a hand down to his chest, tamping down on the throb that filled the inside of my entire chest cavity for him. "Not that I'm really complaining, but the whole hand on my neck, and your thumb doing these magical things to me, and you know, feeling your hips down here and being backed against a wall . . . I mean, a girl can have so many fantasies before one is needing to come true. So could you, um, could you either *do* something or step back?"

"*Do* something?" His eyes went back to mine, holding me in place.

My throat swelled up. "Right. Or step back." But I pressed against him, ignoring the emotional distance, because he was locked back in. He was seeing me, not her. He was feeling me, not her.

"Step back?" He frowned, his thumb moving over my mouth again. His eyebrows pinched together, and he began to bend down, folding over me even more.

Oh man. I was feeling him between my legs, and I said, a faint plea, though I wasn't feeling it in a faint way, "Please."

His eyes flared, and I tensed because I had no idea what he was going to do, but then a whole new intensity exploded from him, and he was reaching for me. "Ashton!"

A female's voice began shrieking from inside the house.

He went rigid over me.

A door crashed open behind us, and that same voice shrieked again: "Ashton!"

I—fuck it.

I reached up and stood up, and I fused *my* mouth to *his*.

CHAPTER

TWENTY-FOUR

ASHTON

I ripped myself away from Molly, my whole body trembling because holy *fuck*, the need to tear down her leggings, throw her up against the wall, and sink my dick deep inside of her was tearing through me at a breakneck speed.

She tore something down inside of me. Something I needed, the last bit of restraint with her.

She didn't just tear it down. She took a battering ram to it, and I was shaken, taking her in. *Only* her in. I was ignoring the emotions clawing through me.

Only Molly. I could only feel Molly.

I was also going to murder Remmi West because I knew who'd just stormed her way in.

"What are you doing here?" I had to get ahold of myself, but I half growled at Trace's sister.

She was coming in, hoop earrings. Leather jacket. Her dark hair swept up, piled high, and she was wearing her usual black pants. Trace's sister liked to dress the Mafia-princess stereotype, but today there was no faux fur jacket.

Remmi ignored me, her neck craning so she could see Molly. "Who's that?" She pointed at her.

I pushed her hand down. "None of your business. What are you doing here, and how did you get here?"

"She came with me." Marco stepped around her, coming into the room, and he was eyeing Molly too.

I cursed, raking a hand over my head as I squared off against my cousin. He was family. Of course he'd know about the compound, but Remmi?

"What are you doing here?"

Marco's eyes narrowed before he turned back to me. "Trace called. Said he couldn't get ahold of you, and it was imperative. I thought this was the one place you'd go where you wouldn't answer his call, and since Remmi had just landed at the airport, I picked her up and brought her here to see if you *were* here, and you are." He motioned to me.

I stared at him. Hard.

He grinned back. "Relax. I know you got this place cell jammed, and I shared with Remmi this place is secret to even her family."

Remmi smiled at me. "Oh yeah. I wore a blindfold, headphones, and a bag over my head. I felt very *Ozark*-like. It was awesome, but really . . ." She approached Molly. "Who are you?"

I cursed, moving forward.

Molly was about to answer, but I stepped in between her and Remmi. "She's no one."

Remmi's head moved back, her eyes widening a tiny bit.

She was Trace's sister, but in many ways, she was also mine. When he couldn't handle her or take care of her, I stepped in. Hell. I stepped in a lot of times even before he was given a chance to be her brother. That was me, taking care of the fires before they turned into infernos, and her being here was the start of another one that would rage out of control.

I took Molly's hand, linking our fingers, still standing in front of her.

Remmi's gaze darted down, zeroing in on the action.

Marco seemed mildly interested, but he went to the bar and poured himself a drink first. "Was that some family business I saw being handled when we drove in?"

I didn't know what he thought he saw, but Worthing would've been taken out of here before they arrived. I ignored his question for now and glanced at Remmi, who seemed captivated by Molly.

Marco saw the look. "I only pulled her blindfolds off once we got into the garage. Secret's still safe, cousin."

"Cousin?" Molly squeaked.

I tightened my hold on her hand.

And at the sound, Remmi's head jerked back up, and Marco's eyes narrowed. A look flickered in his gaze, but he blinked it away before assuming a cool and casual expression once more. He sipped from his drink before meeting my gaze again. "Thinking we should have a discussion before you leave."

Remmi glanced his way. "We just got here."

Marco kept watching me, and he grinned, almost smugly. "My cousin likes to come here when he's beginning to cook something up, but if he brought his latest flavor, he won't want us around. I have no doubt that Avery is already packing their vehicle for their departure. Like me, Avery knows our boss."

I glared at my cousin. "Now is not the time for you to test my boundaries."

His eyes flickered again—something flared there, but he dimmed it just as fast as it showed. His hand tightened around his glass, and he couldn't hide that tell. "You'll have to forgive me. Before getting Remmi's call, I'd been on the phone with my mother and received a nice earful on behalf of our aunts."

He was right. We'd not done the second family dinner.

As if sensing my inner turmoil, Molly touched the back of my wrist, sliding her hand down to replace her other hand. Her palm touched mine, and she linked our fingers as she moved beside me, raising her head and giving me a solemn look.

I couldn't understand what she was trying to express, but she kept moving, and I felt in a trance. Captivated by her.

I wasn't the only one. The rest of the room fell silent.

She ignored them, touching my chest with her free hand, standing in front of me for a moment before she began walking backward. Toward the door. She tugged me, so I followed her. Once I did, she ducked her head down, leading the way past Remmi and Marco and not making eye contact with them.

Our hands were still linked.

I went with her, soundlessly.

She faltered in the hallway, so I took over, taking her to my room in the north tower.

Once through the door, I whisked her around, my hand going to her hip. She gasped, but I guided her against the door, and I was trapping her. I liked doing this, feeling her right there, in front of me. That need was still there. Burning. It had been banked but wasn't out, and now. *Now*, I was done holding back.

My other hand let go of her hand and placed it on the door above her head.

She had some color come to her cheeks, and her mouth parted.

I could feel her pulse. It was so strong, so loud, that I felt the drumbeat even just touching her hip.

"Why'd you do that?" My voice was gruff. I hadn't meant for it to come out that way.

She didn't answer right away, biting down on her bottom lip as she searched my face. Then, with a sigh, she seemed to melt in front of me, leaning fully back against the door. "Because no matter what you do, you still lost your grandfather and uncles not that long ago, and I forgot. I think a lot of people forget."

I frowned. "Forget what?"

She touched my chest, lightly. "That you're in mourning too."

I closed my eyes and swallowed tightly. Her words were like a punch to my system, but then I opened them again and found her studying my face. Her eyes scanned all over me, tracing me until she saw I was looking back at her, and hers widened a little. The top of her lip curved up, just slightly. She wasn't scared of me. Why wasn't she scared of me?

Her eyes even sparkled a little right now. "I don't think I like your cousin."

This woman. I didn't understand her.

I began to pull away, and as if sensing that, her hand grabbed a handful of my shirt, and she held me in place. "I'm going to be honest a little bit here."

I was listening.

She went back to searching my eyes. "I don't know the dynamics of the two in there, or you, or this place, or your men. I don't understand what's happening with you or Jess and her man, but I can tell you that I *really* don't want to know any of that. I *do* know when to hide, when to fold, when to run, and when to fight, but right now, I know there's something else going on between us, and for selfish reasons, I only want to focus on that." She was pulling me to her, slowly, with each word. And she shifted her stance, spreading her legs as I stepped in between them.

The desperation to be inside of her was primal, rushing through me.

My hand skimmed down her leg from her hip, catching the back of her thigh, and I lifted it, stepping fully into her.

She gasped again, a soft breathy sound coming from her. "This"—she trailed her finger down my chest to my stomach and lingered there, toying with the top button of my pants—"is one thing I keep getting distracted by, and I'm just going to reiterate again that I *don't care* about the other bullshit going on."

I lifted her leg higher and moved in.

She gasped again, her head falling back against the door, her chin rising, and her tongue wet her bottom lip.

God.

My dick just shot up at that sight, and feeling me, her eyes opened fully, *seeing* me.

Her hand splayed out over my chest, pushing back but using that momentum to lift both her legs up.

I growled, moving with her. My hands slipped under her ass as she wound her legs behind me, her ankles crossing.

Jesus.

I rubbed against her, slowly.

Looking down, I watched where we were grinding against each other.

She started panting slightly, softly, in my ear.

"This is distracting you?"

"Yes," she breathed out, her hips and ass moving with me. She was pushing against my chest so she could start moving harder, starting to ride back against me.

Well, it was distracting me, too, but I forced myself to stop.

Marco was here. That wasn't good. Remmi was here. That really wasn't good. I was about to lose my head, and that really, really wasn't good. And if reading the past actions, I could predict that where Remmi went, Trace and Jess were about to show up, even if they didn't know how to get here. They'd still show up.

I wanted Molly out of here before any more fireworks happened.

I groaned, separating and letting her drop back down.

Hurt showed from her eyes, but I still peeled myself back from her. "This can't happen." I said it rougher than I intended, but that was happening more and more with her. Everything was coming out backward.

She flinched, biting back down on her lip.

"We're leaving." I nodded for the bathroom. "Use that before we go."

She was blinking rapidly, some wetness shining before she folded her head down, scurrying into the room. She closed the door, the fan turned on, and I cursed. Things were so fucked up right now.

I pushed the intercom button. "Avery."

His voice sounded from the other side of the door. "I'm here."

I opened it, seeing him standing back, but his face was guarded. "Your companion's items are in the car, as well as your items. I've received word that your other guest is about to be dropped off as well. Should they turn back to meet you when that's done?"

"I want Marco and Remmi out of here."

He nodded. "Yes. I can arrange for an 'emergency' to occur. CO_2 alarms can be finicky sometimes."

I hid a smile. Avery was very good at his job. "Thank you."

We both heard the flush from the bathroom.

Molly came back, drying her hands. Her head was still folded down, her shoulders hunched down as well, but she glanced up and braked abruptly at seeing both of us regarding her. "Ready?"

I felt Avery's attention, but I didn't look away from Molly. I couldn't, for some reason. "Yes. I'll be right there."

She blinked again a few times before nodding, her head folded back down, and she skirted around me. I still felt Avery's gaze. "Would you like an espresso for the ride back? I think we'd have time for me to make one."

"Oh, no. Thank you, though."

They started down the hallway, but I sent Avery a text on his phone.

Me: Make the espresso anyways. Thank you.

I saw him check his phone and glance back, giving me a nod.

After that, I went to have a private word with my cousin.

———

Marco was ready, leaning against the bar in the main floor's library. He had a drink in hand and another was poured and sitting on the corner. "Made you a beverage for the trip back."

I took it and threw it against the wall. It whizzed right past him, but Marco knew me. He didn't flinch, didn't even blink. He just lifted his own glass, the ice clanking as he took a long and deliberate sip. "Feel better now that that's out of your system?"

Fuck him. I advanced, taking his drink out of his hands, and this time, I smashed it down on the desk, right behind him.

He cursed, jumping away, shaking his hands of any liquid. "Jesus Christ! You're insane, Ashton."

"You brought Remmi West here. Here! Are you fucking her?"

He was reevaluating me, his eyebrows pulling down. "Yeah. Why is that such a problem?"

I grabbed him now, yanking him away from the desk by his shirt, and I pulled him close, growling in his face, "Because she's a walking tsunami and her father *just* died, you idiot!" I threw him against the nearest wall, and as he hit against it, I was there again. Catching him. "She's *here* in the Walden compound. Even Trace doesn't know where this place is and you brought her here? Here?!"

He was frozen, and the blood was starting to drain from his face. "No—"

"Yes!" I snapped. "She'll put a tracker in the house. She'll have a second cell phone. I don't know, but she'll figure it out, and again, her father was just murdered. She doesn't know what he did, and Remmi is uncontrollable. She's unpredictable. You know what she did to Jess Montell."

"I thought her father was presumed missing."

"You know better." I glared at him. "You know *who* made him go missing."

"That's—"

"She's a loose cannon."

He shoved me back. "You brought someone here too. And who was that, by the way? She's not your flavor of the month. You don't get like this with those women, and you're not this worked up just about the compound being at risk. You don't even like this place. You only come here if you have to. I know you, Ashton." His face was moving into my space now. He was going on the offense, but I held my ground. "You're forgetting how much I know you, too, and that puta isn't—"

My hand moved in a flash, choking him off as I wrapped it around his throat and held him against the wall. I tightened it. "Don't *ever* call her that." Another squeeze. "You hear me?"

He couldn't speak, but he pushed me away enough so my hand slipped away. "Jesus, Ashton!" He bent over, coughing. "Yeah." He looked back up, rubbing at his throat. "I'd say I got that one right. Whoever she is, she ain't worth this shit." Still bent over, he motioned between the two of us. "We're familia, and are you forgetting how much family we've lost? You're going to turn on me?"

I stepped in, close. "You should really stop underestimating my intelligence."

He paused, jerking back up, but he didn't comment. He only regarded me, a flicker of wariness showing.

"I want you and Remmi out of here within the hour."

"But—"

I began walking for the door. "That's not a request. Cut her loose once you get her back to the city."

"You can't tell me who to fuc—"

I stopped at the door. "Yes. I *can*."

He stared at me, measuring me.

"Both are orders." I tilted my head to the side. "It would be very *stupid* of you to challenge me." That was it. That was all. If he did, he'd learn. If he didn't, I had no doubt he'd still learn at a later date. Marco was officially on my watch list.

Avery had a small cup waiting for me as I went past him into the garage.

I took it, pausing.

"She was quiet, but she took the espresso."

I gave him a slight nod. "Thank you." We both turned as Marco was coming out of the library. He paused, taking us in before he headed down the hallway, disappearing from sight.

"Your hand is bleeding." He handed me a towel as he said that.

I took it, grimacing because I hadn't even noticed.

Avery was watching as I wound the towel tightly around my palm. "I'll put a first aid kit in the back seat before you leave, and I'll clean the office right away. Do I need to plan my 'emergency' tonight?"

"Notify me if they don't leave within the hour."

"And if they don't?"

"Then do the plan."

He nodded, beginning to leave.

"Avery."

He stopped. I was watching where Marco had gone. "Watch him on the monitors until he leaves."

"Consider it done."

CHAPTER

TWENTY-FIVE

MOLLY

I was *such* a moron.

Throwing myself at him. Doing the whole hand-to-his-chest thing. Being seductive. And it failed! Crash and burn. He rejected me, but man oh man. I felt him. He wanted me. He was into it, but agh. I was so humiliated.

Was it me?

What was I thinking? Of course it was me.

Me. Who else would it have been? Something was wrong with me. I wasn't pretty enough, or tall enough, or I don't know. It was just me. Who was I kidding? The universe did not like me, but dammit. No. I refused to go down this path. I'd done too much, endured too much, etched out a damn good life despite my parental seeds. Screw him.

I mean, that's what I'd been trying to do but aghhhh!

His loss. Right. Totally his loss. He'd be regretting it, except, and this was hard for me to admit, I didn't think he was regretting it at all. He was quiet when he got in the vehicle, and despite performing some first aid on his hand, he hadn't done anything on the whole drive back to the city. Total silence. Which was uncomfortable, and I didn't know the driver. He was a new guy.

I knew Elijah and now Avery. I didn't know this guy.

When we passed the turn for my place, it was then I remembered what else Sophie had said. "My place!" I jerked forward. "Soph said all my stuff was gone. Did you do that? Where's my stuff?"

He barely reacted, barely looking my way. "Your things were put into storage for safekeeping."

"What about me? I can't go into storage. My clothes. My things. My . . ." Okay. I wasn't big on bonding with material things. There were a few items that I'd kill for, but it was mostly Easter Lanes and my friends. I'd slit a throat for them.

And yes, total darkness. I had some in me, but that was an area I liked to pretend wasn't there. I'd been doing swell for so long. I wasn't counting "the switch" as part of that, but who was I kidding? I knew it was connected.

Still. I could be pretty dark, and I was back to pretending it wasn't there. One identity crisis at a time.

"I had your necessities put into a guest room at my place."

"What?" I thought my humiliation had a time limit. Now it was on a perpetual circling motion, like when the internet wouldn't connect. "Why? No. I want to go *anywhere* else. I don't—"

"It's for your safety." His head turned my way.

I was ignoring the whole jaw-clenching thing or how his eyes flashed not to push him on this. I was so pushing. "I don't want to be around you any more than I need to, and that's enough of even that. I'll stay at Pial—"

"Like fuck you will!"

I clamped my mouth shut, my pulse skyrocketing. I was getting heated. "Then Jess—"

"It's for your safety!" he snapped, through gritted teeth. "The subject is closed."

"No—"

"*I don't want you dead!* How are you not comprehending that?"

"How are you not comprehending that I don't give a damn what you want anymore!" I shot back. "I'll stay with Jess."

"And put her in danger? Her and her mother—because they stay at her mother's half the time. Give Jess one more thing to worry about after she lost her best friend?"

God. He was right.

One last thing for Jess to worry about.

I settled. I had to. He was right.

He took a deep breath to calm himself. "I am trying to keep you off the radar of my best friend and Miss Montell for that very fact. The sooner we find out who killed Justin and Kelly, the sooner all of this can be put to an end."

That was true. Jess. Justin. Kelly.

This was all for them.

But I was *still* embarrassed. The rejection had been swift, and yeah, it stung. Plus, I needed to pee, and the feeling just got worse after I folded my arms over my chest. I had no idea how that worked except that gravity must operate in amazing and complex ways.

I squirmed a little in my seat.

"What's wrong?"

"That espresso was really good, but . . ."

"You have to go to the bathroom?"

"I mean, if you felt the need for a Slurpee, I'd use the bathroom."

Ashton stared at me for a long time.

I was trying not to squirm, especially under this newest round of attention, but I couldn't stop myself. I even did what you're not supposed to do. I pressed my legs together, but man oh man. Sahara. Think of the desert. Dry. Camels. The heat. The sun. Being delusional and seeing water in the distance.

It wasn't working. "I have to go bad."

He nodded, touching a button. "If you could swing through the nearest gas station, please?"

His driver lowered the privacy divider. "We don't have the usual amount of guards."

Ashton was studying me again.

I was trying to sit on my hands. Maybe if I tipped my bladder this way, it'd help?

It wasn't. I glanced at Ashton, and he took that as my response, saying for me, "We'll have to make do." He stared at me without blinking. "You're like a child sometimes."

"I'm aware." I huffed, sinking low in the chair. "I'm working on it. There's a whole list."

He blinked now, but his gaze was still dry before he looked away. "There shouldn't be."

I glanced at him, frowning. What did that mean . . .

The driver hit the turn signal and began easing into the next lane toward the exit. "There's one a block over."

Ashton watched me as we got off the ramp and turned in to the gas station. The place itself wasn't heavily populated. It was run down, bars around the clerks and on the windows and doors. Ashton took my arm, holding me in place as the driver went inside.

"He'll check it first."

I nodded, still thinking Sahara in my head until reality clicked into place when I saw Ashton pull a gun out of his coat. "What are you doing?"

He frowned. "Are you kidding?"

I flushed, *remembering*. "Sorry. I forget sometimes. I mean, I don't, but I do. You're you, and I don't know. It's like I have my own privacy divider to you and what you do in my head. We're constantly in the back bickering while what you do is in front, you know, with the guns and the guards."

The driver was returning, so I ignored a very different feeling that came over the back of the car. I pointed at him. "He's back."

He opened the door. Ashton got out first and stepped aside to let me lead the way.

I did, ignoring the clerk and a couple other customers inside. The bathroom was empty, thank god, but the lock was pitiful. Holding my bladder, as if that worked, I hauled the giant garbage bin over to block the door. The thing was hella heavy, so it'd do. After that, heaven and relief and yes.

That's when my phone pinged in my pocket.

I pulled it out, seeing that reception had come back at some point, and saw thirty text messages, sixteen voice messages, and a whole host of other alerts. Holy shit . . .

Pialto: WHAT THE HAT, WOMAN?! WHERE ARE YOU?

Pialto: Sorry. What the what. Auto-duck.

Pialto: Your cousin won't tell us anything!

Sophie: Where are you? Are you alive? Did you have a one-night stand and it's amazing and you're taking a day? Please please please tell me that's what is going on and not something else.

Sophie: Your cousin! Asshole!

Sophie: P is here and we're both worried. Your cousin told us we could take a week off. What is going on? I'm really worried about you.

Pialto: WE WERE JUST AT YOUR APARTMENT AND THERE WAS NOTHING IN IT?

Sophie: did you mean to move and get a new door?

Pialto: Mrs. Tulip just got back from visiting her sister. She's beside herself that you're gone and she didn't know. She's blaming herself.

Sophie: Oh, dear. Do you know Mrs. Tulip's phone number? Could you let her and myself all know you're okay?

Sophie: Super worried.

Sophie: Love you so much.

Pialto: Is this because of your father? I swear, I SWEAR, I will crack his head open on the pavement the next time I see him.

Pialto: Where are you?

Sophie: Where are you????

Pialto: That's it! I'm tracking down that cop friend of yours. She will get it done. I know she will.

Pialto: Do you have her phone number?

Sophie: P's going to get ahold of Jess. I'm not saying this is the best plan, but we're really worried about you. Your cousin could tell us you're okay, but he refuses. He's holding this over our heads. I think he's enjoying that we're so worried.

Pialto: Glen is an asshole. Also, I got Jess's number.

Pialto voice mail (8)
Sophie voice mail (7)
Jess voice mail (2)
Unknown number voice mail
I couldn't listen to them all, but I'd do what I could do.

Me to Pialto and Sophie in a group message: I'm okay. I'm still with Ashton Walden. Some stuff is going on, but I can't tell you or you'll be in danger. I'll be fine, though. Ashton's made it very obvious that he doesn't want me dead.

Pialto calling.
Sophie calling.
I declined both.

Me: I can't talk now, but I'll call as soon as I can. Promise!!!

Me: Can you get Mrs. Tulip's number for me?

Me: Jess, I'm fine. I'm okay. My dad is in something. I'll call and tell you what's going on as soon as I can.

Gahhhh. I didn't want to lie to her. She was a friend and a good friend, but I couldn't get Ashton's words out of my head. *"I am trying to keep you off the radar of my best friend and Miss Montell . . . the sooner we find out who killed . . . the sooner all of this can be put to an end."*

My phone was going crazy, so I silenced it and stuffed it in my pocket as I finished in the bathroom. It kept buzzing, but I ignored it. I'd have to turn it off and was just pulling it out to do that when I moved the garbage bin aside and left the bathroom.

Two steps out, the hairs on the back of my neck stood up.

It was silent. No voices. No scuff sounds from sneakers on the linoleum. No register ringing up customers. No bell over the door as people would come in and out. Total and complete silence.

I looked up and froze.

Three customers were huddled by the freezer section while Ashton and his driver had their guns up, aiming at two other men who were just inside the entry door. Those guys were in jeans and bomber jackets, and they looked like middle-aged men. Dark features. Greasy hair. They weren't slim, but they looked almost solid muscle except for a bit of a paunch in their stomachs. Both were white, their skin was almost puffy and blotchy. One looked flushed. The other had tanned way too much.

They had their guns up, but were more relaxed in their stance, or looking like it.

One was saying, ". . . you wanna come into our territory, you gotta call ahead. Pay the toll. You think you can use our toilets without getting our permission? I don't think so. Times have changed."

Every single hair on my body was standing up—not because of the guns or what that guy just said but because of Ashton.

A whole different look came over Ashton, like instead of a snake shedding their skin, I was seeing him pull his skin on for the first time. His eyes went into the glittering look that was dark and ominous, and I knew, without a doubt, that these men were going to die. Ashton would be the one to kill them, and it would probably happen in two seconds. But those guys, they didn't know that. Their whole demeanor was off, too confident and smarmy.

"You work for Worthing?" Ashton's tone was low and cold. Deadly.

Another chill went through my entire body. Head to toes. I fought against letting it slither up and down my spine, like a snake.

Suddenly, I was pulled back against someone's chest. Something metal and cold being pressed against my head. "Put your guns dow—"

Whoever spoke, he didn't finish.

As soon as he started, Ashton turned my way. It happened in slow motion.

My heart paused.

Our eyes locked, and I knew, I knew what I needed to do.

Decision made, and he *knew*, somehow he just knew what I was planning, and then I did it. I let my body drop to the ground.

Bang!

And then,

Bang! Bang! Bang!

Pop, pop, pop!

Smoke filled the room, along with other smells that I'd never forget, of bodies sweating, defecating, blood, tears, piss.

Thud.

Thud.

Thud.

People were screaming.

Someone was shouting, and then hands touched my shoulders and I flung my arm up, intending to fight at whoever was going to try to take me.

It was Ashton. His eyes looked feral.

I gasped on a sob, but I couldn't move. Ashton swept me up, an arm under my legs and another behind my back, and he turned. He was looking around, saying something over my head, but I couldn't make it out. My ears were ringing.

My eyes were stinging, too, and I was blinking back tears, because oh my god, they were hurting.

His arm shifted, pulling me tighter against him. A hand went to the side of my face, and the pain sliced through me. I bucked in his arms, but he held on tight, and then we were moving.

There was a car, a door opened, and we were inside.

Ashton went with me, so I was sitting in his lap, but I couldn't let go. I'd wrapped my arms around him. I was clinging to him, and he kept me firmly in his arms. The door was shut behind us; then we were speeding off.

I had no idea what was going on.

Terror.

My body was cold.

Everything was spinning around me so fast. I choked out a sob. A hand began smoothing down the side of my head, pulling me to rest against Ashton's neck.

I burrowed into him so hard that if I cut into him, I didn't care. I would've climbed all the way in as long as he was holding me.

A phone was ringing. I could hear it distantly. The murmur of voices.

I saw the light. Ashton was speaking on his phone, his other arm anchoring me to him.

I tried to look to see who was driving, if it was the same driver or not, if he made it out, but it wasn't. A different guy. Ashton had so many guys.

Then I felt the chest behind me. The gun next to my head—the words being spoken and Ashton. He looked. I looked. I knew what to do.

I started shaking again.

Ashton shifted me so I was completely in his lap. My side against his front. My feet were tucked over him, resting on the seat to his side, and he had one arm behind my back, holding me steady. He went back to smoothing down my hair, but he was still talking on the phone.

The phone—I don't know why I did what I did. It didn't make sense and wouldn't make sense to me later, but I reached up. I took his phone from him, and I hit the "End" button. The phone went dead. It lit up again, but I looked up, meeting Ashton's gaze, and he took it from me.

He spoke over me, pulling my head back to his chest, and he put his phone away.

His other arm came around me, and I felt him rest his cheek on the top of my head.

This. This was the only way to leave or go or whatever we were doing, but whatever we were doing, it was the only way to do it after a shooting.

Just. Like. This.

I decided that was the best time to check out.

CHAPTER TWENTY-SIX

MOLLY

He was cleaning my face.

We were in a bathroom. I was on the counter, and Ashton stood between my legs. A first aid kit was next to us. He was dabbing a cotton ball at my forehead.

I felt the sting and hissed.

He pulled back. "Can you hear me?"

His voice droned through an invisible barrier, but I nodded. I could.

"Can you talk?"

I closed my eyes and started to lower my head, but he touched under my chin. "I need to clean some scrapes you got. They can't get infected."

Another nod. Fine. But I kept my eyes closed.

It felt better this way, somehow. And I reached back for what I'd been holding on to, my fingers touching bare skin.

I looked, seeing that I was holding on to Ashton's side.

I took all of him in.

He was in his black pants that he'd worn earlier, but his shirt was unbuttoned. It hung open. The ends tucked over my hands as I was gripping onto him, as if I couldn't let go, but it felt right to put my hand there again, so I did.

Ashton moved even closer, his head angling over so he could get a better look at me, and after a bit, it felt nice.

He kept cleaning me, a gentle swab here and there. He never pushed hard. He never rubbed. He was doing a methodical and delicate cleaning of whatever cuts I had on my face.

I didn't leave my body again because in a way, I felt safer this way.

———

He cleaned me up, all of me. The cuts got washed, antibiotic cream was put on. Bandages were set over those. After that, he took another fresh and warm washcloth and dabbed it all over me. My neck. The rest of my face. My throat. He moved my shirt aside until I finally lifted it up.

He moved back, his eyes meeting mine for a second, and then he took it and handed it off into the bathroom. I was in my bra. He began cleaning my shoulder. My arms. My back. My front. My chest.

My stomach.

He cleaned all over me until I was shivering from the air wherever we were.

That's when he held out a hand into the other room and brought back a blanket. Either he had the magic of countertops on the other side, or someone was there, handing things to him. The clothes-and-blanket fairy. I liked that idea the best.

The blanket was settled over my back and pulled over my shoulders to drape in front of me.

When he began to step back, my hands moved of their own accord, sliding back to his waist. Not even there. They went lower on his hips. I felt I had a better hold there, and he stopped before he nodded.

"Okay." It was such a soft murmur, I didn't know if he said that or me.

He moved in, helping line up my legs to wrap around his waist, and I moved my hands to his shoulders. I wrapped around him, all of me. Arms. Legs. He pulled me flush against him, his hands lifting me up, and carried me from the bathroom into a bedroom.

The blanket fairy was Jess.

She stood just inside the room, my shirt in her hand, and smiled at me. Her eyes were shining, unshed tears.

"Jess." I couldn't totally hear my voice, but I felt it vibrate out of my chest. I reached for her, and she stepped in. I wouldn't let go of Ashton, though. I didn't know why, I just couldn't do it, so she wrapped an arm around my back, and her head came onto my shoulder.

"Hey, sweetie." I could hear her voice like a whisper and feel it graze over my face. She looked up, still blinking back those tears. Her throat was bobbing as well. "How are you feeling?"

I didn't answer. I didn't even want to.

She nodded, as if understanding, and ran a hand down the side of my face, framing me before a shudder went through her body. "I know. It's—it's scary, having a gun against your head. I'm so sorry you went through that." She choked off, stepping back.

Someone else was there, and they—he—came up, touching her shoulders, drawing her back against him. Trace.

I tried to smile and wave a hand to him, but everything in me was feeling wonky and tired. I couldn't lift my hand, so I just smiled, or I was trying, and I rested my head against Ashton's shoulder.

"Hi, Molly. We're glad you're safe." He gave me a smile back, but his was sad.

I was sure mine was loopy.

Ashton was moving again, going to the side of the bed. "I'll be down in a minute—"

"No." Jess said it just as I tightened my hold on him. "Stay with her. She shouldn't be alone."

Ashton pulled back to see me. I knew that's what he was doing, but I didn't lift my head to look at him. It felt right and nice against his shoulder.

"Here." Jess pulled away from Trace and went to the other side of Ashton's bed, then pulled back the blankets.

"Thank you."

She came back and reached for my hand. "I'm here. Okay? I'm right here." She was blinking back tears once again, and I knew she was thinking of Kelly, so I squeezed her hand. She choked out a sob but squeezed mine back, just as hard.

"We'll be in the other room." Trace touched her shoulder, drawing her with him. "Take your time, Ash."

There was no response.

Ashton was setting me down on the bed as they left, closing the door behind them.

"I need to change clothes myself."

I tried protesting but stopped because that was ridiculous. They were acting like I was some fragile kid. I might've been in shock or not in my body earlier, but I was now. I could think. Reason. I knew he needed to change clothes, but I wasn't going back to that gas station, and I wouldn't return to our old roles of how Ashton couldn't stand me. Not now, anyways, but I was still rational.

I moved back in bed, climbing in.

He seemed surprised, standing, waiting until I was settled in.

I gave him a thumbs-up but still didn't talk.

Everything was just hurting so bad. Aching. I felt like I'd been hit with a semi, and at some point, I might've dozed off because the next thing I remembered was the sound of the shower.

The door was open. Light spread out from the room. A couple other lamps were on in this room, but I was starting to feel warm. Slightly.

Finally.

I was only shaking a tiny bit.

Then the water cut off. Ashton came out of the bathroom a moment later, a towel around his waist as he was running a hand through his hair. He paused, surveying me, but we didn't talk. He went into his closet and came back in sweats. Nothing else, but the tattoo on his hand stood out. A dove, wings stretched out, rays of sun shining from behind it.

He went over, turned off one lamp, and went to his side of the bed.

He watched me. "You want Jess to come in instead?"

He meant if I wanted her to sleep with me. I shook my head.

I wasn't questioning any of my decisions right now. I didn't have the strength.

He nodded, reaching out, and turned off the second lamp. The bed depressed as he crawled in, and then I felt him against me. I felt his heat, and I made a sound. I felt it in my chest as his heat engulfed me. It was so abrupt but needed.

"You okay?" His hand touched my arm. The one with the tattoo.

I grabbed it, holding it up so I could feel it. I couldn't see it anymore in the dark, but I knew it was there. I traced my fingers over it, feeling his skin. "Why do you have a tattoo that usually means peace?"

He tensed. "What?"

"The dove. The rays of sun. Your life is not about peace."

He didn't answer right away. "Because there was a time in my life when I needed some. So I got it."

"Did it work?"

Another pause. "No."

"After our mothers died?"

He sighed. "Yes."

I crawled to him, wrapped my legs around him, and burrowed into his chest.

God.

Warmth.

I wouldn't shake so much now.

He was still tense, and then slowly, muscle by muscle, he relaxed until he was lying on his side, his arms around me too. He moved again, rolling to his back, and I moved with him, settling into his side. My head to his chest.

He lifted an arm, and softly, gently, he began smoothing it down the side of my face, my shoulder, my arm, and he'd repeat the motion.

Over and over again. One. Two.

Ten.

Twenty.

Thirty-nine.

Forty-eight.

I wished for a flying dove right before I fell asleep.

Then I stopped counting.

CHAPTER

TWENTY-SEVEN

ASHTON

I stayed until long after Molly fell asleep, and even then, I couldn't bring myself to leave her.

This—I didn't know what the fuck this was, but needing to take care of her, the terror that went through me when that gun touched her head. It was nothing to how it felt when she looked at me.

I felt struck by lightning.

She was scared. She knew she would die, and she looked at me for help. It was in an instant. One look. Not even a second and we both knew what we were going to do.

I hated her while growing up and now this? This? What the hell was happening with me? I untangled myself from her. It'd been my fourth attempt. The first two she'd fought back, waking up. The third, I hadn't had the heart in it myself, but this fourth time—I needed to separate. At least for a bit. I needed to think clearly again, to even remember how that felt.

Pulling a shirt on, I headed out and toward Trace's basement. He had a whole TV lounge area, and in the last month since he'd bought this place for him and Jess, it was where they spent the most time. He was at the bar mixing a drink when I came down the stairs.

"Heard you get up." He brought it over, his own in hand.

I took it. "Thank you." I looked around, but no Jess. "She's sleeping?"

He snorted. "Are you kidding? She was already riled up when she got the call from Pialto, and you called, showing up with Molly covered in blood? She's in the gym, trying to kick ass in there so she doesn't kick your ass here."

I almost grinned. "I might enjoy that."

He chuckled, shaking his head. "You and the love of my life. I don't know what I'm to do with both of you. You make her want to rip out your throat, and I swear that you enjoy it."

I smiled now. "I do."

"Well, get ready, because any thawing that she's done toward you, that shit is up in smoke. She wants to put a bullet in you."

Fuck. But I almost laughed at that too.

He motioned upstairs. "How is she?"

Molly.

All my amusement vanished. An image of her looking at me when she felt the gun against her head flashed in my mind again.

"She's been through a lot."

"What's going on with you both?"

Trace had been asking me this same question since Molly Easter came into our lives. I never answered before, not really, because I hadn't wanted to get into anything about our mothers, but now . . . it was different. I was different. She affected me, and I shook my head. "I was planning to use her. I was going to take her away, stash her in some house, and leak her location. Then I would sit back and wait and see who showed up to kill her. Course, I'd kill him first, and voilà, we'd follow the lead back to whoever killed Justin and Kelly. Jess *would* be better. You would feel better if she was better, and you and me, we could handle things and *end* this war we're in." That same image. A gun against Molly's head. How she looked at me. How I felt it. How I knew what she was going to do. "All that's gone. Everything is different now."

Using her as bait that way was something I would've done before, without blinking an eye or giving it a second thought. Another person, another situation, it'd already be a done deal. I knew who I was. I knew the darkness in me, and I welcomed it. I wrapped myself with it, savoring it, but her. She'd broken through, giving me different thoughts. Different feelings.

A different outlook.

If that gun had gone off against her head . . .

I greatly and intensely wanted to rip someone's head off their shoulders. I wished I hadn't killed the man. I wished that I'd kept him alive and he was strapped to a chair in one of my warehouses and I could be feeling his blood all over me.

I wished for that with every fiber of my being right now.

Trace had been observing me. He always did. It's how we were. Him and me. We watched each other, but we watched out for each other. So because of that, he murmured, "You're in too deep."

"Yeah." Fuck. "Yeah."

Trace let out a sigh and came over, clinking his glass to mine. "Shit's different when you care about someone."

Goddamn. Care.

I hated it, but yes. I cared. I cared about Molly.

Shit was so *very* different now.

"It was Worthing's men."

"You sure?"

I nodded. "I recognized them. Molly had to go to the bathroom. They'd been tailing us. I think they saw a chance and took it."

"Were they there for you or Molly?"

"Me. They didn't know she was there. She went inside first, so I don't think they even saw her until she came out of the bathroom. They had a guy positioned at the back door. He came up behind her. My source said that on the camera, he saw her on her phone. That's when he approached her."

My mouth was so very fucking dry, just talking about it.

The whole thing played out in my head. Slow motion. It was on a continuous loop.

I shot him first, right in the forehead. He was dead before his body hit the ground. My guy Cal was shooting next to me, and I'd turned, taking out the last guy standing. He had wavered between shooting me or Cal. That'd been his mistake.

"Jess talked to some people she knows. She said the shooting was clean. You guys took down all three. Boom, boom, boom. That's how she made it sound."

"They got off a couple of shots. Cal got hit in the leg and arm."

"She said it was still pretty clean."

"I don't think they thought we'd shoot, or maybe they didn't think I would shoot. They were surprised. I remember that at the end, the last guy was stunned we were shooting back." My gut was twisting and churning. Worthing. He'd sent those men. Those same men who put Molly in danger . . . and I'd been about to do the same thing myself.

"That makes no sense. If they were Worthing's men, they'd know we would shoot. Or you would shoot. You recognized them as Worthing's men?"

I nodded. "I have a file on every single man who works for him. These guys are low on the hierarchy. They're the guys who open the car doors, the restaurant doors. They're the lookouts. Why would he send them to tail me? If they weren't going to kill, then why did they approach?"

"What are you thinking?"

I shook my head, taking a drag from my drink. A long drag. I needed it. I barely felt the burn. "I thought it was Worthing who had killed Justin. He found out something, and that's why he and Kelly were running and asking the 411 to hide them, but Nicolai Worthing wouldn't have sent these guys to make a move how they did. It wasn't thought out. It was lazy work. Careless."

"You're thinking we have another player?"

I shrugged. "I have no idea, and that pisses me off. I don't like playing chess against someone I don't even know is playing."

A door opened above, then a stampede as someone was coming down the stairs. Jess arrived, holding up her phone. "Just got off the phone with a friend. All three of those men were texted orders from Jake's phone."

"What was the order?"

My own phone beeped, and I was getting the same information she just got.

I read my text out loud. "Find and tail Ashton Walden. Scare the shit out of him. It's time we stepped up this fight."

Another beep.

I continued, "Worthing was at the hospital when he sent the texts."

Trace frowned, stepping over to stand beside Jess. His hand went to her shoulder, and he began rubbing her back. "Excuse me because I don't have an enemy or work relationship with him, but that doesn't seem like an order Detective Worthing would send out."

He was right.

"The order would've gone through Nicolai, not Jake." She was watching me intently. "Why was he at the hospital?"

"Hmmm?" I shook my head. "No idea."

Trace snorted, turning to refill his drink.

"You asked to take over finding Kelly's killer. Since then nothing has happened except Molly's apartment was blown up."

"Her door was blown up, and it was a small blast. Contained."

Jess kept on as if I hadn't spoken. "Her coworkers called me, worried out of their ever-loving minds because she's gone and they have no idea where she is, and her cousin, a guy that I found out you also pay, is manning the bowling alley. Then seconds after I get a text from her that she's fine, but she'll explain later, Trace comes tearing through the room saying that you've been shot at. And *then*, you show up here with Molly in your arms. She's terrified and covered in blood, and the only person who can help her is you because she freaked every time you tried to let me have her. Why is that?"

She was speaking through gritted teeth, her tone clipped.

I took a sip of my drink. Oh, screw it. I tossed the whole thing back, eyeing her. "To which one?"

Her eyes flashed. "What?"

"You had a lot of statements in there, but you're asking me a clarifying question. I need to know which one to address first."

Pure venom flashed before she reached for her gun.

Trace moved in, his hand covering hers before she could pull it from her holster. "Okay. Since I'm aware how close Jess is to actually shooting you, and because he's my best friend and also business partner, I'm hoping we don't get to that." The last part was directed at her.

She scowled in response.

He sighed, moving toward me. "You asked to handle finding Kelly and Justin's killer. We pulled back, giving you that freedom. But Molly's involved, and Jess doesn't want to lose a second friend. It's time you brought us in on what's going on."

I was almost disappointed at how he was talking to me, all reasonable and sensical. "Would've been more fun if your woman brought the gun out."

Now she growled.

Trace was fighting back a grin. "You already made the decision to bring us in on this when you brought Molly here."

I was aware, but crossing to one of the leather couches, I still tossed Jess a smirk. "Maybe I just wanted to hand her off? Maybe I wanted Jess to babysit one more person?"

"You did not go there! That's a crack about my mother. You fuck—"

"Okay." Trace stepped in again, his back to me, and he used his hip to keep her in place. "He enjoys messing with you. You're aware of this. You're both aware of this. Maybe not indulge him, and he'll get to the point."

She was half snarling. "He's *such* an asshole. Why do you have to be best friends with him?"

I was smiling because this was helping. Some of my tension about Molly was easing.

Trace said, almost gently, "Because he's like my brother."

"Agh!" Jess craned her head around him, barking at me. "Talk."

Trace sighed.

I smiled even wider. That was the worst thing to say to me.

"Now he'll go on a whole tangent that has nothing to do with anything, and he'll do it because you *just* ordered him to do something he was already going to do." Trace came over, took my drink, and went to refill it. He brought it back, then sat on one of the couches across from me. "Come and sit, Jess. Ashton, stop needling my woman, or I'm going to take it personal pretty soon. You both seem to have forgotten that we have limited time before a certain female might wake, and then our discussions will come to an abrupt end. Remember?"

If he meant to chide us like we were children, it worked.

"You're right." I shot Jess a look.

The back of her neck was getting red, but she clamped her mouth shut, walking over and sitting next to Trace.

I almost grinned but sighed because the fun was over. "The usual ways we get answers weren't working, so I tried a different method." Both were watching, waiting. "I sent Marcus Easter out."

"You sent Shorty out for you? He's not loyal to you. He was loyal to your grandfather."

I held up a hand, halting Trace. "He was properly motivated. He has no idea it was for me. I used someone as my front—"

"He used me."

The words came from the stairs, and they were quiet. Almost weak.

My stomach took a plunge, but I was up and crossing the room before Jess and Trace could comprehend that Molly wasn't in bed. Molly was here. She was sitting on the stairs, just out of eyesight. She had a blanket wrapped around her, and she looked up at me. Her eyes were big and wide but hurting. Dark bags were smudged underneath them. Her skin had an unhealthy pallor to it.

Jesus.

She looked like a scared teenager, so young and as if she'd waded into a world she'd not been prepared for.

I *hated* it.

I hated it because this was my fault, her father's fault, her mother's fault, my mother's fault. It was all of ours, but swallowing a curse, I went and squatted in front of her. I patted my thighs. "Come on."

She moved in a flash, like a spider monkey. She came in, wound her legs around my waist, her arms around my neck, and I stood, a hand on her ass to keep her in place. She got even tighter to me, burrowing her head into my neck.

Both of us sighed at the contact.

Fuuuuuck.

This was bad, so *fucking* bad. One touch and I felt right with her in my arms.

This hadn't been in the plans.

But I couldn't get myself to stop holding her.

Trace was watching me more intently than he *ever* had before, and I was ignoring him, more than *I* ever had been, moving back to the couch and sitting. Molly moved to sit sideways on my lap, her head still against my chest, so she could see Trace and Jess.

"Molly." Jess gave her a smile. All the hostility from earlier was gone. "How are you feeling?"

Molly stretched her leg out, just a bit, shifting and getting more comfortable. "I'm okay. It's—I've had guns pointed at me before, but this one was a first. Never had it against my head." She gave her a sheepish grin. "I'm a little embarrassed, but I'm okay. Really."

Jess was skirting between Molly and me. "Do you want something to eat? Drink? We can go up and I can make you broth?"

"No." Molly's tone was firm. She sat up a little straighter too. "I want to hear this." She looked at me, her eyes determined. "My dad stirred this up. I'm *going* to hear this."

I swallowed, reading her right. She wasn't going anywhere.

I gave in, a small nod, and she relaxed.

Jess's head was inclined forward, her mouth parted. "Wha—okay then." She jerked back in her seat.

Trace was trying to contain a laugh and failing. He looked down, his shoulders silently shaking.

"Glad to bring some entertainment tonight."

Trace looked back up at me, his face wiped clean, but the amusement was still in his gaze. "Can you blame me?" He indicated Jess.

No. I couldn't. I thought it'd been hilarious when he fell for a cop. PO, whatever. They were all the same in my eyes. Law enforcement.

"Ashton."

"Mmmm?" I looked down at Molly.

She'd tipped her head up to me. "Tell us what the fuck's going on."

Jess started laughing, but I did as Molly commanded.

I told them everything, or mostly everything.

CHAPTER TWENTY-EIGHT

MOLLY

I was watching from the bed as Ashton moved around the room, sweats on, a T-shirt not hiding how very toned he was. Shock and trauma aside from being shot at and everything else, *man*, the man had muscles. He was the definition of muscle definition. And those sweats were dipping so nicely low on his hips.

I wasn't trying to work myself up, but it was just happening.

Ashton had given me and Jess and Trace the info on what he thought was happening because my dad was scurrying around out there. And also that he'd sent in an order for Marcus to reach out, but that he hadn't yet. That was either good or bad. I checked my phone, but he'd not messaged or called me there either.

"Do you think he'll be alarmed when he goes to your apartment, Molly?" Jess had asked earlier.

I snorted before remembering she didn't really know the dynamic between my father and me. I shook my head. "Number one rule surviving being Shorty Easter's daughter? Never let him know where you live. He only knows to get ahold of me at Easter Lanes."

"And if he shows up, Glen will let us know. I have other men in place as well."

Ashton. The Mafia man of the men. He had them everywhere, had ears everywhere, eyes all over the city. I watched him now as he came to the bed and reached for his shirt's hem to haul it over his head, but he paused upon seeing me studying him.

He asked, "What?"

"The Worthing family sent men after you."

His eyes grew wary until he masked them.

He was doing that less and less, or I was starting to be able to read him better and better. I was going with me. Woman power. I was awesome.

"Yes."

I reached for the blanket, my finger running over the end, playing with it. "So according to Mafia street rules, that means you guys are going to hit them back?"

His shoulders rose as he took in a deep breath. "It's not normal for me to talk about who I'm going to murder before I do it."

If he meant for that to be cutting, I let it roll off my back. "They hit you before? With your uncles. Your grandfather. Trace's uncle too."

Ashton's mouth dipped down. "What are you getting at?"

"I'm getting at, why haven't you hit them back yet?" My pulse began to pick up pace. "Ashton, you are not the guy known for restraint. What is going on?"

He stared at me before a slight grin curved at the corner of his mouth. Reaching for the sheet, he moved it back and got underneath. He rested against the headboard, looking at me, so I moved forward, facing him and kneeling on the bed. He laid a hand between us, palm up, but other than that, he didn't move to touch me.

"Most women don't advocate for murder."

I snorted at that. "Most women don't own a business or have lived in a community where the Mafia runs it either. They get to live in fairy tales and castles. I don't. Hit them back."

He frowned a little. "We're planning on it, but no, I'm not telling you the details."

"I don't care about the details. I just want to know you're going to do it."

He rested his head back, still looking at me. It gave him an almost softer look. "You and Jess are friends."

I shot him a frown. "Yeah?"

"Then why am I the one in here with you?"

I shrugged at that, turning so I was sitting with my back against the headboard with him. I was still playing with the bedsheet in my hand. "Because Jess thinks I'm fragile, and she talks to me as if I'm an egg about to crack open. Yes. I'm not tough in hand-to-hand like she is, and I didn't have to deal with parolees like she used to, but in a way, I'm more street than she ever was."

"Her brother is in prison. Her father was murdered."

"She was never homeless, and she lived in a decent community." I'd stopped looking at him when he asked about Jess, but I chanced one now. "You don't treat me like that. You don't talk to me like that."

A dark understanding was looking back at me. "I wasn't? Not when I was carrying you around?"

I grinned. "That was me milking the situation. No matter how old we get, there's always a little girl in us who wants to be picked up by her knight."

He lifted his hand up, his thumb coming to rest on my chin, right in the dip. His gaze fell to my lips. "I'm not your knight."

I swallowed over a lump. "No, you're not. You're the bad guy."

His eyes darkened, and his thumb moved down to my throat, farther, gliding between my breasts. "Yes. I am."

"You're the murderer."

That should scare me. It didn't. It really didn't, and it wasn't because I was attracted to him or whatever else might've been unfolding between us. It had to do with something more, something underlying everything. Something in him that recognized something in me. Something that I felt, knew, was there but still wasn't altogether ready to address.

And until then, I was willing to address a whole other "something" I was feeling for him, right now, something in a very physical manner.

His chest rose, but he ran his finger over, pulling the side of my tank down, exposing one of my breasts. His finger moved up, circling my nipple. "I'll always be the murderer."

"I know what you were planning to do, you know."

I was watching him as I said it, and he paused, his eyes steady on mine. My pulse was skyrocketing, and a deep ache was beginning to pound between my legs. Still, I held firm. "You were going to use me as bait for Kelly's killer."

His voice was raspy. "You knew?"

I nodded, silent, before murmuring, "I guessed."

The thought of what he could've done, maybe should've done—my gut shifted, sliding to the side, because a part of me understood. The part like him, the part that helped me survive the streets, the part that contributed to when "the switch" happened, but the other part, of actual thinking what that would've been like? Sitting. Being bait?

"I understand, but I'm not happy about it." I reached up, pulling my tank down on my other side, letting that breast free as well.

We shared a long look. Him, I don't know, but me, I was letting him know that I wasn't stupid. I wasn't wide eyed. And I wasn't totally sure if I was going to be pissed about what he might've done.

"And your response to what I was considering doing?"

I shook my head, instead answering in a whole different away. I moved up, lifting my leg and coming down to straddle him. Both of us paused at the contact because he was right there.

He felt good. *So* good.

I bit down on my lip and began to move over him.

He groaned, his hand moving to the back of my ass, clamping on. I was learning it was one of his favorite places to hold on to me, but he was guiding me so we were both grinding against each other.

I leaned back, my hips still riding him, and I gasped against the onslaught of pleasure. "I'm not the girl who thinks sex is love. I know it's not. It's never been that in my life."

"Molly. About what I—"

"Shut up." I rose and paused, then ground against him, going slow, savoring.

He frowned a little, but he moved me harder, more insistent over him, distracted at the same time. He reached up, one of his hands resting on my neck, the rest of his fingers, his palm, spread out over the side of my face. He was half holding me in place, half somewhat cradling me in a touch that might've been gentle, but it was also slightly aggressive. We both knew it.

His eyes flashed, hard, as I rolled my hips forward. "What kind of girl are you then, Molly?"

Need and carnal desire were pulsating through my body, spreading, and I knew he wouldn't say no this time. Or if he did, that'd be interesting as well, but because of that, because of what we were doing, because he was rock hard underneath me, I reached down and pulled his pants low. I moved up, shoving my own pants down, and then I paused.

His dick was fucking long and hard.

I was in love with that part of him, but shooting him a slight grin, I didn't share.

I just panted, "Condom?"

"Molly." He was gritting his teeth.

I shook my head. "You messed up. That's what I think."

"How?" he rasped out, his other hand kneading my ass.

I knocked his hand away from my face and neck, before grabbing ahold of his cock. He hissed at the touch, but his eyes only closed for a moment. I said then, when he wasn't looking at me, "You should've used me when you had the chance."

His eyes opened, and they were molten. He reached over to the nightstand and grabbed one from the drawer. He handed it to me, content to watch as I worked my hand over him before putting the condom on, and then, I rose up. I positioned over him and sank down, both of us groaning at the feel of him inside of me.

That's when I said, in a pant, "Because I'll never give you the chance again."

He cursed but shoved up even higher inside of me.

God. He felt so good.

I added, answering his other question, "I'm the girl who doesn't know how to be treated right, so treat me right tonight."

He froze at my words, but it didn't matter.

I bent my head down, resting on his chest, and I rode him for myself.

———

Round two, he flipped us over.

I was on my back, he was above me, and he thrust inside, grinding in. He rode me, sometimes hard, sometimes slow, but always so fucking delicious that I was screaming by my second release, and he started pounding me for his own release.

———

Round three was in the shower.

I was smashed against the wall, water pounding over both of us.

My hands were up, his were linked with mine, and he was moving up into me from behind.

I think that was my favorite.

———

Round four was when the sun was coming up.

I'd lost track of time and was starting to lose energy, but Ashton was still going.

This time it was slow and exploratory. If the others had been straight sex, this was the slow-sex round.

He worshipped every inch of my body, kissing, tasting, caressing, and I was panting, grabbing onto the bedsheets as his mouth brought me to climax before he rose back over me.

His gaze met mine, and we both paused. I was panting, trying to catch my breath, and his eyes were dark, so dark. Our last words had been mine, telling him to treat me right, and he had.

The night had been a fuck fest.

Something flashed in his eyes, something hard and primal and something that sent a shiver down my spine. Whatever it was, he reached for my legs and raised them up, pushing them so they were above my head. I had to scoot down, but rising back, he held my legs in place. His hands would leave handprints on the backs of my thighs, but he shoved inside, and I was wrong.

This wasn't the slow-sex round.

This was the hard: "I'm going to ride you so hard that you have absolutely nothing left, and I will enjoy fucking the life out of you"—it was that round.

He watched me the whole time, his strokes almost punishing. I held his gaze. We were in some sort of fight, even just now. I just panted, not caring about whatever was going on in his head, because I was loving this. The harder, the better, and I grinned as he growled, bending over me, his forehead next to mine. His head was turned, and we still watched each other. Our lips were grazing against each other, but neither moved to seal a kiss.

We hadn't kissed the whole night.

Suddenly, he let go of my legs. They fell around his waist, but he held a hand against the headboard so he was able to pull back, almost coming out of me, only to slam back inside.

I gasped, moaning. He was making my entire body shake, and somehow I knew this round was him taking out some form of frustration on me. But, almost grinning at how I was about to mess with that, I reached for his ass and lifted myself up, plastering myself against him so he couldn't give me the punishing strokes.

He made a guttural sound, almost like a growl, and I was moving to meet him so we were both punishing each other. I was doing it to piss him off, and he knew it, growling before he took charge. A hand came around me, and he flipped me over. I was slammed down on my stomach. I reached up, trying to grab a place to hold on the bed, but he took my ankles and slid me down in one yank.

"Agh!" I squeaked.

His hands were on the insides of my thighs, spreading them. He was back at my entrance.

He slid in, thrusting a little slower, but he was back to fucking me, and goddamn, I gave in, my head falling to the bed.

I lay there, and I enjoyed every second of this as he was pistoning into me.

We came together.

I felt his release at the same time mine ripped through my body. I didn't think that was planned and half laughed about it, but he lay over my body for a minute. He was gasping for breath. I was doing the same.

My pulse was slowing, normalizing.

He began to pull out, his hand sliding under my legs, but I ceased being aware of anything . . .

I was asleep. Bliss.

CHAPTER

TWENTY-NINE

ASHTON

We'd slept through the rest of the morning.

I was sitting on the edge of the bed. Molly was still conked out behind me. She'd fallen asleep after our last time, so I'd moved her, positioning her back under the sheets, but I couldn't sleep. My body was a mix of satisfaction, exhaustion, and also readiness for whatever was to come.

I liked this next stage. Not in a Mafia war, but in our businesses. I enjoyed where the next move was ours to make, where our adversary was wary, where we were the predators. But the stakes were different here.

They'd hit us last night, and before we'd even retired to our separate bedrooms, Trace and I had already coordinated our attack. Each of us still handled what our families handled before, with Trace's family covering transportation and distribution and mine handling the cops and higher-ups, but it was different now that he and I were the heads. We could coordinate better. There was no more needed time to call for a meeting or to decipher if that was necessary. Trace and I just did it. Together. We made the decisions where to hit, how to hit, whose men would do the hits. We no longer had "boards" or "uncles" to get permission from in order to make an order. Our men were dispatched with their missions, and a part of me was up, waiting for the notice that they were successful.

My phone buzzed, and I was expecting that text.

I got something else instead.

Avery: Keeping you updated. Your cousin and his guest left an hour after you did. I put a tracker on his car. Here's the link for his coordinates.

I checked it, and Marco was at Katya. What the hell?

I was standing, reaching for my clothes, when my phone buzzed again.

Trace: You awake? We need to talk.

Me: Give me two minutes.

Trace: Dress to leave. I'll be in the garage waiting.

I hurried to dress. When I was done, Molly was awake, watching me. The sheet was tucked over her chest, under her arms.

"Hi."

She looked rested. There were shadows under her eyes, but overall, she looked better than the night before. "I have to go."

She nodded, solemn. "I figured."

"I think Jess is still here."

She nodded, again. The bags under her eyes looked more pronounced. "I want to talk to Pialto and Sophie."

I frowned.

She was reading my expression, and she sat up, keeping the sheet tucked under her arms. "I won't leave. I won't do anything else, but they're my family. That's nonnegotiable. If you don't let me talk to them, I'll sneak out myself, and don't think I won't be able to. I have crazy cat burglar skills, except breaking out, not in."

My gut tightened. "Wait for me to come back or arrange something. Please."

"What if Jess takes me?"

"I'd prefer you waited for me. Montell tends to run toward bullets when she hears them. I'd like for you to run away from the gunfire."

"Okay. I'll wait for you."

I gave her a nod, still studying her because . . . I didn't know why.

Because I didn't want to leave her. Because I thought she would find a way to get in trouble the second I left. Because . . . I liked being around her.

Goddamn. My gut was tightening all over again, but I left without a goodbye.

Elijah was at the kitchen door when I came through. He had a fully cleaned gun ready for me. I took it as I walked past, heading into the garage. Our other men were there, and all moved into their places.

Trace's men were in his car. Elijah would get into a following SUV this time.

I'd ride with Trace. All of this was already worked out.

I grunted in greeting to Pajn and Demetri, Trace's men, and I slipped into the back seat. Demetri shut my door, then climbed into the front next to Pajn.

"What's going on?"

Trace let out a long sigh, showing me his phone.

I read the message.

Unknown Number: This is Nicolai Worthing. We were informed this morning that members of the Walden Family shot and killed three of my men. Upon inspection, we saw the aggressors were my men. I'm reaching out for a meet. This is an act of good faith. I did not send my men to kill Ashton and his guest. I have not broken the ceasefire. Will you accept my invitation?

The next text was the location and details.

"He's going to make himself vulnerable to us."

Trace took his phone back, putting it away. "I believe that's the point."

"Also a nice incriminating text to any authority reading your messages."

"Yes, he's letting whatever authorities watching us know that he was not behind his men coming for you."

"Marco is fucking your sister."

"What?" Trace's head whipped to mine.

"After everything that happened, I forgot to tell you. He brought her to our compound."

He shifted so he was turned more toward me. "The compound that even I don't know where it is? The one that you have mixed emotions about. You hate, but you use anyways. That place?"

I shot him a grin, ignoring the latter part. "He reassures me that she doesn't, either, but we both know your sister. She probably set a building on fire behind her."

He shifted back, sitting beside me. His tone was resigned. "Destruction does tend to follow her wherever she goes." I could almost hear him grinding his teeth. "They're actually sleeping together?"

"I asked if he was fucking her"—I ignored his swift intake of air—"and he said yes."

"Shit."

"And they're at Katya right now."

"How do you know?"

"Avery put a tracker on Marco."

Trace growled. "I don't know which I'm more frustrated about, your cousin or that my sister is at our nightclub after we've told her to stay away."

I grunted. "I think the latter. Remmi's more likely to destroy Marco, so I'm not too worked up about the two of them. Though, I'm wondering if I should ask the details how that started or if I don't actually need to know. I know I don't want to know. I told him to stop sleeping with her."

"He's your blood, so I'm not expecting that to happen."

I smirked. It was true.

Trace rubbed at his forehead. "She's been a mess since our dad's death. She was never close to Uncle Steph, but she was clinging to hope that our dad would someday actually be a dad. To her credit, he was somewhat loving to her."

Neither of us were commenting on the details surrounding his father's death. Remmi didn't know any of that, and she wouldn't if it were up to Trace.

"She's in mourning, reaching out to who was receptive."

"That makes me worried that Marco was receptive."

"Not me. He's always had a thing for her."

I ignored Trace as he turned to observe me again. "Since when?"

"Since forever. He took her to prom."

"That was a pity date."

I shot him a look. "That wasn't a pity date."

"Are you serious? You've known all these years he had a thing for her, and you never told me?"

"She's always had a thing for me, so no. Why would I?"

"What? You and her?"

I scowled. "I never went there. Nor would I. Your sister is, one, *your* sister, and two, like a *sister* to me. A bratty, young, 'somewhat materialistically spoiled because she's not spoiled in the getting-love-and-attention way' kind of sister. I've cleaned up more of her messes than you."

He relaxed a little. "That's true. You have."

"You're welcome, by the way."

"Let's not get ahead of ourselves."

"She is *your* sister."

He groaned. "That's true." A pause. "Thank you."

"What's the plan going into this meeting?"

He gave me a look this time. "I thought I'd let you handle it while I sit back and observe."

I smiled, liking that *a lot.* "Excellent." It was time to make some people bleed. We were leaning into our strengths. I liked hurting, and Trace enjoyed analyzing.

We were the West and Walden Mafia family. If I were Nicolai Worthing, I'd be scared.

I couldn't wait.

CHAPTER THIRTY

ASHTON

Nicolai Worthing was a smug prick. That was my opinion when we'd first met, and it remained today. We went in. He was already outside his vehicle. His men were spread out. He'd picked a place where he would be vulnerable if we chose to take him out then and there. But I didn't believe that. He'd never let himself be as open as he was. I had no doubt he had a sniper set up somewhere.

Because of that, I had sent Avery a text to come.

He was an hour out, so we stalled as long as we could. We couldn't stall any longer.

As we got out of our vehicle, our men spreading, I got a text.

Avery: Ten minutes out.

I almost whistled. He must've been speeding and beyond to make that time, but it was Avery.

I tucked my phone back in and walked the distance toward Nicolai.

He grew up in privilege, and he dressed like it. Three-piece suit. He probably got his shoes shipped direct from Italy, and he had a smarmy look with his hair combed to one side. I'm sure females thought he was attractive with his boxy-looking face, but I just saw a punk when he looked at me.

He was still smirking as I approached. There was a single flicker of emotion when he noticed Trace was staying back. I'd be the one leading this meeting.

"Ashton."

"Punk." I grunted.

Irritation flared over his face, tightening his features, but he covered it almost right away. Not as quick as I would've assumed. That told me he was slipping a little from the hold he thought he had.

"You walk into a meeting and insult me?"

"Save it." I started walking around him. He and Trace didn't know each other, but we did. I knew his cousin—not Justin, another cousin. I'd done coke off her stomach at one point, and Vivianna had spilled a lot of secrets about her various cousins. Nicolai had never been mentioned, not because she didn't know him but because he'd been an afterthought. How he'd sprung up with so much power and how quick it had happened, I had doubts about whether he was the real front man or if there was someone behind him.

"I know you. You forget that," I added.

His mouth went into a flat line. Yeah. He hadn't forgotten.

"I assumed this meeting would be done with both you and Trace West."

"No. He's given me the reins here." I stepped closer to him, getting into his space. "You know, since it was me that your men tried to kill. Since it was me that killed your men instead."

"I never gave them an order to do that."

I moved back, studying him. "So who did?"

His mouth tightened again. There was a little tic right behind his eye. It pulsed before he blinked, and it was gone. "I'll be doing an investigation into who sent that order, but I reached out. I put myself at the disadvantage to show you that I did not send those men."

My phone buzzed again.

Avery: Two minutes out.

"I have a theory that you're not as vulnerable as you're making us think, but we showed up because while you apparently haven't got a fucking clue, we do know who sent the order to your men."

He went still.

He really didn't know, and that tic was back. He was pissed.

"The orders came from someone in your family."

His eyes narrowed. "You kidnapped one of my men and held him for questioning."

I almost laughed. Fucking Jake Worthing. "That's right. He probably went to the hospital and got treated, for the very minimal rough handling that might've been done to him?"

"He got checked out, yes." Nicolai wasn't amused. He wasn't showing any emotion, but I knew him. Could read him.

He was so pissed.

He thought he could control Trace. He knew he couldn't with me.

"You're saying because I questioned one of yours, it's okay that you sent three men to kill me?" I stepped right into his face, leaning in, purposely making him uncomfortable. "After you killed three of my uncles, my grandfather, and Trace's uncle? Eye for an eye, right? That means we're due for way more than just three of your men."

I wanted to flick him in the forehead. I wanted to, so badly. It would've been a humiliating insult, but I couldn't. However he got where he was, Nicolai held too much power.

He was holding firm, staring right back at me, seething but holding his ground.

I narrowed my eyes, cocking my head to the side. What the hell? Let's go with my theory here. "How'd you get where you are today?"

"What do you mean?"

"You. I mean, you." I sneered at him. "I know you were a nothing in your family's business, and now look at you. Head of the family, or is it someone else?"

He tensed, his face schooling in concrete. "Tread carefully, Ashton. I also know you."

He knew nothing that I was scared of him knowing about me. I liked fucking people up. I liked being cruel. I was also smarter than people thought, and I loved that people didn't know how to read me.

Except Molly. She could read me.

"You got someone else behind you? Pulling the strings? Or is it really you? You this hard-ass Mafia head? Did you really order those hits on us? Or was it someone else?"

A new shift came over. I felt it, felt his true weasel self showing, but he laughed at me. His tone was hard, his eyes rageful. "I ordered the hits against your family, and I loved it."

I reacted swiftly, bringing my gun up and putting it against his temple.

He froze.

I didn't. I moved in *even* closer, staring down at him.

There was a burst of activity behind us. Shouts. Threats.

"Say it again." I said it softly. Taunting. I took the safety off. "Say it again, how much you enjoyed issuing the order to kill my family."

He looked away, staring beyond me.

Fucking coward.

I pressed my gun harder, clenching my teeth. "Say it again, dipshit. Say. It. Again."

A presence moved up behind us. I knew it was Trace before he spoke.

"I'm not here for Ashton," he said.

Nicolai sucked in a breath, just slightly, but I heard it. I felt it.

I started laughing. "He's here to double down."

"You called this meeting for what purpose?"

Nicolai swallowed. "I told you—"

"He didn't give the *latest* order, Trace. The one that sent those three men after me. That's what he's going to say. But dumbass." I angled my head over his so I could look him in the eyes, moving the gun to the side, but still right against his head. "We already knew that. It's why we came here."

Nicolai's eyes were chilled.

I grinned. "You wish you could redo that order, don't you? But send a special team after me. Right?"

He didn't answer that, looking at Trace. "Can you get your psychopathic pet off me? A man can only stand so long with a gun to his head before he makes an order that's going to involve a bloodbath."

Trace was quiet.

So was I.

Then, a gunshot rang out not far from us.

Nicolai cursed, jerking before looking at me.

I held still. My phone buzzed. "Something tells me that wasn't my man going down."

Nicolai exploded with curses, but he couldn't shake me. I was on him, my gun against his head. He tried moving left; I was there, blocking him.

"Get off me!" He shoved me back.

I went, but my gun remained up, pointing at him. I took a shooting stance. "Tell me how much you enjoyed giving the orders against my family again. Do it. Forget the last three men. I want to hear about the first orders you made."

Nicolai's eyes were wild. He had shifted. He couldn't hide any longer, and that's what I wanted. I wanted in there. I wanted to be so far in his head that I would haunt his every thought.

Trace was lapping up this opportunity too. He was better at the psychological stuff.

Me, I just saw a weasel killer and wanted to snuff him out.

"I want the ceasefire to continue." Nicolai was making a concerted effort to keep in control, but he was sweating. The restraint was costing him. "Until we know who killed my cousin."

"And Kelly," Trace said.

Nicolai stiffened.

I narrowed my eyes. He'd forgotten about the girl.

Trace's voice went low. "And Kelly too. She was loved by someone in our camp."

"Of course. Justin loved her. She would've been family one day."

I snorted at that.

Nicolai sent me a dark look.

"Somehow I doubt that." I put the safety on, seeing our work was done here.

We saw him. He wanted to keep the ceasefire in place, and I'd rattled him enough. In my eyes, he was a coward. I was sure Trace would have a whole different take on him, one that was more convincing and more intellectual, but I didn't care. I was going to kill Nicolai Worthing one day.

I couldn't wait for that day.

"The ceasefire will continue, but if there's one more aggression, we'll stop waiting."

Nicolai stared at Trace before dipping his head in a brief nod. "Thank you." He glared at me before he went to his vehicle. His men moved immediately, swarming him.

They all were in their cars and speeding away within seconds.

"Tell me that gunshot was ours?" Trace looked at me.

I checked my phone.

Avery: His man is down. Orders?

I called him. "Is he alive?"

"He is. I have his gun packed up."

I slid my eyes to Trace, seeing him cursing and shaking his head. "Bring him in. Take him to the downtown warehouse."

"On it."

"You serious?" Trace asked as I put my phone away. "Who'd you call in?"

"Avery."

He swore again but took in a deep breath. He was aware how good Avery was. "He had a man out there?"

"Sniper, or I'm guessing from the distance. Avery didn't specifically say he was a sniper."

Trace's eyes closed for a respite before he shook his head. "We just agreed on the ceasefire, and one of our men took out one of his right after?"

"No."

"What? Yes!"

"No. It was in the middle of negotiations. The gunshot happened before you both agreed on the continued ceasefire."

Trace rolled his eyes, but I was right, and he knew it.

I was grinning, enjoying this moment. I got one over him, my genius analyst best friend. He flicked his eyes upward again but gave me a half grin back. "You're such a cocky shit."

"I'm a cocky shit that's right."

Trace nodded, and his whole demeanor shifted. I knew this look. He was moving into the mulling phase, where he was pulling up all the information he had taken in from our interaction, and he was sifting through it. He was a computer, bringing everything up on the screen so it could get studied and grouped in the right category.

"This ceasefire doesn't make sense."

I grunted. Now he was getting it.

"He wasn't worried about Kelly. He forgot about Kelly. He was only worried about who killed Justin . . . or was he? I couldn't read him when he mentioned Justin. But it's like he's more worried about the ceasefire than anything else."

I was figuring that too.

Trace kept on. "You kidnapped one of his cousins. You killed three of his men. You just had his sniper taken out, and he is *still* insisting on the ceasefire. Why? That makes no sense in our world."

The answer came to me, and it was glaringly obvious. "Yeah, it does."

Trace looked my way.

"He's planning something else, and he needs time. We're *giving* him that time."

"There's no ceasefire then."

"Exactly."

We shared a look.

"That means we can hit him back."

I smiled. "Finally."

He grinned back. "It also means he has no idea we already took his cousins."

Crispin and Penn. General dickheads, but yeah. Nicolai left without saying one word, so he had no clue.

"His sniper isn't dead. We got that man, too, and his gun."

It was a good coup for us.

Trace nodded. "We need a big hit."

"We need to find out why he wants a ceasefire so damned much." I remembered something else. "We still need to take care of Marco and Remmi."

His grin vanished. "Let's handle the sniper first."

CHAPTER

THIRTY-ONE

MOLLY

I got my dad's voice mail, again. "Dad, you need to call me. I'm actually worried. For once." I hung up before I could say anything more, like how I wanted to murder him, because if he heard that, he'd never find Kelly's murderer.

"No luck?"

I straightened, hearing Jess come into the kitchen.

I'd left the bedroom around six because my stomach was doing its best rendition of a pterodactyl squawk, or how I was assuming they would've squawked. It would've been more like a roar.

I'd realized this was not Ashton's house or another one of Ashton's places when I went down the stairs and saw a picture of Trace and Jess together. The next picture over was of her mother. Her brother. There were more people, but I didn't know them, and then I meandered into the office and was captivated for the next hour because there was an entire wall of pictures of Trace during his high school and college years. A lot of those pictures had him and Ashton, and yeah, my stomach was doing all these little flutters seeing Ashton smiling and looking young and dare I say . . . cute?! He was hot, but he was cute too.

I was looking forward to teasing him about the dichotomy.

"No, but that's typical with Shorty Easter. He finds you, not the other way around."

Jess motioned to the coffee machine. "Want some?"

"That'd be great." And of course, I fought back a yawn at that moment. "This is your new place with Trace?"

She was grabbing the coffee, and a soft smile came over her face. "It's not far from my mom's house, so she's close if anything happens."

"It's nice. It's . . . adulting."

Jess glanced back, a short laugh escaping her. "What?"

"It's adulting. You and Trace. You're doing it, despite, you know."

Some of her smile faded. "Yeah."

"Um. Hey." Shit. I was an asshole friend. "I know I reached out when it first happened, but—"

"That's not on you."

"What?"

She finished the coffee machine and hit the switch, then turned to rest her back against the counter beside it. "That's not on you. I know what you were going to say, but you did reach out when it happened. You were there when Trace and I were going through our thing, and you tried being there for me after Kelly's body was found. I—I wouldn't let anyone by me, except my mom and Trace. That was it. I kinda went insane after I found out." Her voice shook. "I—it was my fault and—"

"Hey." I shoved off the stool, and closed the space between us.

Everyone thought Jess was this tough parole officer, and to be honest, she was. No one wanted to mess with her, but she was—well, she wasn't really soft inside, but what she *was* was an amazing friend, and she had an amazing heart. I went to her, ignoring how she started to put her arms up. I wrapped mine around her in a hug. "It wasn't your fault. I don't care what you're going to say. I don't care about what you do for a living, who you fell in love with, anything else you might say.

The person responsible for Kelly's death is the person who killed her. Period. You do not blame yourself. You hear me?"

She was stiff, at first, and then she let out a shuddering sigh and leaned into me. She didn't put her arms around me. Jess wasn't that kind of friend, not really, but it said a lot that she stood and let me hug her. So I had to hug her with everything I had in me. I was pretending Pialto and Sophie were here helping me hug her.

They gave the best hugs. We always did them three ways too.

I heard her sniffle, so I kept on squeezing until it was long after the coffee was done.

"Thanks, Molly." Jess stepped back, wiping a hand at her eye before she showed me where the coffee mugs were.

I nudged her aside, taking over from there. Selecting a mug, I asked her, "You want some?"

She nodded, blinking a little and wiping her face as she went to sit on the stool I'd left. "Thank you."

I poured both of our cups and went looking for some cream in their amazing fridge. "I was going to say earlier that I'm sorry I haven't checked in lately. I guessed you'd like some space, but I meant to reach out, but then . . ."

Jess's grin was knowing as I brought her coffee over and slid onto the stool next to her. "Then a guy tried to rob your place and you went a little insane?"

"Who wears green makeup to rob a bowling alley?"

"I'd like to think that if you're planning to rob a bowling alley, the only makeup I'd want to wear *is* green makeup."

I shot her a grin. "Maybe I almost shot him too fast. I should've asked his thoughts on what makeup to wear when robbing a costume shop?"

"That'd be hard. I wish you had asked him. I don't know if I'll be able to asleep tonight not knowing what color he would've worn."

It felt nice to be joking with Jess again.

I swallowed over a lump in my throat. "Maria, Dex, and Jimmy come every Sunday night still."

The coffee cup went down so fast and almost forcefully that I hesitated, thinking I'd pissed her off, but her head folded over, and I heard the sob.

She'd dropped the mug. She hadn't put it down.

"Oh." I moved in, putting my arm under hers, and I stood from the stool, pulling Jess into me again. This time, she leaned her entire weight into me. Her hand was covering her mouth, and she seemed to collapse. She was crying so hard.

One of her hands lifted, gripping onto my shirt.

Her whole body shuddered.

I was half cradling her head, my arms up in an awkward hold, but it was me. It felt like the most natural way to comfort a friend. It was a bit before she quieted.

She took a deep breath, leaning back a little.

She was blinking rapidly. I reached over to a Kleenex box and grabbed a bunch for her.

I eased back onto my stool, watching Jess the whole time.

Breaking down in front of someone? I had no idea she had it in her. I was honored it'd been with me. I reached over, touching her arm. "Sorry for that."

She laughed, letting out a few more tears. "No. I'm—it's me. You said that about Sunday night, and you know. Sunday nights were our night. They still go?"

I nodded. "Every Sunday night. Jimmy comes in, wins the first game, and he's started to just walk out. His mom brings back his shoes and pays now."

She laughed, wiping at the corners of her eyes. "No more mentions of pop and pizza parties?"

"Nope. He now mentions that he's going to go to the next WrestleMania event with Kelly, and then the whole walking-out thing. Those are the new routines."

"Maria and Dax stay after?"

I nodded, my throat swelling up because I remembered a time when they were acting, well, not sane. "They, uh, they pretended to bowl for Kelly and Justin one night."

"What?"

"Jimmy had left. I noticed they were pretending to hand off the bowling balls to people who weren't there, and then pretending someone had bowled. They put up fake scores too."

"Really?"

I nodded. "I cried the whole time when I saw that. Kicked everyone else out, which was like Bob and Monica, some of the regulars. They knew that I knew what they'd done, so they sat, and all of us pretended to have a drink with Kelly and Justin." A few more tears slipped down my cheek. "It was one of the best nights of my life, drinking with ghosts."

"I wish I'd been there."

I checked my phone, saw the time. "They're probably arriving right now. We could get there in time to witness Jimmy's victory walk off."

"That sounds epic." She quieted. "It *is* Sunday night."

We shared a look.

She said, "Your life could be in danger. I mean, if you're looking for the person who owns a bowling alley, there's probably a good chance she'd *be* at the bowling alley."

"Um."

"I have a gun."

"Um." Oh, boy. I could already hear Ashton railing into me.

She added, "I know how to shoot a gun."

"Uh . . ."

"At this stage, you might be immune to gunfire. It might not faze you anymore."

"Oh, boy."

Her eyes danced. "I know we shouldn't go. I know it's stupid, but I want to go for two reasons. One, Kelly. She'd love it. She would already be changing and planning for the nightclub after."

Kelly would *so* be doing that already. "She called me before they left."

She went still. "What?"

"The night they left. Or before they were going to leave. She called me at the bowling alley. She said goodbye and asked me to watch over you because despite your stubbornness, you do need a friend to check in on you. She said it's kinda like how you check in on your mother."

She was blinking again. "I'm surprised she didn't ask you to send pigeon videos to Sal."

"She did that too."

"No!"

I nodded. "She did."

"That was her. Thinking about everyone else before they left."

"That was her."

We fell silent until Jess choked out, "I really miss her."

I reached over and took her hand, and I held it while she cried some more.

"What was the second reason you want to go?"

She smiled, already standing from her seat. "To piss off Ashton. He deserves some payback."

"Oh."

She held her phone up. "How about this? I'll call Trace. He'll okay it, but he doesn't need to tell Ashton?"

I sighed. "I'm going to get in so much trouble."

But we went bowling, and I was hoping some ghosts would join.

CHAPTER
THIRTY-TWO
MOLLY

"Is that supposed to say closed?" Jess asked from her car.

The sign said CLOSED. Easter Lanes was *closed*.

I growled. "I'm going to take a fork and stab my cousin. I'll keep stabbing him, little cuts, over and over again, until he's bleeding out and he can't move. The slowest and longest death possible."

I was fully aware I was saying this in the presence of an ex-law enforcement worker, and that she was giving me a look as if, "Do you know who you're saying that to?"

I didn't care. Sunday was always a decent day for work, and he had closed my place! Also, I felt the switch starting to turn. It wasn't just my dad who could flip it. It was family in general.

I turned to Jess. "I guarantee you that my cousin is still in bed, hungover from wherever he went last night, and if I find out that he closed early last night, I will blow a gasket."

She stared at me and blinked once. "What's his address?"

God, I loved my friends.

I gave it to her, and she programmed it in and took off. "Do you want to call Ashton?"

"Nope. I'm saving my breath until I figure out what I'm going to do."

"Do you have an idea of what you'll do?"

"Kill my cousin."

"Obviously. That's step one," said the ex-parole officer.

"I'll go back to running Easter Lanes. I'll sleep there if I have to. I'm not letting this mess with my livelihood."

"I'll stay with you."

I glanced her way. She was driving and paying attention to the street, but I was studying her.

"You sound serious about that."

"I am." She glanced my way for a second. "Ashton sidelined me, and I'll never admit this to his face, but he had reason. But you working, I can help with that. That gives me something to do."

"How's the painting?"

Jess's mouth flattened, and she swallowed over a knot in her throat. I could see it. She ducked her head down briefly, her hand tightening over the steering wheel. "It's—not well. I've tried, but the only thing I can paint is Kelly. Over and over again."

Jess was an up-and-coming artist. Her paintings were getting picked up by galleries, and there had been an article written about her not long ago. I remember thinking it was one shining spot for her amid everything.

"I go in. I try to paint. I *want* to paint, but then I go into a catatonic state, and when I come out of it, it's Kelly. I can only paint her." Her voice was hoarse. "So." She cleared her throat, forcing a smile my way. "Besides taking my mom in for her doctor visits, I can hang out at Easter Lanes." She let out a sudden laugh. "Consider me your personal bodyguard. What's Ashton going to do? Mafia wars can take months, years even. You have to work."

She was right. I had to work.

Also, months? Years? Talk about bleak.

Wait. "Your mom? Hospital visits?"

Jess flinched, just a tiny bit. "She had some weird test results come up, so we've been taking her in to get that checked more. They're not sure what it is yet."

Oh man. "I'm so sorry."

"It's okay. I mean . . . it's okay." She glanced my way. "What's your plan with your cousin?"

"Oh! I do not need a plan for him."

———

That wasn't totally true.

We got to his building, and I buzzed his neighbor. She was my version of Mrs. Tulip, but instead of my own Mrs. Tulip—"Hello? I didn't order anything."

"Hi, Mrs. Navarro!" Upbeat and happy. She really loved that side of me. "This is—"

Bzzzzzz!

Jess smothered a laugh. "I could've used you when I went to visit some of my parolees."

I grabbed the door and went inside, bypassing the elevator. "That gets stuck every third day between floors twelve and fourteen. It's the thirteenth-floor effect. I swear by it."

"Hmmm." Jess grunted, heading up with me.

When we got to his floor, his neighbor's door was open, and Mrs. Navarro was waving a blanket in the air. "Oh, it is you! I thought I might've reacted a little hastily."

"Hello, Mrs. Navarro." I went to her, hands on her shoulders, and I kissed both of her cheeks. She grew up in Spain, so I kept up with her custom.

She was beaming at me and patted my hand. "How are you, honey?"

"I'm good." I glanced toward Glen's door. "I gotta handle something with my cousin, but how are you? You look amazing. Tan hermosa."

"Oh!" But she was beaming and waved a hand to me. "Dios te bendigo."

My Spanish was rusty. I'd given up trying to get better, but I nodded and smiled back. Anything Mrs. Navarro was saying, I loved it. She kept talking until her phone began ringing. "Oh, honey. I need to get that. You come by next Sunday for dinner. I never need an excuse to make paella, but I'll make it just for you with extra spices."

I was so totally down for that. "I'll be here. Tell me the time."

She reached inside, grabbing her phone and speaking into it before handing me a key. "Come over around six, and here you go. Slide it under the door when you're done."

"Gracias, Señora Navarro. Gracias."

"Ooh!" She came back, kissing my cheeks and giving me an extra pat there. "Tan hermosa! You!" The person on her phone was speaking fast and loud, so she motioned to it and stepped back inside, another wave of her free hand.

Jess had been holding back, but she came closer, looking at the key. "That was . . . amazing to watch."

I chuckled, stepping over and fitting the key into the lock. I turned it, unlocking it, and I took it back out, sliding it under Mrs. Navarro's door before I forgot. After that, it was Glen Ass-Kicking time.

I shoved open the door, expecting to hear—I had no clue.

I was greeted with the sounds of nothing.

I stepped inside, and a wave of tension went through me. My stomach tightened up.

I expected to hear snoring. The sounds of his fan. I thought I'd find a whole sink full of empty beer cans, because that's where he tossed them. He never took out the garbage until days later, even washing dishes around his beer cans.

Nothing. The apartment was completely silent.

Something was wrong. As if on the same wavelength, Jess touched my shoulder. "Move back. Behind me." I saw the gun in her hand and gulped.

Oh man.

Glen.

He would piss his pants if he was in there, just sleeping.

She raised her arm up, her other hand steadying her gun, and she called out, "Anyone here? I am armed. I'm here with your cousin. Is anyone here?!"

She kept on, clearing each room as she moved down the hallway.

I didn't know what to do, so I moved farther into the living room. We hadn't cleared the closet. There was one right behind where we came in, so I went over to it, opening—a man was there!

I gasped, my throat opened up, but he had a hand up, smothering my scream. His other hand held a gun. Dressed all in black, a ski mask. The whites of his eyes were bulging.

"Hello! Is anyone in here?" Jess was still going through the apartment.

Glen had a two bedroom, but there were closets, an extra bathroom. She hadn't heard me.

"Don't say a word and you'll live," he hissed at me.

No.

He did not say that. To me! No, he did not because if he had, then that meant that I was *once more* in a situation where a gun was being pointed at me.

And that *was not* happening. Not *again*!

I felt the scream coming. His smothering hand be damned.

The *switch* was starting.

I was going to do something I always did.

I was staring at this guy, whoever he was. His hand was over my mouth.

An inferno was lit, and the flames were fast spreading until—"Get this *fucking* gun away from my *head*!"

I charged him. Well, no. I first bent my head down and head-butted him. Envision a mountain ram: that was me, and this asshole was going down. A shot went off. I was impervious by now.

The guy went down. His arm went to the side.

He was trying to hit me or kick me, but I was on him, and I grabbed his head, both sides of his head, and I was knocking his head into the floor underneath him. Over and over and over again. Ram. Ram. Ram.

"Ahhhhhh!"

"Oh my god!" Jess came running in.

She was on the right side.

The guy was losing his steam, but so was I, and I clued in, noticing he was trying to turn the gun back toward me. I had my knee on his arm, holding it pinned and aimed the other way. I hadn't even known I'd done that, but then Jess was there.

She plucked the gun out of his hand and yelled, "Get off him. Molly!"

I stopped heaving his head, but my strength was leaving me and fast, so I scrambled backward. I couldn't stand up, not yet. I scooted to the kitchen.

"Behind me."

Oh. I changed position, crawling to sit behind Jess. She had her gun up, and she was talking into her phone like it was a radio. "You!" she barked at the guy. "Get—can you get up?"

The guy shook his head before passing out. His whole body did a shudder and shake before I was guessing he went unconscious.

After that, I curled in, bringing my knees up to my chest, my arms wrapped around them. Jess was calling the police. I heard her say, "We need an ambo and—" She hesitated. "We have a DOA here."

DOA.

What? Not this guy. I didn't kill this guy, but that meant—I knew what that meant, and now the adrenaline was wearing off. I *was* getting immune to that, but my cousin. Jess had been back there.

I had to see him before they came to get him.

I pushed up, choking back a sob.

"No, Molly. Don't go in there."

I hauled myself up, pushing past her. She had to stay, keep the gun on the guy in case he woke up, so I slowed right before I got to Glen's bedroom. I took a breath, one breath, and went to the doorway.

I—huh?

There was a dead body in the bed, his head turned my way. I refused to look at the rest of him.

I glanced at Jess down the hallway. "Where's Glen?"

"What?"

"My cousin has neon-blue hair. That's not Glen."

CHAPTER THIRTY-THREE

ASHTON

We were leaving the downtown warehouse, which at one point had had three guests, but we made the decision to separate the Worthings. Avery would take them to the compound and put them into the warehouse their detective cousin had vacated earlier. Their interrogation would be a much longer process.

"Marco is still at Katya?"

I was checking my phone, then cursing when I saw all the missed calls and texts.

"What?"

I called Eze, my main guy I'd left on Molly. "What's going on?"

"Molly and Jess left the house earlier today."

"What?" I put him on speaker. "You've got me and Trace."

"I followed. Your orders were to stay back if Montell was in the house with her. Well, they went to Easter Lanes—"

"Where are they now?"

"The police station."

Trace jackknifed forward. "What?"

They kept talking, but I went scrolling through the rest of my phone. My sources from all departments were alerting me. I clicked on the last one.

34: Homicide had them, but OC is pulling rank. I can't get any more information.

I swore long and low under my breath.

"What is it?" Trace asked.

I spoke into the phone. "You're outside the station?"

"Yeah."

"Get out of there."

"Why?"

"They're not there. They'll be moved to a second location. Move back three blocks and wait for my call."

"On it."

I ended that call and hit dial on another number. While it was ringing, I told Trace the latest information.

"What the hell did they do?"

Jake Worthing picked up. "Are you fucking kidding me?"

"Detective."

"I'm not doing shit for you. Not after the last time we talked. I'm hanging up—"

"Three of your cousin's men followed me last night."

He was quiet on his end. "What?"

"They followed me into a gas station."

"Why are you—"

"Molly was there."

He was quiet, again, which I'd been banking on and which was making my stomach grind. When he spoke, his tone was low, raspy. "I got no call about this. What are you talking about?"

"We need to meet up."

"We're in a war!"

"Your cousin is fully aware of what happened last night, but you aren't, and I'm having a hard time believing that, considering their orders came from your phone."

"Bullshit. You're full of shit."

"Your phone says otherwise. Meet me."

His growl was savage. "Jesus Christ. I want nothing to do with any of this. Do you hear me? I want to find Justin's killer, and then I'm out. With you, with my cousin, with everything. I don't even want to be a cop anymore. Get off my back, Ashton."

"Meet me. Trust me, Jake. You need to hear what I have to say."

He was quiet again. I was gambling here. Those texts were from his phone, but it never felt like a Jake Worthing move to make. We had two cards that he seemed to care about: his brother and whatever he felt for Molly. If his unit had her, I needed to see him in person.

"Fine. I'll text you the location and time."

"Now."

"What? No. I just got called in—"

"It has to be now."

"Goddamn you, Walden. Goddamn you!"

I waited, still gambling. Always fucking gambling in this life.

"Fine. Now. Jesus."

He ended the call, and a second later, his text came in with the location. I relayed the location to Pajn, and he immediately hit the turn signal, getting us in the right direction.

"What are you doing with this guy?"

"He used to work for me. I have a feeling about him."

"Fuck your feeling. He hates Jess."

"He doesn't hate me, and I don't think he hates Molly."

Trace started shaking his head, curses spilling from his mouth. "Does he know about you two?"

"I told him we were fucking."

"You did?"

I shrugged. "I was saying it to mess with his head at the time, but he seems to react to her. I don't think he knows his unit swept her up, her and Jess. He didn't want to meet me, said he was getting a call to go in. If that's true, I want to get to him first."

"What *the fuck* are you doing, Ashton? This is my woman. She's not exactly Miss Popularity with her old colleagues."

I scowled right back at him. "Molly's not a game to me."

He snorted, sitting back. "Since when?"

I would've retorted, but he was right. She had been. She wasn't anymore.

———

Detective Jake Worthing was waiting for us at the end of the tunnel walkway, and as soon as he saw Trace, he began shaking his head. "Nope! No way, Walden. You're loco, thinking I'm going to talk with this motherfucker around."

Trace was glaring just as hard back. He snapped, "You think I'm happy about this? You threatened my woman."

"Because she made my brother disappear."

"Jess didn't do shit to your brother. If anything, he condemned Kelly. If he hadn't been with her—"

"What?!" Jake went at him.

Trace met him, within inches. "Then she'd still be alive, and Jess wouldn't be in half the pain she's in. That's what."

Jake's eyes went feral. The air charged, but I rolled my eyes upward. "Molly and Jess were picked up tonight."

Trace was still in the fight, but Jake's head jerked to me. "What?"

"That's the call you got, having you come in tonight. I don't know the details, but I know Homicide had them, and now Organized Crime is taking them."

He stepped back, keeping a wary eye on Trace. "They'll move them to a different location."

"I know."

His eyes grew chilled. "How the fuck do you know that?"

"You weren't my only source. You were always aware of that."

"If you know that information, what am I doing here?"

"OC has loopholes, and they're going to use them on Jess and Molly. I need someone to get them out."

"Are you kidding me?! Do you know how that'll look?" He took a few more steps back, shaking his head more and more. "No. No way."

"Eyes are already on you. You're a Worthing. I need you to pull them out. Sooner than later. They can't stay in there."

"Why? They'll just question them about why they're in there, but knowing both Montell and Molly, they'll get cut loose eventually. I can't think either of them would do anything to be arrested."

Okay. He *didn't* know Molly.

Trace snorted softly behind me.

Worthing apparently didn't know Jess either.

I used a different card. "Because they're sitting ducks in there. Once your cousin becomes aware of a few details, I don't know how he's going to react."

This Worthing went eerily still at my words. His head tilted upward, slowly. "What are you talking about?"

Trace must've figured out what I was planning because he moved forward, turning his back to Jake. He said, low and a warning, "Ashton. Think about this."

I had. Unfortunately. I stepped around Trace, and he cursed, moving off.

"Your cousin's not filling you in on what's going on."

"What are you talking about?"

"I told you three men were sent to follow me last night. Did your cousin tell you about them?"

"No. Why would he? I'm sorry if Molly was there, but what's the problem? They just followed you, right?"

"I told you Molly was there."

"Yeah, but . . ." He was starting to frown, glancing to where Trace was watching us, his head tipped all the way back. "What happened?"

"One of them put a gun to Molly's head—"

Jake swore.

"—your men were killed."

"What?"

"All three of them."

"Jesus Christ, Ashton! I'm a cop. You're telling a cop that you killed men who work for my cousin?! My own family. And I'm a cop! What the fuck?!" He was hissing and whispering all at the same time. "Jesus—there was no call about a shooting at a gas station, and there would've been. There should've been. Homicide would've kicked it to our unit because—"

"Because the men would come up as working for your cousin?"

"Yeah. I worked years as a cop in this city. That family affiliation has never come down here. They've always been up in Maine. They wouldn't—" He stopped, his head hanging. His hand went to his side. "Shit. Shit! This is all getting so entirely fucked up. They're either cutting me out, but no. They called me for tonight. Unless . . ."

A thought happened, and he let out another low curse, everything in him going slack. He finished his own statement: ". . . my cousin has someone higher up handling this for him."

Both options were possible.

He swung his head my way again. "Nicolai knew about the men?"

"We just had a meeting with him."

"What happened at the meeting?"

"Nothing," Trace bit out. "We're still in a ceasefire."

Jake narrowed his eyes, frowning. "But that doesn't make sense either."

I shot Trace a look because he was forcing me to show my cards sooner than I wanted.

Jake was looking between us. "What else is going on? You want Molly and Montell out sooner than later. That's implying you think they're in danger. Why would they be in danger if there's a ceasefire? As much as Montell is hated right now, no cop will move against her if that's what you're thinking . . ." His eyes narrowed even more. "That's not what you're thinking. You're calling me. Asking me specifically. Why?"

"Molly's been through some traumatic experiences lately. I'm worried about her mental health."

"Bullshit. I know Molly Easter. She can go nuts at times, but that woman is like leather. She's too tough to break. I've been on the other end, having to notify her about her father's various mishaps. I've gotten a good sense of Molly Easter. Stop fucking with me. Tell me the reason, or I'm walking, and I won't answer your calls anymore."

I was gritting my teeth. "Because pretty soon your cousin will realize that he's got two other cousins missing."

I let that hang, and Detective Worthing picked it up real fast.

His mouth was open. "Are you kidding me?! Oh my god, Walden! You took out two of my cousins?!"

"They're alive."

His eyes were bulging. The lines around his mouth were turning white. "Alive? But missing? You kidnapped them. You're telling me that you kidnapped *my* cousins, and you want me to help get *your* women out?"

He let loose a myriad of curses just as he lunged for me.

His hands went to my shirt, but Trace was there, getting in between us.

"Stop!" He shoved Jake back. "One more move, Worthing."

"What?" Jake snapped at him, hitting his arm down that was extended toward him. "Fuck off. Both of you. I cannot believe—"

"Your cousin is doing something."

"Fucking hell, Ashton!" Trace whirled on me. "Just tell him *everything*. Let him run right to Nicolai with it."

My gut had never been wrong with this Worthing. I stepped around Trace, saying to Jake, "We killed three of his men. He never told you about that. We also took you."

"Because I told him."

"He didn't seem that upset about it."

Jake's glare turned to a whole new level of hostility. "Fuck off, Walden. Just seriously fuck off already."

"I took you. I killed three of his men, and in the middle of our meeting, one of my men took out your cousin's sniper. The only thing he cared about was the ceasefire. He's keeping you in the dark. You were my man before he shoved in, and then Justin was killed. You switched when that happened, but your cousin didn't blink an eye about Justin in our meeting. You said it yourself just now. That side of your family was in Maine. It wasn't anything for you to worry about being a cop down here. Your cousin's keeping things from you. He cares about the ceasefire, not about Justin's killer. Don't believe me? Push him. Read him. Make up your own mind."

Now was the time to pray. If I still knew the man he was when he worked for me, or if I was wrong the whole time.

A whole minute passed before Worthing started to leave. "I'll do what I can to get Montell and Molly out."

"Thank you."

"Don't—" He turned, one last dark look from him. "Just don't anymore. I'll get them out, and I'm gone, from both you and my cousin. I'll do my own investigation into Justin's murder. Seems I'm the only one who gives a shit anyways."

Trace waited thirty seconds for him to get out of hearing distance. "What the fuck are you thinking?!"

"He was my man."

"What?"

"The night we got raided. He was my man. He was the one who told Jess about the raids. He was the one giving her the test, for me. I knew the raids were going down, and we got our shit together in time because of him. Him." I pointed in his direction. "I'm gambling, I know, but I think I'm right. I think *he's* the one who'll help us pull the rug out from under his cousin."

"If you're wrong . . ."

If I was wrong, we were screwed.

CHAPTER THIRTY-FOUR

MOLLY

I was taking stock of my life. It felt appropriate to do that while I was in the slammer.

Except I wasn't. I didn't think.

We were in a building with cement walls, uncomfortable benches, and metal chairs. No windows. I didn't think we were at a police station, but there were police here. Across from me at a metal table in the front lounge area was my new pen pal. Ritalicious was fabulous. Her pink nails, eyelashes, and feathers were on point. I now had a new obsession with feathers, faux feathers though. Not real feathers. But also, she gave me the name of a gay bar that she promised had the best shows.

I was basking in the future excitement of attending Gary's Hairy Heels and waiting for Jess to stop fighting with whatever cop came through the door. It'd not been easy when the first cops showed up at Glen's apartment. Once they knew who Jess was, their attitude went south.

It was like that with each one who approached us, and now we were somewhere I didn't know where, and I was hoping for that one phone call you always get promised.

Detective Worthing walked through the door.

The lady who was arguing with Jess shut up, and Jess groaned.

Not me. I perked up. Jake wasn't that bad—or hadn't been in the past. He went to a back office. There was a heated argument, and he came out three minutes later. He walked past the female detective, picked up Jess's handcuffed wrists, and took the cuffs off.

He glanced at me, but I showed him they never put handcuffs on me.

He said something to the female before motioning to Jess and me. "Come on."

Jess was unnaturally quiet and stiff. "What are you—"

He gave her a look. "I wouldn't question my kindness right now."

She shut up.

I jumped up, said goodbye to Ritalicious, and followed him. My insides were feeling like I was at a disco. I had a whole new purpose in life. I didn't know when it happened, if it was when the gun was pointed at my head, when I was fighting him for it, when Jess helped, or after we kicked his ass? Or maybe it was a combination of everything and all, but we'd gone to Easter Lanes to bowl with Kelly and Justin, and somehow I came out of this recent scare with a new outlook.

I saw things in a different light.

"Do you have everything with you?"

"They didn't strip-search us, if that's what you're implying."

His eyes were so cold, staring at Jess for a beat without blinking.

She frowned, a little.

So did I. For doing something nice, he was being abnormally chilly.

He led the way, taking us down a back stairway and opening the door to an empty street. He motioned to the left. "Down the block—you have vehicles waiting for you."

Vehicles?

Jess took off at a brisk clip.

I moved past him, studying him from under my eyelids before choosing to leave without saying anything. I stepped down to the street, but it didn't feel right. I turned. "Hey."

He paused, starting to close the door. He didn't say anything.

I motioned toward Jess and myself. "Thank you."

He nodded, that cold look not thawing at all.

I started again for the vehicles.

"Hey."

I stopped.

He nodded beyond me. "Be careful with him."

Him? Ashton.

"He's the reason for this?"

Jake didn't answer right away. "No. You're the reason for this." He went inside after that.

Me? I didn't understand.

But as I headed to where Jess was waiting at the end of the block, I glanced over my shoulder. He was gone. The door shut firmly behind him.

"You okay?" Jess asked once I got to her.

I nodded. "Yeah, just a weird feeling. That's all. Also, I want to talk to you about something."

She nodded beyond us to where two SUVs were waiting. "Okay, but heads up. They're not happy."

I almost laughed because at this point, that was the norm for Ashton and me.

She indicated the first one. "That's me."

That meant Ashton was in the second one.

As we approached, Elijah stepped out from the front passenger seat in the second vehicle, and another large man did the same from the first one. As if they'd rehearsed it, they both opened the back doors, and we separated. Jess looked back, mouthing, "Call me."

I nodded, giving her a thumbs-up. She would be my bodyguard. Hell yeah.

I moved to Elijah and paused, grinning up at him. "Heya."

His eyebrows flickered, and the corner of his mouth twitched. "Heya back."

"Molly," Ashton groaned from inside the SUV.

I flashed Elijah a last smile before climbing in, and I beamed at whoever Ashton was to me now because I hadn't the first clue anymore. "Do I have a day to tell you about."

His face schooled into a mask. "I heard. Another gun in your face?"

I nodded. "I went a little nuts. The switch happened. And I got violent, super violent."

He eyed me. "Did you like it?"

Did I?

If anyone else had asked me that question and looked at me with a seriousness like Ashton was, I would've laughed it off. I would've denied it and shoved that down inside of me, deep down. That was anyone else. Not Ashton.

And since it was Ashton, and since he seemed genuinely curious, I told the truth. "I don't know."

His head cocked to the side, like he wanted to look at me from a different angle, as if that would help him study me better. Maybe it did this time because he said, softly, "There's darkness in every one of us. We have to do what we have to do to survive at times. You've been in a few of those situations."

Maybe. This didn't feel like that, though.

"Also." He had me looking back at him. "I'm glad the switch happened. I'm glad you're safe and alive."

I smiled.

He smiled back.

It felt right. I sighed and relaxed back into the seat as the vehicle pulled into traffic. "So, my cousin is now missing."

"No, he's not."

"He's not?"

"He works for me. I've known where he was this whole time."

"Where was he?"

"He's staying at a safe house in case something happened, which just happened at his place. When he's at Easter Lanes, my men are there."

I flattened my mouth. "He closed Easter Lanes on Sunday. That's not cool."

"He closed Easter Lanes at my request. I was worried about retaliation."

That made me pause. "Retaliation?"

He nodded, studying me.

"For what?"

"For business that's none of your business."

I glowered. "You saying that and half smiling when you say that isn't helping, and it is my business since my father's involved. Remember?"

His smile faded. He grew solemn instead. "It's bad guy shit. I'd rather keep you out of it as much as possible."

"Does it have to do with my father?"

"No."

"Oh. Well, then you have a point."

He reached out, taking my hand, and linked our fingers. "Tell me about your day."

"I thought you already knew?"

"I'm finding I like to hear you say it anyways."

That was . . . a whole warm feeling pulsed through my chest, deep inside. "You're not mad we left the house and went to Easter Lanes?"

"I've come to expect the unexpected from you, and also, I know what today is."

Sunday night. The old Kelly-and-Justin bowling night.

"I wanted to bowl with my friends."

"I'm sorry."

My heart was melting with each new word he was saying. He was being kind and even a little gentle with me.

I looked down at our hands. His were big and strong, swallowing mine up, but they felt like a perfect fit. A lump formed in my throat at the sight, at the feeling sweeping through me. "We're holding-hands friends now?"

"Who said we're friends?"

But he was teasing. I shot him a look. "Detective Worthing got us out of there."

"I know."

"He said he did it because of me."

His head inclined forward; he was studying me a little more intensely than normal. "What if I told you that he might have a thing for you? How would you feel about that?"

I looked down, playing with our fingers. My free hand tracing over his linked fingers. "I don't know. Never liked cops, so that would make me feel odd. I guess."

His attention was so heavy, but not in a bad way—in an uncomfortable way, because I was feeling he could see stuff in me that even I didn't know was there.

"I have a mission, a new one in life."

"What is it?"

"It hit me earlier, when I was waiting in the police place. It suddenly came to me. All this stuff happening to me, there's gotta be a reason. Right?"

He didn't respond. He was frowning.

I kept on. "And there's issues between you and Jess. Right?"

His frown just deepened.

"So, like, in groups there are roles. Do you know what I'm talking about?"

"No idea."

Right. That wouldn't deter me. "Well. Okay. There are. There are roles. There's the thinker. There's the doer. And then there's the in-between people. I'm the in-between person. You're a doer. Jess is a doer. Trace is the thinker. I mean, you're a thinker, too, but you're mostly a doer. I kinda think that's why you and Jess don't get along. You guys are both competing for the same role in the group. But me and Trace. We don't compete. No one else is our—well; you're a thinker, but again. You're more—"

"Doer. Yes." He was watching me with a strange expression. "All this came to you when you were at the police station?"

I nodded, then shrugged and leaned back against the seat. "I keep getting into situations where there are guns pointed at my head or bombs exploding my door. If this all had happened before you, I would've blamed my dad. Shorty Easter. And yeah, there's an argument that could be made that this *is* all because of my dad, but my cousin. There was a dead guy at my cousin's apartment. Who was the dead guy?"

"A guy that heard your cousin's apartment was open, so he crashed there. The guy who killed him was the guy you beat up. He works for Nicolai Worthing, so we know Worthing is sending people after you. He sent a man after your cousin."

"Wait. What? I thought you said there was a ceasefire."

He lifted a hand and cupped the side of my face. His thumb rubbed over my face, so gentle, matching his tone. "I don't think there was ever a ceasefire."

"Oh." And the lump kept growing in size.

His hand dropped to my hand, and he laced our fingers together. "I'm still interested in hearing about the roles in our group. It sounds interesting."

Maybe I was wrong about it all. "It's all because of my dad?"

"I think this particular bad string of luck, yes. It was kicked off by your dad, but Molly." He leaned forward, inclining his head.

I lifted my head up to see how soft his eyes were watching me back.

"If you are saying that you're an in-between, and you could help fix the issues between Jess and me, then I'm going to say that I don't think another person could get better results than you."

"Are you serious?" My throat swelled up. My heart began beating so fast.

He nodded. "I think your idea makes perfect sense. You're the glue."

"I'm like added sealant."

"That too." His lips quirked.

Right on. I was still in a good mood, and I didn't want to think about the bad stuff that just happened, that seemed to always happen to me. "Can we do something fun tonight? Can we forget, for one night, about everything going on?"

I lifted my head, waiting for his answer.

He was looking so intensely at me. He nodded. "We can do that. What do you want to do?"

I shook my head. "The last time I really took a night off, I went to the hockey game, and then we went to Octavia. What about Katya? You own it, right? Can we go there and just, just be there?"

He leaned over, reaching up, and a finger traced a strand of my hair, tucking it behind my ear. A tingle followed in his trail. I found myself waiting, holding my breath, warmth spreading all over my body. The fuzzies were in a flurry.

"Yeah." He said it so softly. "We can go to Katya."

"And forget everything, for one night?" I leaned toward him.

Closer. So close.

He nodded, his forehead now almost resting on mine. "And forget everything, for one night."

I held up my pinkie. "Promise?"

He flashed me a smile. My heart jumped in my chest. He linked his pinkie with mine, keeping them entwined. "Promise." Sitting back, he pushed a button, relayed our new location, and sat back. He kept our pinkies linked so now we were doubly holding hands.

I scooted over, getting closer until my side was touching his.

He let go of our pinkies, putting his arm behind me, anchoring me more firmly against him.

I leaned in, resting my head to his chest.

I was kinda loving this.

That scared me.

CHAPTER
THIRTY-FIVE
ASHTON

I took her to the private floor that Trace and I usually used when we were at Katya. There was a small patio-like extension to the side, a bench that sat far back in the shadows. I knew Trace used to sit and watch Jess when she worked. She didn't know, but it was private, and we could still be a part of the atmosphere below.

That's where I took Molly tonight.

Trace and Jess went to their place, and when he or I were here, we were the only ones allowed on this floor. Elijah was at the door. A few guys were on the other side, my personal guards. Anthony came in, Katya's main manager, and had a debrief with me quick, but now he was gone.

I was sipping my bourbon, and she was dancing on the end of the patio, overlooking the floor, lost in the music.

She was the most beautiful woman I'd ever seen.

It sounded so fucking cheesy, and it wasn't something I usually would think, but with Molly Easter, I found myself unable to think anything else.

God. What was I doing with her?

Even I didn't know, but there was a pulse between us. It grew stronger each day we were together, each touch, each look, each word shared. It was a long tether, growing more powerful until I was so bound to her, if I cut it, it would be to both of our detriment.

Her mom.

My mom.

That was still a mess, something no one knew who was alive anymore. Just me. Now just her. Even Trace hadn't a clue. I'd never told him. It was too hard, too painful, but I gave birth to it the second I told Molly the truth.

That burned me, deep down.

She hadn't asked a question since. I didn't think she thought about it, but maybe that was how she survived? Not thinking about who defined us growing up. Or not letting them define her?

Me. I was defined. I knew it.

I liked the shadows. I lived in the shadows. I excelled in the shadows.

My mom put me in the shadows, *what* she did, who she was.

Her drug addiction was just the tipping point.

Watching Molly now as she was dancing, seeing she was like sunshine right now—she was the opposite of me. I was darkness. She was light, though she had darkness in her. I knew it, felt it. Just like she did. It was another reason we connected. She and I. We were the opposite, but also the same. I was cruel. She was . . . whatever she was. She had a switch. Happiness. Half-crazy?

Now she was saying she was the in-between?

Jesus. She was. She could be.

She was exactly what I needed, and I never knew. But no, that wasn't true.

I *had* known.

Fuck. All those years ago. I had known. One look at her in that hallway, knowing she shouldn't have been there, and knowing what was happening—I knew it then. I needed her in a way that I should've needed the woman who just died.

The burning was too intense, trying to claw out of me.

Molly didn't have a care in the world right now. Everything was put away, shoved down in whatever drawer it was supposed to go. And for now, her eyes were in a daze. Her body glistened from some sweat. She never stopped. Her hands were in the air, twirling, creating a spell, and she turned, circling. She could've been in a field, enjoying the feel of the sun on her. It was the same movements, but more whimsical.

Beautiful. Stunning. Powerful.

She was mine.

I wasn't letting her go.

She owned me, and god help anyone who tried to take her away from me.

As if sensing my thoughts, something she'd done before, she looked my way before she began coming to me. She was bringing her sunshine to me, lighting up my corner.

I sat back. Waiting.

She moved in, holding her drink.

I opened my legs wider, and she stood between them, looking down at me. Still moving to the music.

The look in her eyes, I didn't think she wanted to talk, and knowing that pulse was still pulling, I leaned forward, running my hands up the backs of her legs.

She closed her eyes, feeling my touch while I was feeling her. Enjoying her.

She was magnificent.

The need to be deep inside was pounding in me, but I savored this moment, trailing my hands up her thighs, over her ass, pulling her even closer to me. She came, her eyes still closed, her head now thrown back. I moved my thumbs to the insides of her legs, finding her clit and gently pushing on it through her jeans.

Her body floated toward me. One of her legs lifted.

I caught it, my other hand running behind it, lifting it so she was half kneeling over me.

Her clit was so close to my mouth.

My mouth was fucking watering, like a goddamn waterfall. I wanted to taste her.

The music was still playing. The neon flashes of light behind her, below us, but we were in the complete dark. No one else was as high up as we were. No one in another box could look down and see us. There were no cameras positioned here. Trace and I talked about this place, wanting a corner we could go to be in the club but not a part of the club, to do whatever the fuck we wanted. This was why. Right here, with just this woman, I was thankful for this corner.

Moving my hands to the sides of her hips, I tucked them over her pants' waistband.

She stilled, and I unzipped them, pulling them down. Taking them off.

She looked down, her eyes now open, looking drunkenly at me. That was the lust since she'd barely touched her drink.

I settled farther back, tugging her over me so she was kneeling on the seat to the side of my legs. Smoothing my hands down her sides, to her ass, I pulled her even closer, hooking over her panty straps.

She swallowed, her throat moving, and she parted her lips. Her chest was rising, deep and slow. Carnal pleasure looking back down at me.

This woman. She drove me crazy, but she was mine. Just mine.

I moved my mouth, closing over her clit first and sucking.

She gasped, her body leaning into me even more.

I ran a hand down her ass, my thumb circling her before I leaned in better, a different angle and I was tasting her. My tongue moved inside of her as her body rested against my shoulder. I could hear her moans, the vibrations through her body.

I could die worshipping her body. Touching every inch. Tasting her curves.

I'd never get enough of her. That pull, it was unbearable but undeniable, and I couldn't fight against it any longer. From hate to want, to need, and now something more. I didn't know. I didn't want to know—I just needed to have her.

I kept tasting her. Over and over again. Moving inside of her, licking, caressing until I felt her body rip apart in my mouth, her hands digging into my shoulders. Her head was resting against the back of the booth behind us, her entire body trembling.

I still took my time, enjoying this.

The buildup. The desire. The touch. The crescendo. Then the peak, the climax, and the aftereffects. How her nails were cutting into my skin, but I loved the pain. I needed my own release, but this, smoothing my hand back over her ass, her stomach, shoving her shirt until I could touch her nipple.

I could do this every day and night and return for seconds.

A goddamn heavenly dip.

When she could breathe steadily, her eyes peeled open, and she grinned down at me. A small but crooked grin. I reached up, tugging at her bottom lip. She drew me in, sucking me. After that, I held back, waiting to see what she would do.

She could go back to dancing. She could pull my pants down and suck me. She could do anything she wanted.

I just wanted to see what she was going to do, this woman I never intended to want.

A soft and playful grin teased at her mouth, and she ducked her head, as if shy, before she settled farther down on me. She'd done this in the bed, our first time, and I leaned back, my pulse skyrocketing to my dick as she skimmed a hand down my chest, moving to my belt buckle.

She moved her mouth to my ear, tugging open my belt buckle at the same time. "I like this."

"Yeah?"

She undid my zipper, opening me and reaching in, finding my cock. She smoothed a hand over him, pulling him out, stroking.

I swallowed, my hands sliding to her hips before moving up, pushing her shirt with them.

She leaned back and took her shirt the rest of the way off. Her bra was next. I reached for her breasts, her nipples, and leaned in, taking one in my mouth.

She kept stroking my cock, squeezing, smoothing over me, cupping me too.

My teeth grazed over her nipple, went to the other, and I ran my tongue around her, suckling.

Her body trembled, and she was breathing heavy in my ear.

Even this, just tasting her, having her stroking me, I could do this for hours and relish it. Who the fuck was I becoming?

She moved her mouth back to my ear, panting, "I need you."

I growled, her words my undoing, and grasped her hips, tugging her over me. I was at her entrance, a brief pause as we lined up, and then I yanked her down as I thrust up into her.

She gasped in my ear, her whole body plastered to me. She wound her arms around my waist, holding tight as she rode me while I was driving up into her. I was holding her hips down so hard, pounding up so I wasn't sure who was riding each other more.

Up. Higher.

The need. The pleasure.

Lust.

I loved this.

Pleasure shot through me, and I couldn't stop thrusting into her. It wasn't enough. This angle, none of it. I moved us. Her back on the seat, and I moved into her from above, and now my body was plastered to her. Reaching over her, I grasped onto the seat's handle and lifted, getting a deep angle.

It still wasn't enough.

Christ.

She'd be the death of me, but I needed more.

I ran a hand to her back, to the arch, and then spread down, lifting her up, higher for me, and I sank in. I sank as low as I could, bottoming, and she was writhing underneath me.

There. Right there.

My strokes were lined up, perfection.

I could see every emotion on her face. Her mouth opened, a cry forming, but she was right there with me—and then her body convulsed, exploding. A sensual masterpiece. I wanted to record that, watch it over and over again, but then my own release was coming.

It hit me, shattering me, and I let out a guttural roar before holding still, waiting as the waves went through me.

Jesus.

Watching her watching me, I needed to taste her mouth again.

CHAPTER THIRTY-SIX

MOLLY

The night was a dream, which was the point. I wanted a night away from guns and people dying and missing family. And so far from my normal life that it was laughable. This wasn't my normal. I wasn't the girl who got this type of life. Work. Grind. I fought to keep what I had, and even that was almost conned out of me. That's the girl I was. My dad made it very clear what kind of girl I was growing up, what I deserved, but Ashton. He was something else.

He wouldn't last. I knew this was all temporary. I didn't get the happily ever after. That had never been in my stars. I'd known from the beginning what to expect.

That's how I knew I would enjoy every minute I got with him while this lasted.

I was going with it, and if that meant seriously hot sex, sign me up.

I was there for it. I was going to savor every second of it, because we both knew that one day, we'd find Kelly's killer. My dad would come back, and all this would be over.

Just the thought was making my heart palpitate in a painful way, but nope.

I wouldn't go there. I already knew I'd crossed over into the "feelings" land.

Until all of this was done, I was in the moment.

No more worrying about the future. Enjoy the moment. The here and now, while I had it.

"It's almost closing." Ashton came back from the inside area, a new drink in hand and a plate with some hors d'oeuvres.

I took the plate, moving as he sat beside me. We were both in various states of undress.

Me, I was wearing only my shirt and panties. Ashton hadn't let anyone into the area we were in, and he reassured me we were private, so I was lounging. I mean, seriously. To be in this state in a nightclub? And no one could see? Once-in-a-lifetime moment. Totally enjoying it here.

As for him, he was wearing his pants. His shirt was unbuttoned.

That's when I thought about how I'd gone barefoot from our patio area to the inside to use the bathroom. "Please tell me you've had this floor cleaned?"

"What?"

I lifted one of my bare feet.

He chuckled. "Yeah. We have this place cleaned before and after we leave."

"Oh, good." I could eat with ease now and reached over for another—I had no idea what these were. They looked like fancy mini cheeseburgers. They were delicious. "Do we need to go soon then?"

He gestured out over the dance floor. "I like to leave before lights go up, otherwise Anthony will be up here."

"Who's Anthony?"

"He's our main manager."

I popped one last mini thingy in my mouth and took my drink before getting up. "I'll go and get dressed." I began heading off, but a tug to my shirt pulled me back. I looked over my shoulder, seeing Ashton's eyes right on my ass and darkening.

He pulled me back to his lap and took my drink from me, placing it farther down on the seat so it wouldn't get knocked over. Then he positioned me, straddling him, but with my back to his front.

God, I loved how he touched me. Possessive. Alpha, but tender, and so very hot. He ran a hand down my back, tunneling into my panties, and I felt his fingers slip inside of me at the same time his mouth opened over my shoulder. His teeth grazed against my skin, and I relaxed back against him, my whole body melting as he began thrusting up into me, his fingers moving deep, and then rotating. Grinding. Pulling out, his thumb moving to my clit, working me like magic.

My body was conditioned to him by now. It wasn't long until I was combusting over him, my legs sprawled out. He was completely holding me up, but I felt his dick underneath me. He lifted me up, moving aside his clothes and mine, and sank deep into me.

I leaned forward, my hand to his knee, and I rallied my bones to reform so I could move with him.

He went in bare our first time tonight, and we'd had a conversation right after. I was on birth control. He was clean. I was clean, and that'd been it. He went bare again, and now it was the third time tonight.

If this kept happening, I'd well and truly be addicted to him. I knew I already was, just to having sex with him, but man. The heart stuff always got in the way—and when I felt his mouth move down my back, I stopped thinking.

I really, really loved having sex with this man.

———

It was after closing. Lights were on in the main area, and we were both dressed. It gave the nightclub a whole different feel to it now that you could see the corners and nooks and crannies.

I was coming out of the bathroom when there was a knock on the main door.

Ashton was at the bar and lifted his head up. "Yeah?"

The door opened. Elijah stuck his head inside. "Remmi West is requesting to come up."

Ashton's eyebrows furrowed together. "Remmi? Now?"

He nodded, grim. "She's by herself, and I'm told she's irate. It's about Marco, doing what you told him to do."

Ashton cursed before sending me a look.

I'd picked up on the last name. "Trace's sister?"

He gave a nod, almost grim like Elijah. "I should talk to her."

My own eyebrows went up because he did not sound like he wanted to. "You want me to . . . ?" I motioned for the patio.

He shook his head, turning to Elijah. "Put her in Anthony's office. We'll come down."

He nodded, leaving.

Ashton didn't move, not at first. He was staring at the floor, his hand resting on the bar before he dragged himself out of whatever he'd just been thinking. "Remmi is . . ."

"A handful?"

He frowned. "Jess talked about her?"

I shook my head. "The expressions on both Elijah's face and yours said enough."

He grunted before pushing off from the bar, rubbing his hand over his face. "That's fair. Listen." He moved in, not quite looking at me but more over me, but standing so close that I could feel his body heat. "I don't want her to see you. When we get down there, I'll have Elijah take you to the main floor. Just hang out at the bar, have a drink if you'd like. If you hear screaming, don't come running. It's just Remmi's melodramatics."

I nodded.

I'd been uneasy with her before, but now I was all sorts of reluctant, except if she was going to be Jess's future sister-in-law, then I had a whole friend duty to adhere to. As we went down in the elevator, Ashton's hand to the small of my back, I made up my mind that I would not seek this Remmi West person out, but if we happened to cross paths . . . so be it. Friend duty. Or at least that's what I was telling myself.

The elevator landed, and he cupped the back of my elbow as we stepped out. His thumb swiped over my skin, sending sensations through me. I glanced back, seeing a heated look from him. One that went straight to my core. Man. My body's reactions to him were getting worse. I was so highly sensitized and in tune to just a thumb graze over my elbow.

Still. I shared my own heated look with him before he nodded in the direction Elijah had gone and was waiting for me. We separated. He went down a back hallway, one of his guards standing outside the door. A second one remained at this corner, and Elijah walked me into the main area.

A few employees were cleaning up. A couple were behind their own bars, doing inventory checks. Another guy, dark slicked-back hair, a shirt unbuttoned, some comfortable-looking loafers on his feet, was leaning against a bar, tapping his finger when he saw Elijah and me. He perked up, an idle hand reaching for his shirt, and he began buttoning his shirt as he straightened to his fullest height. He looked just under six feet. His eyes narrowed, growing determined on Elijah before focusing on me and staying there.

He started toward us, but Elijah held a hand up. "Not this one."

"But—"

"Walden's orders. Not this one."

Not this one what?

The guy moved his head to get another look at me, giving me a different reassessing look and lingering on my lips.

I frowned. His gaze jumped to my eyes.

"I've seen you before."

"Seriously, man. Not tonight. Not this one."

He gave Elijah a distracted nod before turning my way again. "You're friends with Montell."

I frowned. "How do you know that?"

"I saw you here with her the other night."

"You know Jess?"

"She used to work here, at that bar actually. That was hers that she manned."

I looked down, giving it another perusal. I knew Jess had worked here, but I'd never come when she was working. Her or Kelly . . . a knot was forming in my stomach, a reminder about everything. All the bad stuff, but what brought some good stuff to my life. Ashton.

When this was all over, I'd go back to being just a bowling alley owner. Although, what was I doing? I used to be proud of that. I was. I *am*. Owning and running a successful business was nothing to sneer at. That was me. Screw anyone who made me feel otherwise, and in this case, that was me. *Screw you, Molly.*

You survived Shorty Easter—that alone deserved a commencement speech delivered by the president. Fist-pump in the air to yourself.

I raised my chin up toward this guy, who Elijah was still blocking and he was ignoring, trying to talk to me around him. "You knew Kelly too?"

I ignored Elijah's quick glance my way.

The guy nodded. There was no reaction on his face. He didn't warm up, but he didn't look sad either. "I knew Kelly. She was a good shots girl. You know Kelly, then?"

Was he being serious?

He caught my look, frowning. "What? Those two fall out or something?"

That knot in my stomach jumped to my throat, lodging right there, smack in the middle.

Elijah must've read my face because he turned, completely blocking the guy from me. "For real. Step back. I'm not joking this time."

The guy snorted. "Were you joking before? What's your problem? I can't do anything. My office is being used. Just let me talk to her. I kinda miss Jess."

I folded my head down, but I sensed Elijah's look before he said, more firmly, "I said no. You want to talk to her, you wait till Walden comes out."

The guy snorted again. "Yeah, right. He's probably dick deep in that chick—"

I tensed, pain lacing through me.

The way he said that, as if it happened all the time, as if it happened all the time with that girl or any girl, and me—I was a no one. That's why I was feeling how I felt before, because that's what this guy was thinking about me. He thought I was just another girl. He knew I was here with Ashton, but he didn't care what Elijah was saying. That spoke volumes.

And I remembered, *Not tonight. Not this one.*

More pain was slicing through my inside, down my chest.

Ashton had done this before, brought a girl here, had her waiting for him, and this guy was what? What was he doing? Why was he saying these things to me?

I swallowed that knot. I was raised by a con. No one could hurt me unless I let them.

"Shut up," Elijah hissed. "This one's different."

This one. Because I was one in a long line of ones. Just another girl.

No. No, "this one" wasn't. End of the day, I was just Shorty Easter's daughter after all. That said enough.

I cleared my throat, spying a bathroom sign beyond the bar. "I'm—uh—I'm going to use the ladies' room." I didn't ask for permission. I grabbed my purse and headed over.

Later I would admit to being hurt and being irrational.

I'd blame some of it on the alcohol, or that's what I was telling myself because as I went to that bathroom, I knew I was going to do something very, very stupid. Then again, I'd done a lot of very stupid things in my life, but I wasn't so helpless.

And thinking all of that, not wanting to feel the pain that that guy's words inflicted on me because they shouldn't hurt as much as they did, I did something my instincts were telling me to do because I was in a situation where I was *only going to lose.*

Physical danger or heartbreak danger? I chose.

I ran.

Slowing down at the bathroom, I reached for it, pushing it open a little, and looked back. Elijah wasn't watching. That guy wasn't, either, and I sailed right past.

Yes. So very dumb, but I'd had an amazing night with Ashton, and hearing I was just another girl had way too much power over me. Too much power.

I'd been fooling myself.

Stay. Ride the ride as long as it lasted.

Nope. Not now, not experiencing that pain, though it was fleeting.

The universe was telling me to cut my losses. I'd deal with the fallout later.

Walking to the hallway, I glanced where Ashton's guards were, but a door opened suddenly across from me, and I darted in. It was a locker room. There was a girl inside, coming out of a dressing room. She frowned at me. "You new tonight?"

"Yeah. I—" I smiled. "I got lost. Sorry."

"Oh." She laughed, motioning over her shoulder. "Exit door is out this way. You're not taking the train by yourself, are you?"

"Uh."

She shook her head. "I'm Amy. I work on the second floor."

"I'm Molly. I . . . I'm not even sure where I work. I kept getting turned around tonight."

She laughed. "You'll get the hang of it, but do you want a ride? My boyfriend is picking me up. We usually head to a diner with some of the other staff to unwind. You could come if you wanted?"

"Uh—" Talk about another gift from the universe. "That'd be great. Thank you."

She took me out another door, and we turned left, down a short hallway, and out another door. We were in a back parking lot alleyway. A vehicle was idling, a guy behind the wheel, who waved at seeing us.

"That's my boyfriend. Nick." She motioned to the back seat. "My boxes are on the other side, so climb in here." She opened the door. A wave of warmth blasted us, along with some rap music. "Hey, honey."

"Hey!" He glanced back, giving me a chin lift. "New friend?"

"This is Molly. She's riding with us to Nancy's."

"Solid. Nice to meet you," he said as I got in.

Amy got in on her side. "It was Molly's first night tonight."

"Oooh! How was it?"

"It was . . ." My smile was forced. "Interesting."

Amy smiled as we left. "It'll get better. I promise."

No. No, it wouldn't.

I just did a very stupid thing.

CHAPTER
THIRTY-SEVEN

MOLLY

My phone started blowing up a block away.
Ashton calling.
I hit decline but texted:

I'm sorry. I overreacted. I'm with some of your staff, and I'll tell
you where we stop.

My phone buzzed.

Ashton: Where are you?

Ashton: The security monitors are showing me that you
WALKED OUT ON YOUR OWN? Where are you going?

Ashton: Have them turn back.

Ashton calling.

I declined.

Amy frowned back at me. "Everything okay?"

"Yeah, I . . ."

Ashton: Answer the goddamn phone or I will fire that worker you left with. I'm assuming she has no idea what she did, helping you.

Ashton: ANSWER YOUR PHONE

Ashton calling.

I declined.

Ashton: She's fired. Want to keep pushing me?

Ashton: I won't stop with her. I will find out who that driver is. I'll find where he works, and I'll get him fired too. Keep pushing me. I have no qualms about blowing up lives for your safety. Pialto and Sophie are next. Give me enough motivation. I could get them evicted by the end of the night.

Me: Stop! I'll ask them to bring me back.

"God!" I hit dial, and as soon as he answered: "Don't do that to them."

"Where are you?" Now he was all calm. Now he was. Now, after he'd already issued all those threats.

"We're—" I leaned forward. "Do you think we could turn back? I—"

Amy's head twisted back to me, her frown deepening a little bit more. "Back?"

"I think I left my keys back there."

She frowned at me, glancing to her boyfriend, who hit his turn signal. He was watching the traffic.

"I'm not hearing them saying yes fast enough," Ashton growled from his end.

"Ashton." I was mortified. At myself. At my behavior. At the situation.

"Ashton?" Amy squeaked, starting to pale. Her eyes widened. "As in Ashton *Walden*?"

"Who's Ashton Walden?" her boyfriend asked, but quickly jerked the car over because there was an opening. "Score. It'll be a bit before we can get back, but—"

I looked up, seeing the diner's sign. "No. Hold on. I see the sign a few blocks up. We're going to a diner named Nancy's. I'll be there."

"Be outside."

I ended the call, shoving the phone back into my purse.

Amy was watching me. "Was that my boss, as in my boss over my boss over my boss? The guy who owns Katya?"

"Yes."

She paled. "How do you know him? What was that about? Did you really forget your keys?"

"It was . . . nothing."

She didn't look reassured. "That was nothing—I mean—it'll be fine. When we get to Nancy's, he'll pick me up."

"Uh . . ." Nick spoke up, staring in the rearview mirror. "Guys? You seeing this too?"

Two sets of headlights were speeding behind us, and one SUV jerked around us, slamming on its brakes and swerving to block us in. The other did the same behind us. Nick hit the brakes. Amy screamed, reaching forward to stop from hitting the dashboard, but her seat belt held her in place.

Me, a part of me had started to dissociate because by now, how many life-and-death situations had I been in? But I was still thinking.

I had to by now, so because of that, I twisted backward, seeing if I recognized the driver in the second car.

I didn't. I had no idea who that was.

Ashton said he'd pick me up at Nancy's, so that meant . . .

Two guys got out from the first SUV. I didn't know them either.

It was the sight of guns in their hands that had me yelling, "*Drive around them!*"

I shoved out before they did, not thinking, my heart in my mouth, and I ran into traffic.

So foolish—but I braced myself to get hit.

There were screeching sounds, horns being blasted. I was being yelled at. A *ping ping* next to me, but ohmygodohmygodohmygod—I kept running, only looking over my shoulder once I hit the sidewalk. Two of those guys were coming after me, but Nick and Amy—thank god—had driven off, speeding around them.

They were safe. They were safe. I had to keep telling myself that, but then one of those guys behind me raised his gun back up and I tensed, preparing to try my rendition of some *Matrix*-style bullet dodging, but already knowing I was screwed.

Then, suddenly, I heard from ahead of me, "*Police! Stop!*"

I screamed, looked, and saw two cops running toward me. Their guns were drawn.

I yelled, pointing behind me. "It's them. I'm being chased."

The one looked behind me, but yelled at me, "*Stop! Stop, right now.*"

Wha—but I looked. The guys were gone.

I heard screeching sounds again and looked over. Their SUVs were fishtailing around the corner, turning and racing in the opposite direction.

They were gone.

Oh, thank goodness.

"Miss."

Shit. I forgot about these cops.

"Put your hands in the air."

Fuck me.

"Get on your knees."

I'd been foolish. Dumb.

"And link your fingers behind your head."

The dumbest.

I needed to stop doing these things.

CHAPTER

THIRTY-EIGHT

ASHTON

We pulled up to Detective Worthing's place, and I called first.

"Yeah?"

"You have her?" I asked, looking toward his building. Getting a call from Jake Worthing after threatening him, then asking him for a favor, wasn't what I had expected for the night, but when he told me the events of the evening, I was thankful he'd stepped in. Again. Even though, there was a part of me where I wondered, really wondered, if I was good for Molly. This war would pass. She wouldn't be in danger at that time. She'd be normal, could be normal. Live a normal life, but not if she was attached to me.

I brought this to her. Guns. Wars. Mafia. That was me. That was this life, so while she ran from me, while I was worried to the point that I wanted to strangle someone, there was a deeper part of me that had to ask the question: Would she be better with someone like Jake Worthing?

Or someone else. Someone normal.

I thought about it and felt like I gutted myself.

I was so far in, too far in. And that was on me because I was too dark, too selfish to let her keep running. That was on me, would be on me. God. I really hated that she'd called him. Though I understood it, I still despised it.

"I do. Gotta say, not liking how she was looking when I mentioned your name."

My lips thinned. "Can I come up?"

He snorted. "Sure. I mean, what's the point of hiding our connection anymore? Just come on in. Let's have a Sunday barbecue while we're here."

I ignored the sarcasm. "She spooked before, and I don't know why. Let me come up and talk to her."

I heard rustling from his side of the phone before his voice came back, clearer. "I'll come out."

Great. Fucking great, but he ended the call, and I couldn't do anything else except wait and twiddle my fucking thumbs.

Molly was upstairs, in this building. In his apartment.

She'd had the police call him.

I never usually cared about women, about this game, but yeah . . . with Molly, I cared. And she'd called *him*.

The back door to his place opened, and he came out, a hood pulled low over his head. He was hunched down, in case of security cameras, but cut past the dumpsters, through his parking lot, and into the alley where we were parked.

I got out as he neared the vehicle and motioned for Elijah and Derek to stay inside.

Worthing paused, looking to me, his head craning to the side before he identified me and came the rest of the way. He stopped a few yards away, his eyes smug.

"Is she okay?" I hated that I had to ask him, and I couldn't ask her.

He laughed. "You are hating this, aren't you? You actually care for her, don't you?"

I didn't answer. I wanted to punch his face but didn't think that would be wise right now.

He laughed again, shaking his head, but came closer. "She's okay. You know what happened?"

"No."

"She was in a car with some of your employees. Two vehicles came up, blocked them in. She recognized they weren't your men, and said that she yelled for them to drive, while she ran out into traffic."

My heart stopped. I ceased breathing.

She ran into traffic? *Into traffic?*

I grated out, repeating, because it was taking everything in me to keep myself here, and not tear into his building, destroying everything in my way until I got to her, "She's okay?"

"She's okay. Really. Pissed, but she wouldn't tell me why. Said it was none of my business, but I swear, Walden."

I stilled.

He was shaking his head, and the anger was coming off him in waves now, tightly reined in. "If you fucking hurt her, I'm moving in. I never took my try before but fuck you. Fuck you for whatever you did to move in on her. She doesn't deserve your criminal ass, and you know it. I know it. The only one who doesn't know it is her, because she's got no idea how much better than you she is. And she is. Mark my words. She's better than both of us. You and her, you've got something. That's obvious from both sides, but the second you mess up again, I'm coming in. Consider this my warning."

I really, *really* wanted to hit him, but he was right. About all of it. Still, she was mine. I wasn't a good enough guy to walk away when I knew I should, he knew I should, and Molly probably knew in her subconscious that I should.

I was all fucking in, and it took until today for me to realize it.

"The men after her, they were your cousin's?"

He shook his head. "I don't know. I'd assume. At this point, who else is going against you? But I've not seen any security footage yet. Things take time on our end. I'll let you know when I do."

That surprised me. "You're suddenly on my side?"

"Fuck no, but Molly's a game changer. My cousin goes after her, and I'm not okay with that."

"What about what I told you earlier?"

He looked ready to pull my head off my body, but that made two of us here. I wasn't happy about this either. Not anymore; the game changed with Molly. Everything changed with Molly.

"It's under advisement. That's all I can tell you, but don't ever call me to a meeting with Trace West present. I'm aware of your brothership with him, but I loathe him. I loathe Montell."

"You blame Jess for Justin leaving?"

"*Trying* to leave, remember?" he bit out.

Yeah. He blamed her. "She's not the reason he was going."

His jaw clenched, and he shoved his hands into his hoodie's front pocket, hunching over again. "Doesn't matter. He never told me he was leaving. She's the one who told me. Logical or not, I'll always hate her for that."

Fine. Fuck. Whatever. "I want to see Molly."

He shook his head. "Not at my place. No way can you come in. It's too risky, but I'll bring her here."

"I don't like that. I don't like waiting."

"I don't give a shit. You fucked up. She ran from you for some reason. I'll go in, talk to her, and bring her out—"

"I'm here."

We both shifted backward, seeing Molly darting out from behind a bush.

A bush. She was hiding behind a bush.

I'd never get a read on her. It hit me then. Never. She was made up of some DNA that didn't make sense to me. I couldn't understand how her brain worked, her psychology, but there she was.

A fucking bush.

I almost started laughing while Worthing was sputtering. "Wha—Molly! You can't—"

She scooted around him, coming to me but stopping a foot away. "I'm sorry, for earlier. I'm sorry."

I could touch her if I wanted. She was letting me know that, and I wanted to do that. I wanted to do more than touch her, but she ran. From me. And I had no idea why.

I sighed, giving in, but not even knowing what I was giving in to. "Get in the vehicle."

She nodded before moving to hug Worthing. "Thank you, Detective."

I growled. She was touching someone who wasn't me.

He shot me a look over her head before softening it when he said to her, "It's Jake by now, Molly."

"Jake." She nodded, stepping back from him. "Thank you for coming and getting me."

He nodded. "It's no problem."

She looked my way before giving him a half grin, and then darted inside, scooting to the far side. I shut the door behind me.

"She's yours."

"You're stating the obvious."

"You're such a dick."

I shrugged. "The war is here. We're in a remission right now, but that's going to end. Second act is coming. I suggest you make up your mind which side you're on before that happens."

He clamped his mouth shut, but he didn't have a reply to me. He knew. I was reminding him again. I motioned toward my SUV again. "Thank you."

He gave me a small nod. "Treat her right, Walden. My last warning about her."

I flicked him off before getting inside.

"Take us to Nancy's Diner."

I felt Molly's gaze on me, but I wasn't ready. Not yet.

I wanted to question her where we wouldn't be interrupted for a long time. A very long time. And I shared this with her through a heated look. Her lips parted, reading me right, and she slumped down in her seat, a soft sigh leaving her.

She knew what was coming.

I didn't know if I was looking forward to it or not . . . that was a first to me too.

CHAPTER THIRTY-NINE

MOLLY

I had no idea why we were here, but I was also not going to push my luck with Ashton.

I'd done something stupid, let my emotions run me off, and he was quiet, but the fury was simmering under his surface. It was there. I could feel it, but I also couldn't lie and say I didn't want to make sure Amy and Nick were okay.

When we got there, Elijah went inside to check the place first. He came back, and Ashton had me go first. He didn't touch me, like he had when we went into Katya or when we left our floor. I missed his touch. Even a simple graze of his finger would've reassured me a little.

Nothing. He kept a firm distance behind me as I walked in.

Amy and Nick were there, and Amy gasped when she saw me. "Oh my—" She stopped, paling, and her mouth dropped when Ashton stepped in after me.

The whole diner went quiet, more than a few mouths dropping to the ground.

A guy stood up from their table, starting to approach before stopping and moving back a foot. His hands folded in front of him. "Uh. Mr. Walden. Sir. Hello."

Ashton gave him a nod before turning toward the counter. An older woman was coming from the kitchen area, an apron tied around her waist. She had gray hair, but it was her eyes that made me pause and take her in again. She wasn't nervous with Ashton, not a bit. She inclined her head a little. "Ashton. It's nice to see you."

He moved past me, meeting my gaze, before turning to her.

As he stepped toward the counter, Amy rushed over to me. "Hey. Hi. Are you okay?"

I nodded. "How are you? I was worried about you." Nick was watching us, but he remained sitting. He was watching Ashton too. "I'm really glad you guys are okay. I'm so sorry for pulling you into my mess."

"No. I mean, it's okay. I have no idea what's going on, but wow. You actually know the *boss* boss man. We—we heard rumors when Jess quit about who really owned Katya, but we weren't sure. Then yeah, he and Mr. West both started showing up on the main floor. They never used to do that, not till Jess. And you know him. I, uh, I'm kinda in shock." She touched my arm. "We went to the police. We weren't sure what to do. You ran into traffic, but you yelled for us to leave and Nick saw the guns, and we're so sorry we didn't stop and help you more."

I shook my head. "No, no. It's fine. I'm just glad you guys got away, and you're okay."

She was nodding, her eyes big and scared, but she gave me a faint smile. "The officer at the station said they already had you. They told us to go home." She motioned behind her. "Nick, uh, he wanted to go home, but I was shaken up. I wanted to be here, with the rest of the group. We didn't tell them about, you know, about you. I don't think they know you."

Oooh no. She was still operating under the assumption I worked at Katya. "No. I—I don't work at Katya. I was there, and I—" I looked

Ashton's way; he was now moving to sit in a back booth. Elijah remained just inside the door. The other guard was outside. "I overreacted to something tonight, but I don't work at Katya. I'm really sorry I pulled you into my mess. I'm just grateful you're okay."

"Yeah. Of course. Yeah." She looked back at where Ashton was sitting. "Do you, do you think you guys would want to join us?"

"No!" I gentled my voice. "No. But thank you for the invitation."

Her head was bobbing up and down. "Oh. Yeah. Cool. I mean." She giggled a little. "That's cool that you know him. He's—yeah. You know. Wow."

I did. I really did, and giving her another smile, then one to Nick, too, I moved toward Ashton.

He was sitting with his back to the wall, his front facing the rest of the diner, and his eyes were on me. They pinned me down as I slid into my side of the booth. I could feel Amy's and Nick's attention on us, probably the rest of them, but I reached for the menu.

"Nancy is making you something."

His tone was so rough. Brisk. Cut off.

I . . . had so royally messed up. "I'm sor—"

"Save it," he clipped out.

Really, really messed up.

"If you don't want me to apologize, why'd you bring me here?"

"To see that your friends are okay." Those cold eyes locked onto me, and he leaned forward. "And to let them know I know you. To let you know the extent of what I can do, will do. And to let Nancy know that I'm aware my employees come here after working at Katya. I need to press upon you that there are not many twenty-four-hour diners open in a safe area. This is one of them. I say the word, Nancy will shut the doors to them. I own Katya. My family owns other businesses here. She knows how it works."

I slumped down. "I'm aware. I'm a business owner too. I bet Nancy is the rightful owner of her diner. I wonder how she'd feel if she found out the person she thought she bought it from had conned her, and actually gave it to a Mafia family. I bet she wouldn't be as warm and welcoming then."

He didn't reply, just glared at me.

And fuck him, but it was affecting me.

He'd been inside of me not long ago, and then I realized how much power he had over me, freaked, and ran. Now everything was up in smoke.

I lowered my head. "I really am sorry."

He sighed. "I know. We'll talk about what happened in private."

God. He gave in, an inch. The knot in my chest loosened, just slightly.

Nancy came over, bringing coffee and a plate of food. She placed it in front of me, not him, and even though it smelled delicious, looked delicious, I couldn't eat it. My appetite was gone.

"You're not hungry?" Ashton asked when Nancy left.

I shook my head. "I'll have the coffee. Thank you."

———

I was in the bathroom and coming out, seeing a woman waiting to use it.

I moved aside, holding the door for her, but she didn't go in.

She was insanely gorgeous. Sleek black hair. Dark almond eyes. Long legs that supermodels had, and she was dressed in the cutest outfit. Hemp sandals. A faded jean miniskirt with an oversize corduroy sweater. Underneath, she had pulled the collar up from a button-down shirt so it folded over the sweater. The tail ends peeked out from under too. Her hair was pulled back, two long braids trailing down her back while the rest was shiny. So beautiful.

Her eyes were icy.

"Can I help you?"

"He takes women up there regularly. Three times a month. Don't think you're special." Her lips pressed in a flat line. Her message was delivered, so she started back for the others' table.

Ashton was watching our exchange, but no way had he heard. He was too far away.

I stood there, the same feeling happening all over again. Like a knife came up and punctured my stomach, my insides were spilling out onto the floor.

It was becoming increasingly and alarmingly obvious how incredibly stupid I had been because Ashton was *inside of* me. He wasn't a fun time. This wasn't sex with no emotions. There were emotions. So many, and while they were curling inside of me, what that woman just did—I felt the switch.

The. Switch.

I began marching for her when Ashton rose swiftly. He touched my arm, stopping me. "What did she say?"

I swung my gaze up, seeing his eyes starting to heat up.

I started to go past him. "Nothing. Just tired of hearing about your other women."

His hand tightened, then changed so he wasn't hurting me. He slid down, catching my hand, and moved in again, blocking me from seeing their table. "I have no idea what you're talking about."

"How could you? You wouldn't let me apologize."

His eyes narrowed, some of the hard mask slipping. "What are you talking about?"

"Why I left. I wanted to explain, but you shut me down. Now she threw it back in my face, and I'm sorry, but I'm tired tonight. I did something irrational. I get why you're mad at me, but I'm not going to take attitude from her."

He went eerily still, and the feeling, whatever was going on with him, was starting to puncture my anger. Unease and something else, something I couldn't place, went through me, but he lifted his attention from me and looked, finding her. He turned back to me. "What did she say to you?"

I told him, repeating it word for word.

He frowned at me. "I have never taken a woman up there before."

I had to take a step back. "What?"

"I only go there with Trace. We've kept our ownership low profile. It recently came out that we own it because of Jess."

I—had no idea what to say to that. "Before, that manager guy said something about your women too."

Ashton straightened fully, letting go of my hand. "What did he say?"

God. This was embarrassing, but I told him, including how Elijah tried to shut him down.

"I will question Anthony, but again, I've never brought a woman there with me. He was making assumptions."

And that was . . . I had no idea what to even think now.

Ashton turned, motioning for Elijah.

"What did Anthony say to her at Katya tonight?"

His story was the same, but he added on, "He took one look at her, and he wanted her. I tried shutting him up, but he was saying shit that didn't make sense." Elijah gave me a pitying look. "How he operates isn't how Ashton operates. He was wrong. I didn't get that in earlier."

I was mortified as the pieces were starting to come together.

I was with Ashton Walden. Who he was, how he looked, his power, his money, even how he walked. It made other people act crazy, which was starting to make sense.

Ashton's face was unreadable as he studied me, saying to Elijah, "Take her outside. Please."

Elijah nodded, and I moved ahead of him.

We went past their table. I gave Amy and Nick a small smile, another last way to apologize, but when I saw that woman staring at me, I stopped and leaned into the table. "It's not that he brings women there on the regular. It's that he doesn't bring women there. He brought me tonight, and sorry, honey, but I think I'm pretty fucking special. I got a glimpse into how you think and how you feel, and I can draw comfort. The universe will give you what you deserve. So knowing that, have a nice fucking life."

Ashton was behind me, then moved closer. "Whoever you are, you're fired."

She paled. Others gasped. Mouths dropped again, but Ashton took my hand and led the way back outside. I risked it, squeezing his hand as we got into the waiting SUV.

He linked our fingers in response.

We drove off, and I couldn't hold back a smile.

I hadn't completely Shorty Eastered this whole thing.

CHAPTER FORTY

MOLLY

We went to Ashton's Manhattan apartment. I was dead on my feet when we finally walked inside.

"Do you want a drink?"

Ashton had thawed toward me, significantly. Which I was grateful for, but which also alarmed me because man, when he was pissed, he was like *ice*. Like the Antarctic ice that doesn't get thawed.

I shook my head, leaving my purse, impressed with myself that I had kept ahold of it through everything tonight. "No."

He tossed his keys on the counter, putting his phone and wallet down. Then went to the liquor cabinet and poured himself a drink. "You sure you don't want one?"

"Do I need one for this?"

His gaze locked on me. His eyes trailed down my body, and I looked away. I didn't want to get heated. I didn't want to want him. I just wanted to go to bed, alone, and wake up and regroup because my head was spinning. No matter what, the fact I reacted so quick and so intensely was scary.

I didn't like how much he could affect me.

"You were jealous?"

Here we go.

"No. Yes. I—when I kissed you and when I made the first move, it was just sex in my head. It really was. I've never looked a gift horse in the mouth. I enjoy the gift and keep it moving. It's how I've survived, so yeah. I was jealous, but I was hurt, and that terrified me. I wasn't supposed to catch feelings for you. That was never what this was about." I motioned between us.

"What was it supposed to be about?"

I closed my eyes, counting to five. My chest burned. "Sex. Enjoyment. To feel good for a short time until this is all over. That was it."

"And how are they now?"

He was so in control, his cool eyes on me, sipping from his drink. He was unruffled, as if he'd been attending a charity event among the rich and famous.

"They're confusing. Shit got real with me."

"Define real." Another sip.

I wanted to take the glass away from him and throw it against the wall, see some sort of reaction from him. He'd thawed, but not enough, and my chest squeezed, because that was on me. All and only on me.

"I caught feelings, and I don't want feelings. Not for you."

"Molly." A low warning from him, but he was still sipping that drink, still looking unruffled, but he wasn't. He was so ruffled. I felt it under his surface. The dark and dangerous Ashton was there, right there, just simmering. He took another sip, a long sip. "Why not feelings for me?"

I almost laughed. Then I did. "Are you messing with me?"

"Why not me?"

"Ashton! Be serious. You walked in, intending on using me. I was supposed to be bait. You never went through with it. You still could. You should. Tonight *proved* they want me. I was away from you for thirty seconds, and they were on me." I raised my chin up, feeling tears coming and needing to stop them. "I'm the perfect bait. You messed up so bad, not using me already. Or hell, too bad those cops were there. They could've taken me. I would've survived. I come from Shorty Easter. I would've gotten away, or worse, let loose my switch on them. I could've—"

"Shut up." His jaw clenched. A vein stuck out.

I kept on, shaking my head. "I could've gotten free. Told you where they were, who they were. You should've used me all over again when you had the shot. Now you don't know what I could've done for you. You already used me for my dad. You're getting what you wanted. He's shaking the tree. He's the dog that goes out to scare the birds up. That's happening, and whoever killed Justin and Kelly, what? They're coming after me to stop my dad? We're so far down this rabbit hole that I don't know what's happening anymore."

I wanted him to come out, so bad. I wanted to play with him, not this cool and calm Ashton. I wanted to see the monster that I knew lived inside of him.

I was almost smirking, feeling my chest pinching, pain slicing through me. "But you asked why not you? Because of who you are. Because of who I am. I'm the girl who gets left behind. I'm the girl who survives everyone walking away. That's me. That's my story. I'm not a Jess Montell. I'm not the girl who gets the hot, wealthy, and powerful guy. I'm a disaster. I'm fucking chaos. You could have anyone, so why me? *Why me?* I'm Shorty Easter's daughter. Even *he* didn't want me. I'm the girl no one wants, so I blackmail my dad into selling me a dying business and I hole up, making that my world. That's my everything. And you come in, saying it was never mine. *That's* who I am."

I looked away. "I'm the joke."

"Is that what you want?"

I froze. "What?"

That simmering look was still on me, and I felt knocked back. "You ran tonight. Now you're saying this. Is this because you want to be free? Should I have let you keep running?"

I was staggered. A pit opened up inside of me, and the thought— no. *No!* I couldn't speak because my god. To think it. To be scared of it.

To run from it, but to hear him say it? I felt emptied out, all of me. He had reached in and taken everything that made my blood pump and pulled it out. He let it drop at his feet with just the question.

I was so far in that I couldn't think straight. I was that far in.

I could only shake my head. Not that. I didn't want to run. I didn't want to keep running.

I wanted him. "No. That's not what I want."

I felt his gaze on me, long and hard. And intense. So intense. "And if I wasn't Mafia?"

I bit out a hard laugh. "It doesn't matter, because it's you. *It's you.* When I heard your manager say that about you, that you were probably already fucking Remmi West, it hurt. Really hurt. It was pain that I could get over, but that was after you and me being together for what? A full day? Two? Imagine how much worse it would be for a month? Even a week? I'm more scared of what you could do to me than what a gun aiming at me could do. I cut my losses and ran. It's an old habit, and it rose up tonight. You, what you could do to me, is what I have fought against every day being Shorty's daughter. I never let him beat me. I never let anyone beat *me* down, but you could do it just by making me fall in love with you."

Jesus.

I just said that. "And now this? You asking me if I want to run? If I want you to let me run?" I was shaking my head. I was mixed up, all mixed up. I wanted him. That's what I kept coming back around to. Him. I wanted him, no matter who he was, what he did. It was him. Every part of him.

I needed all of him, not parts of him, not slices. All of him. His darkness included.

My insides were on the outside of my body. I'd never felt as exposed as I did now.

I hated it.

It almost made me hate him, almost, but I knew better.

Ashton's eyes were still narrowed on me. He took a sip, another fucking sip. "Are you in love with me?"

My heart squeezed. I didn't blink an eye, lifting my head back up. "I could, yes."

He finished his drink, gritting his teeth as he swallowed it, and then came toward me.

I began backing up. "What are you doing?"

He moved past me, taking his things into his bedroom.

I followed, at a sedate pace, but I was following him. I stood in his doorway, watching as he disappeared into his closet. "You've had a long night, Molly. Shower and change."

I . . . we weren't going to finish this conversation? Or was this a one-sided thing? Only I told him how I felt. But I guess, in a way, it was just me that fucked things up tonight.

My shoulders fell down. A heavy weight pressed on my chest. "Yeah. Okay." Maybe he was right. A shower would make me feel better. Clean clothes. Comfy clothes.

I was so tired.

He came back from the closet, in his sweats from the other night and a T-shirt. It wasn't fair, how good he could look. "Use my shower."

I nodded, still feeling like an idiot, but moved past him.

I was beyond worrying about things like clothes. Knowing Ashton, and I was getting to know him, he'd find some new ones for me while I was in the shower and have them ready for me. Or he'd put a robe out while he ordered someone else to go and buy me some. I was beyond thinking of the details, so I stepped into his bathroom. His very spacious and gorgeous bathroom, with a clear glass wall that separated the shower from the rest of the room. It was partitioned off so the shower was deep back.

I turned the shower on, stripped my clothes off, and went under the spray.

I drew in a breath, my head hanging forward, feeling the water beat down on me. Trailed down my back. All the grime, dirt, tears, blood, everything that I hadn't cleaned earlier was running to the drain now. It felt good. Refreshing. That's what I needed. A fresh start. A new start.

Then, suddenly, a body was behind me.

I started to yelp, but he moved in. My body recognized his, and I sagged in relief. Ashton.

He reached past me, taking the shampoo, and lathered it into my hair, massaging my head, still pressed up behind me. His mouth was to my ear as he began to rub his hands over me. He was washing me. "You think I enjoyed getting a call from Detective Worthing?" His hand moved down my body. "Finding out that you called him instead of me?"

He moved all the way, half lifting me in his arms and moving me to the wall, pressing me against it.

He continued moving his hands over me.

"I had to go to *his home*, because that's where he had taken you. To another man's place? I had to ask permission to come and talk to you. You think I enjoyed that?" His hand smoothed down, sliding between my legs, and I felt him at my entrance. He circled me, teasing. "I'd come to terms with how I was beginning to care for you and then bam, I'm asking another man to talk to *my woman?*"

My heart spiked. He had—his finger slid inside of me, grinding deep. All the way.

I gasped, my head swimming, as a second finger thrust in. He pulled them out, sliding back in, and he kept thrusting, his mouth nipping at my ear.

"You have an issue, you wait and discuss it with me. You don't bolt. Ever. They could've *taken* you." His whole body was vibrating on those words. "You think I'm still the guy who wants to use you as bait? We're past that. Long past. They *shot* at you. Another man had a gun to your head. How many fucking times do you need to get that you don't leave my side? Everything changed the second a gun was put to your head. Everything did. You. Me. Us. This." He wrapped a firm arm around my stomach and hoisted me in the air, kicking my legs apart. His fingers pulled out, and his dick surged inside.

I let out a sound at the fullness of him, but then he was moving, and this man was made to fuck me. My soul was purring. In and out. He was riding me, moving up, his hand gripping my thigh, holding me in place so he could pound into me.

He grated against my ear, "I asked if you wanted me to let you go, because for a moment tonight, I thought maybe it would be better for you. Safer for you. I am who I am. I am what I do. Make no mistake, I am the bad guy." He kept thrusting inside of me, slowing as he grated out, "And I asked you if you wanted to be free, and the look on your face—" He shuddered behind me. "I can't do it. I can't let you go. You've become the reason. You're no longer the woman I'm going to use to end this war. You're the reason for this war because if anyone hurts you, touches you, I'll kill them. Are you hearing me? All of them.

"I am sick of hearing that *another* gun was pointed at you, shot at you, or getting calls from another man that you went to instead of me. You only wanted sex between us? Too fucking bad." His mouth closed over my ear, his teeth grazing my lobe as he shoved so far up, he could've been in my stomach. "Mine, Molly. Do you know what that means?"

I was starting to get it, but I couldn't talk.

My toes were curling from the pleasure he was giving my body.

He was holding all of my weight. I couldn't move, didn't want to. I gasped against the shower wall, the water sliding down my side as he pistoned into me. He was fucking me hard, and it was punishing, but he was cementing one fact.

I wasn't alone on the feelings factor.

"You are mine." He grunted, moving back and almost dropping me, but only to turn me around. My legs went around his waist. My arms wound around his neck, my hands into his hair, and then he was back inside of me. Moving deep. "Never run from me again. Do you hear me?"

I heard him. I so heard him. "Never."

He lifted his head, his eyes searing into mine. "You run and I'll burn the world down for you."

A deep shiver went through me, curling my toes up, a good shiver. A delicious shiver.

"No more running."

He wasn't asking. He was ordering me.

I nodded, almost unable to talk.

"Promise me, Molly." He slid out, repositioned me, and slid back in, pushing all the way to the hilt.

I groaned before I squeaked out, "Pinkie."

That was enough for him.

His mouth caught mine, commanding, and a wave of euphoria ran through me, racing down my spine, to my toes, back up and making my fingers spasm from the sensations.

His tongue caught mine, sweeping, claiming me. I gasped for breath, only to be reclaimed by his lips.

The universe just exploded around us.

Ashton thrust up into me, over and over again. Both of us came together, and even during all of that, as my climax erupted inside of me and left me weak, he still held me and he still kissed me.

He didn't stop kissing me until later, a long time later.

———

"Wait." I lifted my head in bed, moving so I could see him better. The lights were off. We'd moved from the shower to the bed, and hadn't left, but the next day's light was peeking under his window shades. I didn't want to fall asleep. I didn't want the next day to come. "You have feelings for me too? I want to make sure I got that right."

Ashton reached over, tweaking my nipple before he growled lightly. "You're mine." He rose over me, bracing himself on both sides of my head, his legs moving between my legs, and sliding up, lifting them as his knees parted them. "No more leaving."

He was back at my entrance.

I'd lost count of how many times I'd had sex with this man over the weekend. It wasn't natural. We weren't teenagers anymore, but his mouth caught mine in another soul-engulfing kiss, and he slid inside of me once more.

I sighed, giving in, winding my arms around his neck and pulling his body to rest on mine.

I was glad we'd had that talk.

CHAPTER

FORTY-ONE

ASHTON

Both our phones lit up almost at the same time.

I jumped up first, curled around Molly. It took her a little more time since we'd fallen asleep two hours ago. I cursed, two hours of sleep, but grabbed my phone and hers.

Unknown number so I answered. "Who is this?"

"Is that my phone?" Molly was yawning, rubbing at her eyes before she sat up.

A harsh laugh came from the other end. "I didn't believe it, but now I do. You're screwing my little girl?"

"Easter."

Molly woke up with a snap after that. She sat up and took the phone from my hand. "Dad?!"

My phone had quieted but started again, so I answered it. "What's wrong?" It was Trace.

"We've been hit, again."

Fuck. Though, not surprising. I moved to the closet, grabbing clothes and beginning to pull them on. "Where? Who?"

"Two warehouses, separate locations. They bombed the warehouse that we leaked was where we were holding Molly. The other place was where we had his sniper. He got his man back."

"Our men?"

"They got out. We didn't lose any men, but I got a report that someone tried to take Molly last night?"

"I called in some sources. They were working on getting the footage and running down the license plates."

He swore from his end. "Where were you?"

"I was—it doesn't matter. They didn't get her."

"We have to move forward thinking that Nicolai knows we have his cousins. Have you talked to Avery? Has he gotten any information from them?"

"He said not to check in for a few days. It's a whole program to break them down. Real torture doesn't get good results. We know this. Psychological torture breaks better."

"But not faster."

I was fully dressed and moved through the apartment. Molly was still on her phone, huddled in the corner of the couch in the living room. I said to Trace, lowering my voice, "Shorty just called."

"Interesting timing. Has he gotten anything?"

I studied Molly, but she seemed to sense me and moved even more into a human ball, the phone tucked close to her face. She was whispering into it.

I frowned. "I'm not sure. Waiting on that."

"Enough's enough, Ashton. Let's put our first move into play."

"On it."

"I'll send my orders. You send yours."

"We'll convene at the safe house."

"I hate this world. Why are we in it?"

There was my best friend. Hearing him taking his old role, I felt like I could step into mine. The old Ashton coming back into place. It felt good. "Because we were forced into it. We're not the guys that roll over either."

"True. Okay. Let's talk later."

We ended our call, and I sent a text to Avery.

Me: War's officially on.

Avery: Okay.

It didn't change much on his end, except he knew to fortify the compound even more than it was. I called Marco and moved back into my room, grabbing the rest of everything we'd need.

"Are you serious? It's six in the morning."

"It's nine, and the war is on again."

He changed his tune immediately, a lot more alert and somber. "What happened?"

"They attacked the warehouse. I'm putting you on notice."

"What do you want me to do?"

"The familia is your responsibility. Watch them. Guard them. You need to get more men."

"I did. The men are ready."

"Call them in. If you can, talk our aunts into staying at the same house. Those men are to protect our family. You get me?"

He quieted before responding, his voice low, "I get you, cousin. What about Remmi?"

Fuck. Remmi. "She's Trace's sister. He'll take care of her."

"But what if he doesn't? He forgot about her last time. He could again."

"You were supposed to stop fucking her."

"I did."

"Then she's not your problem, at least not now. If you actually care about her, we can discuss later." Because, catching sight of Molly still on the couch, who was I to tell someone they couldn't be with someone they'd fallen for? "I have to go."

"I'll take care of the family. Kick ass, Ashton. I know you will."

That was the plan.

I ended the call and texted Glen.

Me: Board up Easter Lanes and take a trip.

Glen: I will. Is Molly okay? I heard what happened.

Me: She will be.

After that, I saw Elijah at the door. He would've been notified at the same time I was. We had an alert system coordinated that if the boss got notice, his higher security got an alert to be ready to move. He was ready to move, with three large hockey bags hanging over him.

I frowned at him. "Do you have war paint on?"

He shrugged. "I got excited."

"Fine, Marcus!" Molly's voice rose before she shoved up from the couch. "I can't stand him!" She turned, saw us, saw our bags, saw Elijah's war paint, and her mouth turned into a small O. "What'd I miss?"

Jesus. I think I loved her.

"Change. We have to go."

She frowned but didn't argue and hurried into the room.

Elijah and I began moving as almost one entity. We took all of our items to the SUV, and came back, doing another trip. On the way, I sent my orders out for our first coordinated attack against the Worthing family, but there was one more person I needed to give the heads-up to.

I texted Jake.

Me: We were hit last night.

Worthing: Okay. See you on the other side.

I grimaced because that wasn't what I had been hoping to hear from him. Then again, I wasn't sure myself anymore what I thought Worthing would do.

I started to text him but deleted it and pocketed my phone again.

When we went back, Molly was ready. She had her own bag. I wasn't sure where she found it or what was in there, but knowing her, it had literal magic inside. I wouldn't have been surprised.

Elijah took it, walking back to the vehicle. Molly began to go past me, but I caught her, dipping my head for a quick kiss.

I needed one taste, just one, before we were about to go into this. I savored the feel of her lips under mine, how I could capture her breath, how her tongue felt against mine, and how she rose up on tiptoes so she could wind her arms around my neck.

I took my time kissing her. I took all the time.

CHAPTER
FORTY-TWO

MOLLY

The safe house was an entire building that was hidden in plain sight.

We drove into a parking lot, went down, and somehow we were going through a tunnel and parked in a basement. There were a bunch of men in the room as we got out. Ashton took my hand, walking with me to an elevator, and up we went. We got off on the sixth floor, the elevator opening to an apartment that spanned the entire floor.

"Make yourself comfortable." Ashton pressed a kiss to my forehead, staying back with Elijah and a few other guards. I wandered around. For safe houses, this one was luxurious, but I wasn't surprised anymore. Everything Ashton did was thought out. He had the reputation for being more impulsive, and Trace was the analyst, long thinker, but Ashton was underrated. Severely.

It wasn't until later that day, after I headed right back to bed and slept, that I realized we were next to Octavia.

I'd woken later in the afternoon, heard the music, and went to see what was going on. There were floor-to-ceiling windows that surrounded the entire apartment, all sides, so by the kitchen area, I could see a line of people on the street waiting to get into the nightclub, winding around the corner. From the front side, there were flashing lights and the traffic was nuts from cars stopping and speeding through. A few large security guys were milling around.

"Windows are blacked out. They can't see in."

Ashton had come into the kitchen, wearing what he'd worn when we first came.

"You haven't slept?"

He had slight bags under his eyes, his hair messed, but in a whole sexy way, and he yawned, coming toward me now. He rubbed a hand over his face. "No time. Trace and I have been in meetings all day."

Right. Meetings. For a Mafia war. Made sense . . .

"Can I ask what's going on?"

He leaned against the counter, his eyes gentling as he took me in, up and down. I had changed into some black leggings and a black hoodie, clothes that he already had waiting in the closet for me. He shook his head. "We're moving in a thought-out plan, but one to cut down on innocent lives lost. If that helps?"

My mouth went dry. Innocent lives.

Like mine. "Oh."

"Molly, I need to ask about your father. What did he say on the phone call?"

I flinched, just remembering the conversation. "He'd heard about you and me and was pissed. Basically, he wanted you to know that he won't do shit if you fuck me over. His words, but I cleaned them up a bit."

"Had he found out anything about Kelly's killer?"

I shook my head. "No, but he said he was onto something else, something big. He wouldn't say anything more except to keep my head down because whoever or whatever it is, they had deep pockets. Legal pockets."

Ashton frowned. "Legal?"

I nodded. "Well, he said pigs, but yeah. Legal."

He continued frowning before clearing his throat. "I'd like to put a program on your phone. The tracker will be directly connected to my phone. It'll locate where your dad is when he calls again."

"Not just his call, though. Right? It'll locate other calls too."

"Is that a problem?"

I opened my mouth. Normally, I'd say hell yes because Shorty Easter installed a good paranoia about the government tracking me, but this wasn't the government. It was Ashton. He had reason. I'd had four guns pointed at me within a short amount of time.

I shook my head. "No. That's fine." I took my phone out, sliding it to him on the counter.

He caught it, but his eyes remained on me. "Are you doing okay?"

I nodded. "I'm good. I mean, we're in the lap of luxury for places to hide out in." I gestured to Octavia. "Though, I'm confused about that place. Doesn't a different mob family run that?"

"Cole Mauricio. They're active in Chicago, but Trace's family and mine have an understanding with them."

"Do they know we're neighbors?"

"No, but they've agreed to reach out if any of the Worthing family shows up. Trace and I have a chain of restaurants in Chicago, and we do the same, or did when they were in their own war."

Gah. My mouth went dry again. "Will they be pissed that you're literally right next door to them?"

He shook his head.

My phone beeped at that moment.

He murmured, "You have a text from Pialto."

That had my mouth going dry again. "About Easter Lanes?"

His grin faded, but his eyes were still soft on me. "You don't need to worry about your bowling alley."

"I am. I'm losing business if Glen's not keeping it open during my peak days."

"Glen's not doing anything with it right now."

"What?"

"I told him to board it up and take a trip. So he's safe."

I snorted. "To Glen that means holing up in one of your family's casinos and gambling the whole time. His definition of 'take a trip' is different from yours."

"I'll have my men locate him, and if he's not safe, we'll make him safe. Does that work?"

I nodded, surprised. "Thank you for that." And on to the other matter. "What do you mean I don't need to worry about Easter Lanes?"

"Just that you don't have to worry. We closed it down during this time. That'll affect your business, so whatever revenue you're losing, we'll reimburse you."

"What?"

"It's business, but ours is affecting yours. I don't want that to happen."

I—had no clue how to take that. "I want you to reimburse double what I'm losing." A businesswoman was a businesswoman.

Ashton cocked his head to the side, his eyes sparking. "Deal. Also, it'll be Trace who will handle this. It'll be between you and him."

I nodded. "I'll give you that number, what I would make in an average during the time period I'm closed?"

Still sparking. He nodded. "Yes. We'll do double. I promise."

"Okay. I'm going to consider this a vacay in a weird way."

"What do you usually do on a vacation?"

I shrugged. "Never been on one, so I don't know."

His eyes sharpened. "You've never taken a vacation?"

I shook my head. "Never had time. Taking time off a while ago and going to the hockey game was a big deal for me. I couldn't pass it up."

His gaze was thoughtful. "Good to know. You're a workaholic."

"I am, I guess, but it's my home. I love it."

"I've noticed."

"Hey, boss." Elijah interrupted us, coming from a hallway that I didn't even know was there. He saw me and stopped. "Oh. Sorry. I can—"

"What is it?"

Elijah grimaced but held up a tablet. "We've got movement at the compound."

Ashton swore, coming to me and pressing a kiss to my forehead. He took the tablet from Elijah in one hand, his free hand trailing down my arm and side before heading in the direction Elijah had come.

It was then I realized that I didn't know if I could text Pialto back, but I looked and never mind.

Ashton had taken my phone with him.

That answered that.

CHAPTER

FORTY-THREE

MOLLY

I tried fifty different pizza places in New York. Course, they didn't know I tried them because we ordered delivery to a place that wasn't even remotely near here, and there was a whole elaborate system for security guards who picked up the food and transferred it. But I tried them, and I was now an expert.

I was considering creating an app just about New York pizza places. Though, there probably already was one, and so . . . maybe I'd look into that.

I asked about Jess and Trace, but Ashton said they were in a separate place.

"We want to keep you separate, just to be safe. Less exposure."

That was three weeks ago, and we were still going.

Ashton left at all hours of the day. Sometimes he'd crawl into bed for a few hours, then leave for three days. It was insane, but they were in a war. The news was reporting a huge uptick of criminal shootings, all places with mob ties.

I wondered if those were either Ashton's or Trace's places because I didn't know much about the Worthing family, what base they had in the city or not. I was going crazy. Ashton left me one of two bodyguards. Eze and Matt. I think there were others in the building or downstairs, but when Ashton left, one of them was always here. Today was Eze, and I went about my new routine.

I made coffee, took one for me and one for him.

Eze always gave me a look, but I'd worn him down. He took the coffee but would place it on the counter where he was standing.

I went over on the other side of the counter and had my coffee with him. I don't know if Ashton frowned on them relaxing with me, but I knew my ways around that too. Like sitting on the same counter, sipping my drink, and every now and then Eze would relent and drink his coffee with me.

Matt was different. He was less stoic than Eze, and he'd drink his coffee almost right away, almost before I even had time to sit, so I started setting my coffee down first before handing Matt his. I'd race back to my seat and then start sipping away.

When he was done, if he finished before me, he'd give me a crooked grin, placing the cup back down and saying thanks. After coffee, I'd head to the gym area and either work out or do yoga. Late breakfast or early lunch was next, whichever worked out. And no matter who was with me, I'd make food for them as well. It was the same deal as the coffee except the guys would sit at the table with me to eat.

The afternoons were spent on educating myself.

I didn't know how long this would take, and I couldn't relax enough to read for enjoyment, so I started watching business lectures on YouTube and videos about group roles. I was convinced I had enough education in me to be a group therapist, or an assistant to a group therapist. Yeah. More like the assistant to the assistant of the group therapist. I could be the note taker.

Then, early dinner and a movie.

After the movie was the real treat I started to enjoy.

Spying on Octavia customers, or more specifically the line waiting to get into Octavia.

I started to notice the regulars. The newbies. The people who'd stay out there all night, and the people who would get in right away. They had a whole system. I was able to see the front door from one side of Ashton's floor, and if I snuck out to a patio, I had an even better view.

I went out there again, my usual time, because people really started showing up around eleven.

There were blankets out there, a snack pile, and I never had to worry about being quiet because the music from the nightclub was somewhat loud, especially when the doors opened, but it was mostly the people or the traffic. Where I sat on the patio, I was half-hidden by a post and who'd be looking where I was? The windows behind me were all dark. The only time any light shone out was when I'd open the door to go in and out, but tonight, I was having a drink, my snacks next to me, when I saw a vehicle pull up.

The bouncers approached, their radios in hand. One went to the front passenger door. The window rolled down. They were talking.

This didn't happen. People rolled up in their cars and got out, then went to the bouncers to get let in. There was none of this where the bouncers went to the vehicle. I expected it to be a quick convo of yes, they can come in or no, keep moving. That didn't happen.

The main bouncer guy was having a whole conversation, speaking into his radio. Then, a guy from inside the club came out. He looked all official, and he joined the conversation.

The back window was lowered. The official guy went to have a conversation.

I was riveted.

I wrote down the license plate. Then the official guy and bouncer began backing away from the vehicle, shaking their heads. Their hands were out. They were yelling.

A shot rang out, and the vehicle sped off.

I gasped.

The official guy was down.

The bouncer dropped to his side, his radio in hand, and more security people rushed from the nightclub.

People were screaming. Half the line ran off. The other half—I was fairly certain most were regulars—stayed put to watch the newest action.

Within a few minutes, two cop cars pulled up.

The whole neighborhood was lit up red and blue. An ambulance arrived a bit later.

My phone started ringing. *Ashton calling.*

I went inside and answered. "Hello?"

"Tell me you are not outside, watching Octavia."

There were loud sounds from his end. "Where are you?"

"I'm coming to you, but you're inside. Right? Right, Molly?"

I glanced back. The door was shutting. "Yep. Totally inside."

He groaned. "You just came inside, didn't you?"

"I refuse to answer that question on the basis that I might incriminate oneself."

"You're not—this isn't a joke. Octavia's people called. It's the night manager who was shot, and they're saying it's from our end. I have to know—" His end suddenly got a lot clearer. "Are you inside or not?"

"I am."

"Where's Eze? Elijah is trying him, and he can't find him."

My stomach dropped down to my feet, and I turned, slowly, as if that would ward anything off—but he wasn't there. "I don't know."

"Get out of there! Now!"

"Ahhh." I was running, not sure where I was running, but I was running. This was supposed to be a safe place. Had my pizza orders tipped them off? Had someone decoded the stool pigeon encryption? What was happening? But I heard the toilet flush, and I stopped, my heart pounding.

The door opened.

I began easing backward.

Eze came out, grimacing. He saw me in the hallway, plastered against one wall, the phone glued to my face. "What is it?"

"Is that Eze?"

I held the phone out. "For you."

He frowned, hurrying and grabbing the phone. I began easing backward all at the same time. "Hell—" He reached into his pocket, pulling his own phone out. "It's dead. I have no signal." A whole different awareness came over him. "What?" He raced to the patio door, peering out. "Cops. Ambulance. Crowds. I'll lock down here, but I think we're good. Her phone has a signal." He moved to find me.

I was all the way in the back, as far away from him as possible.

He spoke into the phone, wincing at me. "She's here. I'll lock down. We'll move locations."

A thought came to me. "Wait."

"What?"

I hurried back. "Give me the phone."

He did, leaving right after, and I heard him engage all the locks on the door.

"What is it?" From Ashton.

"I was outside."

He cursed on his end. "I didn't want you to be out there."

"I saw it."

"Saw what?"

"The shooting. The car. I saw it. Why do the Octavia people say it was from our end?"

"Because someone in that vehicle said they worked for us and wanted to get inside."

"That's a lie."

"What?"

"I saw the whole thing. It was weird. The people wanting to go inside just go inside, or they get turned away. This vehicle had the staff go to them. They talked, and they were arguing, and then the manager guy was shot. It wasn't us."

"I'm aware it wasn't us. Thank you."

I ignored Ashton's dry tone, saying, "I got the license plate number too."

"What?"

"I'm nosy. And bored. And I got it to see if you'd run it down for me."

"What is it?"

I went back outside, ducking down for the pad that I'd dropped and moved back inside. I read it off for him. "What are the chances they would've gotten an entire vehicle registered to you before doing this whole thing."

"Chances are high."

Oh. "What was the point of doing the whole conversation and telling them they were there for you?"

He was quiet on his end.

I had a point. I thrust my fist in the air and doubled down. "I bet they had to do that because they didn't register the plates to you. I mean, it's a genius move to try and alienate you from Octavia's owners."

"We'll run the car down."

"Okay." And I was running in a circle, fist in the air. Booyah.

"I'm still going to have you move locations—"

"No! Come on. I like staying here. If I stay—"

"You'll go where Jess is."

"—that'd be awesome because company. Or could she come here?"

"Eze's phone lost signal. I don't like that coincidence."

I didn't, either, but I wasn't done arguing my case. I went over to the side where I couldn't see the front of Octavia anymore, but the large crowd was as much entertainment. "I have a whole system here. And we have the vantage. If they knew I was here, they wouldn't have tried it where we could see them do it in real time. You said it yourself. No one knows we're here. It works . . ." I trailed off because the same vehicle was parked at the end of the alley. By the back door. Which I knew Octavia rarely used, and I knew this because I was involved on a long stakeout, for my own pleasure.

And I knew no one used that door.

"They're there."

"What?!"

"The same vehicle. Car. The plates are the same."

"Get the fuck out of there."

I got closer, stepping to the end of the floor. "They don't know I'm here. I'm telling you—" I cut off because that door that was never used *was just used.*

A woman and man came hurrying out.

"They're picking people up."

"Who?"

I squinted, trying to see as best as I could. "I couldn't tell. A woman and a man. His head was down, and he had a hand on her back. She stuck out more. She was thin. Tall. Black hair. She had a shawl wrapped around her, and she had silver heels. The heels were killer."

He was quiet again. "If I got you surveillance tapes, could you recognize those shoes?"

I was totally hearing the theme song for *Sex and the City* play in my head. "Oh yeah. I'd recognize them."

Eze was coming back inside. I heard the locks being disengaged.

"Are we staying?"

"No."

"Come on."

"No, Molly. First rule is if you even think your location is blown, you move."

"If they knew we were here, they wouldn't have returned to pick someone up from the same nightclub they just shot."

"Eze's signal might've gotten intercepted because they figured out he's one of your personal guards. I am not taking a chance on your life."

I had a whole argument prepared, but the door opened again and Ashton walked inside, all scowly and fierce looking, and everything melted inside of me.

He cared. It hit me hard in the middle of my chest. He really did care about me.

In my life, with how I grew up, sometimes it took a beat for that to sink in.

Him, Ashton, he was sinking in.

I hung up the phone and ran to him.

His eyes flickered once before he dropped his phone, his arms came out, and I was up in the air. He caught me, my mouth on his. I was kissing him because I wanted to let him know that I cared as much about him as he did me.

"What's this?"

I shook my head, smiling, and tightened my arms. "I care about you too."

His eyebrows dipped. A whole somber look came over him. His eyes darkened, dropping to my mouth, and soon his lips were back on mine.

I sighed, feeling the press of them, the taste as his tongue slid inside. He was kissing me and carrying me at the same time, but then we were in the bedroom, and he dropped me lightly to the bed. He straightened, walked to the closet, and brought back a bag to me. "Get your absolute must-haves in here. We leave in ten. We're going to where Trace and Jess are."

Ten minutes. Got it. I stood up, leaning over, and touched his lips with mine again.

I only needed eight.

CHAPTER

FORTY-FOUR

ASHTON

"She was right?" Trace joined me in the back of the kitchen where I was standing, a drink in hand but mostly watching Molly interact with Jess. They were on the other side of the kitchen, doing meal prep for dinner.

I nodded, indicating for us to head somewhere private.

He followed, stepping out onto the back three-season porch.

"Car was registered to the grandmother of a guy in Crispin Worthing's employment."

"Crispin?"

"Who we still have locked down at the compound. Avery connected when I told him the latest. He's making headway with both of the Worthings, but the biggest information they've given up is that Nicolai has a backer. One big major backer, bigger than anyone."

"That's not good." Trace asked, "Mauricio reached out himself about the shooting tonight?"

"He did. I told him what happened, sent him the registration, and he was fine. The numbers collaborated with their security cameras."

"Is he going to let Molly watch the security tapes?"

"They're being compiled into photos and will be sent over as soon as they're ready. He said they could have it all together within an hour."

He whistled. "That's fast. You told him we had eyes on his club?"

"I told him it was a coincidence, that I had a staff member driving by at the time of the shooting."

Trace snorted. "No way will he buy that. Mauricio is smart."

"I know, but Cole Mauricio doesn't want to war with us. He's brought up more business ventures he'd like to set up in New York."

"It's easier to work with the families you know than ones that are new and suddenly ambitious."

"And unpredictable."

"Still." Trace shot me a grin. "You know Mauricio likes us."

"He likes you more."

I glanced back, watching Molly as she was smiling and telling Jess about Octavia's customers. She was waving a potato skinner in the air. Jess took the weapon from her and gave her a bowl of romaine lettuce to tear apart instead. Jess took over the potatoes. Probably a smart choice.

"How's Jess doing?"

Trace looked where I was watching. "She's okay."

I kept watching the both of them. "They change things, don't they? Having them involved."

"They don't change who we are. They just make us better men."

Maybe he was right, but I felt different. "This war is going too long."

"Sometimes these can take years."

I gave him a look. Molly would not stay in hiding for years.

Trace knew what I was saying to him and inclined his head, sighing. "Jess's mom has to go back to the hospital. She insists on taking her."

"Have one of your men take her."

"She won't go. It's either Jess or no one. Jess knows this, so tomorrow afternoon, my woman is going to be exposed. I can send as many men as possible to protect her, but the truth is that if Nicolai Worthing has any smarts, he'll have her mom under watch and they'll report activity. He'll make their move when they're leaving."

"So let Jess take her and switch up how she gets home."

He looked my way. "He could hit her mom. Just be done with it, deliver a fatal blow because her mom refuses to go into hiding."

"He could, yes; but then we'd reciprocate by killing his cousins."

He nodded, another long sigh. "I know. Tit for tat. We've been hitting his businesses. Trying to hurt him that way."

"Which is working," I pointed out, and it was. "We made this decision to try to cut down on any extra lives lost, on both sides. Businesses. When they're empty. That was what we decided on. And he's losing his backers."

"But he's still coming at us."

He was right. We'd taken our losses—20 percent of our businesses had gotten hit by his men—but we'd taken out 80 percent of his. No matter what Trace was saying, we were winning.

"I got a call from his supplier today."

I grunted. "And?"

"He's open to switching partners."

That was a huge get. "When'd this call come in?"

"Twenty minutes ago. It's why I came to find you."

I studied him, seeing and feeling the shadows in his gaze. "What are you worried about?"

"Who he'll strike out against when he's on his last leg." Trace's gaze was directly on Jess. She had skinned the potatoes and was now slicing them up and putting them in a pot on the stove. "It's tomorrow. She's going out there, and I can't lock her in a room, like I'd love to. We've fought so much about it, but it's why I love her. Part of the reason. She loves and protects so hard. Damn anyone who tries to get in her way."

"Let me have a conversation with her."

He shot me a look. "Right. You just want to piss her off."

Nothing wrong with riling up the cop.

"That shows that you haven't changed *that* much."

I went back to watching Molly. Everything shifted in me. "Yeah. I have."

CHAPTER
FORTY-FIVE

MOLLY

"I'm going." I was following Ashton around the room the next morning.

"You're not."

Over dinner last night, a very, very late dinner, I learned that Jess was going with her mother to the hospital. Right then and there, I knew I had to go. I couldn't explain why. There was no rational logic for me to go, but I *had* to go. I just knew it. My gut was sparking something bad, and I didn't think it was the lettuce I forgot to wash.

I was the fixer in this group. It was my job to go, and he needed to understand this.

I was pleading my case this morning by just repeating that I was going because he'd stopped listening about the group dynamics and roles.

My plan of attack was to wear him down, and it was working.

He picked up a tie, putting it around his neck. "You're not. You have to look at the security photos from Octavia, remember?"

"I have to go. The photos can wait."

He finished looping the tie through the hole, then tightened it. "That look okay?"

It didn't. I stepped in, righting it. "So."

His hands went to my hips. "No."

"I'm going."

He moved aside to look in the mirror. "You're not. Thank you for this."

He was pulling on his suit jacket, and damn. Very business Mafia dangerous-esque. How did he look so good, and I was the one who got him?

Then I switched back to the mission. "I have to go."

He checked his phone, responded to a text, and opened our bedroom door, leading the way down the hallway, up the stairs (yes, we were in the basement, but we had a secret exit and it was so cool), and around to the kitchen. There were voices talking. I recognized Jess and Trace, but I followed him, not done. "Are you ignoring me?"

He entered the kitchen. "Morning, you guys."

Trace and Jess were hunched over a tablet on the far side of the main counter. "Hey." That was Trace. He frowned at me. I was still in my robe, because who wouldn't be if they had an option to wear a fuzzy robe that felt like heaven on you? "What's going on?"

I turned to Ashton. "I have to go. I'm not asking anymore."

He hit the brew button and turned sharp eyes on me. "Excuse me?"

I flushed but raised my chin up higher. "I'm telling you. Life or death—"

His eyes flashed. "Exactly. I'm not risking you."

"—if I don't go. I have to go." I was aware my argument wasn't the best.

"Go?" Trace moved closer to us.

Ashton looked his way. "Genius here—"

I smiled.

"—has decided she has to go with Jess today. Jess and her mom."

"What?" Jess's head popped back up from the tablet. Her frown was immediate. "No."

"Yes." I nodded. Firm.

"No way."

Trace looked at her, stepping back with his own coffee in hand.

The machine started brewing behind Ashton. "I don't want you to go. Jess doesn't want you to go. You're not going."

"Trace hasn't said anything."

Trace held his hand up. "I don't want you to go."

My gut was flaring again, twisting and churning like a tornado with IBS. "I have to go."

"Why?" That was from Jess.

I shook my head, lifting my shoulders up. "It's a feeling. I have to go. Like, if I don't go, I know something bad will happen."

"Have you gotten amnesia about all the times you were *not* around me? How many guns have been pointed at you?"

I flushed again. He was sorta correct about that. "It's a gut feeling, Ashton."

He sighed, grabbing a coffee cup and pouring coffee into it. He put the pot back, added some creamer to the coffee, then brought it over to me. He held it in front of him, stepping closer. His head inclined toward me, his eyes piercing. His mouth was in a firm line. He dropped his voice low, where I was feeling it in my belly. "I cannot lose you."

That same gut did a whole three-hundred-and-sixty spin from warmth. We'd come so far from him wanting to use me as bait. I reached for the coffee, but he wouldn't let it go.

I whispered, looking right back up at him, "Something bad will happen if I don't go."

His eyes flared up.

So did mine, and I pulled the coffee mug away from his hands, slowly, but determined. We were having a conversation within a conversation here. "You need to trust me with this one."

"No." But he whispered the word.

"Yes," I whispered back. "I don't get these feelings often, but when I do, they're always right."

"Ashton," Trace spoke up, a few yards away. "If she's having this feeling, then . . ."

I closed my eyes, praying Ashton would listen to him.

When I opened them, Ashton hadn't moved. He was still looking at me.

"I know you need a better reason than my gut, but that's all I have. I have to go."

"I don't want her to go." Jess's voice rang out, loud and authoritative.

Ashton closed his eyes now.

I angled my head around Ashton to see her.

She had folded her arms over her chest. "I'm only going because my mom is insisting on me. Trust me, if I could stay in hiding during this time, I would." Trace quickly looked her way, and she flicked her eyes to him. "I'm not a fan of this, but I know the dangers. I also know that if I ever saw Nicolai Worthing, that prick, in real life, I'd probably shoot him, but all that said, I agree with Ashton."

Ashton snorted.

"I agree with *this* prick here, that you shouldn't go. Stay here and remain safe."

"I'm not going to react to that because you are *that* important to me." Ashton sent her a short glare.

She rolled her eyes.

I still had work to do with them.

Ashton turned back to me, and since I was holding the coffee, he touched my hips, pulling me closer to him. Leaning down, he rested his forehead to mine and whispered, "I can't let you go."

"But—"

"If something happened to you? Don't you get it? If something happened to *you*?"

He was leaving the question hanging for me, and damn. That was a good tactic. Warmth swirled up in my chest, easing some of the bad gut sensation, and I was getting it. Me. I was important to him.

"Run and I'll burn the world down for you." I remembered his words. A tingle went through me.

"Three uncles. My grandfather. *Not* you." He moved his head, his lips pressing the softest kiss to my forehead. "Not you."

My throat closed up. A different memory was coming to me. I lifted my head to look him in the eyes. His mother. My mother. We never talked about why he wanted the truth out, and I'd forgotten until now. How could I have forgotten about that? Maybe my own mother issues? I didn't know. I didn't like thinking about her, but that was another layer between us, and I felt it pulsating.

I sighed. "Okay. Fine, but if I'm not going today, then you need to have it out."

Ashton straightened, frowning. "What are you talking about?"

I nodded at him and Jess. "You two. Both of you. Neither of you will tell me what happened, but I know something happened. What was it?"

"Now's not the time—" Jess started to say.

"So when is?" I clipped out.

"Molly."

I held a hand up, stepping back from Ashton.

Trace wasn't saying a word.

"There's a group dynamic here. Between all of you. I'm late to the group, but I'm here. I know my role. I know all your roles. Do you?" I gestured to Ashton. "He already knows. I've rambled about it to him, but I'm serious."

"Molly." Jess was already shaking her head.

"I mean it, Jess. You are going to marry that man by you. He is in the middle of a war with the man next to me. There's strained history between you two, and it needs to be resolved. Today. Now. Before you leave because I *do* have a bad feeling."

She didn't say anything.

Ashton wasn't either.

Trace was watching Jess with a pensive look.

"What happened? What was so horrible—"

"I tortured her."

My head whipped to Ashton, to his sudden declaration, and he was watching me back, waiting. Waiting for what? I frowned. "Torture?" I whispered. "You tortured her?"

"It was that night when I came to get her at Easter Lanes." His darkness. I felt it again, but my own was pushing up. The darkness that I liked to pretend wasn't there but was, and I knew it, he knew it, and he accepted it.

He accepted me.

"Run and I'll burn the world down for you."

He fell silent after that, but I was still waiting for more information. More of an explanation. He wasn't giving it to me. "You're going to drop that bomb and not say anything else?"

"We had a mole. I needed to make sure it wasn't her." His jaw clenched. His eyes were blazing before he banked them. A wall slid back into place. I felt the draft by how cold he'd become. He was reverting to his default setting.

My own jaw clenched.

Trace was still watching Jess. I could only shake my head. "You don't have anything to add? He's your best friend."

Trace shifted his attention to me, barely blinking. "He and I have resolved things."

"He put me in the hospital."

Trace echoed. "I put him in the hospital."

Jess wasn't looking at anyone. Her head was down, and her hands were opening and closing into fists. "And you?"

She lifted her head now, her eyes pained. Haunted. "There's nothing that can be said after what he did to me."

I moved toward her. "You're just cool letting him hang out to dry? Between him and his boy?"

I was focused on Jess, but I sensed Trace's head jerking to mine.

Jess's eyes widened, just a fraction. Some blood drained from her face, and she said through gritted teeth, "Not really the best time to go down that memory lane, Molly. Especially considering where I'm going and what news I might be getting about my mom's health. Also, especially considering your 'bad' feeling. Why are you pushing this?"

"What do you need from him?"

She flinched, warily. "What do you mean?"

"What do you need from him to make it better?"

She opened her mouth, then closed it. She shrugged. "He's already doing it."

"I am?"

She didn't look his way but lowered her head. "You're looking for Kelly's killer. Words can't undo what you did." She lifted her head, *now* seeing him. She barely flinched this time. "I know why you did what you did, but you did it to *me*. And you did it behind Trace's back, and even that I get, but no words can take away that damage. You've already laid the groundwork. You apologized. You meant it, and now, doing is the best way to heal anything. I'd let you torture me infinity times over if it meant you found Kelly's killer just once. I *loved* her. She was my family. Mine, and someone took her from me. Justin was a good man too. They took both of their futures. They took her." Her words grew thick. A sob came out. "Her kids would've been my nieces, nephews. I might've not seen them, but I would've known about them. I would've *known* she was happy and had finally,

God, finally, got her happily ever after. They took that from her, so you and me, I don't care anymore. I just want to find who killed her. Find them, and we're solid."

"Trust me," Ashton clipped out. "I *am* working on it."

"We know." Trace moved to Jess, a hand curling over her shoulder. She reached up, grabbing it. He pulled her into his chest. "She's slowly letting it go, but he didn't know that." He looked Ashton's way. "We'll be fine. All of us. I believe that."

The two were sharing a look. It was heated and long, and somehow, when Ashton nodded, blinking rapidly, I was thinking something good had happened here.

"I don't need the words," Jess said to me, holding tight to Trace's hand. "Words are empty to me. Never put much stock in them, but actions. That takes time, and"—she looked Ashton's way—"it's happening. I'm okay with that."

He jerked his head in another nod, blinking again before focusing on me. "How about you?"

"Me?"

"You found out I tortured your friend. Are you going to judge me?" Those eyes of his, so dark and so defiant right now, but I knew better. I knew him better.

I shifted on my feet. "Are you sorry you did it?"

"Yes," he grated out.

I already knew my answer, and he should've known it, too, but fine. I'd string it out. "Will you do it again?"

He frowned. "Not her."

Trace snorted.

Jess shot him a look.

Ashton ignored both of them. His gaze was focused on me. His words were for me alone. "What else?"

He was asking what else I needed to know. What *did* I need? I needed him to know me better. "You should know better," I chided, softly. His eyes flashed, but I added, "If you could do it again, would you have—"

"Never." His answer came so fast after my question. "I would never do it again. There was a time I thought I would." He shifted his gaze to Trace. "A time when I was full of self-righteousness about what was 'best' for the families, but that was before I understood." His gaze slid from Trace to Jess, then to me. An extra fire was lit there, burning at me. "Before I got it."

I felt that burning in my stomach.

"You said I should know better, but I do, and I need you to know this." He said, swiftly, "If Trace ever touched *you*? Took *you*? Put *you* in a chair? Made you feel like you were drowning over and over again? If he dared even consider doing any of that to you, and I'd—"

We shared a look, and a pulse went between us.

"You're no longer the woman I'm going to use to end this war. You're the reason for this war because if anyone hurts you, touches you, I'll kill them. Are you hearing me? All of them."

He cut himself off, before pulling his gaze away. He said to Trace, "You showed restraint when you put me in the hospital."

"You're right. I did. *You're* welcome."

He shifted to Jess. "I am sorry that I hurt *you*."

She drew in a deep breath, blinking as her eyes grew wet, before she nodded. "Thank you."

He held her gaze for a second before shifting his attention my way. His eyes gentled. "Of the two of us, Trace is the better man."

That burning was back inside of me, and rising, spreading throughout me. "You should know better." I said it again. Softly.

His jaw clenched, and his tone gentled. "You should be judging me."

I shook my head. "I'm not built that way. Of the two of us, *I'm* the one who'll do something stupid. Remember?"

The corner of Ashton's mouth curved up. "Sometimes I like when you do stupid things. I get to be the good guy." He sent Trace a look before closing the distance between us. He pulled me to him. His hand slid to the back of my neck, and he dipped down, his mouth finding mine. He whispered there, just for me to hear, "I will *never* lose you. I refuse."

To a girl like me, those words had my fuzzies all aflutter. My job was done.

There was an extra peace among the group.

CHAPTER FORTY-SIX

MOLLY

Matt was outside my bedroom door, and I'd blasted my fan, telling him not to bother me for a few hours. I was going to take a much-needed nap.

All my craziness. All the times I reacted to situations and ended up making things worse. Most of those times, I hadn't made a conscious decision. I'd only felt the switch happening, and then bam, I was reacting and doing stupid things to put my loved ones in danger.

This was different. I was *choosing* to do something stupid, but I was doing it to save someone I loved.

So, I snuck out using the secret exit.

Ashton shouldn't have told me about it because it was going to be my personal front door. Also, it was just plain awesome because there was a tunnel that went under a whole other building. It came out to a side street, but because no one thought I knew about it, and I doubted Ashton thought I'd use it, I totally used it.

The same gray sedan that we'd used to pick up my dad was waiting for me behind a dumpster. I ran over. "Go, go, go." I threw myself into the back seat, falling down over candy wrappers and chip bags.

Pialto squeaked from the front seat but gunned the accelerator and we were off. "Molly Easter! You gave me a heart attack."

I pulled out a Doritos bag and looked inside. There were still chips inside. "How old is this bag?"

"Which one?"

I sat up, just barely, plopping my chin on the back of his seat in the middle section, and hung the bag over the edge of the seat. "These guys."

He glanced at it and lifted up his shoulder. "No clue, but I wouldn't eat any."

I tossed it over my shoulder, keeping my head up, my chin on the seat.

He grinned at me over his shoulder before hunching back over, his ball cap pulled low. He kept driving. "It's good to see you, boss."

I laughed. Boss. It was good to hear that. "You too."

He laughed, holding a fist back toward me.

I pounded it with mine. We both pretended to have it explode. Although, probably not the best idea considering my apartment door. I grimaced.

"I feel like I'm springing you from jail."

"You kinda are."

"We're going to the hospital?"

I nodded, getting serious and checking my phone. "Jess's mom has an appointment there in an hour."

"What's the plan?"

I cringed.

Pialto saw the cringe. "Oh, no. Tell me you have a plan. You're putting yourself in danger for—"

"I have a plan!" I didn't have a plan. Or, well, my plan was to get us inside the hospital, and we should be good. There were so many visitors walking around; no one would think to raise an alarm about us.

So, yeah. I had a plan.

"What is it? I'm risking my neck here too. Your man is dangerous and deadly, and word on the street is that he enjoys being cruel to his enemies." Pialto kept tightening and retightening his hold on the steering wheel. He began muttering in Spanish.

"Hey." I touched his shoulder. "I won't let Ashton do anything. I promise."

"And what if something happens to you?" He craned his neck around, enough to hiss, "*You won't be around to save my hide!*"

"I will haunt him."

He went back to muttering in Spanish. "Not helping, Mols. But it's good to see you."

I smothered a laugh and fell back, but moved my legs up so I wasn't lying across the seat. I was sitting, slumped down. "You too. I've missed you guys. How's Sophie?"

"She's gonna be pissed we didn't call her too."

My heart tightened up. He was right, but that was another person in danger. "When we get there, you drop me off. I'll go from there."

"Yeah, right. We'll argue about that when we get there."

He was right. One fight at a time.

———

Jess's mom's appointment was in the clinic part of the hospital, but we just needed to get inside. That was the first step. The other part of my plan was ditching Pialto because he would argue about going with me, but I didn't need to put even more people in danger. I was following the guideline that if someone was with me, and I was doing something stupid, chances were high they'd have a gun pointed at them. Because of that, the very first time he stopped the car, I darted out.

"Hey!" he yelled through the window.

I flashed him a smile and two thumbs up, then took off, heading for the ER entrance because a car had just pulled up. A guy ran around, yelling for help, and wham bam, I was there. "I can help. What's going on?"

He gave me a cursory look before opening the door. "My wife's in labor."

Got it. I knew nothing about the birth process. "How long ago did her water break?"

"Two minutes."

We both bent in, helping his wife out. I yelled over my shoulder, "We need a wheelchair!"

"You got her? I need to park the car."

"I got her."

"Okay. Here." He gave me a bag, pressed a kiss to her forehead. "I'll be right back, honey."

She was in the middle of screaming but grabbed his hand and squeezed. Hard. I thought I heard a snap before he extricated himself, his whole face twisted up, before he went back to his car.

The nurse was bringing a chair over. "What's going on?"

"Her water broke two minutes ago." *Act like you're supposed to be there. Act like you're supposed to be there.* That was on repeat in my head, and the nurse glanced at me once, a frown on her face, before the woman started screaming again. "Okay, okay." She took over as we got her in the chair.

I followed with the bag.

The security guys waved us in, but they did make me step through the metal detectors. Once I was cleared, I picked up her bag and hurried after where the nurse had gone.

They put her in a room.

I put her bag down and patted her hand. "I'm going to tell your husband where you are."

I moved, going to the left, and kept walking. I was inside the inner sanctum. I could make my way around now. That was until I got to the stair door and opened it, planning on heading down to the basement. Except Pialto was there.

I screamed, then clamped a hand over my own mouth. I swatted at him, stepping inside. "What are you doing?"

"What do you think I'm doing?" he hissed back. "I broke you out. You're my responsibility until you're back and safe. If a bullet goes your way, I'm jumping in the way."

I gave him a look, but that was kinda sweet of him. "No, you won't. Take your grandma's car back before she finds it gone."

"No."

"Pialto."

"Molly." We both had our arms folded over our chests, but I couldn't argue with him long. The appointment was in ten minutes. "I have to go."

I started for the basement.

Pialto was right behind me. "We have to go."

"Agh. Go home." I kept going down.

"Agh back. You go home."

I pushed open the door, turning left for where the clinic offices were. He was right next to me.

I shot him a look. He shot one back.

There were people coming toward us, but we could be down here. I'd been down here other times when my dad had a broken nose or a busted rib. There was a room where we could heat up our own food. It was a secret room, but I'd been there enough, I knew people could use it.

We went past a bunch of nurses, their lunch coolers in hand. None of them paid us any attention.

I *so* had this in the bag.

"Do you know where you're going?"

"I—" We turned the corner, and there was a wall. There hadn't been a wall there the last time I was down here. "Uh." I pushed on the door to the stairs. "We're heading up."

Up and to the left. All the way to the left. I was leading us, moving along the hall and through doors that didn't look like they would set off an alarm until—success. We were in the back—I was so dumb. I looked up. There were signs to the clinic area, and who was looking for us? No one. No one had a clue we weren't supposed to be here. I'd made this all more complicated than it needed to be.

Pialto pointed up. "That says clinic. Which one is your friend's appointment at?"

I opened my mouth . . . and closed it. I had no clue.

But I looked at my phone and squealed because we were going to miss them. I took off running.

"What are we doing?" Pialto was back to hissing.

"I don't know. Just look for Jess, okay?"

"Jess Montell?"

"Yes."

"We're here following your cop friend?" Still hissing.

I was looking in each clinic as we went past them. "Yes. Why?" Also, "She was a parole officer."

"I don't care. She scares me even more than your man."

"Then go home!"

"No!"

An older lady came out of the bathroom and gave us a dumb-founded look as we passed her, both running, both hissing at each other.

"Agh!" Pialto tackled me, his arms coming around me and pushing me to a doorway. There was a big post right next to us.

"What?" I tried to see around him. "What is it?"

"I found your friend."

I perked up. "Great! Where?"

He let me go, edging back a step and peeking around the corner. "They went into the oncology—ooooh. Oh no."

Oncology?

No . . .

I stepped around him, and could see Jess with her mom at the front desk. Jess's guards were with her. One was coming back toward the door.

I squeaked, grabbing Pialto and moving him back.

I scanned the entryway, too, and saw two more of Trace's guards there, but they weren't looking toward us. They were looking out.

I moved back in, almost smashing Pialto against the door behind us. "What is it?"

I peeked back. That one guard was outside the door, but he was on his phone.

I moved in when he began to look our way.

"I don't know," I answered Pialto.

"You wanted to come and find them for this appointment. Right?"

I nodded.

"They're right there. Go and join them."

I shook my head. "It doesn't feel right." If I joined them, Jess would make a call and send me home. I was still having this bad feeling, twisting in a whole knot.

"What are you going to do? We can't stand here the whole time. This door will eventually open."

I turned, assessing the door. It was a janitor's closet. "I think we're good for a while."

"Oh. Yeah. Probably."

We waited.

I had no clue what I was doing, and after thirty minutes I was thinking this was all a foolish idea. That's when I heard a voice clear behind us.

I froze, first thinking it was Ashton. He found us! But no. It was Nurse Sloane.

She was standing in full view of Jess's guard. Her hands went to her hips, and she cocked her head to the side. "What are you doing?"

"Uh . . ."

Pialto jumped out into the hallway and thrust out his arm. "I was thinking this might be cancer. What do you think?" He pointed to one of his moles, and to his credit, it had gotten bigger in the last year. This was not a new conversation or even one in jest. He really was asking her opinion.

She frowned. "What?" She motioned to me. "I'm talking to her. What are you doing here?"

I flattened myself back against the door. "We're here to look out for Jess."

"Jess?" Nurse Sloane paled, her face looking haunted for a brief second. "Jess Montell?"

Pialto chanced a look. His shoulders slumped down as he exhaled a deep breath. "He's not there."

Oh—what?! I jerked my head out. He wasn't there, but the other two guards were still outside. Where was this guard?

That churning feeling was back. Something was off. Something was about to happen.

No, no, no.

I started to run toward the oncology clinic.

"Molly! What are you doing?"

"Get back, Nurse Sloane."

"What?"

I reached for the door, wrenching it open. I could see the other guard who had gone inside with them. He was down the corridor, standing outside a door, and he looked right at me. His eyebrows went up. He reached for his radio.

I looked back. The other two guards were inside. One stayed. The other was coming.

I ignored all reason and raced past the front desk, past the nurses now yelling at me, and sprinted for him. "Your other guy is gone."

He frowned at me, but his radio was crackling. A voice came out. I couldn't make out what he was saying, but it made him stiffen.

"Go. I knew something bad would happen. Something's wrong."

He didn't go. He opened the office door.

Jess and her mom were inside, a female doctor on the other side of the desk.

Jess saw me. "Molly?"

The guard spoke. "Derek is gone from his post. We need to leave."

"But—" her mom started to protest.

The doctor's eyebrows were permanently locked together, her gaze darting between everyone.

Jess's gaze went to me, but she reached for her mom. "Mom, we need to go."

"No. He probably went to piss—"

"Mom!"

"Mrs. Montell." I was having none of this. "In the space of a little over a month, I've had four guns pointed at me, one directly against my head. My danger radar has been fine tuned. You need to listen to your daughter. If she says you have to go, trust me: you have to go."

Jess muttered a curse but pulled her mom up. "We have to go. This is no joke."

"Jess—"

"Go!" Jess yelled, pointing behind her.

The guard had moved back and motioned in the direction opposite to where I'd come from. "We leave that way."

Jess's eyebrows dipped down. "What are you talking about?"

"New protocol. A vehicle will be out there waiting for you."

Jess spared him a look, her frown swinging my way, but she moved her mother in front of her. They hurried past the doctors and nurses, heading straight for the exit. Their guard was behind them, herding them forward, and that's when it hit me.

He didn't care about me.

I was still at their doctor's office. There'd been no order for me to join them. Nothing like that. He was completely focused on Jess and her mom, and that wouldn't happen. This guy's boss was Trace, but Ashton was his partner.

A normal guard would include me.

I knew then. I just did. "Hey!"

This guy shouldn't have forgotten about me. I was just as important as Jess. If Ashton found out he left me behind? The torture he'd do to that guy? Yeah. Something was very, very wrong here. It was this dude.

The guard stopped, looking at me, his frustration evident on his face.

Jess stopped, too, shifting so she could see me better.

I held a hand up, and understanding dawned on her face at the same time it registered on his face. They both clued in that he had fucked up, only paying attention to the "mark." He cursed, reaching for his weapon, but Jess made her move first.

I took off, sprinting for them.

He tried pulling his gun free of his holster, but Jess was literally on him. She was fighting to yank the gun away from him, but she looked up and saw me barreling toward them, and instead of struggling for the gun, she let it go and grabbed onto him.

She was holding him in place.

He looked at her, confused, but then I was there, and I launched in the air.

I hit him with everything I had in me. Since Jess had held him in place, he went down. The gun flew down the hallway, but fuck this guy.

I was up and scrambling.

He went for the gun. I went for him.

Fuck him. Fuck this. Fuck everyone.

I was totally and completely embracing that darkness in me, because right now, this guy was the same as the guy at the gas station who'd put a gun against my head, the same as the guy who'd pointed a gun at me in my cousin's apartment, the same as the guys who'd chased me in traffic, and I was not letting them win.

Never.

I would be standing at the end. I declared it. Every damn time.

Knowing that, remembering all of that, I accepted the last part of me that I'd been hiding from, the part that helped connect me to Ashton because he had it too.

I reached out, and slammed my foot down on his arm, then pivoted and delivered the best soccer kick straight to his face. If it'd been a ball, it would've sailed halfway down the field. I was sure of it.

I wanted to do it again.

His head snapped back from the force.

"Hey! Stop. Stop right there."

I twisted around.

Jess had the guy's gun, but she had it up and pointing at Pialto, who was running for us.

"*No!*" I reached for her, then froze. I didn't want to set off her shooting Pialto. "That's my friend. He works for me."

Pialto made it to us, and gasped, panting. "We—" Pant. "Have to—" Pant. He tried to point back. "That way. Bad guys."

"What?" Jess clipped out.

That churning feeling was back in my gut, and it was swirling, snarling, flipping upside down. I felt it rising, almost overpowering me. We had to go, and we had to go now!

I yelled, "That way." I pointed in the complete opposite direction of anywhere.

"What?" Jess looked my way.

"*Move!*" I screamed.

"Wha—" But I shot past her, leading the way.

She cursed.

Her mom kept asking what was happening, and I heard, "Here, Mrs. Montell. I got you."

I looked back. Pialto had Jess's mom hanging over his shoulder, his face was determined. "Go! Lead the way."

"Uhhh. Okay!" I jumped, turning and racing anywhere but where they expected us to be.

Jess was right behind me. Pialto and Mrs. Montell after her.

We wove through hallways and offices until I found another exit door. It was small and off to the side, and it looked like where nurses would go for smoke breaks. I took it, shoving it open, and we were running down a small ramp of stairs.

We were somehow between three parking lots and another building.

"Where are we going?" Jess ran next to me.

"I'm winging it."

"That's obvious."

I was looking around and saw an SUV slowly casing the parking lot nearest the hospital. "There. We have to get down."

Jess looked, saw them, and cursed. "They haven't seen us yet." She turned to Pialto. "Get down."

He did, or tried. Mrs. Montell was slapping his ass, but he was ignoring her.

"Mom, stop."

"You stop! This guy's bony shoulder is pressing on my bladder. I'm two seconds from drenching him in piss."

"Oh, god. No." Pialto's face turned a bit green at the idea.

"Mom," Jess clipped out. "Rein it in, or we're dead. Get that in your head."

"You're—" Mrs. Montell tried to twist around to see her daughter, and she did, but whatever she saw stopped her words.

"It's like Bear and Leo all over again. This is real shit, Mom. Stop it."

Her mother's mouth pressed into a firm line, and she nodded, visibly swallowing at the same time.

Pialto swore in relief but still tried to hunch over. "We have to keep moving. I ran in because two other mofos came in and shot your guards. I was screeching like a banshee, but they didn't know who I was. They didn't shoot me. They could've, and they will now if we *don't get going*."

Jess swallowed. "We have to get moving."

"Agh. Agh. Agh." I didn't know why I was saying that, but it made me feel better. I kept saying it as we moved forward in the parking lot.

An SUV began to back out of a slot but hit its brakes when the driver saw us.

She had reversed right in front of me. Dr. Nea Sandquist. Her window was between us. She rolled it down, looking at the rest of us. "What are you guys doing?"

"Nea." Jess moved forward, looking in her vehicle. "We need a ride out of here. Will you help?"

Nea, not Dr. Sandquist, looked at Jess's gun but said, "Sure. Yeah. Is that your mom?"

"Hi, Dr. Sandquist." Her mom tried to wave but couldn't and hit at Pialto's back instead.

"Great." Jess reached for the back door and opened it, motioning for Pialto, who was trying to snarl over his back. "Put my mom here."

He did, saying, "Gladly."

"Hey!" Her mom held up a closed fist at him.

Jess said, "Mom, you need to lay flat. Okay? Keep hiding so those men don't see you."

Her mom nodded, now quiet. But her fist was still in the air. I think it was up more on principle against the situation. Who'd want to be thrown over a bony shoulder and bounced around as they ran for their lives?

Pialto rolled his eyes, returning to my side.

Jess shut the door and went to the back. "Can you open?"

Nea looked at me but didn't say anything, hitting a button. The back lifted. Jess motioned for Pialto and me. "Come on. You guys hide back here."

I didn't move at first, looking back at Nea.

She seemed flustered, but I said quickly, "Thank you."

"Yeah." She blinked a few times. "Sure. Yeah."

"Molly," Pialto hissed.

I followed him. We both got in, sitting with our backs to the sides and our feet toward each other. Jess shut the door, her entire face just kick-ass and in charge. She went and got in somewhere up front. "Okay, Nea. Drive out the south lot. They weren't looking for us back there."

Nea listened, driving off.

Pialto was studying me. "You should look terrified."

I wasn't. That was the thing.

I couldn't explain it. I wasn't even going to try with him, but something clicked with me. I hadn't reacted this time. I'd known the consequences. I'd been told not to go, but I *had* to go.

I'd chosen it this time, and somehow, I felt calm inside.

Or calmer.

I accepted something inside of me, something I'd been fighting, and it was there. It was a part of me. And because I was accepting it, I didn't feel the switch in me. It was . . . I couldn't say it was gone, but I didn't feel it.

Huh.

CHAPTER
FORTY-SEVEN

MOLLY

Nea drove for a while. She and Jess were talking, but we couldn't hear much in the back. My phone was buzzing, and I answered, already knowing it was Ashton.

"We're in the back of a vehicle."

"I'm aware."

Oh, boy. His voice was already grim. He was not happy.

"I'll call when we've stopped—"

"We've been following you for the last three blocks. Tell Nea to pull over in the nearest parking lot."

"What?" I looked up, peering through the window, and there he was. Ashton was glaring at me from the front seat, right next to Elijah, whose mouth was twitching. "How'd you find us?"

"I put a tracker on your phone, remember? Tell her to turn off."

"Oh, okay." I twisted back around. "Nea! We have a ride. Pull over."

"What?" Both she and Jess said that at the same time.

I motioned behind us. "The cavalry found us."

"What?"

Jess cursed. "There's a parking lot. Go there."

She hit the turn signal, moving over, and once she had stopped, vehicles swarmed us. Literally. One went in front. Two went on both sides. Ashton's car pulled up behind us. The definition of circling the wagons happened in real time, and it was awesome.

Elijah went over to where Jess's mom was trying to get out of the vehicle.

Nea and Jess were both out when the back door swept up. I didn't get the option of climbing down. Ashton swooped in, his arms winding around me, and he lifted me clear out of the SUV. I gave in. My time of following my gut was over. Ashton was here. I was in his arms, and I was relinquishing control. My arms and legs wrapped around him, and he walked away, returning to his own SUV.

"Ash—" That was Nea, trying to speak to him.

He ignored her.

The back door opened, and he got in, with me in his arms. It was shut behind us, and as soon as we were in, Elijah was back behind the wheel. "Go!" Ashton barked.

"Jess—"

"She won't leave her mother, and I'm not waiting."

Elijah hit the accelerator, and off we went, but as we left, I looked up.

Nea was standing in front of her opened door, an odd look in her eyes. Hurt, but anger glimmered there as she pressed her mouth tight. I looked past her, getting a glimpse of her bag and some other items on her front seat. Then we were past, zooming out of there.

"Jess." I moved my head back, angling to see Ashton. "Pialto."

"They'll be in the next vehicle." He pulled me back to him, his head burrowing into my neck. A shudder rippled through him, and oh man, oh man. I tightened my hold on him, burying my head into his neck, and he just held me, rocking me back and forth.

His words came out against my neck, mumbled. "They would've taken you."

"No."

"They had seven men in place. They killed four of Trace's men."

"Only two."

"What?"

"The one guard outside the clinic was gone. I went inside, and that guard tried to lead them into a trap. He forgot about me. That's what tipped me off, but he was in on it."

Ashton was studying me, then cursed and pulled me back to him. "Jesus."

"I wasn't in danger."

"You put *yourself* in danger this time."

"I know, but—"

"Don't do that again." His words were fierce, and he pulled back to see me again. His hands framed my face. "Please. Don't. Just, don't. *Please*."

Oh. Wow.

I was nodding, and I held on to him. "I won't. I promise. I won't." I meant it. The switch needed to retire, or it had retired. I wasn't sure, but: "I just needed to go this last time. I promise. It's the last time, but Ashton." I framed his face with my hands back. "I'm okay. Really."

"You have to stop doing that shit. I mean it."

I nodded. "I will. I promise."

He studied me for a beat. "Pinkie?"

I flashed a grin. "Pinkie."

A whole shudder went through him.

I was in the arms of a guy who was my next chapter. Whether it was good, long, bad, brief, or whatever, wherever Ashton planned to take me, he was the next chapter. Everything after would be affected because of this time right now.

A lump in my throat doubled in size.

He lifted his head, like he couldn't stop looking at me. He lifted a hand, tracing a finger down the side of my head, picking up a strand of hair and tucking it behind my ear. "This feels like something more than just me freaking out over you."

I didn't have the words because I couldn't explain how this whole event was sweeping through my body, where I knew I was changed from today on, and he was part of that change. It was deep and painful but beautiful, and I felt like a crying, molted butterfly. Not that I was flapping my wings for the first time, but that I'd remembered they were there and I was fluttering them, remembering there was a thing called love. I was on that path, walking toward it.

That's what was going on inside me, but I didn't want him to look at me like a freak, so I just leaned in and grazed my lips over his. "Thank you."

He kissed me back. "For what?"

That lump. It was so strong and powerful. "For you being you."

His eyes went dark, but he nodded. "I care, more than I want to, but I do."

I grinned, feeling some of my tears hanging on over my nose.

He laughed shortly. "Most women wouldn't be happy about that statement." He reached up, wiping those tears away too.

I shrugged. "I'm different. I get it." I settled back over him, getting comfortable.

His arms tightened around me. "That's a good thing?"

I just smiled. "I'm a molted butterfly."

His arms went stiff. "What?"

I patted his hand. "You're not supposed to understand."

His arms relaxed. I felt him nudging my neck, but then his phone began blowing up.

He answered. "Is this the other side? You're calling to tell me you're seeing me there?"

Now I tensed, half twisting my head so I could see his phone.

He pulled it from his ear and put it on speaker.

Detective Jake Worthing's voice came over, all gravelly. "Dr. Nea Sandquist is saying she was forced at gunpoint by your woman, Jess Montell, Jess's mother, and another male."

The whole air in the vehicle changed. It went from being beautiful and emotional to being charged and deadly. Ashton didn't move, but the hairs on the back of my neck stood up. He was close to doing something dangerous. I eased back so I could see his face better.

His eyes were like ice. The old Ashton was stepping forward. The one whose reputation was how *very* cruel he could be. "You know that's not true."

"We're aware. We have security cameras backing up what Officer Montell is saying. She had the weapon in her hand, but it was never pointed at Nea Sandquist. She never issued a threat. Her mother is backing up her statement, as did Mr. Pialto. I'm calling to see if Molly corroborates that statement."

"I do. We never threatened her. Jess asked if Nea would help us. Why would she say that?"

"Hello, Molly."

I gave the phone an impish smile. "Hi, Detective."

Ashton's hand dropped to my leg, and his thumb was rubbing over it in a slow caress.

"I'm calling to let you know that's what she is saying. It's up to you to figure out the reason."

Ashton's eyes closed; the bags under his eyes seemed a bit more pronounced. "She's scared."

"Possibly. I was under the impression the doctor and Jess were on friendly terms." Detective Worthing paused before he added, "I'm also letting you know that I received a phone call minutes ago. A couple phone calls. The first was that whoever was my cousin's backer, the publicity from the shooting at the hospital was too much for them. They're pulling out. The other phone call was from my family members. It's been decided that Nicolai will no longer be speaking for our family."

Ashton's entire body relaxed. An entire shudder went through him, and I tipped even more into him from the sudden shift. "So that's it. It's done."

"I told you I'd see you on the other side. Ashton, I'm letting you know that they've appointed me in his place."

Ashton lifted his head back up from the seat rest. He was nodding at the phone. "You're taking over?"

"I will be leaving the New York City Police Department."

Ashton snorted. "You gave Jess such shit for choosing Trace. How is you choosing family over your career any different?"

Jake sighed. "The bigger irony not lost on me is that it's *you* giving me that statement. Your last free information from me: my cousin is not going to go down lightly. This is a warning. Be prepared because I'm sure he'll still try to throw a Hail Mary."

"Jake."

"What?"

"Who were your cousin's backers?"

The detective didn't answer, not right away. "Honestly? I'm not sure. They only worked with him, but who would find it too threatening when there's a shooting in a public hospital?"

"Someone big. Public."

"Yes."

"Someone legal." Ashton's jaw clenched. "You have a theory?"

"I do, and if I'm right, we're all lucky that they pulled out." Jake ended the call on his end before we could say anything.

A slight smile tugged at the corner of his mouth. Both his hands settled on my legs.

"Does that mean what I think it means?"

He nodded, the slight smile forming to a real smile. "It's over. The war is over, but I still want you to look through the photographs Mauricio sent."

I nodded. "I will. It's not over until he's *gone* gone."

"It's mostly over. Jake won't push to come into the city like Nicolai was doing. That was Jake saying he's heading back to Maine and focusing there, and that's even if he keeps with the family business. Knowing Detective Worthing how I do, I'd bet he'll go in, say he's with the program, but he'll end them from the inside. He'll make that family go legal."

"He was on the pay from you?"

Ashton nodded. "He was, but Jake walked the line. He never totally stepped over. I was aware of what he was doing. He gave me information that would help me against our enemies, against guys who did worse things than my family did. He picked the lesser of the two evils, and he knew that I knew what he was doing. It was an unspoken thing between us."

I was starting to see that.

"Jake's the reason Justin worked for us."

I frowned.

Ashton wasn't really saying that to me. It felt like he was saying it just to say it. "I knew another one of their cousins, Vivianna. She made a call one night. Asked if I'd give her cousin a job. She was doing a reach out, trying to see me. But it was Jake's call if his brother was hired as a bartender, and considering I had him on the payroll, I needed to know the parameters for this hiring. He said yes. He said it wouldn't look right to his colleagues if his brother had an option to work at Katya and *not* take the job so . . ." He looked at me, a haunted expression in there. "In a way, because of Jake, because of their other cousin, because of me, we're the reasons Kelly is dead."

"Ashton."

His phone began to ring once again, and seeing it was Trace, he put it on speaker right away. "Hello, brother." His voice was hoarse.

Trace asked, "Are you guys okay?"

Ashton didn't answer that, instead asking, "You have your woman?"

"I do, but uh, that's not why I'm calling."

Jess's voice came on next, saying, "We're getting married!"

I gasped, taking the phone from Ashton. "What? When? Where? How did this happen?"

"Today. Just now." Jess sounded happy. "We got the news that my mom has cancer. Then we were almost taken, and who knows what would've happened. Now, in a weird way, my mom has to go into hiding with us, and it feels right. What Molly did is what Kelly would do. No matter the guns blazing, Kelly always wanted her happily ever after. She would ignore everyone's warnings and follow her gut. I'm doing this for Kelly. I'm done waiting. I want to get married. Now."

"Now?" Ashton leaned forward, blinking some of the ghosts away.

"Or as soon as we can. Do you know of a place that would be safe?"

Ashton and I shared a look. A part of me was gleeful, but the other part was worried. The bad guy was out there, the real bad guy, and my gut knew.

He was still coming.

CHAPTER

FORTY-EIGHT

ASHTON

"Thanks for letting us do it all here."

I was fixing Trace's tie as he was doing his cuff links. He was talking about my family's compound, and I grunted, stepping back. "It's the least I can do. The Worthing family stepped back and pushed Nicolai out, but he's still out there. This place seemed the obvious choice so we're all safe while being ridiculous and having a wedding."

"Has Molly had time to look over those pictures from Octavia?"

"She started. I brought them in case she had time later. They're in my office."

"But she's not recognized the woman?"

I shook my head. "Not yet. She will, though."

He cleared his throat. "Thanks again for letting us do it here. I mean it. I'm aware that this was your safe place if there was a world apocalypse."

I paused, remembering how happy Jess had been, how Molly was trying to "fix" the group. I shrugged. "It's the least I can do for you guys."

"Tell the truth. You're already scouting locations for a new compound, aren't you?"

I shot him a grin, feeling some of the tension ease from my shoulders. "Maybe."

He barked out a laugh before moving closer to the mirror to brush off any remaining lint on his shoulder. "Demetri told me how Sloane looked when he told her she needed to be blindfolded in order to come to my wedding."

"Jess got tight with her and the doc? Nea Sandquist."

He nodded. "With Jess's mom's health, both of them have been there for her. Molly likes Sloane too."

Trace had been waiting for the perfect time. He'd had the ring for months, but somehow it seemed fitting that Jess was the one who proposed. Now everyone was at my family's compound. Trace. Me. Demetri and Pajn were ushers. The other guests included Marco, who was Remmi's date. Molly. Pialto and Sophie. Jess's mother. There'd been a question if her old partner should come, but it was decided a more intimate dinner with Val and Officer Reyo would be more appropriate.

"Nea apologized for what she said to the cops, took it back, said she was scared."

"As long as Jess didn't hold a grudge."

"Old Jess, maybe. New Jess." Trace gave me a look. "What Molly did the other day, having us talk about what you did to her, that went a long way with her."

I nodded, starting to move back.

"Ashton." His voice was serious.

I glanced back, pausing.

His gaze was serious too. "What we said was true, that you've laid the groundwork for the group to move forward, but that wasn't what had the most effect with Jess. It was you, seeing how you would've reacted if I'd done the same to Molly. She saw it then, how much you regretted it. She told me that was the first time she really felt like there was healing happening." His voice grew thick. "Meant a lot to me, brother. I know you blame yourself for Justin even meeting Kelly."

I went still, just holding still. I'd only said those words to Molly.

"I know you. Known you all my life, so I know you'd never say the words. I still know that you blame yourself, and you need to let that go. Justin met Kelly. It is what it is. You blame yourself. Jess blamed herself, because if it wasn't for her, Kelly would never have gotten a job at Katya. You both blame yourselves, but Jess is starting to let that go. I need you to let yourself off the hook. It's time. I'm getting married today. Make it a wedding gift to me."

I gave him a look. "The compound is your wedding gift."

He grinned. "You know what I mean. You have a good woman. I don't understand the history between you two, but thinking I'm not meant to. What I do know is that she's changed you for the better. It's time to let some happy in."

I swore. "You're not supposed to make me cry before *your* wedding."

He laughed. "Minute I see her walk down that aisle, I'll start bawling. You'll love it. Now, fix this thing so we can go back to being tough mafiosos."

I fixed his tie, then asked one last time, "Ready to get hitched?"

"Since her? Been ready."

Right. My brother and best friend was all grown up now. I reached up, cupping the back of his neck, and moved in. Forehead to forehead. "Love you man. Be happy."

He reached up and clapped my shoulder. "You too."

I loved him. He loved me. Nicolai hadn't broken us: just the opposite.

"You got the ring, right?"

I patted my front pocket. "It's secure."

"Good. Let's get married."

CHAPTER

FORTY-NINE

MOLLY

My stomach fuzzies were on drugs. I could barely stand still, but Jess, total cool. All cool. She was the definition of cool. We were in a back room in one of the towers, and I kept moving the flowers around. Dress was perfect. Hair was perfect. Makeup was on point. Shoes were on. So, flowers. They needed to move from the left. That wasn't right. To the right.

Back to the left.

No. They looked better in the front—"Stop, my beautiful sunshiny boss and soul sister." Sophie moved in, taking the flowers from me and putting them on a counter.

I sucked in my breath. "That's a *perfect* location for them."

Her smile was a little tight. "I know. You've put them there seven times in the last hour. You need to calm down. You're not the one getting married."

My hands were tingling, so I began wringing them, shaking them out. What were the tingles from? Why was I all tingly? The fuzzies had begun to invade the rest of my body. The fuzzies usually only came out to play when Ashton was around, or in a mood, or in bed, or in a mood in bed.

"Mi querida, sit. Por favor."

I blinked a few times but sat where Sophie was guiding me to sit.

She was shaking her head as she went and grabbed a drink that Pialto had brought in earlier at her request. "Here. Drink this."

"What is it?"

"It's lemonade."

I sniffed it. "It doesn't smell like lemonade." But I raised it to my mouth and began to sip it.

Sophie tipped the whole glass up, and I sputtered but had to open my mouth or risk spilling and ruining everything. The dress. The makeup. Could not risk anything. Choking on a large amount of bourbon in there, I glared at her. "Not cool."

She patted my head, taking the glass away. "You'll feel so much cooler in a few minutes. You're welcome."

Jess was standing in front of the mirror, smoothing her hands down over her dress, watching us. "She's got the nerves I should have."

She looked like a fairy princess, a calm one too.

Her hair was pulled up and woven around a sprig of baby's breath tucked into a back roll. She wasn't wearing any jewelry except her engagement ring. The dress was a mermaid-style, spaghetti-strap silk gown that molded to her body. She looked elegant and stunning. Her bouquet was a handful of white and pastel-pink roses, wrapped together with a greenery ribbon. I was her bridesmaid, her one and only, and she hadn't cared about colors. I'd plucked out a dress that Sophie nabbed from her sister, who was a dress designer. She'd brought both dresses, for me and Jess. I had a similar style of dress, but mine didn't fall all the way down. It ended just above the knees, and it was a dark matte pink color to match the flowers.

At Jess's words, I had a job to do. I stood and walked over to her. "You are stunning, and you are marrying the love of your life, and you are surrounded by people who love you." She started to tear up, but she swallowed, blinking a few times.

I wasn't done, saying softer, "Kelly is here. I am holding her place for her so when I hug you, Kelly is also hugging you. You know how she'd be on your wedding day. That's how she is today, just on the other side. She is happy and shining so much love over you."

The tears fell, but she was holding it together.

"Oooh." Sophie jumped over, fanning her hands over Jess's face, trying to dry the tears. "It's okay. It's okay. Kelly would be crying too."

"You're not helping." But Jess was smiling as more tears came to her eyes.

I grabbed her hand, holding it in both of mine, and squeezed lightly. A sudden new calm came over me, and I let it go through me into her. It worked. The tears started to slow. She squeezed my hands back. "Thank you." She looked at Sophie. "Thank you both. I know Val can't be here for obvious reasons, but I also know you're right. Kelly *is* here. I swear I can smell that lotion she loved so much."

I laughed, my chest growing lighter.

She held her arms up. "Thank you, Molly. For everything."

I moved in, hugging her, and I didn't think it was a coincidence when I felt another pressure added around us.

There was a soft knock at the door, and Pialto stuck his head in, his eyes covered. "Are you decent?"

We were all sniffling.

Sophie said, "We're decent. Is it time?"

He dropped his hand from his eyes, and his eyes got big. "You— you all look amazing. Holy—"

"Pialto."

"—just beautiful," he finished, a serene smile beaming at us. "The local priest arrived."

CHAPTER FIFTY

ASHTON

The night was about Trace and Jess, but the second Molly showed up, my eyes never left her.

We had dinner, speeches, and I was doing my thing. Toasting Trace, telling him how much I loved that we'd grown together over the years to where we both were now through loss, grief, but blessings. Trace was looking Jess's way for the blessing part. I was looking Molly's way, and now someone pulled out a playlist, and people were dancing.

Jess's mom was dancing with Avery.

Sloane was dancing with Demetri.

Me, I was heading right for Molly, who was standing with Pialto and Sophie.

Their heads folded together, the freaking three musketeers, until I got to them. They went silent. I waited until Pialto's head popped up, and he blinked, pretending to see me for the first time. "Oh, hi, Ashton." He nudged Molly with his shoulder, who looked up, looking all shy.

She ducked her head down, the same shy smile showing over her face. Her cheeks were a good blush color by now. I glanced at the wine-glass, seeing it might've been the red wine too. "Ashton."

I had pounded her body thirty different ways, and she was blushing, looking at me.

The final crack in whatever wall I had inside of me broke. It shattered, and all the pieces landed hard. I felt it in my gut.

I loved her.

Jesus. I loved her.

I'd known. I'd had an inclination. I'd been obsessed with her, but this look, this shy look after everything we'd gone through and she was so far inside of me that I felt fused with her soul. My happy. That's what Trace had said.

He was right. Molly was my happy if I deserved it.

I held out my hand. "Dance?"

She placed her hand in mine, and a tingle shot up my arm. It went straight to my dick.

Yeah. I was in love, totally, and so fucking clichéd in love. I was thinking all this, feeling all this, as I curled my fingers over hers, giving her a little grin, and tugged her for the dance floor.

The feel of her so close to me, it was the most natural thing in the world.

I pulled her in, my hand sliding over the small of her back, enjoying the feel of her soft dress but mostly the feel of her. Her pulse was racing. "You look beautiful."

She tipped her head back, her pink lips opening a little, matching the color on her cheeks. "You too."

My grin deepened. "I look beautiful?"

A half grin tugged at her lips. "You look *hot*." She folded her head back to my chest, settling in, and her whole body relaxed against me. "And beautiful."

I laughed, right next to her ear, and felt a shiver run down her back.

I pulled her in so there was no space between us.

"I want to take you away, push you against a wall, and slide so deep inside of you that it's only me in there. Forever."

A slight tremble went through her. She pressed her cheek harder against my chest and didn't respond.

I moved my thumb up and down her back, enjoying the plunging back on her dress where I could touch her skin. It was designed just for that purpose, to make all men groan from desire.

We moved together, in silence.

My mouth was almost touching her shoulder, and I let my head fall just a little bit, until I could taste her there.

Another tremor went through her. She trailed her hand down my back, dipping in my jacket, and slowly, she began to pull my shirt up from my pants.

Now I was the one experiencing shivers going through my body.

That need was deep. I had to be in her. Inside of my woman, my soulmate. *Mine.*

Once my shirt was undone, her fingers went under. She spread her palm out on my back, and then began moving her hand over me, slowly and torturously.

I held her against me, knowing we were still technically moving to the music, and no one could see what she was doing, but they all could see how I wanted her.

She moved her hand in front, between us, and we needed to separate a little. As her hand fell to rest just over my dick, I smashed our bodies together, not letting anyone else see what was going on, and I tasted her shoulder again, moving to her neck.

Her whole body was shuddering, a tremble after a tremble racking through her as I kept exploring her, moving to her chin, her jawline, her cheek. I was taking my time, and she was pressing her hand so hard over my cock, but she couldn't move it. She was trying. We were plastered against each other, and I just gripped her by her hip, half my hand spreading to rest over the top of her ass, holding her anchored against me.

I found the corner of her mouth, and I tasted, a slight nibble.

She rose up on her toes, not dancing anymore, and turned her head, her mouth seeking mine.

I found her mouth, warm and inviting, and slid inside, tasting her again.

Her whole body was shaking, just slightly, but she pulled her hand from between us and rose, standing still. Both her hands caught my face, and she explored me right back, taking *her* time. Thoroughly.

I groaned as her tongue flicked against mine, teasing me, and pulled back, just barely. "Get out of here?"

She breathed into me, saying, "Yes please," right before she sealed her lips back to mine.

I picked her up, knowing that I had moved us so we were dancing in the far corner. The tables were on one side, the houses behind them, but where we were, there was a shed not far from us.

I carried her back there, went inside, and pressed her against the door, my hand immediately sliding under her dress.

She was helping, panting as she lifted, her legs half winding around my hips. Her hand went to my pants, undoing them and finding my cock. She wrapped her hands around me, but I couldn't wait. I pulled her panties down, she had my dick in her hand, and then I paused once at her entrance.

She shuddered, lifting up, giving me a better angle, and I slid inside. Deep inside.

We both paused, both groaning at the feel. Goddamn fit so perfect.

She wrapped her arms around my neck, pulling herself up, and I began moving inside of her.

"Ashton," she moaned into my ear.

I grabbed her hands, raising them up, and pressed them against the door behind her, our fingers lacing. I kept sliding inside of her. She was rolling her thighs with me.

This time felt different. More raw. More real if that was possible. More needed, like I was desperate for her. Just more.

I slowed, thrusting in and holding as far as I could go.

Her whole body was straining against me. Her insides clamping down on me.

I lifted my head to see her.

She turned hers, looking back.

Her eyes were somber, hungry, but there was more. Again. A deeper feeling. I felt it inside of me, moving around, opening sensations I didn't know were there. A wave of such intensity and tenderness rose, overwhelming me, and I ground up into her. She gasped, her head falling back, our fingers rubbing against each other. Her thighs pulled me in, and I groaned, sliding out and thrusting back in. Her whole body moved from the motion, parting her lips.

"Ashton," she panted again. Her chest moving up and down.

I moaned, leaning in and nipping at her lips again. I said, poised right above her mouth, "I love you."

Her entire body lifted in one breath. She whispered, "I love you too."

Her mouth sealed to mine. My darkness. Hers. We were connected.

The last separation from us fell away. It was her and me. I was still in her, moving, our hands holding on to each other, and our mouths were fused, but nothing would be the same after this. I felt it, an internal knowing, and it was rocking my foundation. But that was Molly, claiming me right back.

I pushed in, holding, as I felt her release explode through her, her whole body trembling once again. I held off, waiting until she'd come down from her wave, and I began thrusting inside of her again, bringing both of us to a release.

Her hands broke from mine to wrap around my neck, and she clamped onto me as her second climax ripped through her.

I was just coming down from my own when—*bang!*

CHAPTER

FIFTY-ONE

MOLLY

Oh, god.

Not again, but *again*.

All that flashed through my head in the space when Ashton let me back down, and *bang*!

Bang!

He cursed, pulling up my panties, then fastening his own pants. He had a gun out, and where did he get that gun? But he had it pointed down, and he took my hand, pulling me to the back of the shed.

I looked around, hearing the screams but knowing I had to follow Ashton.

Another scream. God. That was Jess's mom.

And another—that was Sophie.

I started to turn, to run for her, but Ashton caught my hand. "No. No, babe."

I could hear Sophie crying. A guttural scream left me, but Ashton yanked me against him, clamping a hand over my mouth and wrapping an arm around my stomach. He was hurrying backward, carrying me with him, and he had the gun in his hand. "Ssssh. Please, Molly. Please."

I was crying, already knowing I was about to lose someone. I didn't care if it was me. Just not someone else. *Please.*

I stopped fighting to get free, and Ashton put me back down at the end of the shed. There was a door here, and he opened it a crack, peering at me first.

I nodded, telling him I'd be quiet, so he took his hand away, turning so he was between me and whoever was outside.

People were running. I could still hear someone crying.

Then, silence. Everything and everyone stopped.

Ashton took a deep breath, like he was preparing himself for something.

He moved back in and put his mouth to my ear. "This place is surrounded by a fortified wall. Whoever is shooting was let in by someone, so remember that," he said, so quietly. "I need you to not overreact. Okay? Don't flip the switch."

I gripped his hand tight, his free hand. "What are you planning?"

He shook his head, putting his lips back to my ear and turning his hand around so he squeezed mine back. "I'm going to run right." He pulled his hand free, and something hard and metallic was pressed into it. "Take this. You run left, keep going until you hit the wall, and then follow it north. Do you understand me?"

I was shaking my head. I wasn't running away. I wasn't leaving him or anyone behind.

"Molly." He cupped the back of my head. "You run to that wall and turn right, and then you follow it until you hit a door. It's the guard post. Inside is a phone that'll work—"

"I'm not going anywhere." I moved away from him, stepping ahead.

He caught the end of my dress, pulling me back.

I shook my head and gave him the hardest glare I could muster in this moment. I cocked the gun, taking the safety off. "I already told you. I'm not running." My tone was hard, and *I* was hard. Fuck being scared.

I was enraged. Whoever came here, shot at people I loved, I was done. They were going to get their ass handed to them, possibly literally with me. But he was right. My switch was retired. I wouldn't put people I loved in danger, but I wasn't running. He couldn't ask me to do that.

"We all have phones that'll work. I'm sure there's one in the house."

"Molly." His hand was twisting in my dress, but I saw the fear in his eyes.

I still shook my head. "Do not send me off on a fool's errand because you want me to be safe. I'm not safe, no matter what. Heartbreak or physical pain, it's all the same to me."

He straightened back up, his eyes glittering, and he pressed his mouth in a firm line.

I clipped my head in a nod. "Right. I'll lead." I took a step forward but was hauled back.

Ashton was glaring at me. "Leave!"

"No," I hissed back.

He groaned.

"We don't have time for this."

"I'm aware," he shot back.

Bang, bang, bang!

Pop!

There were more screams, more shouting.

I couldn't make them out, but Ashton leaped into action, turning in midair, and he shoved out of the shed. His gun was up, and he was shooting before I could see what was ahead of us.

"Agh!"

Bang!

That was Ashton. He kept running, and he kept shooting, until I heard a sudden thud ahead.

I moved around him. A man had fallen to the ground, and Ashton went right up to him, nudged him over, and shot him in the face.

I gasped, jumping back.

Ashton spared me a look, but his eyes were hard. The cruel Ashton had returned. I fought down a shudder because he was so different from the man holding my face, telling me he loved me.

A shot rang out from our left.

Ashton moved, his arm sweeping me behind him, and he was shooting back at the same time.

That guy fell, too, his gun falling far from his body.

A hand appeared, and Ashton barked, "Don't!" His gun was still up, and he walked over until whoever was reaching for the gun froze. It was a female hand. Her other hand showed. "Get out here. Now."

Nea came out, standing on shaking legs. Her face was pale, her lip trembling. Her eyes were so big and scared. "It's just me, Ashton."

I frowned. I didn't like how she said his name, like she *knew* him, knew him.

"Step away from that gun, Nea."

"Ash—"

"Now!"

Her whole body jumped, but she scrambled away, coming more into the open. Her hands were still out. "I was just scared. That's all. I don't know what's going on here." She pointed behind where she'd been hiding. Her finger was still wobbling. "There—others. There are others hiding back there."

Others? Every part of my body wanted to run around him, get in there, save who else was in there, but no. I cursed but held back.

Ashton went first, and I peeked right behind him. Instant relief flooded me, seeing Nurse Sloane, but also Sophie and Pialto. Nurse Sloane was sitting, her knees to her chest, haunted eyes looking at me. Sophie and Pialto were huddling together, their arms and legs around each other.

I cursed, first touching Nurse Sloane's knees, but then I put the safety back on before I threw myself into Pialto's and Sophie's arms. Both circled me, pulling me into their huddle. Their arms wrapped around me. Sophie was crying. Pialto was smoothing down my hair. "Oh, thank goodness. You're okay."

Sophie held me so tight I couldn't get air. "Thank God, thank God, thank God," she kept on repeating, and Pialto was thanking God, too, looking up in the air and giving a cross motion with his other hand.

Then, suddenly, a hush came over them.

I turned, seeing Ashton standing there. Nea was a bit away from him, farther back. He had his gun, and he motioned to us. "Everyone, come out here."

We did.

Ashton pointed ahead, to the right. "Go that way. There's a safe room where you can hide."

Pialto's sigh of relief was loud.

Sophie choked on a laugh, tucking her head down.

Ashton was giving me a slight "WTF" look, but I motioned for him to leave it alone. Both did odd things when they were uncomfortable. Sometimes, I thought it was the basis of our relationships, besides me employing them.

No one had moved, so Ashton barked, "Now!"

Nurse Sloane gave him a nasty look, but she moved. Nea was next.

I brought up the rear as Pialto and Sophie ran ahead.

I fell into step next to Ashton. He pulled me to him and pressed a kiss to my forehead. He whispered, urgently, "Please be safe. Please."

Ashton guided us to the back of a warehouse, and he opened a door. Everyone filed into what looked like an office. He went ahead, checking some things before racing back. He pulled me to the door, indicating the others. "Keep them in here. Barricade the windows and doors unless you know who is on the other side."

I nodded.

He cradled my face, smoothing my hair down with his hands, and took a moment. He bent down, his forehead to mine. "I love you. Be cautious, my only request."

I was nodding with each word he said, my one hand touching his.

He kissed me and left.

"Lock the door, Molly." His voice came through the door.

Right. Lock.

I locked it, and then he was gone.

Oh, god.

Oh, god.

No more, please.

But I heaved a deep breath, turned, rested my back to the door, and slid down to the floor.

This was happening.

———

"He loves you."

I looked up at Nea, who had come over what seemed like hours later, but I checked my phone. Ten minutes had passed. She turned and slid down to sit next to me. Her long, model-like legs pulled up as she hugged her knees to her chest. "I didn't think he was capable of that emotion, except for Trace."

Okay. If she had approached me with this thirty minutes ago, I might've been upset. Obviously, she knew Ashton in a way I wished she didn't. But also, obviously, she was saying this for a reason.

I glanced in Nurse Sloane's direction. She was holding Sophie in her arms, and Pialto was standing next to them, half turned away. He noticed me noticing them and shot me a look.

I raised my eyebrows back at him, conveying whatever he took that to be, and his nose wrinkled before he turned away. Then he looked again and winked my way.

I had no idea what any of that meant.

"Ashton and I dated."

Right. I didn't want to do this. It wasn't the appropriate time, but I just closed my eyes at this point.

"It was a while ago—"

I held up a hand with an "I don't care" expression on my face. "I'll stop you there. Save us both some time."

She closed her mouth on a snap, sitting up higher. Straighter.

I inclined my head. "I would've cared thirty minutes ago. I would've been jealous, not insecure, but yeah, jealous because you're insanely gorgeous. Or I would've started that way, then shut down and blocked it off until either Ashton noticed or one of my friends noticed and gave me a pep talk that I do, in fact, ooze amazingness. Also, so you know, I'm not normal. I don't waste energy on being down in the dumps. I mean, yes; thirty minutes ago, I might've considered booking a day in the Misery Airbnb, but that was thirty minutes ago." I motioned around the room, doing it with my gun, the one Ashton gave me. "Thirty minutes ago, Ashton told me he loved me. And thirty minutes ago, the place where all my loved ones are at is under fire. Someone broke in here, and they shot guns at people I loved. That was thirty minutes ago. Whatever this is"—I motioned between her and me—"I don't give a fuck about."

Her eyes caught on it and held. She frowned, a little bit.

There. Right there. She was looking at the gun, and she was annoyed. That was it.

She wasn't scared, but she'd been a whole lot of scared when Ashton first showed up with the gun and barking orders. Now, she was cozying up to me for what?

I gestured to her with my free hand. "What are you doing?"

"It wasn't supposed to happen this way," Nea said.

And at the same time Nurse Sloane whispered, "Nea."

I frowned at Nurse Sloane, who was standing by the back desk and looking down at a pile of pictures. Then my phone started ringing.

Thinking it was Ashton, I pulled it out as I got up. "We're safe—"

"Get out of there! Now!"

Not Ashton. I had to look at the screen, seeing the unknown-caller identification. "Dad?"

He cursed. "I'm coming to you. Did you have to go so far fucking north of the city? Get out of there. Now!"

"Dad? What are you—are you driving here?" But I was moving to Nurse Sloane because she wouldn't stop staring at whatever was on Ashton's desk.

"I got everything, honey. Everything. I know who's behind everything."

"You know who killed Kelly?"

Everyone's head snapped in my direction.

"What?" a few asked.

I was ignoring them, only focusing on my dad. "Do you know who killed Kelly and Justin? That's what I asked you to find out, remember?"

"Honey—"

The line went dead.

"Dad?" I waited, but nothing. The call was gone.

"Was that your dad?" Sophie had come over, her eyes on my phone.

I tucked it away. "It doesn't matter."

"What was he saying?"

I frowned. "I don't know."

"Yeah, but—"

"If she doesn't want to talk about her dad, especially in these circumstances, leave her alone." Pialto moved up, touching Sophie's arm, his gaze on me. He steered Sophie away. They went back to the desk Nurse Sloane had been studying so intently.

I nodded, letting him know I was fine, but I wasn't. I was suddenly so tired. And worried.

Ashton was still out there. Jess. Trace. It'd been quiet except for an occasional gunshot, and quiet again. I couldn't handle the silence. I felt like my skin wanted to come off my bones.

"Your father knows who killed Kelly? Jess's friend?" The question came from Nea, who was staring at my gun.

I shrugged. "I don't know."

She lifted her gaze to me, her eyes narrowed, focused. "That's what he was trying to find out? Who killed them?"

I frowned at her. "Yeah. Why?"

"Nea." Nurse Sloane was coming around the desk, fixated on her friend. "Don't—"

Nea shook her head, her eyes looking a little panicked. "He knows. He knows, Sloane."

"Nea, don't—"

Her voice hitched up. "It wasn't supposed to happen like that."

She'd said that before. My body went cold at her words. "What wasn't?"

"Um . . . ," Pialto said from behind me. "What are these?"

"What?" I glanced back. He was staring at the desk, at the pictures there.

Nurse Sloane stepped away, coming toward me. Her face was stricken. Pale, like she'd seen a ghost. "Nea." Her voice was so low, like a warning.

"Molly." From Pialto again, more insistent, more alarmed. "These. What are these?"

I held up a hand. "One second."

Something was happening. Something between Sloane and Nea.

Something . . . why did my stomach take a nosedive?

Dread started lining my insides.

"Molly!" Pialto said it again, sharper.

I looked his way, seeing he was holding a picture, and he was slowly lifting it. "What is this?"

"It's—uh—Ashton brought pictures for me to look at."

But the picture he was holding up to me. His eyes were darting from it to Nea and back again. A deep frown on his face.

That picture.

He kept looking from it to Nea and back.

He was confused, but me—dread was lining my organs.

The room was suddenly shrinking in size.

I felt the ground starting to shake under me. It was going to get pulled out from under my feet. I knew it. I felt it coming. I was transfixed by that photo Pialto was holding up. I couldn't make it out, not all the details, but it was of a woman. Red dress.

It was the woman from outside of Octavia.

It was the picture I'd been looking for, and Pialto had it.

And he was staring, confused, at Nea.

The dots were slowly connecting. Horror began to fill me.

I began to turn, slowly, feeling as if I were moving in mud.

His eyes were jerking from me to the picture to Nea and back again, and again, and again. "I feel like this is important. Why do I feel that? Why do you have a picture of *her*?" He nodded at Nea.

But Nea was saying right next to me, as if he hadn't spoken, as if she hadn't even heard him, "None of this was supposed to happen how it did. None of it. I fell in love, and I shouldn't have, but I did. He's a bad guy. I'm trying to tell you, to explain because I was hurting after Ashton. You have to see that. You have to understand that. When you're so lonely, and then you think you're getting sunshine, only to have that sunshine taken away . . . you'll do things to replace it. Things you're not proud of. Things you regret."

"Nea!" That was Nurse Sloane.

Pialto's gaze was solely focused on Nea.

She added, also a whisper, "He's not the good guy."

"What?" I was so confused. "What are you talking about, Nea?"

She looked torn, looking at me. Stricken. "I thought I loved Ashton, but he ripped my heart out and then—my guy came after, and *he* filled me up, but I was wrong. My guy filled the void that Ashton had left behind. I think . . ."

My bad feeling turned into dread.

"Nea," Sloane hissed again.

Nea wasn't even seeing her. She wasn't seeing Pialto. I didn't think she was even seeing me anymore. It was like she was seeing something else, someone else.

I held my hand straighter, now moving away, turning. Walking backward. Putting space between Nea and me, holding my gun firmly. The safety was still on.

I didn't want to take it off.

I needed to be safe. Smart.

People I loved were outside, but people I loved were in here.

Nea *was* almost talking to herself, her head looking down. "I was so stupid, but I was a doctor. And my parents. I wanted to make them so proud of me. I worked so hard for them. I was ambitious. Naive. Trace's father came in, and no one seemed concerned about how he ended up in the ER. I raised the question, asking if I should call the police. The next day, my patient is gone and Ashton was flirting with me in a coffee shop."

Oh, god. Ashton. My heart sank.

She kept on, a second tear falling, "I had no life in medical school. Undergrad. Med school, biology, chemistry, anatomy and physiology, none of it came naturally to me. I had to study, for hours. I didn't go to parties on the weekends. I didn't get wasted after my finals. I studied for the next exam, the next class. I studied ahead, and it's all moot now, but I need you to understand."

I blinked, looking around, but it seemed she was solely focused on me. "Understand what?"

I was trying to understand what she was telling me, even if it wasn't making sense. She was saying *something*. I had to figure it out.

"I was lonely. Sometimes, you get *so lonely*. You sacrifice so much. Give up so much, and then you get a glimpse at something you never had, and you only want *that*. I only wanted that. To not be lonely. When Ashton asked me out, I fell for him. I didn't know better. I couldn't read the signs that he wasn't into me, that he was using me. I'm so pissed at myself for caring, for still caring." She closed her eyes, and she almost started talking to herself. "He showed up again, but not to ask for another date. He *educated* me"—she was sounding bitter—"on who he was. On who Trace was. On how I should never call the police if any of their victims end up in the hospital, or I'd learn the true meaning of what Mafia meant. He intended to scare me, but he just hurt me. I asked around, learned the real deal about the mob. They exist. They operate where I work. I needed to get with the program. I learned. I got with the program. I never told a soul. I never raised another alarm about anyone who mysteriously showed up when the security cameras were on the fritz, or when there was *a look* from one nurse to the other. It's always the same look. The same knowing look. Sloane wears it in eighty different shades. The nurses always know." She looked at Nurse Sloane. "You always knew."

"Nea." Nurse Sloane took a step toward her, saying softly, "Please stop." A lone tear slipped down her face.

Nea was shaking her head, her eyes not in this room. They were elsewhere, seeing something else or seeing someone else. A tortured expression was deep in her gaze. "I can't. It's too late, Sloane. It's been too late for too long."

"Molly, why do you have this picture here?" Pialto hissed, holding the picture. His entire arm was stretched toward me, straining. "I really, really feel like you need to answer me, and I don't know why, but I do."

Sophie was frowning, inching closer to see the picture.

Sloane looked, and her entire face blanched before she focused back on Nea.

Everything was happening in slow motion. Slow, but I wasn't fast enough.

What was going on?

The picture. Ashton told me he brought the rest of the pictures here, if I wanted to keep looking, because we still didn't know who that woman was.

I just hadn't gotten through that group of pictures.

Sloane looked like she was going to have a heart attack, and then, the dots were connecting faster.

There was a sudden barrage of gunfire.

I jumped, swinging my gun toward the door, but cursed and lowered it again. Pialto and Sophie both screamed. Sloane almost collapsed to the ground, shaking her head, repeating Nea's name over and over again.

But Nea—she was looking at her phone.

Her screen flashed.

All of that happened at the same time before she looked up, met my gaze.

An expression flashed over her face. Regret? Then she blanked. A wall slammed back down over her, and she turned for the door.

No . . .

I began raising my gun. "No—"

Sloane's head lifted, and she began to stand again.

No. No. No!

"Nea!" I yelled, lifting my gun all the way up.

She ignored me, rushing to the door.

"Don't open that door!"

She did, pushing it open.

A hand reached in from outside, grabbing it, and it swung the rest of the way open.

I took my safety off. At the same time a man I didn't know walked inside.

He had a creepy smile on his face, with his slicked-back hair. A tight black long-sleeved shirt and dark pants. I kept the gun up even as I was noticing the gun he was holding. One that had a long silencer barrel clipped on top. "You're Molly Easter?"

Recognition hit me in the gut. I didn't know this guy, but I *knew* this guy.

He introduced himself. "I'm Nicolai Worthing."

CHAPTER
FIFTY-TWO
ASHTON

I was going to murder whoever was doing this, whoever was putting my loved ones at risk, whoever dared to bring this fight here. *Here.* My compound. My family's compound. The one I loathed.

I raced from building to building, tearing open every door to find everyone.

Marco and Remmi were in a back closet.

Avery and Elijah found me when we moved to another building. They helped take my primo and Trace's sister to another safe room.

I kept going. I had to keep going.

Everyone had to be safe. We couldn't lose anyone.

I swept through the staff building now.

Trace was inside, holding a gun up and aimed right at me. He cursed, seeing me. "Thank god."

I grated out, "We need to find the rest."

"Molly?"

"They're safe. They're in my office."

I turned, my gun in hand, and I kept going. Always keep going. Always.

Never stop. Never stop fighting.

"Ashton. Jesus." Trace touched my arm. "You're shaking."

Avery's radio sounded. There was another barrage of gunfire before a voice came over, yelling, "Warehouse! He's going for his cousins."

Trace cursed; his men were with him. My men were with me.

We tore out of there. Avery and Elijah were on each side of me. Demetri and Pajn were surrounding Trace.

I glanced back at one point, yelling at Trace, "Jess?"

He continued to run by us. "She stayed back with her mom. They're going to join the others in your office. Your house was clean."

Avery was listening to his radio as more information was coming in from the rest of my men. "They've got Worthing's men surrounded, but they're saying a car got through from the south entrance. It's empty, but whoever was in there is on foot inside the compound."

I stopped running.

God. My heart was pounding. Molly.

Avery was listening again before he said, "We have control of the compound, but we need to find whoever that person is." His radio crackled again. "Our men are in the security room, and—"

"Nicolai Worthing" came from Ben, the guard now in the security room. "We lost time on the cameras, but—shit—he's in the primary office."

I tore out of there.

Primary office.

That was my office.

That was where I'd sent Molly.

Molly . . .

No, no, no.

I would not get there, open that door, and find a body inside.

I would not lose her.

I heard Trace asking behind me, "Is that—Ashton!"

They were coming after me, but the only one faster than me was Avery. I still had a dead sprint ahead of him.

I was the outcast in the family. The black sheep. Marco should've taken over, but *I* had. I was the one who'd work in conjunction with Trace. That's what I'd said when Marco had questioned why it was me stepping forward, but it was more than that. I wanted control over my fate. I wanted to be the narrator of my place in my family, because I would never hold another secret again, not like the one my mother made me hold.

The opportunity to step forward and take control was given to me. I took it.

I never wanted to be controlled again.

I'd been close to getting everything I never knew I needed in life. Love. Security. Power. Peace. And now Worthing was here, and he was trying to take it away. I wouldn't let him.

Molly was mine. He could not have her.

I raced to the door.

It was already open—my heart was pounding. What did that mean? As I reached for it, stepping into the opened doorway and—a gunshot went off.

My heart stopped.

CHAPTER

FIFTY-THREE

MOLLY

He laughed. "I see my reputation precedes myself."

Christ. He was laughing. I opened my mouth, but what was there to say?

He nodded at my gun. "You should put that away."

I blinked. "I should shoot you."

Everyone else ceased to exist for me. It was him and me. My gun against his. He hadn't raised his yet, but he would. I knew he would.

I was going to kill someone. That knowledge seeped through my spine, like a cold trickle.

I was going to kill him because I wasn't going to let him hurt anyone else. It was me or him.

His eyes were still cold, but a different glint appeared. A cruel one. One I'd seen come over Ashton a few other times. He cocked his head to the side. "You know what I'm doing here. My men"—he motioned outside—"are out there, killing your man and his friends."

That cold trickle turned into ice. "You're lying."

"You've not heard the gunshots. I'm here. I got in. What does your common sense tell you to believe? Me, who is here and telling you, who's not threatened by your weapon? I could lift my own gun up, you know. So quick. I've killed before. I wouldn't hesitate, but you, you might hesitate. Have you shot someone before?" His eyes took on a whole pitying look. "It'll be okay, Molly. I'll let you and your friends go."

He was lying.

He was calling my bluff, and as soon as I thought that, he started to raise his gun.

My mind wasn't blanking. I wasn't leaving my body.

I was here. I was present. I wasn't flipping the switch, but this time, this time I knew exactly what I would do. He gave me no other option.

This was no overreaction.

I pulled the trigger.

Then I heard, from a distance, Ashton yelling my name.

He tore into the room as soon as I finished pulling the trigger.

"Molly!"

I was having a sense of déjà vu because I hadn't shot Nicolai. My bullet had grazed him. What was wrong with me? I still couldn't shoot right, but then a bloodcurdling scream sounded out next to me. *"No!"*

Nurse Sloane moved in, slamming Worthing's arm away. The gun went off, but the bullet zipped past me. I still felt the burn and touched my cheek, falling back a step.

An arm swept around me, almost throwing me out of the way. Ashton was in front of me, blocking me. He had his own gun out, pointing it at Nicolai and looking way sturdier than I had been. "Don't move!" He was barking orders at Worthing, who was temporarily stunned by the sudden change of events.

"Sloane!" Nea ran to her, and both of them reached for each other, moving to the side.

A stampede of feet came into the room right then.

Avery. Elijah. Two other big guys I didn't know. Trace and Jess were behind them. Marco and Remmi were looking in from the outside, along with Jess's mom, until security guards moved them aside.

Jess's voice sounded from the other side of him. "Sloane? Are you guys okay?"

Nurse Sloane was crying, but I couldn't look away from her because *she* wasn't looking away. She wasn't crying like she was scared. She was crying . . . I didn't know why, but that haunted look was back, and it got worse since Jess came into the room.

"Jess—" she started.

Nea cut her off. "He threatened me—"

"Let it go, Nea!" Sloane yelled, flinging her arm out. "It's over. You let him in. *You* let him *in*. You did that, and you already started talking about how Ashton broke your heart. What were you thinking?"

I frowned. That didn't feel right to me.

Sloane frowned too. "Nea."

"No. I didn't know. It's over." She was giving Sloane a meaningful glare.

"Molly," Pialto hissed, coming over and shoving a picture in front of my face. "It's *her*." He nodded at Nea.

I—couldn't breathe, because holy gods, I'd connected the dots, but I still couldn't believe it. Not really. It seemed so surreal. I swung my gaze in Nea's direction.

Her dress. Her hair. Her shoes.

Another memory flashed in my mind, as we were driving past her vehicle. The day we ran from the hospital, when she'd helped us. She was in the front, her door had been open, and her things were on the seat behind her. I hadn't noticed then, but there'd been a sparkle behind her—and remembering now, it was shoes.

The same shoes she was wearing the night this picture was taken.

The same shoes had been in her front seat, the day she gave us a ride away from the hospital.

When Ashton grabbed me from her car, and we were driving past.

I looked beyond her, and it was those shoes.

She was wearing them in the picture, the one from outside of Octavia.

She was the woman.

I took it from Pialto and held it to Ashton. "It's her."

I could see her now clearly, coming out of the back of Octavia, out the door that was never used, into the car that had shot at the nightclub's manager moments earlier and the man . . . I looked down at Worthing on the floor.

It was him.

That's how I knew him.

Nicolai Worthing had been at Octavia with Nea.

Nea was a part of it.

"You let him in."

She frowned, her eyes flickering to me, but she didn't say anything. Her chest rose. She took a breath and held it. She was fighting back tears.

I added—the dots had all clicked and were now settling inside of me; I said it as it was making sense to me now—"You knew he was out there. You looked at your phone. You kept watching my gun. You went to the door. You let him in. You . . ." She hadn't been scared. She was talking about Ashton, but she'd never been scared.

We were all scared.

She should've been scared. She hadn't been.

But she was now, and she drew in another ragged breath.

"She killed Justin."

Everything stopped, *again.*

All eyes went to Nurse Sloane, who was looking at Jess, that same haunted look on her face. I didn't think I'd ever see her without it again. "Nea killed Justin, and I saw it."

Jess fell back a whole step, her mouth dropping slightly. "What?"

"They called me. I told you." She looked my way, including Jess. "They called to say goodbye, but it wasn't the night before. It was *that* night. I heard a security guard in the background, telling them they needed to move out of the parking slot. I knew where they were, and hurried down there. I wanted to talk some sense into Kelly. Why was she leaving? It didn't make sense. She could've stayed. None of it made sense. Kelly sounded happy, but they were saying goodbye, and she was asking me to look out for you, 'cause you'd need it, you'd need all the help you'd never let anyone give. That's what she said as she was laughing, so I knew she was okay, but she was still sad to be leaving you. I wanted to talk them into not leaving." She stopped, swallowing before looking away. "I heard the shot as I was coming around the corner. Nea was standing over Justin's body. She had the gun in her hand, but before I could say anything, Kelly attacked her. She was—she was screaming, and she was out for blood."

Tears began to fall from Jess's face, but she didn't show anything else. She was locked down.

"She wouldn't stop, Jess. She was going to kill Nea. I knew it, and I—" She stopped, her whole face twisting up. Tormented.

"You what?" Jess asked, her teeth gritted.

"Kelly got the gun out of Nea's hand, and it fell to the ground. It stopped a few feet from me. They didn't notice. Nea was yelling for her to stop, and I—Nea wouldn't do something unless her life was in danger. But Kelly *wouldn't* stop. She wouldn't—she kept slamming Nea's head into the pavement and"—she took a shuddering breath—"I picked up the gun."

Jess's face was pure white but so hard. Her eyes were inflamed.

"She's lying." Nea coughed, her eyes troubled. Wild. "She's the one who killed Justin. I came out, and I was the one who heard the shot. Kelly turned on her. Sloane was the one who said we could make it look like a Mafia hit. She said it happened all the time, that no one would even think twice since they were already leaving."

Sloane was staring at her, dumbfounded "You . . . you're the one who—you killed Justin! I saw it with my own eyes."

Nea barely reacted. "Security cameras were already down that night. How are you going to prove that? Besides, I only went out there because Nico called. He said Justin knew about—"

Bang!

Her head went backward; half of it was missing, and her body slumped to the ground. Nurse Sloane let out a muffled scream.

Nea was gone.

Turning, looking, Nicolai had shot her. He was sitting up, a second gun in his hand. He started to point it at me next, until a guttural growl left Ashton as he started forward, his own gun already aiming at Nicolai.

He shot him.

I barely reacted to the sound this time. My eardrums were continuously ringing.

His own head went backward, too, his body falling the rest of the way back down.

Bang, bang, bang!

Ashton kept moving forward. He *kept* shooting Nicolai. His jaw was clenching hard. His shoulders rigid. His back as straight as could be, and he kept shooting. He emptied his entire clip into Nicolai Worthing's body.

No one said a word until his clip ran out.

Even then, he kept trying to shoot him.

"Ashton." Trace stepped for him, but Ashton whirled, only seeing me.

He took two steps, coming back to me, and he pulled me to him. His arms went around me, and he held me, half lifting me off my feet, his head burrowing into my neck. His one hand went up, smoothing down my hair, and he said into my neck, "Never again."

I clasped onto him as hard as he was holding me.

Nothing else mattered in that moment.

CHAPTER
FIFTY-FOUR
MOLLY

The rest of the story was pieced together.

Sloane filled in the initial blanks.

"You killed Kelly. Didn't you?" Jess said rather than asked.

Sloane nodded. She'd been void of emotion by then, sitting in a separate room at the compound. Nicolai's and Nea's bodies were both—well, I didn't know. I didn't ask. I didn't want to know, but now it was later, and it took time to learn the truth.

Everyone just wanted to know the truth.

"I did. I thought I was protecting her, but now I realized that Kelly was trying to protect herself. I came in at the wrong time. I—I'm so sorry, Jess. I'm so sorry."

"Why did Nea kill Justin?" Trace moved to Jess's side, his hand on her back.

Sloane raised her chin up. "She was dating Nicolai. They met a month after." She looked Ashton's way and at me. "I think that's what she was saying earlier. She was hurting after." She glanced in Ashton's direction. "Then Nicolai came in asking questions. I don't know what drew him to her, but she was beautiful. She meant well, in the beginning. I don't think she went this way because of Ashton. It was Nicolai. She talked to me a little bit about it, but that was after she was already dating him. I knew who he was, but he was different. He wasn't a Trace or an Ashton. There's a difference. They might do the same work, but he wasn't like them. Ashton, Trace, they're good men who do bad things. I don't like what they do, or didn't, but I wasn't scared of them as people. Well, except that one time." She directed that statement to Ashton. "She was hurting because of you. He used that. He exploited that. He made her change, in ways that people sometimes do that, molding them or whatnot. He did that to her, but I thought she'd turned a new leaf over. She promised she had, said she wanted to make things right. It's why we both came today. It's the only reason. Jess, I . . ." The haunted expression hung over her like a dark cloud. "I can't say I would've told you what I did, but I can say that I'm sorry. I liked Kelly. I am so sorry, for everything. I—"

"Three men were given orders from Jake Worthing's phone to attack me. One put a gun to Molly's head. Do you know anything about that? The GPS said it came from his phone at the hospital." Ashton was standing behind me, his arms crossed over in front of me, and I was holding on to his arms, leaning back against him.

I loved standing like this, in his arms.

Nurse Sloane's face shuddered before she nodded. "Nea did it. Said they'd do what he said, if it came from his phone. It was her plan, trying to turn one family against the other. Or that's what she said to me . . ." She trailed off. "Now I'm not so certain."

"None of that has anything to do with why she killed Justin." Trace moved toward her. "She must've said something. Anything."

She flinched away from him but shook her head. "She only said that he attacked her. That's all. I couldn't keep asking, or she would've turned on me. I—I'm so sorry. I should've pushed harder on her."

"She killed him because Nicolai asked her to."

A new voice, a new presence.

I tensed, looking for and then seeing Detective Jake Worthing in the doorway. He yanked someone else forward. My dad.

"Dad!" I started for him, but Ashton held me back.

That's when I saw that Jake had a gun on my dad, pointed into his back.

"Worthing." Jess's tone was like ice.

He barely gave her a look, finding Trace and then Ashton. "This fucking piece of ferret asshole almost got himself killed tonight." He shoved my dad farther inside, releasing him.

My dad ran forward, coming my way until Ashton growled in warning.

He reined it in, pausing but holding up his hands. "You okay, Mols?"

I nodded, looking him over because I couldn't help it. He was still my dad. Moron.

"Get over there." Ashton pointed to the corner where no one was standing.

My dad went over but glared as he did. Then he saw a pot of coffee and poured himself a cup, adding half the sugar bottle to the Styrofoam cup.

"What are you doing here, Detective Worthing?" Trace was asking, his tone as cold as Jess's.

Jake ignored them, looking at me first and then focusing on Ashton. "You remember my theory?"

Ashton's jaw clenched, but he nodded, just barely. So stiff.

"I was right. And that weasel has the proof." He motioned to my dad, who was making a face after tasting the coffee. "I don't know where he has it, or what he has, but I followed the trail enough to know it's true. Nicolai had Justin killed because Justin found out my cousin was working on behalf of the DEA."

Ashton went completely still, his arm like cement on my waist.

Trace's voice was eerily low as well, saying, "You want to say that again?"

Jake barely flicked him a glance, only focusing on Ashton. "He was approached and backed heavily to go up in power in my family. DEA wanted to get a player in the mix, in the city, to help maintain control over the drug trade. They pushed Nicolai to get in our city, thinking a player from NYC would have more power than from where we were from in Maine. They were the backer, and when the fight went too public, hitting a hospital, they pulled out. Nicolai came here as a last effort to maintain control. It wouldn't have worked."

"What does that fit in with Nea being the one to pull the trigger on Justin?"

"She overheard him and Kelly calling to say goodbye to that one." He indicated Nurse Sloane. "She was on the phone with Nicolai and mentioned it to him. He asked her then and there to stop him, by any means necessary. He told her Justin was planning to go to the authorities, but Nicolai would be killed. He wouldn't just get arrested. He convinced her that someone had cops on the payroll, and they'd go after him. She killed Justin to save Nicolai."

"How do you know that?"

"Anonlinediary."

We all turned to my father, who was drinking his coffee, and now he was munching on a donut. Where he got the donut, I had no clue, but he waved it in the air, now at center stage, and swallowed his coffee in one big gulp. "A diary. Online too. She logged in every night and added to it. I got everything in there up until today. It was her failsafe, I guess. In case something went wrong. She'd have something to plea her way out. She was thorough." He frowned at me, narrowing his eyes at Ashton. "She talked a whole lot about you two. That's how I knew the both of you were doing what you're obviously still doing, unless I'm taking that hold in a different way than it's intended?"

Ashton growled, low in his throat. I felt it through my back, vibrating.

I snapped at my dad. "How did you get ahold of her diary?"

He grinned at me, taking another bite of his donut. "There she is, so spunky. I love you, Mollykins." He leaned around me as if to talk to Ashton. "You know she's got this thing called a switch—"

"Dad!"

He swallowed before taking a sip of coffee. "Right. Right. I broke into her place and holed up."

I was dumbfounded. "You what?"

"I needed a place to stay, and I'd been asking around to find out who killed Justin. Paulie over on Fifth said the shot happened at the hospital, that's the word on the street, so that's where I headed over. Asked around and saw the doctor acting weird around me. So"—he shrugged—"I broke into her place. Course I thought she'd be heading home that night, so I was quick, looking around, and then she came home, but she didn't even notice. I ransacked her place, and she only rushed in, packed a bag, and was gone. Heard her on the phone with that one, I'm guessing. She was saying a guy with my description was asking questions about who killed Justin Worthing. After that, I got comfortable, but she never came home, so I took my time snooping."

I wanted to hit him in the forehead. "You've been at the doctor's apartment *the whole time?*"

He nodded, then cocked his head to the side. "Mostly. She came back one other time, but it was the same thing. Rummaged around looking for something and went crazy when she couldn't find it." He grinned. "Good thing I'd already found it. Her laptop and diary. Got it all there. She changed her password, logging in from somewhere else, but I already had access to all her accounts."

"*When* did you find all that out?"

Another one of those shivers went down my spine at Ashton's tone.

My dad noticed, too, going still and looking a little more wary. "It might've been a bit ago."

"How long ago?!" Ashton barked.

My dad's face went slack. "A few weeks."

A few weeks . . . I surged forward. "How long?!"

His eyebrows dipped low, and he began edging backward. "I don't know. Why's it matter?"

"Why's it matter?" I taunted him, still going at him but going slowly. "Oh, I don't know, because maybe an entire war might not have happened? Maybe that's why it might've mattered. How long?"

"I don't know. A while, okay?" he shouted back at me, before tossing the last of his donut on the desk. "I came through! That's all that matters. I came through." He held up his coffee. "For you."

"You said you couldn't find who killed Justin. That's a lie."

"I didn't lie. She never said in those diaries that she was the one who pulled the trigger. Just went on saying how Nicolai called her and there was an incident, but I know you. You wouldn't want to know unless there was foolproof evidence. I didn't have that, so I waited until I had enough to bring you all of it. Just got into the last diary today. She put it all there, a full confession. I have no clue why. That's when I called the upstanding police officer himself, Detective Worthing. And we came right here."

"You left a tracker here?" Ashton asked Jake.

Jake barely reacted, but I caught a glimmer of amusement in his gaze. "You're not the only one who knows how to do things."

"Right." Ashton's tone was dry, but he sighed.

I tugged his hands down in front of me, linking our fingers.

———

Jake arrested Sloane. "I brought him here so you could hear straight from him what happened." He was putting handcuffs on Sloane as he said to Jess, "So you know, too, who killed Kelly. Felt it was the right thing to do, bringing him in person."

She nodded, her face stoic until Trace pulled her back into his arms. Then she turned her back to everyone else, and buried her face into his chest. He held her like that the rest of the time.

Jake studied her a moment, a flicker of sympathy showing before his own face went stoic. He glanced in Ashton's direction. "I have enough wherewithal to know when a battle went down, but I'm expecting that when I leave, I won't be seeing any bodies lying around?"

Ashton's voice sounded behind my ear. "What bodies? What are you talking about?"

Jake smirked, a faint one, before he dipped his head forward again. "I'll be charging her, and I'll be taking that one with me as well." He nodded in my father's direction.

"Wha—huh?!"

"We'll be downloading the online journal, too, for evidence." He gave Ashton a significant look before moving Sloane forward. "But first, I'll put this one in the car."

As soon as he was out of the room, Ashton was across the room and in front of my dad. "Let's go."

"Hey—ouch! What are you doing?!"

Ashton marched him right out of the room and down the hallway.

"He's getting to the journal first. The detective is letting him," Trace said to me.

I nodded, not surprised by anything anymore.

The only ones in the room were Trace, Jess, and me. The rest of the guests, they'd all been taken to the nearest hospital to get checked out. From there, Ashton told me the plans had been to have them driven back to the city. Except for Jess's mom. She stayed and was already up in her own room.

Pialto and Sophie were being taken back as well.

"Sloane will be charged. So that means Nea's and Nicolai's bodies will be released into evidence." Trace added, saying to me, "And guarantee he'll charge your dad too. Breaking and entering. Anything else because he just confessed to a whole list of crimes."

I was dazed but nodded. "I'm not posting his bail."

Jess shuddered, breaking free from Trace's arms. She crossed the room to the liquor cabinet and poured herself a hefty drink. "It's our wedding night, honey."

He had a faint smile on his face as he watched his new wife. His eyes were cast in shadow before he said to me, "Something happened with Ashton out there."

I frowned. "What do you mean?"

"When we were running around, trying to find everyone. He was shaking. I have never seen him shake like that, and he already thought you were safe. It wasn't that he was worried about you. It wasn't that he was worried about me. It was something else, something entirely else, and I have no clue what it was."

Jess turned our way, holding her drink against her chest. "Molly, you started to talk a while ago about your place in our group. Or about group roles? Something like that?"

I nodded, distracted by what Trace had just said about Ashton. "Yeah. Why?"

"Could you explain that again? Or explain more?"

I frowned, but okay then. "In a group, there's different roles. There's a thinker." I nodded in Trace's direction. "That's you. The analyst. Then there's doers. I feel you and Ashton are mostly doers. Ashton thinks, too—I mean, we all do—but you and him. You guys get shit done. And then there's me. I'm the in-between. I bring everyone together. I'm the connector." I kept frowning though. "But why are you asking? Why now, I mean?"

She drew in another breath, her chin starting to tremble. "Because when my brother finally gets released from prison, we're going to start a whole new battle to try to keep our mother around as long as possible. And right now, I'm feeling a little raw. I lost Kelly all over again today, so I need to remember who else I still have." She was blinking rapidly, lifting her glass and using the back of her pinkie to wipe away a tear. "I like hearing how we're a group, and we all have our roles, because it makes sense to me. I need something to make sense to me."

I walked over to her, my heart breaking, and hugged her. Drink and all.

She was right. We were all a new family, and one I had no intention of losing.

"Just call me the group sealant."

She barked out a laugh, her one free hand hugging me back. "That sounds so wrong but so right."

Wrong and right and sometimes inappropriate. That sounded about right.

CHAPTER

FIFTY-FIVE

ASHTON

We were at Katya two weeks later.

The place was closed down, except for the small group on the dance floor. A DJ was booked, and he was enjoying every time the girls wanted a song changed. I was in our private box, coming up here because Avery told me a certain detective wanted to talk to me.

He came in now, stopping to grab a drink that'd been poured for him on the bar. I was standing at the end, overlooking how Molly was dancing with Jess, Sophie, Pialto, Remmi, and half the staff, who Molly had insisted be given the night off. She wanted to extend another "sorry" to them for the night she'd left and put two of them in danger. I didn't think the boyfriend was in attendance, but Molly had insisted. I wouldn't be surprised if the boyfriend showed up sooner or later. So far, everyone was having a good time.

Her cousin Glen joined as well.

"What are you guys celebrating?" Jake joined me at the window, sipping his drink.

I gave him a cursory look, noting his badge wasn't out. "A few things. Jess's brother is officially out of prison."

His eyebrows went up, but he wasn't surprised.

"And Jess sold a large painting to a gallery in Europe."

The last part had been kept private, or Jess didn't want to blast it out to everyone because she didn't want to answer any questions anyone might've had.

Jake glanced my way. "And the third?"

"Easter Lanes is officially in Molly's name."

Jake had been about to take a sip but choked on his drink. "When wasn't it in her name?"

I inclined my head. "Her dad was involved."

He grimaced. "Never mind. I don't want to know."

I caught a look from Trace in our direction. He knew about the meeting and agreed maybe he shouldn't be in attendance.

"What's going on, Jake? You are pulling me away from a night of celebration with my woman."

He took another drag of his drink. "I came to let you know the case is officially closed against Sloane. She pled guilty, so nothing will get dragged out. And you don't have to worry about your family being pulled into anything."

"I wasn't worried." He was forgetting I had judges on my payroll.

He nodded. "Also, as of today, I've officially resigned from the force. I'll be moving back to Maine tomorrow. And I wanted to thank you for handing over my cousins. They were in better shape than I expected."

"We went the psychological deprogramming route, but turns out they were just stupid. Didn't know anything that could be useful against Nicolai."

"Listen. Ashton." He looked my way. "DEA already made a play with me. They know I'm taking over the family position, and I'm here as a courtesy. They want in on a player in this city. I said no. My family will back me, but don't get relaxed. They were behind Nicolai, pushing, which meant they were pushing him hard. If they can't get a player in this city, then they'll set their sights on you guys. Do not get lax. Ever."

I nodded, reaching over and clasping him on the shoulder. "Jake, that's just business. It's always been like that, and it'll always be like that. That's how our world works. We'll handle it."

He studied me, his face grim. "I've been on the other side. I know how they think."

"And I've always been on *this* side. I appreciate the warning, but we have fail-safes set in place. They move on us again, and we'll be ready. We *are* ready. Every day is a different type of war for us. I'm not looking at what I do through rose-colored glasses. Never have. Never will. I know who I am."

He drew in a breath.

"I'm the bad guy, Jake. Except for a short period of time, I got to be the good guy. Thanks to your cousin for that."

He shook his head, draining his drink. "Something tells me I'm the one who's not ready for this life."

"But you won't be in it for long." I was going with my gut now, seeing if I was right.

He looked my way, frowning. "What do you mean?"

"You're going in, but you're going to make them go legal. Aren't you? Isn't that your plan?"

He stared at me, long and hard, a steel wall looking back at me. "How the fuck do you know that?"

I broke out in a grin, my hand falling away from his shoulder. "Because I know you too. You were a good man to have on my payroll. I'll miss that."

He cursed, raking a hand over his face. He indicated Molly with his empty glass. "You got a good one there. Don't fuck that up, or I still mean it. I'll come down and try for her."

"Okay. Now you're starting to piss me off."

The corner of his mouth curved up. He gave me a slight nod. "Maybe see you never again, Walden."

"Yeah," I said, almost to myself, knowing that was his form of a goodbye. He left, and I waited until the elevator took him back down before I added, "Hopefully we'll never see each other again, Jake. Hopefully."

I meant it with respect.

Molly was looking up, but she was also seeing Trace, who was leaving the floor.

I waited, knowing he was coming up for a debrief.

It wasn't long before the elevator signaled his arrival.

"What'd he have to say?"

"About what we figured." I gave him the short notes.

Trace's eyebrows went low. He was going into his analyst mode, or his "thinker" mode, as Molly put it. "He's right, though. We can't get comfortable. We can never get comfortable in this life."

I nodded, knowing that. "I'm okay with the decision I made. Are you?"

Trace went back to watching the dance floor, his eyes seeking out his own woman, who was wearing his ring. She was laughing, and that was a sight I never thought I'd see his woman doing, enjoying life.

He let out a sigh. "We fought hard to be here."

"We did."

"We're in. I'm in."

I nodded. "You already know I'm in, but Trace."

He glanced my way.

I wanted to make sure he heard me right. "We fought to be here, so I'm here, but if *we*"—and I was stressing that word—"ever decide to leave, we leave on *our* terms. We don't leave ratting each other out, or begging for our lives, or pissing in some bucket in the woods and hiding out. We choose when we leave, just like right now. We're choosing our place in this city."

His head moved up and down as he took in and released another deep breath. He clasped me on the shoulder this time. "Brothers in, and brothers out. That's what you're saying?"

"That's what I'm saying."

"Let's see what life is like running two Mafia empires."

"We're not just running two Mafia empires. We're the kings of New York."

Trace's mouth twitched. I could tell he liked hearing that. "We're the *goddamn* kings of New York."

He held his drink up, and I met it with mine.

His phone buzzed, and a second later he asked me, "Why does your cousin want to talk to me?"

I choked on my drink before smirking. "Because he's going to ask if he can officially take your sister out on a date."

"*Why* is he asking again? I thought the wedding date was a one-off?"

"He's planning to ask you because I already told him he could keep fucking your sister."

"Jesus Christ," Trace said. He said another string of curses. "Why would you give him permission?"

I gave him a long look, sobering. "Because he's going to tell you that he's not pursuing Remmi for a brief fling or to get her out of his system."

Trace glared at me, because he knew what that meant. He swore again, low and long, before looking away. The man we were both talking about was on the dance floor, and after having a word with Demetri, he looked up our way.

I clasped Trace on the shoulder, squeezing at the end. "My primo is in love. We're going to be family in a whole official way, brother."

"Jesus Christ."

I made a praying motion before glancing upward. After that, it was time to celebrate.

CHAPTER

FIFTY-SIX

ASHTON

Three months later and Elijah was directing Shorty Easter to my new place of business. It was just one of many. I'd moved it farther north of the city, and we owned a good acreage on the Hudson River. This particular new building was a warehouse, one that no body of government was aware of. Yet.

It was also the perfect place for me to fulfill my second promise to Molly.

Elijah brought him inside. We were both ignoring his protests as he put him in a chair and whisked off the bag from over his head.

Shorty quieted, blinking a few times for his gaze to adjust to the change. It was daylight outside, the sun fully shining down, and in here, all dark except for a few lamps in the corner.

"Ashton Walden?" Shorty's hair was greasy, as always. He had his usual homeless-esque attire on. A cargo jacket with holes for the elbows. The pocket was pulled off. The ends of his jacket were shredded and frayed. His jeans were just as bad, and I couldn't see what kind of shirt he had on under the jacket.

He had money. That was always in the pictures sent to me. A good wad of it, always kept in one of his back pockets. Maybe that's the reason for the jacket? That pocket zipped up in the back. It was one of the only pockets that remained intact. We were nearing the end of September, but after getting briefed on him regularly over the last month, I'd come to realize he had a penchant for this jacket. The temps were still hot, but he never went without it. Even during the summer, after he'd been released from jail—which I knew he'd taken a deal and turned evidence on what he knew about Nea for the reduced jail term.

"What am I doing here?" He was twisting around, trying to guess his location.

I only had Elijah here.

Shorty had been bagged before coming in, and he'd be bagged when he'd be leaving here, but he would not be returning back to the city.

"What's going on?"

I tossed a thick file on the table in front of him.

"What's that?" His tone was scared, nervous. But I knew Shorty. He always scurried out of whatever predicament he landed himself in. He never needed to be nervous. I had full faith in his cockroach abilities, as Molly liked to put it.

"You lied to my grandfather."

"What? I'd never. What's this about?" He was starting to sweat, twisting around more frenzied. There were only two doors to leave this particular warehouse. He came in through one. The other was behind me. And as he kept looking for any other exit routes, Elijah moved closer. His gun was on full display.

"This is a nice greeting to your future pops-in-law, don't you think?"

I'd let him talk. For now. I only raised an eyebrow.

He went back to eyeing Elijah, his gaze falling to the gun. "Yeah, yeah. I mean, I wasn't really ingratiated"—he sneered as he said that last word—"when I found out about my little girl and you, but I got ears. Ears to the streets. I know people, know people you don't even know, and the word around town is that you're in love. You actually love my little girl." He laughed, some of the nerves easing from him. "The fellas I know—"

"Shut up." My tone was low, calm.

Shorty knew me. He knew this wasn't a good sign, and he quieted, his gaze locking right onto me.

"You told my grandfather that Molly's mother was homeless. That wasn't the truth."

His eyebrows went low, and his gaze went to the file. He wet his lips, but he didn't move to pick it up. From how I tossed it, pictures slid out from inside the file. There was a glimpse of one of those pictures, a woman.

"Look familiar to you?"

He swallowed, his Adam's apple bobbing up and down. "Those people weren't good to Molly's mother."

"Those people were goddamn saints compared to you." I went over and flicked the file. More pictures spread out from it, and he was getting a front seat viewing of them.

"She has a grandmother. A grandfather. She has uncles, aunts. She has cousins." I leaned over him. "She could've had brothers and sisters. She might've had nieces and nephews by now. But you lied. You took her away from her family. Molly's mother. She was kind. Nice. I told her the truth, Marcus. You piece of shit. I told her the truth about her mother."

His head jerked up, his eyes dilated but panicking. "You wouldn't. That means—"

"My mom was an addict. I have no problem if people know that truth."

He was back to looking for an escape route. His Adam's apple on a continuous bobbing motion up and down.

I straightened back up, stepping out of his space. "I'm not going to kill you. You don't have to worry about that."

"Then what?" he asked, harshly. "I know you, Walden. This ain't a lovely get-to-know-your-future-in-law chat. You're winding up to deliver something—"

"You're out."

Now he shut up.

"Your story isn't even anything remarkable. You saw a girl. You loved the girl. You wanted to take the girl away and make her just for yourself. You didn't want to share, so you controlled her. You manipulated her. You twisted her sense of reality where, like so many sad, abusive stories, she slowly left her family and friends behind, and her life became about you. You and her child. But then she made a mistake, and she became friends with my mother, and that was the end of any hope Molly had in having her mother around for the rest of her life." The table was shoved back, and I placed a hand on each side of Shorty's chair, on his armrests, until he was trying to lean all the way down to get away from me. But it wouldn't work.

I was in his space.

I liked making people uncomfortable, but making *him* squirm? I'd remember this day for years to come. This shit, I ate up.

"My mother took her mother away, so I gave her the truth in return. And then I had my PI look into her mother because I started thinking one day how fucking easy you lie about everything. Why would her mother be any different. I was right. You lied through your teeth. I want you to know that while you took away the chance for Molly to know the rest of her family, I gave them back to her. They're good people. Farmers. One's a doctor. One's a social worker. A couple nurses. Teachers. Molly met them."

He'd been back to looking around, always trying for a way out, but at the last statement, he stopped everything. His gaze jerked up to mine.

I stared down at him, drilling fucking holes into his skull. "They love her. We've been to visit three times already. They'll be at our wedding one day."

His eyes were filling with hate. He did not like hearing any of that, and he sneered up at me. "How's that going to go? When they find out you're Mafia?"

"They live in South Dakota. It's not that big of an issue." I waited a moment because maybe I shouldn't relish this next part? But I did. I would. That was the darkness inside of me, the dark that would never leave because it was so intertwined with who I was. "I'm the one who asked Molly to get *you* to find Kelly's killer. Did you ever put that together?"

His face was etched in stone, but now he let out a grunting sound. It sounded forced. "Course. Only made sense with you railing her."

My fingers dug into the armrests. A whole new level of cold entered my body. "Why am I not surprised that's how you talk about your daughter?"

He swallowed, looking away. Sweat broke out over his forehead; some of it started to slide down his face. "What do you want, Walden? You only 'summon' someone if there's an order you're going to hand out. I'm aware of my deal with your family. I still owe you."

"No."

He frowned, his eyes darting to mine. "What?"

I pushed back from his chair, but I still loomed over him, just staring down at him. "You owe us seven million—that's with interest."

"What? That's—" He quieted himself because he knew there was no reason to argue.

He did, and we both knew it.

"I'm cutting you off."

His eyebrows dipped down again. "What's that mean?"

"That means you're done. You're no longer in the employ of the Walden family. Your debt will remain intact and will acquire interest, but we both know you'll never pay that off, so I'm giving you an alternative. Leave."

He didn't say anything.

"I righted your wrong. I returned Easter Lanes officially to Molly. But she asked me for one thing, and that's for you to disappear from her life. That's what I'm doing right now. I'm putting an order out that if you are seen on any of the Walden premises, that you can be removed the old-fashioned Mafia way. You can take that how you'd like, but I don't want you in my city. If you leave, never come back, you can remain alive. If you come back . . . you're out, Shorty." I motioned to Elijah, who came forward.

"What if she changes her mind? What if she wants to see her father one day?"

I motioned for Elijah to put the bag over his head. "Then that'll be her decision. Not yours. Elijah will take you anywhere you want, anywhere except New York City. I hope to never see you again, Shorty."

A muffled protest was my response as I left.

Avery was standing at the SUV, and he opened the back door for me. "Compound?"

I got inside. "Compound."

I had one more item to extinguish.

CHAPTER
FIFTY-SEVEN

MOLLY

Ashton wanted to take me on a trip, but I hadn't expected a helicopter ride.

I gaped at him when we drove up to the helipad. "Are you serious?"

He smiled before nodding. He'd also asked for me to dress up, so I was wearing a dress. V neck. The material was the softest fabric. Sequined. It looked light pink, but in the right light, it could sparkle and give off undertones of lilac as well. And it was wrapped around me like a robe. I tied it in front. Ashton was wearing a black suit and an off-white shirt under. He looked dashing.

"What's the occasion?"

He squeezed my hand, nodding to the helicopter. "Just get on. You'll see."

A guy approached us, wearing a bright-orange vest. We were given these helmet/visor things with radio pieces for our ears. It helped silence the sound, but we could still talk to each other. After we got in and seat belted, the helicopter lifted off.

I'd never imagined this was something I would do in my life. Never, ever. Not being the daughter of Shorty Easter, and as I was starting to learn, the daughter of Gen D'amperia. I was learning all the ways she was like me, how she wasn't like me, and I kept remembering new things. Memories that my dad used to tell me didn't exist, but they did.

And I had a newfound obsession with the stars. The ceiling in Easter Lanes was getting a whole new upgrade. Actually, the whole place was. The entire interior was getting one giant mural painted over of the night sky, complete with galaxies and stars.

Obsessed. Me.

I was expecting for us to go north of the city, but forty minutes later, we were landing in the Hamptons. It was a private landing spot, behind a giant house. Cobblestone driveway. Grand arches. It looked like three giant villas from Tuscany, but they were transplanted into the Hamptons. A giant pool. A lavish garden. Tennis court. And there were four other barnlike structures.

"What is this place, Ashton?" I asked once the helicopter took off and I could hear my own voice.

He squeezed my hand, tugging me forward. "Come on."

I followed.

He took me inside the home, into the kitchen, and Avery was there. He gave us a small wave, but he was busy cooking. "Welcome, Molly."

"Hi, Avery." But I was so confused.

Ashton kept tugging me forward, taking me through the entire house.

It was all modern, mostly cream-colored palette except for the library, which was filled from the floor to a second floor with books. There were beds built in among the bookshelves, or a few. A reader's dream reading escape.

Then to the primary bedroom, which was its own floor. Its own library.

Through a secret doorway, into a secret room, then to a secret slide.

"What?" I laughed, taking the slide first and ending up in another whole section of the house.

Ashton landed behind me and began leading me again. We were in a glass-enclosed patio area, and then through another secret door, and we were outside. We were on the other side of the house, by the pool, which had its own pool house, and another whole Zen maze and garden.

"I don't under . . ." And then I stopped trying because there was a table set up, just beyond, at the pinnacle of a hill. Pialto and Sophie were there. Elijah too. My breath caught in my throat. "What's this?"

Pialto clutched a bouquet of pink roses. Sophie held a champagne bottle, a giant-size one that was in danger of being dropped.

Elijah had a towel over his arm, like he was a waiter.

"One last stop." Ashton led me over to the table.

Sophie was crying and beaming as she pulled out my chair.

Ashton helped me into it.

She went and pulled his out next.

Pialto moved in. "These are for you, but I know you're going to worry about a vase right away, so I'll take them to the kitchen and handle it. You"—his eyes jerked to Ashton—"stay here and *enjoy*."

He left, and Elijah took the champagne bottle from Sophie. Opening it, he tipped it enough to fill both our drinks. After that, as Sophie was blushing, and giggling, and mouthing, "OMG!" to me, he nudged her to go with them. Both went inside.

Avery came out, coming from a door not far from us, with the first course of food.

"What is going on?" I couldn't get over this, any of this.

We had the first course, then the second. Dessert came last, and I was stuffed. A sweet leaf salad. Potato gratin. Seasonal vegetables. Vegetable cavatappi. Salmon. Torta Rogel, and I was dying. I was so full, and then all the champagne.

I was a full giggling mess by the last course. It was also long past sundown. By the time dessert came out, the stars were up.

I was in heaven.

"Ashton, you've still not told me what's going on."

He stared at me for a moment, his eyes somber, a faint smile lingering.

Everyone had come out to say their goodbyes. We were officially alone in this new place, big enough to be called a compound.

A flash of fear crossed his face before it was gone again. "You asked me a long time ago about what happened at the compound."

I sat up straight. "Jess and Trace's wedding."

He nodded, his face closing off.

"Trace said something happened to you that day, that you were shaking."

His eyes flickered before whatever emotion that surged forward was blanketed again. "I told you that I hated my mother, but I never told you why."

I let out a slow breath of air, knowing, just knowing, we were going down a delicate path.

"You know my mother was an addict, but you don't know the extent of it. Or what else happened the night before our mothers died." He stared off into the distance. "My grandfather refused to give her money. She'd been trying all day to get it. She went to him. He said no. She went to my uncles. They all said no. She went to me. Her son. I said no. The last person she went to was my grandmother. She was strong, fierce, but she had a heart of gold. We were at the compound that day." He turned, looking at me now. There was pain there, but also grief and relief. His shoulders smoothed down. "My grandmother's health had already started getting bad, but my mom, she . . . beat my grandmother. I think she asked her for money, for the drugs."

"Ashton."

He shook his head. "I'm the only one who knew the truth what happened that night. We were at the compound, so the normal amount of security wasn't there. They were outside. We thought it was safe. I was there with my abuela. Grandfather got called away for a meeting, which was normal, but my mom came. She wasn't supposed to be there. I thought she'd been in the city, but she drove up. She was looking for money. I heard the screams and ran in, but my abuela was already on the ground. Bleeding. My mom was standing over her, holding a knife and my grandmother's purse. She didn't hear me come in. She thought I was in one of the other sections of the place. We have a family safe there, and my mom was demanding the code. My abuela wouldn't give it." His words were so bitter, clipping out, "She wasn't happy with the money Abuela had in her purse."

I reached for his hand.

"I grabbed a gun. I knew where there was one, and I pulled it on her. Threatened her. Told her to get the fuck out of there before I pulled the trigger. She left. She made one of the guards drive her to the city. I didn't care where she went. I just wanted her the fuck out of there, but Abuela. She didn't want anyone to know what happened, and she was so weak. She made me lift her body so it'd look like she fell down the stairs. That's the story she gave. We didn't have security cameras inside the house back then, and I never said a word. I promised Abuela I wouldn't tell, but I also wouldn't actively lie for her either. But Abuela, she still loved my mother, even though she'd been hurt so bad that she needed to be airlifted to the hospital in the city. We got word what happened to my mom, and my grandfather called me to the office to tell me. My mom didn't just kill your mom that night. The beating, it was the straw that broke my abuela. She died three weeks later. I've always blamed my mother.

"In my abuela's culture, we revere the elderly. My grandmother never wanted that secret told, so I'll never tell. I never did, but I *can* tell you. I've held that for so long. It made me hate my mother. I know addiction is a sickness. Christ, what I do, I'm fully aware of the hypocrisy, but I can't unloathe my mother. It's just not in me."

"I'm so sorry, Ashton." I laced our fingers together.

"That day I saw you, I have never stopped thinking about you since that day. Maybe it linked us? Maybe I started loving you that day, knowing what my mom took away from you, knowing what she did to Abuela."

My eyes were swimming.

I was flashing back to that same day as well. "Your grandmother loved you?"

"Fiercely." He blinked, some wetness showing. "My grandfather too. I think they didn't know how to help my mom. They didn't believe in therapy, or they would've sent my mother to one. They didn't know. It's different now."

"Thank you for telling me."

He cleared his throat. "I've been reading more of the group role dynamics you mentioned. That's therapy based, right?"

I nodded. "I've been interested. I think because of my own dad, but also from Easter Lanes. People talk a lot to a bartender that'll listen."

His smile was so soft. "I get that." He looked around. "That's why we're here. A new place. A new compound."

I sat back. "What?"

"I bought this place. Not just for us. The familia too. My aunts. Cousins. Nieces. Nephews. And for . . . our kids if we ever have them."

Children.

My heart was pumping.

I wanted to hug him, hold him, cry with him, but now I wanted to kiss him and so many other things. "Kids?"

"If you want." He was back to looking at me, watching me steadily, loving me right back. "I know I'd want, someday."

"I want. I very much want. Children?" I felt full all over again. Full of love, life, and happiness. "I love you."

Those eyes of his, looking back at me with such tenderness. "I love you too."

"Wait. Did you sell the other compound?"

"No." He picked up his fork, taking a last bite of his Rogel cake. "I burned it. It felt cathartic to see it in ashes."

EPILOGUE

ASHTON

I waited until the next morning. I didn't want to be predictable, but as soon as she started waking up, with her coffee already on the nightstand, she rolled over, and I was there.

"Morni—" She stopped because she saw what was in my hand.

The ring. I moved so I was half lying on her, nestled between her legs, and I held it up to her. "Will you marry me?"

"Ashton." She sat up slowly, reaching for the ring.

She'd start crying. She was a crier, at least lately, but she cried when she was happy. She rarely cried from the other reasons anymore.

Those tears were starting. Her bottom lip beginning to tremble. "Is this—are you sure?"

I groaned. "God, I'm sure." I reached forward, brushing her hair back, tucking it behind her ear, and I held her head in the palm of my hand. "I meant it last night. I think I've loved you since we were kids. Just took me a long time to figure it out."

She was biting her lip, still crying, but her eyes were beaming at me. She kept looking from me to the ring, and back again, until she was only focusing on the ring.

I sat up. "Molly."

"What?" Still focused on the ring. "It's a double-stoned engagement ring. Ashton. This is amazing."

One was a princess-cut stone. The other was shaped in a moon. Both were platinum and on a gold band.

"Trace helped with the ring, by the way. If you say yes, he's requested that they're our first call. And they're on standby. Meaning, they're staying in one of the guesthouses here."

She gasped. "They're here?"

I was half cursing in my head. "You need to say yes or put me out of my misery. What—"

"*Yes!*" She launched herself at me, tackling me backward on the bed. "Yes, yes, yes. Oh my god, yes." She went back to letting the tears fall as she kept staring at the ring.

I took it, took her finger, and I slowly slid it on. "There. Mrs. Ashton Walden."

She couldn't stop staring at it, until she burst out, "If we have a girl, we're naming her after my mom. I know your grandmother was like the matriarch, but my mom comes first."

She was so fierce, and I had no idea life could be like this. None.

I leaned forward. "If we have a girl, we can name her after your mother."

"Gen Everly Walden. I've always felt bad for my middle name. Like, it needed to shine more, but it never just got its due moment. You know?"

I had no idea what she was talking about, but I didn't care. I moved in, needing to taste her. So I did, and I kept tasting her, kissing her, and she was kissing me back.

I didn't give a fuck about calling anyone else.

Molly cared, so we called them later. Way later.

Molly also informed me that we could not use the name Kelly because Jess had already claimed it, for their little girl that was coming.

ACKNOWLEDGMENTS

So many thanks to Montlake. You gave me a chance, and I'll always appreciate it so much. To Lauren, Lindsey, and everyone who helped put together this book! To my agent, Kimberly. To Crystal, Amy, Tami. To my entire team, who I couldn't function without (ahem, my agent), Debra Anastasia, Helena Hunting, Rachel Van Dyken, and so many more. To all the readers in my reader group. You guys give me breath for so many days, and you have no clue. To Mercedes, for helping with my questions about Argentina. To Becca.

To so many!

This part is always the hardest to write because there's just always so many who have helped, from responding to a message to posting a meme in the reader group, or even my Bailey, whose entire body wiggles as he runs up to me. (He's my pup!) I don't deserve him.

So so so many thank-yous and hugs of appreciation!

TURN THE PAGE TO SEE
A PREVIEW OF TIJAN'S
BOOK *A DIRTY BUSINESS*!

CHAPTER ONE

JESS

Beer and hockey.

That's where it's at.

I didn't know what "it" was and where "it" was, but I was currently sitting at the hockey arena, a beer in hand, watching some holy hottie hockey gods on the ice, so yeah, I was thinking I was where "it" was supposed to be. Life was good. Beer and hockey.

"I gotta take a piss."

I stifled a grin because only my roommate, who looked like a real-life Barbie, talked in a way that in no way was Barbie-like at all. Made me love her even more for it.

I gave a nod. The second period was ending, and I glanced at my beer. It was a third empty.

I made a decision, right then and there. Because I was decisive—it's a word that I had to recently explain to a parolee of mine, and I had to explain in detail to the nth degree. She didn't know what setting goals was or what being decisive meant. I'd enjoyed the conversation. Her eyes were glazed, and her drug test was negative, so I knew it was the topic boring her. Too bad. We both had to endure that conversation, though it wasn't her that had me needing my current beer. It was the three parolees after her that I checked on. All of them together made me need the last beer, and my *next* beer was being dedicated to the two home visits I'd be doing tomorrow.

Not looking forward to those, but it was part of the job. So as Kelly was making her way to the stairs, I went right behind her.

Kelly drew the eye. Platinum-blonde hair. A slender and almost model-like body. Blue eyes. Barbie, like I said. She got looks from males and females, and I understood, especially after her recent boob job. She'd been my roommate since college and after. The only time we'd taken apart from each other was when she'd moved in with a boy-friend-turned-fiancé, who was now an ex-husband. He'd cheated on her, so she got a decent-size settlement from him, and I got my best friend back. Score for me, sucked for him. But the thing I loved about Kelly was that she was flexible. I came home and told her I needed a drink, and she said she won two tickets to the New York Stallions hockey game. It was meant to be, the way I was figuring.

She glanced back, saw me following her.

I tipped my cup up and drained it to her unspoken question.

She turned, going the rest of the way with a laugh. Almost like we'd done this before (because we had), she went for the bathroom, and I went to the beer concession stand.

"Oh, ho, ho, ho. Hey there."

The jovial greeting sounded out from one of the workers, a big burly guy. I had to take a second to appreciate what I was seeing. I knew this guy. He'd been a parolee in the past, not mine, but I'd been in the hallway a few times he had a disagreement with his current parole officer at that time. He liked to go by the name Jimi Hendrix, but we all called him Jimmy. And with Jimmy, unfortunately, there'd been a lot of disagreements.

So, he was on parole a lot.

"Jimmy." I was scanning him up and down. He'd lost thirty pounds, which I caught because I needed to know that for my job, but on him, it was barely noticeable. The guy was six five and 310. Or now, 280? I was also noting the beer he was serving. "How are you doing?"

He caught my tone, and his grin upped a degree. "I'm off parole. You don't need to be worried about reporting me. Finished it, got a good place to live, and got this job. I'm working at a grocery store, bagging groceries, too, Miss Jess."

That was another thing about Jimmy. I was normally Officer Montell, but Jimmy somehow got away with calling me Miss Jess. A couple of his coworkers were checking me out like I was his ex-lady, and I saw the speculation in their eyes. I had no interest in dating either of them.

"You wanna beer, Miss Jess?"

"Uh . . . sure." Felt odd taking a beer from a past parolee, but okay then. As he was pouring, still seeing some of the interest from his coworkers, I reached into my purse for my phone and my badge. The badge got hung around my neck. I didn't need to brandish it here, but they saw it, and it did the job. The interest fell flat, and I got a couple sneers instead.

I pulled up Travis, a coworker, and sent him a text.

Jess: Jimi Hendrix is off parole?

He buzzed back almost right away.

Asshole Coworker 1: Yeah. Why?

Jess: Just wondering, saw him. He looks good.

Asshole Coworker 1: He in trouble?

Jess: Nope. Bye.

My phone buzzed again, but I didn't like Travis. The feeling was mutual, more than mutual actually. Derek Travis. He'd been up my ass for as long as I'd been working as a parole officer. Didn't know why or what his problem was since they needed female parole officers. I did my job, did it well, and only butted heads with him a couple of times. But I'd asked about Jimmy because I needed to make sure, and he'd answered. The topic was done as far as I was concerned. I wasn't going to give him any reason to bug Jimmy, but sometimes they lied, hence the text.

"Here you go, Miss Jess."

Even with Jimmy's outbursts or disagreements, I always liked him. He couldn't handle his temper at times, but he was usually funny about it, swinging on himself more than swinging on others. Ninety-five percent of the time, he didn't want to hurt anyone else.

"What do I owe you, Jimmy?"

His smile was almost blinding, his two massive hands resting on the sides of the register and his big frame hunched forward and down. That'd been one of his old habits, I was remembering too. He tried to make himself smaller than he was, usually to make others feel more comfortable around him.

"Nothing, Miss Jess. It's on me."

I glanced to his coworkers, seeing one watching us with a bit too much interest for my liking. I leaned closer to Jimmy and lowered my voice. "Are you sure that you got the cash on you?"

He started to bolster up, his mouth opening, a pink color coming to his neck, more than what it was, but I kept on. "Because I know you travel with as little cash as necessary. Your heart's in the right place, but if you find yourself short on the exact cash, I wouldn't want someone to notice and let your boss know, if you get my drift." My eyes darted to that coworker trying to listen in. He'd washed the same two-by-two inches of counter eighteen times now.

Getting my drift, Jimmy's shoulders sank even lower. "Sorry, Miss Jess. You're right." He told me the amount I owed, and I handed over the cash. When he started to give me the change, I waved my hand, indicating he should keep it. He was putting it in their tip jar when I headed off.

Going to the stairs, I scanned for our seats. Kelly wasn't there.

Knowing I'd need a bathroom break myself before too long, I sipped my beer and headed in the direction Kelly had gone.

The line was too long at the first one, but being the slightly buzzed savvy parole officer I was, I knew there'd be more bathrooms farther away from the main area. I kept going, and I had half my beer sipped before I found a door. It said "bathrooms" and had an arrow, so I was following the arrow.

I surged through, and oh crap.

I was in the exit stairwell. I'd made a mistake.

I turned, reaching for the door, when I heard just above me, "—hear about it. I do not care."

I moved back, angled my head. He wasn't all the way up to the next floor, but he was halfway up to the top. His back was turned slightly toward the stairway, and he was talking on the phone. "Yes. Yes."

I should go. That was a private call, not my business.

I pushed the door handle to go out, but nothing. The door was locked.

I was locked inside.

Well, shitters.

I had a beer. I'd soon have a bladder that would need to be emptied, and that guy was still on his phone.

"—wait. Someone is here."

Oh, double shitters.

I turned when he started down the stairs.

I called up, "I'm sorry! I didn't know these doors . . ." I trailed off as he turned the corner, now facing me and coming down the stairs directly to me. And I trailed off because good gracious, this man was one of the most beautiful men I'd ever seen.

He had pretty features. His eyes were a gray-hazel color, and yes, even from this distance, I was struck at how clear they were. His cheekbones were set wide on the sides of his face, but he had such a square jawline that it worked for him. He was rugged but handsome and hot all at the same time. I was putting his height at six four. Weight at 210. He was dressed in some seriously nice threads, all business suit. His shoes were the expensive kind, like what I would joke that a Wall Street dude would wear to a hockey game. At seeing me, he paused, but then a wicked grin slowly spread over his face, and that knocked me back a bit too.

It was almost a nice punch to my sternum, one to shock me more than incapacitate me.

He spoke into the phone: "Excuse me a bit." I could hear the other person talking, but he ended the call and put his phone into his pocket. "Hello."

He was looking me up and down, looking like a bored cat who had come across a mouse and had a new toy to play with.

"I didn't mean to interrupt your phone—"

"On the contrary, thank you very much." He came down a few more steps. "I needed an excuse to get off the call."

I shifted backward, giving him space—or myself space—as he continued until he was on the step right above, looking down. "I was looking for the bathroom."

"These are the stairs." His voice was a low baritone croon, and he was still doing the eye thing where he wasn't just assessing me, but he was reading my soul, and he was enjoying whatever he was reading. If I were a character in a book, I might've likened him to a vampire. I almost started laughing because how ridiculous was I? Getting nervous with this guy, who it was very apparent was in a whole different tax bracket than me. But normal me wouldn't have cared. Normal me wouldn't have stuck around this long either.

I nodded as he stepped down, facing me directly. "I realized. There's a sign that said 'bathrooms' and pointed in here. I came in, not remembering the doors lock behind you."

"Right." He still had that smile, his eyes sparking up. "Because if you read the sign on the door, it would've said 'emergency exit only.' And that it locks."

I refused to flush for this guy. Nope. But the back of my neck did get heated. A little bit.

"Yeah. My mistake." My tone was cool, and I was giving him the look to back off.

That seemed to amuse him even more. "What's your name?"

I bristled. "None of your business, how about that?"

His eyes went to smoldering. This guy wasn't normal. "Sass." His tone went soft. "I like it."

That made me bristle even more. "Excuse me?" I shifted back, getting in a stance as I automatically started thinking how to handle him if he made a move.

As if reading my mind, or feeling the air shift, he drew back. The smoldering effect lessened, but just a little. It was still there. I was still amusing him, and I didn't know how I felt about that either. "You have no idea who I am."

I frowned. "That gets you off or something?"

His grin turned inward, showing off a dimple.

God. The dimple. What female didn't have a thing for a cheek dimple? That wasn't fair. Some of my bristling eased up.

He chuckled, still in that baritone, and it was *sensual too.* "Apparently it does with you. Trust me. I'm just as shocked as you seem to be." His eyes sharpened. "Are you here with someone?"

I straightened out of the fighting stance I'd assumed and relaxed, only slightly. "My roommate."

Another spark of interest in those eyes of his. "Is your roommate a significant other? Or *just* a roommate?"

Damn. He was direct, and fast about it.

If I'd been at the bar and in the mood for a one-nighter, this conversation would have a whole different ending. I liked guys who were direct. *A lot.*

"She's my best friend." I saw the next question forming, so I added, "And she's straight."

His head lowered, those eyes of his softening. "And you? Who are you into?"

My throat swelled up. I didn't know why, but I felt entranced by him.

He took a step closer, slowly.

I couldn't tear my gaze away, and I couldn't take a step back. I didn't want to.

A part of me was railing at myself, in the back of my head, but my heart was pounding, and my throat was still swollen. My body was heating, and an ache was forming between my legs.

This man, what was he doing to me?

This reaction didn't happen to me, ever.

"Who are you into, Miss . . . ?" His head cocked to the side, like he could lure me into answering him.

I wanted to do just that too.

My lips parted from surprise, but then his eyes shifted to my shirt, and everything changed. Abruptly.

He'd been seductive and coaxing. And then nothing. Frigid cold.

I even shivered, feeling his withdrawal though he hadn't moved a muscle.

I followed his eyes down to my sternum. My badge was sticking out from my jacket, but when I looked back up, I sucked in my breath. His eyes were on me, and they were *not* friendly. They were hostile. All that flirting was gone in an instant.

"You a cop?" His tone was flat, cutting.

"I'm a parole officer."

His phone started ringing again, and he fished it out of his pocket. Without saying a word to me, he hit accept and turned to go back up the stairs. "Hey. Hold one moment. I'm heading for the door. Open it for me."

I couldn't suppress a shiver as he disappeared around the turn, going up the last set of stairs.

Thump!

The door opened. Sounds from the hockey game filtered into the stairwell, and then they were muted again.

I waited, but nothing.

He'd gone.

What the hell had just happened?

Also, I was still locked in.

ABOUT THE AUTHOR

Tijan is a *New York Times* bestselling author who writes suspenseful and unpredictable novels. Her characters are strong, intense, and gut-wrenchingly real with a little bit of sass on the side. Tijan began writing after college, and once she started, she was hooked. She's written multiple bestsellers including the Fallen Crest series, *Ryan's Bed*, *Enemies*, and others.

She is currently writing many new books and series with an English cocker spaniel whom she adores. Connect with Tijan at www. TijansBooks.com, on Facebook at www.facebook.com/tijansbooks, and on Twitter (@TijansBooks). You can also check out her Instagram at www.instagram.com/tijansbooks. Tijan is represented by Brower Literary & Management Inc.